Praise for ~~Robert Ray's~~ Murdock Mysteries

Murdock Tackles Taos (2013)

"Robert Ray is a gifted writer and the Matt Murdock series displays all his many talents. The prose is crisp, the characters vivid and the plot captivating. Read him now! Matt Murdock is part Jack Reacher, part Dave Robicheux. Fans of Lee Child and James Lee Burke will love *Murdock Tackles Taos*. A brilliant murder mystery with a splash of romance. The Matt Murdock series is one of my guilty pleasures!"
—Robert Dugoni, *New York Times* bestselling author

"In *Murdock Tackles Taos*, Robert Ray takes risks that every good novelist has to take in order to push the limits of the genre without leaving his readers behind. As with all of Ray's books, this one is so well written it's a pleasure just to say the words. When Ray brings Helene Steinbeck, his second sleuth, on stage he drags Murdock into the 21st Century with a bang .... In this book, the rich eat the poor. Steinbeck and Murdock set things right."
—Jack Remick, author of *Blood*, *Gabriela and the Widow* and The California Quartet series

"Robert J. Ray has succeeded in doing what Michael McGarrity excels at: developing characters that you want to take home. *Murdock Tackles Taos* is a can't-put-it-down kind of book. Ray seduces the reader from the first paragraph, pulls them in with enticing promises, and doesn't break up with

them until the last page. Murdock is the perfect character. He keeps you at the edge of your seat waiting to surprise you with his next move."
—Marie Romero Cash, artist and author of the Jemimah Hodge Mystery series

"Game, set, match. Murdock Tackles Taos puts readers through their paces, serving up breakneck action, intrigue and murder in this winner-takes-all mystery thriller set in serene Taos, N.M. Can't wait for Murdock's next case!"
—L.M. Archer, freelance author and wine blogger

Murdock Cracks Ice (1992)

"Hard-nosed P.I. fare, with romance singeing the edges while our hero tries to toe the no-commitment line. Good reading, with frisky Chen and Hana definite scene-stealers."
—*Kirkus Reviews*

"The novel, crammed with action, moves rapidly on Ray's smooth prose and strong characterizations. Unlikely as it may be, Ray and Murdock make it believable."
—*San Antonio Express-News*

"For all the violence of the drug scene, the lean, rich characterizations provide a break from the grim realities that feels very much like life, in which love and the companionship of others bring relief and hope. Then, too, the plot moves briskly, with a kind of spare clarity that reflects Murdock's personality."
—*Cape Cod Times*, Hyannis, MA

"Robert Ray has woven a complex web of crime and intrigue that is sure to snare the reader and keep him hooked. And Murdock's chili recipe (page 8) is a good one, too!"
—*Mostly Murder*

"A welcome addition to the ever growing ranks of fine Seattle mysteries."
—*Seattle Times/Seattle Post-Intelligencer*

Merry Christmas Murdock (1989)

"*Merry Christmas Murdock* delivers a knockout punch. It comes wrapped in action and violence. But inside its rough exterior there is warmth and humor. Much like the hard-boiled detective whose story it tells."
—*The Clarion-Ledger*, Jackson, Mississippi

"Riveting. Private-eye Murdock is a sophisticated Mike Hammer, and Ray writes with the sardonic wit of a Mickey Spillane mixed with the insight of a Parker."
—*Tribune*, South Bend, Indiana

"It may be the best Murdock yet, representing a stylistic plateau for Ray …. the reading experience is immensely pleasurable. Ray has become the proverbial incurable romantic and some of the turns of phrase in *Merry Christmas* are irresistible, the kind one wants to read more than once."
—*The Register*, Orange County California

"It's nicer still when there's a decent yarn to spin, decently told, and this latest of the Matt Murdock capers is better than decent. …. This is an easy, unpretentious read. And Murdock is really awfully nice to be around."
—*The Drood Review of Mystery*

"It's a fast-moving, what-will-we-find-out-next story, with some likable characters and some you love to hate."
—*Chronicle*, Houston, Texas

"What a find author Robert J. Ray is …. Perhaps best of all, Mr. Ray has the rare ability to build tension bit by bit

by bit and keep much of this throughout the last two-thirds of the book, almost without pause .... A crackerjack piece of plotting and writing and unhesitatingly recommended."
—*Mystery News*

"The style is punchy, the fast talk is zippy and the final shoot-out a honey .... I'll be on the lookout for Robert Ray's Matt Murdock in the future."
—*Trenton Times*

"I liked the action-packed story line, the resiliency of the hero and the nifty, lucid prose."
—*Cape Cod Times*, Hyannis, MA

"Robert Ray's style is constant action leavened with antic laughter and surprising flashes of romance .... Murdock, a classic tough guy type, thrives in the land of gridlocked freeways and transplanted Midwesterners. He brashly confronts a host of foes, sorts through an avalanche of clues and finally prevails in a climatic shootout, Just another day for the irrepressible Murdock ...."
—*St. Louis Post-Dispatch*

"Fast-paced and easy to read, the adventure mystery won't be disappointing to the folks who like to get away from it all for a few hours by using someone else's imagination."
—*Press Register*, Mobile, AL

"Murdock is as hard-boiled as a 10-minute egg."
—*The Plain Dealer*

Dial "M" for Murdock (1988)

"Ray's well-wrought consideration of what can happen to those overtaken by 'greedy little-boy dreams' will leave

readers eager for the next Murdock adventure."
—*Publisher's Weekly*

"Fast, accomplished and slick."
—*Kirkus Reviews*

Murdock For Hire (1988)

"The Robert Ray talent unfolds with every book and Matt Murdock becomes more and more likable and his friends more lovable."
—*Amarillo Sunday News-Globe*

"The central character is a rare find—tough, lonely, and incurably romantic."
—*Booklist*

"The writing is clear and direct, there is plenty of action, and even a romance."
—The *New York Times* Book Review

Bloody Murdock (1986)

"The Austin scenes are brief, but if you are a fan of the hard-boiled but sensitive private eyes of Raymond Chandler and John D. Macdonald, you will feel at home with Ray."
—*American-Statesman*, Austin, TX

"The story never stops and the lushly decadent southern California life was never more so."
—*Publishers Weekly*

MURDOCK
TACKLES
TAOS

MURDOCK TACKLES TAOS

Robert J. Ray

CAVEL
PRESS

Seattle, WA

CAMEL PRESS

Camel Press
PO Box 70515
Seattle, WA 98127

For more information go to: www.camelpress.com
murdock.camelpress.com

This is a work of fiction. Names, characters, places, brands,
media, and incidents are either the product of the author's
imagination or are used fictitiously.

Cover design by Sabrina Sun

Murdock Tackles Taos
Copyright © 2013 by Robert J. Ray

ISBN: 978-1-60381-925-1 (Trade Paper)
ISBN: 978-1-60381-926-8 (eBook)

Library of Congress Control Number: 2013935133

Printed in the United States of America

For Margot,

Another Murdock

Thanks

Acknowledgments

THIS BOOK GOT IMMENSE help from Jack Remick. He read every page, more than once, and his insights were incisive.

I also got help from Anne Sweet, Joel Chafetz, Karen Heines, Roxana Arama, Mindy Halleck, Max Detrano, Zack Hoffman, Jerry Jaz, and Frank Araujo.

Thanks also to Catherine Treadgold, the courageous publisher and editor who allowed me to keep going with the words. Thanks to Louisa's Bakery and Café, a sanctuary for writers, where I have crafted more than one book.

And huge thanks to Margot, my wife, who urges me, with word and gesture, to keep hitting those keys.

Prologue
Running Girl

SHE HAD THE DAY off and she was lonely in Taos so she took her laptop and her sketchpad and sat in the shade at the Hard Wire Café. She was sketching a guy for money because she was broke.

He was handsome, with a great tan and a gorgeous smile.

When he left her with a twenty she felt even lonelier. She bought a coffee, sweet iced latte, and hung out—was he gone forever or what?

An hour passed, then two. She did another sketch—ten bucks, thank you—and then the handsome guy was back.

"Come to a party," he said. "Artists and writers, Colony People. Our kind, okay?"

The guy drove a silver Humvee.

She kicked off her sandals and settled into the comfy seat smiling. The guy had this really great profile. The Humvee climbed up, past the Pueblo, and crossed through a gate into Never-Never Land. Roofs, aspen trees turning, a lawn so green it came from England.

The first person she met gave her a drag. The smoke invaded her brain, curled like a cat. The people were beautiful, some her age, some younger. The food was out of this world.

Smoked meat, soft and succulent. "Have another bite, hon?"

What is this meat, anyway?

There was wine, beer, tequila shooters, Scotch whiskey so smooth it raised your hopes for a better world. A world for starving artists like herself.

She danced around the campfire, barefoot. Her feet were tough from pounding New York streets.

A pretty girl, Tammy with a Texas accent and a bouncy blonde ponytail, whipped off her blouse and kept dancing— torchlight on bare tits, sell that sketch, make a killing.

Another girl, another blouse, and another. Blouses tossed like leaves in the wind, until she was the only one left, the only girl not on display. So she said, "What the hell?" and they clapped their hands, chanting, as she flung her blouse away.

THEY SLEPT UNDER A blanket, under the stars.

She was naked now, her skin cold, and the guy with the Humvee was warmth incarnate and she was stoned or bombed or whatever. He said, "Marry me, Sofia."

The words shot into her like venom, words arching her back, the vaunted Universal Spasm, sex with bronze gods, her body in a spin, a planet orbiting, her soul synched with the cosmos, her lips curled and the Tantric Voice whispering—*Spread your wings, your thighs, open your soul, open and breathe, breathe and weave, weave with each breath, and there it comes—*

And he was inside her, a god coming.

DAWN—A WALK IN THE woods to clear her head. A walk drenched in beauty. She was in love. She would marry this guy. He drove a Humvee. Humvees smelled of money, money in her life was like manna, manna made her thighs quiver.

She came out of the woods into a field of flowers. Red flowers, and blue, flowers of yellow, purple, and gentian. She was still barefoot, feeling nature rise up through her feet.

A dog's baying sent a shiver along her spine. Another dog joined in. Her brain told her to run. A game trail led through the flowers. The dogs charged from the trees, dogs with bright teeth and rhino shoulders.

She was a runner in high school. A dancer dancing, fleet of foot. She ran down the trail, the flimsy flip flops flapping.

Get to those trees, get away from the dogs.

A pain in her back drove her down. Sharp pain high up, the left shoulder blade. Sharp white pain that swept away her joy of running. As she fell, she twisted, and there was the archer, standing up the hill, looking down. A cartoon bow-person from a computer game on a screen in a nightmare arcade. A death god, bronzed and handsome.

She knew him from somewhere. She reached out.

He looked at her, smiling. Then he fitted another arrow to his bow-string.

1

Helene

THREE THINGS HAPPENED TO Helene Steinbeck on Angel Mountain.

First, she saw a sparkly bracelet, a hand, and a shock of blonde hair.

Second, a faint whistling sound turned out to be an arrow aimed at her heart.

Third, a man in green Army camos slammed her down, just off the hiking trail, and right onto a dead body.

Helene's knee exploded when she hit. She opened her mouth to scream, but a hand clamped her mouth closed. The hand smelled of man-sweat.

The man in the green camos had a rough beard. He wore dark glasses and a boonie hat. His finger was on his lips—*be quiet*. One minute the man was squatting beside her. The next minute he was prone, beside her on the rocky trail. Good. She wasn't the only one feeling the harsh rocks. The hand released her mouth. Her lips felt bruised.

"Who are you?"

"Help me off with this backpack."

The man wore a slim day-pack made of the same green camo

cloth. Who was he? What was he doing on Angel Mountain? A pain shot through her knee as she helped him get loose from the straps. From the little back-pack, a top-loader, he pulled out binoculars and a vintage Army .45 caliber automatic. Helene knew weapons from her dad—an NYPD detective who had carried a .45 for thirty years—and from her last job—Town Marshall on an island off the coast of the Carolinas. Propping himself on his elbows, the man swept the area with the glasses.

"Visitors," he said. "Two, maybe three."

"I suppose you know I'm lying on a corpse?"

"Lucky for you. It broke your fall."

"Why did you knock me down?"

"Look over your right shoulder."

Twisting, gritting her teeth at the pain in her knee, she saw the arrow meant for her driven into the trunk of a thin tree. The man held out the binoculars, and she fitted them to her face, moving from left to right, sweeping the terrain, seeing the trail twisting into the trees. And two men wearing hunters' khaki. One carried a red recurve bow, the other a black crossbow. They were bare-headed and coming this way at a trot.

"Who are they?"

"Not military," the man said. "What were you doing up here?"

"Hiking," she said. "What's your excuse?"

"Recon," he said. "You got a weapon?"

"A clasp-knife," she said.

The man nodded. As he steadied the pistol with both hands, she noticed the rear sight was a hexagon shape instead of the usual V-configuration. The binoculars felt heavy and her hands were sweating. She heard the beat of blood in her ears. As the hunters got closer, she saw they were young men, late teens or early twenties. Their grins looked vicious.

"They're stopping," she said.

"Strategy pow-wow," he said. "Or maybe deciding who gets the first shot."

Through the binoculars, Helene watched the archers separate. The hunter with the red bow took an arrow from the quiver strapped to his back. With the arrow fitted to the drawstring, he fiddled with a black slider mechanism attached to the bow. As she saw him draw the string taut, she wished she was watching an old Robin Hood movie, where the archers plotted an arc between themselves and the enemy. If you were the enemy, you would look up to see a thousand arrows raining down, like divine retribution. But here, on this sunny fall day on Angel Mountain, Helene Steinbeck was not the archer arcing the arrow—she was the target.

"He's going to shoot!" she said.

"Tricky shot," the man said, "with this breeze drifting sideways. Before we panic, let's see where it goes."

"What if it goes to me?"

"Roll sideways."

"There's a steep drop-off, bud."

"Roll the other way."

"It's uphill," she said.

"Then stick tight."

"Stick tight?" she said.

"He's a hotshot," the man said. "Probably made a bet with the cross-bow guy."

"Why don't you shoot him?"

"When the arrow misses, they'll move in closer."

"Try a warning shot," she said, "and maybe they'll run away."

"We're witnesses—they want us dead."

"Great," Helene said. "Just terrific. I love your optimism."

SHE TRACKED THE ARROW'S arc as it sprang loose from the bow-string. Lost it against the wide expanse of New Mexico sky—and then shivered as the arrow arced down, coming right at her, Helene the Target, right for her heart.

The man's hand was on her shoulder, a light touch.

"Easy," he said. "You're good."

The arrow sliced into scraggly underbrush fifteen feet away.

"Here they come," the man said. "You ever hear a gunshot up close?"

"I shot someone once."

"Plug your ears with this. Use your knife."

He handed her a brown khaki handkerchief, faded from many trips through the washing machine. Using her knife, she sawed off two strips, rolled them into little ear-plugs and plugged her ears.

The two hunters were closer, the crossbow leading, his turn for a shot. The man beside her looked relaxed. His beard was shot with gray. His eyes conveyed wisdom and intelligence. His voice was calm. He was trying to settle her down. She had so many questions. What was his name? Where had he come from? Had he been following her? That last thought made her heart flutter.

"How far away is the first guy?" the man said.

"Fifty yards?"

"Maybe sixty-five. That crossbow looks like a Horton. If he's an expert shooter, he might come close. And the bolt comes faster than that recurve arrow."

THROUGH THE BINOCULARS, HELENE saw the man with his eye to the scope mounted on the crossbow. His frozen smile had her rigid with fear. She was shivering when she heard the .45 fire, a single shot that echoed along the ridge. The shooter dropped the crossbow. She couldn't see his face, but his body collapsed as his legs gave way. He dropped to his knees and keeled over, holding both hands to his chest. His companion rushed to his side. Helene heard the .45 fire again. A long moment of waiting and hoping and then the second man twisted, a troubled torquing motion, as if he'd been clubbed on the shoulder. Helen removed one earplug.

"How did you make that shot?"

"Hexagon sights," he said. "Plus, luck with the wind and

elevation. I'll give you a demo when we're clear."

"That was amazing."

"Use those glasses. See that line of white rock just above the tree-line—maybe a couple hundred yards out. Train your eyeballs on that. Tell me what you see."

"Nothing," she said. "Rocks and scrub, and the rock is very white, I don't see—no, wait. Something's moving. The sun just glinted off metal. It's a man. He's standing up, holding something black, could be a satellite phone. Now he's moving away."

"Two shooters and a spotter," the man said. "Check the shooters."

"The crossbow guy is not moving," Helene said. "The other guy is crawling back up the trail. I see a dark place on his shirt."

"We need to clear out," the man said. "Get off this mountain before the relief column arrives. Give me the glasses, then check our corpse. See if you can find some ID."

Helene's knee was stiffening as she levered herself up. The corpse was a young girl, late teens or early twenties, blonde hair and fair skin. The broken end of an arrow stuck out of her back. Dried blood was caked on her blue T-shirt. She wore hiking shorts with those bulbous pockets. Her skin, even in death, looked white and smooth, with a patina of sunburn starting. It was hard to estimate the height and weight of a corpse, but she was perhaps five feet five, weight around one-fifty. Her feet were bare, white, and scabby with blood. One green flip flop lay in the dirt beside her left foot.

"You okay?" the man said.

"She was wearing flip flops," Helene said.

"What's your estimate on time of death?"

Was he testing her? What made him think she had that kind of expertise? Helene touched the inside of the girl's wrist. It was cool, but not cold. She touched the girl's leg.

"Still warm," she said.

"You got a vehicle?" the man said.

"At the Cerdo Falls Trailhead. What about you?"

"You're closer. Can you walk on that leg?"

"Yes."

"Okay. Grab her fanny pack. I used to know a guy with the cops. We'll let them take it. You want help getting up?"

She said "no thanks." But then her knee folded on her and she felt the sizzle-tingle of new blood rushing in. The man held out his hand and she grabbed onto it and nodded. Without effort, he pulled her up off the rocky trail and onto her feet.

"My leg went to sleep."

"Lean on me."

"Wait," she said.

Helene leaned on him as she framed the corpse in the view window of her camera. A soft click, her throat contracting. Then a quick shot of the downed bow-hunters. Without the man's hand on her arm, without him to lean against, she would have fallen. As they started down the hill, her hip bumping his, she still didn't know his name.

2

Murdock

MURDOCK CAME AWAKE WHEN the moving vehicle slammed him against the passenger door. The canyon road twisted and whoever was driving was over-confident. When they took the next corner, Murdock grabbed the support bar above the passenger door.

He looked to his left. The crazy driver was the woman from the mountain. Her last name was Steinbeck, like the guy who wrote *The Grapes of Wrath*. Murdock blinked, tried to focus on the curves in the road. He had forgotten her first name.

Steinbeck was tall, built for stamina, late thirties or early forties, and not bad to look at. She had dark hair and olive skin and a Roman nose that was almost craggy. Her face was not pretty, but the features were strong and the eyes didn't waver when they looked you over. Her hiking hat was a battered Tilley, pricey and built to last. Her tan shorts had hiked up, showing tanned thigh. Had she smiled yet? He couldn't remember. He did remember her wounded knee and the solidity of her body when he had boosted her the first few steps down the trail. Also that she smelled good.

MURDOCK YAWNED. HE NEEDED a stretch, a bath, a massage. Two nights sleeping in the woods and he was ready for food and beer and fourteen hours in the sack. He felt old and out of it.

"You don't snore, Murdock."

"I forgot your first name."

"It's Helene," she said. "With an E."

"French?" he said.

"My dad's a Prussian Jew. My mom's folks were from Ventimiglia."

"Right on the cusp," Murdock said. "But totally Mediterranean."

"You know Europe?"

"Just the bread and the wine and a good bowl of soup," he said. "How far to town?"

"Maybe ten minutes. Are you okay?"

"I'm beat," he said. "I'd like to sleep for a week, but I feel things escalating."

"What things?"

"I wish I knew. Where's that fanny pack?"

"Behind you."

THE DEAD GIRL'S ID was a New York driver's license. Her name was Sophie Orff. An apartment address. Numbered street, numbered unit. Murdock didn't know New York. Couldn't tell Soho from Upper Manhattan, Brooklyn from Queens. Sophie Orff was twenty-two. Her photo showed a blonde girl with a flashy movie star smile. Her listed height was five feet, three inches. Her weight was 158.

Other stuff from the fanny pack: lip gloss, moisturizer in a little envelope, pills in a tiny pillbox, a compact mirror. A lipstick. A stub of a drawing pencil with brown lead.

"Do you remember why I'm here?"

"Writing and painting," he said. "A teacher named Natalie."

"Why are you here?"

"A buddy of mine has a daughter," Murdock said. "She's an artist. She busted up with her boy-friend, came to the Land of Enchantment to re-boot. Had a work-study deal with an art colony, one month in duration. The month ended and she headed back east with a new friend from the colony. That was two weeks ago. No word from the daughter since."

"Male friend?" Helene said. "Or female?"

"She didn't say, which raised the hackles of suspicion in her folks. Her dad—he's an old Army pal—came to Taos to see for himself. The cops are stretched thin, a budget thing. The art colony folks didn't have a clue. So here I am."

"How did you get on that mountain?"

"I hiked in from the northwest."

"No vehicle?"

"It's on the other side of the mountain."

"How long have you been up there?"

"A couple days," he said. "My grub ran out this morning and I was breaking camp when the crossbow guy came trotting by. Moving easy but still with some stealth. He's young and tough so he got ahead of me. When I came up over a rise, I spotted you on the trail. There were two shooters; the crossbow guy had joined up with the recurve guy. And I thought I saw a spotter on that little ridge. You said he had a device. Any idea what kind?"

"I only saw him for a second," Helene said.

"Satellite phone?" Murdock said. "Maybe a camera?"

"You don't think they'd be photographing murder?"

"Just a hunch," Murdock said. "The police station is located on a side street west of Taos Plaza. If you go through this light, then turn right at the next corner, you'll be on Salazar, which will take you right there. I know the chief from way back. His name's Obregon."

"I know where the station is," Helene said. "And I think the old chief resigned. There's a temporary guy, some kind of ex-fed, while they do a search. I met him at a party."

"Changes," Murdock said. "Even in peaceful Taos."

She patted his knee. He looked up. She was smiling at him and her eyes were soft. He felt the rush. Female sympathy, female passion, female mystery. He put his hand atop hers. Today, they were survivors. They rode with their hands touching. They rode without talking along the back road, skirting behind the shops that girded Taos Plaza. At the police station, Helene Steinbeck took her hand back. She picked up her camera.

"Has the ex-fed got a name?"

"Savage," Helene said. "Everyone calls him Sammy. No one calls him chief."

"A big blond guy with a red face?" Murdock said. "Big hands, big shoulders?"

"You know him?"

"Leave the camera," Murdock said. "Don't mention the photos."

"We need the photos—to corroborate our story."

"That was a planned hit up there," Murdock said. "Those guys were not pros, or we'd be dead. This is a small town and we don't know who's connected to what. Leave the camera in the car."

"We hardly met and here you are bossing me around."

"Just a hunch," he said.

3

Helene

HELENE STEINBECK WAS NO stranger to police stations. When she was twelve, her dad had taken her on a tour of the Tombs, Manhattan's criminal holding facility, before it was christened the Bernard B. Kerik Complex. After Kerik's fall from grace the city renamed the place the Manhattan Detention Complex. She had grown up with cops and cop talk. Murdock was holding the door for her. His face was etched with fatigue and his shoulders sagged. As she crossed the threshold into cop-world, Helene saw a bullpen, three women at desks—two in uniform, one in a bright green summery dress. One of the uniforms was Sally Jo Catton, from the writing workshop. Sally Jo left her desk to give Helene a hug. She was blonde and hard from exercise. Great figure, Helene thought. The woman in the green dress brought alcohol and a big bandage for Helene's knee.

When the knee was bandaged, Sally Jo led them back to the chief's office. In the center of the door, there was a bare space, room for a new nameplate. Sally Jo was about to knock when the door opened and there stood Sammy Savage, dressed in khakis and a short-sleeve shirt, sandals with no socks. He looked bigger than she remembered, heavier, with more gut, his face an unhealthy red. In his shirt pocket was a cellphone.

"Helene Steinbeck, famous writer," he said. "To what do I owe …" And then he looked at Murdock. "Foxy Murdock, what the hell?"

The two did a man-hug, one arm around the shoulders, pat-pat-pat. Helene could tell that Sammy was not happy to see Murdock. And what about that surprise name, Foxy? It fit what Helene knew about Murdock—crafty, shifty, every move clandestine.

The office was bare. No flags, no photos, no glory wall. The furniture felt temporary. A laptop next to a telephone, next to a plastic water-bottle. Sammy sat in a wooden swivel chair. Helene and Murdock sat across the desk in saggy chairs. She waited while the two men played catch-up, Sammy in Iraq, Murdock in California. "They let me go, Foxy. The bastards pensioned me off. I was going crazy when an old pal invited me to peaceful Taos. I don't have the creds for the Chief's job—when they find their permanent guy, I am back to the bread-line. But you're here on business. I can tell from the anguished looks. What's up?"

As Helene reported on the killing, Savage stared at her.

He did not take notes.

His face grew pale and he looked away.

He shuffled his feet. He took a drink of water. He shook his head. He said, "That sounds grisly. Any photos?"

"No."

"A tourist with no camera?" he said. "What court would believe that?"

"It's broken," Helene said.

"In agency parlance," he said. "A tourist without a camera is an aberration."

HE WALKED TO THE door and called for Sergeant Catton to bring a map. When she came in, they unrolled the map on the desk. Sally Jo located Flatrock Ridge. Helene put her finger on the trail where she had found the corpse. Murdock used the map to describe the action.

"The shooters were here," he said. "They had the high ground. They could shoot downhill. We were here, dodging arrows. I got off two rounds. We think there was a third guy, a spotter, on this ridge."

"You think, Foxy? You mean you aren't sure?"

"We saw movement. We saw sun glinting."

"Sally-girl," Sammy said. "Have you got enough Intel to run a crime scene op?"

"I do."

"Well, then get cracking. Whoa, there I go again, sounding like a Brit."

SAMMY'S CELLPHONE RANG. HE looked at the call-screen and frowned. He excused himself and left the office. Sally Jo asked Murdock and Helene to go through the location one more time. Where was the body? Where were the shooters? How many arrows?

Murdock said, "What happened to Chief Obregon?"

"His wife got sick and he wanted to be with her," Sally Jo said. "His replacement didn't work out, but the city council heard about this ex-CIA guy, big-time, big-league experience, already in town, so they brought him in. He didn't want to be called Acting Chief. Asked people to call him Sammy … and I'm talking too much, better get … cracking."

SAMMY CAME BACK IN. His smile was twisted and his eyes were darting around. He let out a sharp laugh, like a hyena barking. He had to run, he said. A goddamn pre-lunch meeting, followed by a lunch meeting, followed by a talk to a group of business guys. Even with all the meetings, he would work overtime to solve this crime. "If this was ten years ago," he said. "I'd run up that mountain myself, lead my own crime scene detail. I love this town, these people. I'm not gonna let a filthy thing like this happen on my watch and …"

Sammy stopped talking and swung his head around. The office door was open. A man stood in the doorway. He was handsome, dark, medium-height, wearing a pale gray suit, a blue shirt, a red tie. His hair was full and healthy. His smile showed great teeth. He had the kind of lips that made a woman want a taste. The man nodded at Sammy and said, "Agent Savage, sir." He gave Helene a good long look and nodded hello. Then he saw Murdock and grinned. "Mateo? Hey, man, good to see you. Why didn't you call?"

Murdock said, "Captain Calderon." The two men shook hands. Then they hugged. Another man-hug, but with more emotion, more trust. Helene was impressed. Murdock liked the new guy. But what was going on between Murdock and Sammy?

"Okay, Calderon," Sammy said. "What is it now?"

"I just saw the Sergeant," the man said. "She asked to borrow my top crime scene person. Something cooking I should know about?"

Sammy's cellphone rang again. He turned away to answer. His shoulders were hunched. He was having a bad day.

Murdock introduced Helene to Julio Calderon, a captain with the New Mexico State Police. Helene liked him. His handshake was warm. He told Helene he had read her book. "Great job," he said. "When can I get my autograph?" His teeth flashed. He was so good-looking. How did he know Murdock?

SAMMY'S VOICE HAD AN edge of anger. "All right. I said I'd be there. Yes, I know where it is." He stabbed at his off-button. He shook his head. He said, "I thought when I came here I'd be through with meetings. Not so. Listen, I want to thank you, Foxy and Helene, for ruining my … Just kidding. Sally Jo will come back with enough DNA to blow these dragons out of the cave."

"Where's the body?" Julio said.

"You worried about jurisdiction?"

"We work together, right?"

"You got the budget, Captain-sir. Foxy, we'll catch up. I know some great bars. Helene, a pleasure. Watch out for these bums."

Sammy's cellphone rang again. "What?" he yelled.

Helene walked out with Julio. The hallway was narrow, so Murdock dropped behind. Passing through the office, Helene felt eyes tugging at her, making her the center of attention. She had found a body. Someone had tried to kill her. Someone wanted her dead. She loved Taos. After only two months, she felt like a native. She loved the food, the colors, the people. Her writing was going well. Only this morning, she'd been making plans for another workshop. What would happen now?

Outside on the street, Julio gave her a business card. He asked where she was staying. He wanted her signature. He also wanted something else. Murdock stood off to the side. Not interfering. What did Murdock want? Why did she care?

She gave Julio two phone numbers. One for her cellphone. One for her room at the B&B. Julio's cellphone buzzed and he walked off, talking in rapid Spanish. Murdock said, "Can you haul me to my motel, Steinbeck?"

WITH MURDOCK SILENT IN the passenger seat, Helene drove along the back street called Placitas. The sun was out. The time was close to noon, and Helene was feeling wasted as she drove along the Paseo. When she pulled into the Sleep Inn parking lot, Murdock grinned at her. She wanted more than a grin—she wanted answers.

"So you knew Sammy Savage from where?"

"The jungle," Murdock said. "Sammy was CIA-liaison."

"When did you see him last?"

"Sunday," Murdock said.

"Last Sunday?"

"Yeah," Murdock said. "Around brunch-time. I had just

set up my camp, doing some light recon, found this ridge overlooking a compound—and there was my buddy Sammy Savage, partying it up. Sammy's East Coast, a Yale graduate, Fire Island, and he looked right at home. The party folks at that table were plucked from the Society pages. The men looked like CEO material; the women showed lots of skin, and between toasts they watched kids playing bows-and-arrows."

"You were looking down on Angel's Nest," Helene said.

"What's Angel's Nest?"

"What you described. Well-to-do people from Denver, Houston, Dallas. It used to be an old monastery. What room is yours?"

"Twenty-four, near the staircase."

Helene braked next to the staircase. The September sun pounded down on her SUV, and she decided that she liked her little B&B better than this stark motel.

"So because you saw Sammy having brunch on Sunday, you forced me to withhold evidence?"

"When Sammy asked about the camera, he got uptight. Why?"

"I was wondering about that, too. Why don't we discuss it and—?"

"I'm beat, Steinbeck. And Julio's gonna ask you out."

"Is this another hunch?"

"I know Julio. He was lunging at you like he'd just smelled fresh meat," Murdock said. "Make him take you to a good place. The Taos Inn's safe enough. Have him see you home. And don't tell him about the photo."

"How do you know Julio?"

"Served under his dad in the jungle," Murdock said. "His name's Enrique. When he left the service he signed on with the Albuquerque cops—and since I was a cop we did some business. Julio was a star quarterback, went to school on a scholarship, got his law degree before he blasted through the academy to become a top cop."

Murdock exited the SUV and came around to her window. The noonday light was bright, putting him in shadow. His voice was even when he asked, "Up there on the mountain, you told me that you'd shot someone?"

"I shot a killer."

"How did that happen?"

"I was a Town Marshal, a little island off the Carolina coast."

"You still have your Town Marshal weapon?"

"In my room. Why?"

"Let me guess," he said. "A lady's pretty little Air-weight Colt five-shot twenty-two?"

"The Airweight is Smith and Wesson," Helene said. "Not a Colt. The caliber is thirty-eight, not twenty-two. And I pack a Glock Nine."

Murdock grinned. Though not a gun-freak, Helene did like the smooth feel of a good weapon. When he grinned she felt a little tingle. Or maybe it was a *frisson*.

Murdock said, "Make sure it's loaded and keep it handy."

"I feel perfectly safe in my little B&B."

"They saw the camera, Steinbeck. Now they want you dead. Taos is a small town, nowhere for a beautiful stranger to hide."

Murdock yawned and his shoulders slumped. Helene wanted to ask more questions—about Murdock, about Savage, about what he was not telling her—but this was not the time. The man was obviously beat.

"Get some sleep, Murdock."

"Have yourself a good dinner," he said.

He grinned at her, slapped the roof of her SUV, and walked away. A solid man, six feet, maybe 6-1. A tired man who had saved her life on the mountain. She wondered how old he was. Then she noticed her armpits were wet. She rolled up the window and cranked the air-conditioning to high. As the cab cooled, she remembered what he had called her: *A beautiful stranger*.

Helene smiled to herself. She felt another little tingle and the smile stayed put. How long had it been since a man had made her tingle?

4
Helene

HELENE TOOK A NAP. When she woke up she went into the shower, closed her eyes, ordered herself to relax. At the end, she stayed under the cold water for a ten-count—a trick she had learned from her father to activate her immune system. Her hair wrapped in a towel, she phoned the number for Julio Calderon.

He was at her B&B in seventeen minutes. They sat in the patio with shade from the cottonwoods, sipping iced tea. She replayed the scene on the trail: the dead girl, the two hunters shooting arrows, Murdock's reply with his pistol, the third man who was watching from a little escarpment. As she talked, Julio made notes on a tiny iPhone screen, his thumbs flying. When she finished, he asked questions.

"So how far away were the bow and arrow guys?"

"They were uphill and I was on the ground. Maybe fifty yards?"

"Where did Mateo come from?"

"Out of nowhere," she said. "I didn't see him until I was on the ground."

"He was an Army shooting champ. He tell you that?"

"All I know about him is that he lives in Seattle and he's here helping out a friend whose daughter has gone missing."

Julio scrolled to a page in his little device. "The friend's name is Charles Bellini," Julio said. "His daughter's name is Barbara. We know because Mister Bellini logged her with Missing Persons. They found no registration at the art colony. Bellini's got some bucks to send Mateo out here. He don't work cheap."

Julio checked his watch. Said he had to make a phone call. And left Helene alone. When he came back, he said, "I've got more questions and I haven't eaten since yesterday."

"So that's how you stay so lean."

"And I was wondering if I could take you to dinner."

Helene paused, remembering the words of Murdock, and said, "I've heard good things about the Taos Inn."

THE TAOS INN WAS vintage old-frontier New Mexico. Dark wood, red pavers, lots of flower pots. For the summer, the street-front had been turned into a sidewalk patio. You walked through the patio into a lobby with a high ceiling and a balcony. You bypassed the registration desk and heard the murmur of conversation as you entered a pleasant dining room. Their table was stage center and people kept looking over. While Julio talked, Helene wondered about Murdock. How was he after shooting two people? What was he doing right now? Sleeping? Was Murdock right about the danger she was in? Did he have a woman? Helene stuffed herself on enchiladas verdes. Her mouth tingled; she was drinking too much. She was happy to be alive.

"I like your book," Julio said.

"Thank you."

"How did you get a gig like that? Town Marshall on a fancy island resort?"

"My dad's a cop," Helene said. "He taught me to shoot and how to handle bad guys. I finished college and worked at a publishing house in the city, where I read really awful manuscripts. I knew I could do better, so I started an MFA in creative writing, where I got into some emotional stuff with one of my instructors—he stalked me—so I went to my dad and he connected me with a woman cop who taught me a few moves that were like Aikido. The guy kept after me until I broke his finger. Meanwhile I became friends with the woman cop. One day she said there was scholarship money for qualified women who wanted to join New York's finest. So I went back to school, studied criminal law, hung out with cops, almost went to law school, went to the academy instead, did the push-ups, the squats, the sit-ups. I could outshoot most of the men."

Julio smiled at her and held up the wine bottle. Little chunks of ice clung to the glass. Helene nodded and he gave her a refill, stopping just above the halfway mark. Julio knew his wines. He also knew how to look good just sitting in a chair in a restaurant, like a photographer's model posing for the camera. She was enjoying talking about her cop days. He asked her to keep going.

Helene said, "While I studied for the detective exam, the department plopped me into a patrol car. I hated sitting in a car all day, rousting underclass kids, but then I made detective and worked with some older guys, friends of my dad's, who taught me about eyeballing a crime scene. When this job opening came up on Drake Island, I went down for an interview. I had more training than any of the men applicants and there were two women on the Town Council. Proactive feminist gals. I got the job."

"So. Enough about me. Murdock said he served with your dad."

"Yeah," Julio said. "A special rescue unit in Southeast Asia. They ran rescue ops after the President pulled the troops out and left the country hanging. Back then, Mateo was Special Forces. He was barely twenty and already had a reputation as a small arms hotshot.

"When my dad retired, he worked as a cop in Albuquerque.

His buddy Mateo was a cop in Los Angeles, then San Diego, then Newport Beach, and they got back in touch. Mateo would visit us every year, around deer season. Mateo refused to shoot a deer—he would only shoot something that could fight back—but he liked the country and so he went along with my dad to help with dressing out the kill. He really knows his anatomy."

"Dressing? As in skinning and gutting?"

"All this interest means you're into him. Right?"

"He saved my life."

Julio's phone rang. He excused himself again and walked away. Helene could hear a voice on the other end but she couldn't make out the words. The voice sounded female. When Julio came back to the table, he was shaking his head.

"What is it?"

"Crime scene people," he said. "They found the girl. Said she'd been torn up pretty bad. Coyotes maybe. They're not sure until they get some expert to verify. That means Santa Fe for me. I better get you home."

"What about the arrows?" Helene said.

"Can't tell you," Julio said. "Sorry. Let me run you back to—"

"You're busy," Helene said. "And it's a lovely night. I think I'll walk."

"You sure about that?"

THEY PARTED OUTSIDE THE Taos Inn. Julio headed for his vehicle and Helene turned right toward her B&B. Taos was high desert. When the sun went down, the temperature dropped. Her arms were cold so she pulled the fleece tighter. She felt like jogging to clear her head, but the wine slowed her down and there was no way she could jog in sandals. Cars passed, honking, pickups loaded with grinning young men. She heard whistles and cat-calls. She passed a couple coming out of the big hotel and was again pleased with her little B&B. "Keep it simple," her dad always said. A big vehicle seemed to be keeping pace with her. She looked to her left. The vehicle was a Mercedes SUV, black, with dark windows rolled up. Helene walked faster and the Mercedes sped up. She stopped walking and the Mercedes slowed. A horn honked and she walked faster. The same horn honked again and she heard her name.

"Helene! Over here!"

She turned to see Julio Calderon waving at her from behind the wheel of his Crown Vic. Horns were honking because he was holding up the long line of traffic. She hurried to his vehicle and climbed in.

"Thanks."

"Something wrong?" he said.

"That Mercedes was stalking me," she said. "Don't think it was my imagination."

"I'm running the plate now," he said, "but it's California. Out of state always takes time."

He held up his little device. It was black with a gray screen. On the screen, she saw numbers whirling—some kind of search engine.

"It's the DMV records," he said. "Department of Motor Vehicles. Sometimes states cooperate, sometimes they horse trade. There's your place. You doing okay?"

He parked in the lot and insisted on escorting her to her door. At the top of the stairs, she thanked him and he kissed her. She knew he was going to kiss her and she decided to let him. Julio had knowing lips, lightened by a boyish eagerness. Lips that knew their way around. Just enough pressure to the kiss, no pushy tongue-thrust. That was good. He held her, but not too close. Waiting for her to come to him. She understood his tactic, but she wasn't ready for him. Not just yet. Maybe never. He was good-looking and smooth with his moves. She wasn't frightened. She even welcomed the closeness because of the stalker Mercedes. But when he went after a second kiss, she pushed him away.

"What?" His voice sounded choked.

"Not tonight," Helene said. "We had a lovely evening, but I need more time, coffee, daytime, maybe a stroll, while we probe each other's secrets. You're attractive and you did get me going. I admit it; I let it happen. And now, Julio, you need to let me go inside. Alone."

"You're so lovely," he said, "and so fierce."

Then he turned and walked away.

ALONE IN HER BED, Helene watched the clock. It was digital, with little numbers that glowed in the dark. She dozed, then woke up when she heard a clunking sound, like boots on a stair step. Listened, but the sound did not repeat itself. She reached under her pillow and pulled out the Glock. Checked to make sure it was loaded, and sat on the edge of the bed. Her window was open, letting in the cool night air. More noises outside. Voices, then a scuffling sound, someone at her door, jiggling the handle. Holding the Glock, she moved to the door. No more jiggling from the doorknob, steps on the balcony. She crawled to the window and looked out. She saw someone going down the stairs. A cellphone rang and she heard a voice saying, "Okay, okay, yeah?" There was a beep, followed by urgent whispers. In the half-light from the street, Helene saw three people trotting away. They moved with the certainty of youth. Car doors slammed. A vehicle engine roared to life. The car drove off with a screech of rubber.

HELENE LOOKED AT HER hand. She was shaking and her body felt cold. She had been here three months—from the heat of June into the Indian summer of September—and she had never felt this cold. Shivering, shaky and vulnerable, she pulled her hiking pants over her pajama bottoms, fished along the floor for a long-sleeved shirt and socks. As she laced her boots, she realized she was holding her breath. She told herself to breathe and felt better. She grabbed her backpack and a down vest. She kept the Glock in her hand while she started her vehicle.

The town of Taos was asleep. No traffic, no police presence. She forgot the speed limit as she headed south on the road to Santa Fe.

Her destination was the Sleep Inn.

5
Murdock

MURDOCK DREAMED OF MONSTROUS man-eating bugs in the jungle—attacking him in the hammock slung between two trees. He felt teeth biting his ass, slapped them away. The teeth bit his arm and blood spurted from the bite and the flashlight beam lit up a platoon of black ants, big as rats. The platoon leader directed the action through a red bull-horn.

Murdock opened up with an Uzi and ant body-parts exploded through the hot jungle air, but the ants kept coming; then a new ant-leader grabbed the bull-horn. He had a British accent. The ant with the bullhorn banged on a tree trunk three times. *Knock, knock, knock.* Murdock heard his name being called. He rolled over. The sheets were sweaty from his dream. The jungle sucked at him as he pulled himself off the bed. His legs sagged and he sat back down and the knocking came again.

When he opened the door, there was Steinbeck, first name Helene—a French name, silent H, with an E tacked on the end. Murdock knew some German because of his first wife, Ilsa, who had left him for a used car dealer in Long Beach. He knew some Spanish from when his old man was billeted in Panama, guarding the canal. But no French except for *L'addition, s'il vous plaît*, which meant "Bring the check, buddy," and *Encore du vin*, which meant "Bring more wine."

Steinbeck brushed past him, hurtled into the room. She carried a backpack slung over one shoulder and a Glock in her right hand. She said, "I'm freezing. Can I use your shower?"

He showed her the bathroom. She did not lock the door behind her. Did not close the door all the way. When Murdock tried to close the door, she told him to leave it open.

While she showered, Murdock made coffee in the tiny little auto-pot. The pot said four cups, but it only made two, because by "four," it meant *demitasses*, another French word. He hated motels because he'd lived in too many. Motels strung up and down the California coast. Motels stretching from San Diego to Ensenada, on down to Puerto Vallarta, where he had gone in search of a woman. What was it the French said? *Cherchez la femme*?

The shower stopped. Murdock took his first sip of coffee. Steinbeck came out wearing pajama bottoms and a down vest over her T-shirt. She sat on the bed and pulled on white socks. Taking the coffee, she lay back against the pillows, looking less scared now. She was breathing deep on purpose, in and out. "Leave the bathroom light on," she told him. "Turn the other lights out. Is there more coffee?"

Murdock carried coffee when he traveled. Because it was a motel, he carried extra filters. When the fresh pot was done, he gave her a refill. He asked what happened, and she told him about the black Mercedes and the noises outside her window, intruders running away.

"You want to stay here awhile?"

"How about forever?" she said.

"The rooms are okay, price-wise, if you do a week."

"I don't want a room of my own," she said. "I want to stay here, with you. I feel safer—with you—okay?"

"You take the bed. I'll take the couch."

"Safer means you climb in with me."

He lay down on his left side and she lay there hugging herself, keeping her distance. Murdock told himself to relax. She scooted closer, raised up, laid her head on his left arm. Then she guided his right arm around her waist. He felt her body heat. Her foot brushed his foot. Her teeth chattered.

"I want to talk about this morning."

"Okay."

"I also want to sleep."

"Okay."

"How much sleep did you get?"

"Couple of hours."

"What do you want, Murdock?"

"Let's get some sleep."

She stopped talking. Started breathing deeper, and dropped into a twitchy sleep. Murdock, filled with questions, dozed beside her.

At 4:30 he dressed, left her alone, and went for a run. He started the run wearing bear paws, black with yellow toes. At the halfway mark, he removed the bear paws, ran back to the motel in his bare feet. As the motel came into view, he felt the eyes out there, someone watching, but saw no surveillance vehicles. When he came back to the room, Steinbeck was in the shower and the bathroom door was closed. She came out dressed in hiking clothes and carrying the Glock.

"Where did you go?" she said.

"For a run."

"In your bare feet?"

"Bare feet on the return trip," he said.

"And you don't get cut?"

"Not today," he said. "Can you drive me to my jeep?"

"Okay," she said. "Where is it?"

"Back through Taos Canyon," Murdock said. "Angel Fire, to Eagle Nest, where there's a turn-off to Little Galilee, and then we hit Indian Land and drive to the end of the road."

"So you're not kicking me out yet?"

"I like you, Steinbeck."

"Could you please call me Helene?"

"Sure."

"Julio called you Mateo. That means your real name must be Matt, but I knew a really mean man called Matthew, so until we get to know each other, I'm gonna call you Murdock, okay?"

Light from the bathroom door divided her face, one half in shadow, the other half gleaming. Good bones, classic good looks, lots of character. Murdock was a loner, but right now, with Steinbeck fresh from the shower and close enough to touch, he did not feel so alone.

6

Helene

MURDOCK WANTED HER TO go armed 24/7. But she had no pistol-carry permit, and the police station wasn't open until nine, so Helene carried the Glock in her daypack along with her wallet and lipstick, her compact mirror and moisturizer.

She was still feeling on edge as they drove through Taos Canyon. When they passed the road to the Cerdo Falls trailhead, Helene remembered yesterday, the dead girl, the arrows zinging at her, the hunters with their expensive bows, the stillness of the corpse, the lone flip flop. Shivering at the memory, Helene told Murdock about Julio's report. When she finished, he had questions.

"So the body was torn up and they assume coyotes?"

"Yes."

"They ruled out dogs?"

"I didn't ask."

"And they didn't find any trace of the shooters?"

"No trace."

"No blood? No scratches on the rocks?"

That's what Julio said. The only blood came from the dead girl."

"Who was in the search and rescue party?"

"He only mentioned Sally Jo Catton."

"Did you show him the photo?"

"I wanted to. But I decided not to."

"We need to get back up there," Murdock said. "Check it out."

"Today?"

"Nope. Today is car day. I'm hungry."

"There's a place in Angel Fire," she said.

"You hungry, Steinbeck?"

"Starving."

THEY HAD BREAKFAST IN Angel Fire Village at Mountain Espresso—whose sign said: "We got Coffee, We Got Eats." Murdock had eggs over easy, pancakes, and country sausage. Helene had oatmeal and a bran muffin, but when he gave her a bite of sausage, her mouth watered. She weighed her desire for sausage against her dwindling bank account. When the waitress asked if she wanted something more, Helene shook her head

AS THEY DROVE TOWARD the town of Eagle Nest, the Moreno Valley spread out before them like a portrait of Heaven. Cows grazed on green meadows. The Indian paintbrush glowed orange, then red. The Short Grass Festival, combined with the tennis tournament and Drusilla's writers' conference, made the traffic heavier. Helene saw license plates from California, Texas, Utah, Oklahoma, Kansas, Delaware, and Washington State. At the American Eagle travel court, on the edge of Eagle Nest, Murdock told her to turn left.

The narrow asphalt road felt private, but the sign said State Highway 68. Her tires bumped across a cattle guard and the asphalt turned to pale orange road base. A big sign read:

"Welcome to Little Galilee—a Christian Community."

The road curved through the community, Murdock explained. Little Galilee was a summer place. Things opened up on the Fourth of July and closed down in mid-September.

The road flattened out and Helene noticed that the cabins were better constructed and more luxurious—ranch style, lots of square footage, party decks everywhere. There were people unloading huge SUVs. One Lincoln Navigator, one Cadillac Escalade, four Humvees. After a curve in the road, she saw a woman coming away from a red Humvee, carrying a suitcase. She looked like she had just stepped out of a TV commercial for Land's End or Chico's. "I know her," Helene said. "Elise something—we met at Angel's Nest."

BEHIND THE FANCY CABIN, a blonde was driving arrows into a target set up on a tripod. The girl was fifteen or sixteen, with pretty legs and she took her time aiming and shooting. She stopped as Helene drove past. They crossed a cattle guard, headed down a road into a picturesque valley dotted with alpine flowers that reminded Helene of Switzerland. The road climbed past small chalets set back in the trees and then they came to a big gate and a sign that said, "Indian Land, No Trespassing." The gate was padlocked, but Murdock had a key.

When they were rolling again, she said. "Where did you get that key?"

"From a guy named Jimmy Little Deer."

"Your friend needs to work on this road."

"Potholes discourage visitors."

"What are you driving, Murdock?"

"An old Jeep," he said.

"How far is it?"

"On this road, maybe another thirty minutes."

Helene drove for half an hour. The road got worse and worse. Dodging potholes made her palms sweat. And her underarms. Beside her, Murdock rode with eyes closed, arms folded. She liked it that he didn't bug her about her driving. She didn't know he'd opened his eyes until he told her to park under a giant Ponderosa.

She switched off the ignition. The sun slid behind a cloud, and the bright morning got dark; she felt the onset of winter. Alerted by the sudden cold, she followed Murdock up a dry creek bed, her boots scuffing gravel. When he stopped, she looked around for a vehicle. He led her into a copse of dead twisted trees, where the bare branches looked like witches' arms. He handed her a pair of gloves. *Where had they come from?* He pulled on his own gloves and they both started pulling dead branches off a pile.

She was looking for the glint of chrome, a rearview mirror, a bumper. The first thing she saw was a car window. As the brush and dead limbs came away, the Jeep emerged. The exterior was camouflage—dim yellows, multiple greens, streaks of black crossing.

"Does it always look like this?"

"Special paint job," he said. "For a special job in the wilds of New Mexico."

THE JEEP'S ENGINE KICKED over right away—no grinding of the starter, no fear of being stranded in the bush. While the engine warmed up, Murdock used a special screwdriver to open a panel behind the driver's seat. Inside was a stumpy little rifle. The barrel was fat, with little holes punched in. The shoulder stock was a strange-looking metal triangle that folded out on hinges. The rear sight was that same hexagon design she had seen on his .45 automatic yesterday. Thinking about the hexagon sight brought it all back. The dead girl. The crack of the gunshot, the bodies sagging. Her own fear mixed with sharp excitement and a flood of relief that she was not going to die right then.

"What is it with those hex sights, Murdock?"

"If you're in a rush, they line up fast. You swing the gun up, look through the rear sight, no time wasted locking down the front sight. The front sight collects light. You get a better look at the target."

"I've shot with a scope," Helene said. "Are these that much better?"

"Not if you're doing a thousand yards," he said. "But up to three hundred, most guys can hit the target. I broke a scope once. I was in the field, and came close to dying. The hex sights don't break easy. Take a look."

He handed her the rifle. It was lighter than it looked, and very easy to handle. She fitted the metal stock to her shoulder and looked through the rear sight. Like magic, she found the front sight lining up for her. There was no sudden magnification—you got that with a scope—and no cross hairs, but this simple hexagon sight gave her an incredible feeling of clarity.

"Do we have time for a lesson?"

"Not right now," he said. "I want to get back to town and start working on your carry permit."

"Where do you do that?"

"Start with the cops. A word from Sammy should smooth the paper work."

"You keep looking around like you're worried about something. What is it?"

"Your black Mercedes from last night. I think I caught a glimpse."

"Where?"

"When we turned onto Highway 68."

"Why didn't you say something?"

"No reason to rattle the pilot," Murdock said. "And you were lost in the beauty of place."

She wanted to kiss him, so she gripped his arm and pulled him close. She found his lips then held the kiss until she felt him respond. She had the crazy urge to make love right here, right now, her back against the Jeep, her bare knees—but

Murdock had smelled danger and she was grateful that she was not alone.

7

Helene

WHEN THEY CAME TO the gate, the boundary to Indian land, Helene saw it was open. There was a red pickup parked just inside. And two men in jeans and plaid shirts. One of the men was young, seventeen or eighteen, and doing his teenage best to look tough. The other man was older, with a thick head of hair and a bandana headband. His eyes bored into Helene when they shook hands. The older man was Jimmy Little Deer, who had supplied the mysterious key to the gate. He addressed Murdock as bro. The younger man, a handsome boy with a shy smile, was Young Winchester. The boy blushed when he shook hands. Jimmy unwrapped the package. Inside was a pair of hexagon sights.

"So, bro," Jimmy said, "what do I owe you for these babies?"

"On me, Jimmy. And I've got a guy working on your long gun."

"The drums say that you and the lady here found a dead girl on Angel Mountain."

"What did you hear?"

"I heard they blamed wolves or coyotes. I say no way, man."

"What's your take, Jimmy?"

"Dogs, man. Maybe wild, maybe not so wild."

"You hear about city-people hunting with bows and arrows?"

"There's that kid over at Little Galilee," Jimmy said. "Tammy something. Her mom drives a big red Humvee. Speaking of big rigs, I think you got a tail. Big black Mercedes SUV. Ring any bells?"

"Where was it?" Murdock said.

"At the gate," Jimmy said.

"Did it have California plates?" Helene said.

"Sure did. It's a big black hearse-looking rig, sits up off the ground, plenty of horses, no problem climbing these crazy mountain roads. And on top there was this cool little three-armed radar gizmo that kept turning. They give you trouble, bro, give us a shout."

"Will do, Jimmy. Thanks for the heads up."

Helene waved as she passed through the gate. Jimmy Little Deer waved back. Young Winchester shot her with his videocam.

AS THEY DROVE BACK through the community of Little Galilee, Helene saw more cabins getting shuttered for winter. At the bottom of the hill, where Highway 68 took a sharp right, Murdock's Jeep turned left. In order to follow him, Helene engaged her four-wheel drive. She followed him up a steep bumpy road, past more chateaux-like cabins, where he made a hard right turn, drove about fifty feet, and parked his Jeep next to a cabin that looked closed. Helene parked beside his Jeep. Carrying his strange fat-barreled rifle, Murdock trotted to the edge of a cliff overlooking Highway 68.

To Helene's right, maybe two hundred yards down, was the steep road that forced her to use four-wheel drive. When she joined Murdock, he was lying on his stomach in the prone position. Down below, she couldn't tell how far, she saw the big Mercedes from last night. He handed her the binoculars. The glasses pulled the big Mercedes close. The windows were tinted dark, no way to see through. The hood was shiny black and a little black triangle rotated on the roof.

"They're after us, right?"

"They're after you first. After this, they'll be after me."

"What can you do with that little rifle?"

"I'm betting the glass on that brute is bullet-proof. And the hood and roof and doors could be steel plate. So I'm going for the tires. They don't look like honey-combs—that would attract attention in town—but a good high-priced radial can stop smaller ammo. Might take more than one shot. You're my spotter, Steinbeck."

The black Mercedes was moving. With its sleek carapace body and eye-dark windows and toothy chrome grill, it looked fierce. Helene started shaking. Yesterday, on Angel Mountain, she had felt so free. But then her circle of safety had been penetrated by the dead girl and two nutcases who shot her with arrows. How could this be happening to her? The Mercedes turned left and started up the rough road just taken by Helene and Murdock. Coming fast.

She could hear the car's engine. It wasn't straining, just coming on with extra power. Beside her, Murdock looked so relaxed. How did he manage that? There was a break in the aspen trees that lined the rough road. Sunlight winked off the grilled teeth as the Mercedes climbed. Beside her, she heard a hoarse whispery spitting sound like *Pfft*. And then she saw gray smoke puff out from the little holes in the muzzle of the De Lisle. Down below, the Mercedes SUV was still climbing. Murdock shot again. Helene was holding her breath. There was a long moment while things stood still, everything except the hammering of her heart, and then through the binoculars she saw the black monster leave the road.

She heard the crunch as the Mercedes crushed an aspen tree. The big black cab tilted as the front tires left the road and the fancy black deer guard came to rest against a huge rock that jutted up just below the road's edge. There was a metallic groaning sound and the big machine stopped moving. The rear tires spun, throwing a flurry of small rocks. The doors opened and people climbed out. Helene saw a bald man with a mustache and a young, handsome man with a red face. She saw a short, powerful-looking man in a leather vest, and a woman with dark glasses and a baseball cap. The bald man was on his cellphone.

When they were back at their vehicles, Helene said, "How do we get past them?"

"There's a road over the hill. Takes us back to Eagle Nest, where we pick up the road to Taos."

"I wish we could ride in one car."

"Hang tough, Steinbeck. You're doing good."

HELENE FOLLOWED HIS JEEP up the hill, past impressive cabins set back from the road, looking through the trees like medieval watch-towers. They rolled up out of a dense forest onto a leveled hillside. A sign posted on a tree said,

> End of Season Barbecue
> Angel's Nest, Saturday at Twilight
> Bring the kids

The view from up here was startling. Across the valley was a huge, humped-top mountain bare of trees. Down below, in the valley, nestled the tiny town of Eagle Nest. She could see a road leading down but no gate to the main road. The hill was steep, loaded with bumps. Her hands got sweaty on the wheel. She used low gear and was thankful for four-wheel drive.

When they were back on flat land, with the town of Eagle Nest just one barbed wire fence away, Murdock stopped the Jeep. He didn't look around to see if anyone was watching. He walked up to the wire holding a pair of blue-handled wire cutters. He wore pale yellow work gloves. There were four strands of wire. As Helene watched, he made four quick cuts.

He rolled the barbed wire aside and motioned Helene through. She was breathing hard until he joined her. On the way back to Taos, they stopped at the Cerdo Falls Trailhead. It was past noon and Helene was hungry, but Murdock wanted her to try the little De Lisle. When she lined up on a piece of dead wood, she saw what was so great about the hexagon sights. She looked through the rear sight, which led her eye through the front sight, which seemed to collect light. When she pulled the trigger, the rifle made that same little spitting sound and gray steam pumped out of the barrel. The piece of dead wood splintered.

"Good shooting, Steinbeck."

"It's so quiet," Helene said.

"There are two barrels, one inside the other. The small barrel handles the round; the big barrel exhausts the gas. There are baffles inside the fat barrel, to muffle the sound of the explosion."

"I like these hexagon sights."

"We can get some for your weapon, if you like."

"If you had said that two days ago, I would have laughed. But after yesterday—and last night, and today—I say, how fast can you get me those sights?"

"I'll call my hexagon guy," Murdock said. "He lives in Arizona and loves having me as an unpaid salesman. You hungry?"

"I would kill for a hamburger," she said, "with onion and pickle, tomato and lettuce, and gooey yellow mustard, with a beer chaser."

"I know just the place."

8
Murdock

WATCHING STEINBECK EAT, MURDOCK could tell she was a woman who liked her food. She put away a burger, an order of fries, and two draft beers. While they ate, she told him about her life as town marshal of a little island village, where the closest city was Charleston on the mainland. She told him about her dad, the New York City cop—retired now, living in Florida. She told Murdock about her first book, the book tour, the signings, the stupid questions about how to get an agent. "Where can I get a copy?"

"I have a copy just for you. It's back at the B&B. If you went with me, I could check messages and stuff."

"Okay."

"Unless you're kicking me out."

"Maybe the motel has a bigger room."

"Are you kicking me out?"

He reached across, took her hand. "No," he said. "You stick with me."

"You're making me horny," she said.

HER ROOM AT THE Welcome to Taos B&B was a second-story with a view of the patio. While she checked her phone messages, jotting notes, Murdock checked the patio. He was hunting for signs of last night's intruders. The patio was red Mexican pavers. Two tables, two awnings, a half dozen plastic chairs. A path of gray slate led to a white wooden gate. Beyond the gate was the parking lot, then the street. The fence was a cluster of flowering vines, too thick to see through, which made good cover. When he tried the gate, the hinges squealed. He was testing the gate when he heard a screen door bang and then a high-pitched voice, asking what he was doing. The voice belonged to a heavy guy wearing a T-shirt. The guy had a size XXXL gut, and he had squeezed into a *Star Wars* T-shirt that fit him like a Small. He had big, strong-looking hands and forearms like baby hams. The weight of his gut put a strain on the fancy suspenders.

"How you doing?" Murdock said.

"I asked you a question, dude."

"I'm checking the patio."

"You're supposed to check with the office first."

"Sorry. Are you the office?"

The big guy scowled, then turned. He moved like an elephant, slow. If he sat on you, you'd be dead. He came up with a shotgun. Murdock raised his hands. The shotgun was a small-bore, maybe a .410. If it was loaded with birdshot, it wouldn't kill you, but you'd spend hours getting the pellets tweezed out.

"Checking the patio for what?"

"Vandals at two a.m.," Murdock said. "Last night. If you were in the office, maybe you heard something."

"This is an upscale place in the heart of Taos," the guy said. "We got upscale folks here. No history of vandals."

Murdock was ready to dive and roll when Steinbeck called out, "Benny, what are you doing with that shotgun?"

Benny said, "Call the police, Miss Helen. I just caught a thief."

"That's only Murdock, Benny. He's with me."

"I caught him snooping around."

"He does look suspicious, Benny. Send him upstairs. And put away that rifle."

The big guy called Benny kept glaring at Murdock. His upper body trembled. He shook his head and lowered the shotgun. When he looked at Helene Steinbeck, Benny's big round face took on a beatific smile. His eyes lit up and he sighed. The sigh took forever. Benny Big Guy was a man in love. He swung back to Murdock. Said, "Next time, friend, make sure you check with the office."

"Sorry. Next time, I'll do that."

"Were there really vandals?"

"You might check with your other guests," Murdock said. "See if they heard anything."

"You some kind of detective or what?"

"In my other life," Murdock said, "I was a private eye."

"So what brings you to the land of enchantment?"

"The hot springs at Ojo Caliente."

"My idea of heaven," Benny said.

AT THE TOP OF the stairs, there was no sign of Steinbeck. As he walked along the second floor balcony, Murdock noticed that her blinds were drawn. The door to her room was closed, but the knob worked. He crossed the threshold into a warm dimness. She had turned off the air-conditioner. It took a minute for his eyes to adjust to the change in light. He had expected to see her at the desk, filling her notebook with details from the phone calls. But as his vision came back, he saw her silhouetted in the bathroom door. She moved toward him. Her feet whispered on the thin carpet. She was naked from the waist up. There was a white towel around her hips. She came into his arms and he took in the smell of her skin. Perfume, sweat, woman.

"You smell good," he said.

"Lock the door," she said.

"Thanks for rescuing me from Benny's birdshot."

She kissed him. She stuck her tongue in his ear. Whispered, "No screaming, okay?"

She led him to the bed, sat on his lap while she unbuttoned his shirt, then busied herself with unbuckling and unzipping. She was talking to herself. "Buckle, zipper, is this for me? Um, now those boots."

He sat on the bed while she unlaced his boots. She got them off, then shucked him out of his camos and his boxers. She said, "Oh, God, you." She was making him tremble. When he was naked, she sat on his thighs. The kiss started tender. It ended long, deep and breathless. She showed him a condom. "Okay?"

"Yes."

Her skin was hot. The white towel was gone. She maneuvered him to the edge of the bed, and then she took a firm grip on his dick. He felt the tightness as she slipped on the condom. "Okay?"

"Yes."

She lowered her buttocks, her thighs flexing, and slipped him inside. Murdock exhaled as he gave himself up to her. He felt her magic, her mystery. She was all women rolled into one. She was Mother Nature in all her earth-fire force. She was flying.

AFTERWARD, MURDOCK TOOK A nap. When he woke up, she was looking at him with eyes of love. He didn't know how he felt about love. Images of Hana Lakota fluttered through his memory, a silver-white bird with black markings winging away, back to the reservation. The bird slid over the horizon and vanished.

"Do you have a woman back in Seattle?"

"Not anymore."

"There was another woman in bed with us. Who was it?"

"Are you always this direct?" Murdock said.

"Welcome to the Land of Enchantment," she said. "Red rocks, pinon trees, mountains, truth. Yesterday I found a corpse, almost got killed, you had to rescue me ... If I'm too direct, just kick me out. So, who was she?

"Her name was Hana," Murdock said. "She was an artist and she was one-quarter Lakota Sioux. One day she broke off talking to me and started talking to her spirits. Three days after that, she packed up, left me alone at three in the morning, and headed back to the Dakotas."

"You went after her, of course."

"Yeah," Murdock said. "But when I found her she was lost in the spirit-world. She hooked up with a shaman—an old guy, gray hair and weird eyes. We smoked a pipe together— my mistake—because the smoke made me sick for two days. When I could walk, I split for Seattle."

"What was her name again?"

"Hana," he said, "with one N."

"When you were ahead of me, driving your Jeep, I saw her in the passenger seat."

"She's gone. You're here."

"Yes I am."

Her face moved close. Her lips parted, showing straight white teeth. She rolled on top of him. Her belly pressed his belly, her thighs strong against his. She kissed him, he felt himself stirring. Her legs were together, then they opened.

MURDOCK CAME OUT OF the shower to find Helene on her cellphone. The voice on the other end was female and sharp-edged. Helene nodded at Murdock, then pressed her end button.

"So," Helene said, "when you lived in sunny California, did you play much tennis?"

"I used tennis to get close to my clients," Murdock said. "It was a business thing. All those guys with the fancy shoes and the hot cars and the big houses—they carried trouble around. On the tennis court, I could smell their need."

"I saw you brought your tennis gear."

"And this is leading where?"

"That was Drusilla Dorn, my benefactress. Drusilla was a junior girls' tennis champion, ranked and everything, and she wants us for some friendly mixed doubles."

"Tennis is never friendly," Murdock said.

"You know what I think?"

"Never second guess a woman," Murdock said.

"I think Drusilla has heard what happened on Angel Mountain. I think she wants to meet you. I think she wants to introduce you to her guy."

"Who's her guy?"

"His name is Theo. He's a charming Brit who hasn't bothered to shed his accent. He started as a teaching pro and now he's managing a tennis club."

"Terrific, Steinbeck. Mixed doubles with a British professional reared at Wimbledon, on the slick green grass."

"It's a favor for Drusilla," Helene said. "She's been good to me."

"Theo," Murdock said. "Isn't that short for Theodore?"

"Theo is Greek," Helene said. "From 'theos,' which means god. He was a soldier—maybe you boys can be best buds."

9
Theo

THEO'S LESSON FOR THIS half-hour was a blonde female tennis star with blue eyes that matched her tight sleeveless top. On the telly, posing for the camera, she was all teeth and dimples, her hair coiffed by experts.

On the court, however, she was lazy, spoiled, stubborn and snappish—her black mood triggered by her precipitous fall in the WTA computer rankings.

Her name was Marie Claire Benoit. She was a Belgian, nineteen years old. Two weeks ago, at the US Open, her ranking had been number 7. Today, she was down the ladder at number 13. Her future was in jeopardy

She had just fired her coach, a demonstrative Italian named Tomaso Something—nasty rumors said they had been lovers—and she was here on Court One hoping that Theo could slow her descent, cast his spell, boost her back into the Top Ten. She was here hoping for magic.

MARIE-CLAIRE WAS SO DESPERATE that she was happy to pay Theo's going rate, a hundred dollars for a half hour. For his part, Theo was quite pleased to do his bit for the game. His reputation had grown with the sales of his book: *Proper Tennis for Proper Tennis Players*—and the CD with Theo onscreen in his tennis whites, the warrior-smile, that errant lock of hair across his tanned forehead, sounding, with his clipped British accent, like the Prince of Wales speaking to the nation about the latest national emergency.

THE SUN WAS HOT. There was sweat on Theo's forehead, sweat under his arms. The weather in Taos on this September afternoon had the dead feel of the desert air in the Hindu Kush, where Theo had served the Queen, in the days when his weapon of choice had been his trusty L96 PM sniper rifle, chambered for the 7.62mm bullet. Today on Court One, his weapon of choice was a red and black AeroPro racquet by Babolat. Because he spoke French, the corporation had chosen him as a tester for new products.

Unlike American coaches, Theo would seldom raise his voice to a Lesson. On court, instead of a screechy yell, he preferred a stern discipline that led to insight. Step One was the welcome to my home, this court is your home, too—then a handshake, a word, a steady look, how are you today, lovely weather, and how's your game shaping up? Step Two was the analysis, running the Lesson from corner to corner, from baseline to forecourt—to determine how the Lesson moved under stress, because in tennis, timing was all. Step Three was the report, a military briefing delivered in the language of tennis—footwork, torso torque, shoulder-work, racquet work. Racquet work meant the backswing, the point of contact when strings met ball, and the follow-through, that lovely long finish that told even the dullest spectator that you were indeed entitled to play on this court, to provide entertainment for the price of a ticket.

HE BROUGHT THE BELGIAN to the net. Her face was red, her shoulders were taking too much sun, her tight blue top failed to conceal two erect nipples. Theo explained the problem—her backswing was too lengthy, forcing her to hit late, to rush her shot—and to correct it, she should use her left hand as a guide. The look on her face was bleak with disbelief. No more talk, time for action. He situated her in the forecourt, ten feet from the net, the left hand gripping the throat of her racquet.

When the backswing started, the left hand tracked the movement, the shoulders had a cleaner turn, the backswing shrank from that exaggerated loopy clay court wind-up to a short, snappy, efficient, power-filled cranking motion.

He worked her away from the net, one step at a time, setting her up to succeed, until she was back at the baseline, moving better, her smile bright and camera-ready, because she was now hitting forehands that would maim any opponent.

The time was up. The lesson was over. The Belgian gave him six twenties and the money in his hand made him remember his own days on tour, an amateur prohibited by the British Lawn Tennis Federation from using his god-given talent to get recompensed for his labor, and felt a flash of resentment. The Belgian was excited. She threw herself at him. Her hug was fierce, full of unspoken promise—was she selecting Theo to fill the slot vacated by the Italian? It was time for her to go, but she lingered. They stood in the shade.

"Is it true what they say about you?"

"What do they say?"

"I am finding your information from Google," she said. "That you are descended from a duke or whatever. Your father was the something of Ulster."

"That was my father's brother—the Earl of Ulster—but thank you for the attention. I am quite flattered."

"If I came to the party tonight all alone, would you give me a dance?"

"Well, I would be—"

"Would you steal a kiss?"

HIS DOUBLES GAME WAS waiting—he saw them in the stands, Steinbeck the writer sitting close to the new fellow. Theo sent the Belgian on her way. Watching her exit, the smooth thighs, the tush kept tight by exercise and the mystery of youth, Theo thought she looked edible. What was it the Yanks said: she looked good enough to eat.

10

Murdock

MURDOCK WATCHED THE GUY on Court One working with the blonde chick from Belgium. There was a tennis tournament in progress—the Apache Junction WTA Invitational, sponsored by a sporting goods company that was opening a warehouse store in the north end of Taos, close to the Pueblo—and the blonde tennis chick was having major problems with her forehand. She hit wide, she hit late, she hit long, she hit too hard, she framed the ball because her hit was off-center. Theo Ulster, the head pro, was rushing her, hitting a soft one to her backhand, then popping a hard one to her forehand. Theo kept quiet, no words of criticism or encouragement—letting the girl learn from the ball. Good coaching.

Ulster had that look of entitlement—born on the grass at Centre Court, Wimbledon. Like a lot of upper-class Brits, the guy knew how to dress. The fitted white shorts, the perfect white tennis shirt, even the bush hat, with its Aussie-looking headband, just the right touch of casual. But when Ulster moved on the court, he was fluid, relaxed, confident. His strokes were textbook perfect. He was always balanced, he bent his knees for every shot, keeping his center of gravity low. Born to play, born to win.

Murdock knew good tennis because he had played as a kid growing up on Army bases. His dad had been a sergeant, a career-Army topkick non-com workhorse, smarter than the officers, who refused annual offers to attend OCS and join the officer ranks. The Sergeant was a small arms specialist who played tennis to work off the steam from the job. He did not want an Army career for his son. Better to be a touring pro. "Work hard," the Sergeant said. "Bust your balls, learn the game, master the tricks, and go on tour—you'll see what you're made of. Do it while you're young, while you still have your legs, before your muscles scream you out of bed in the morning."

"THEO PLAYED WIMBLEDON," HELENE said.

"Looks like he still could," Murdock said.

"He's awfully good. We'll be lucky to get a game."

"Smart guy," Murdock said. "He mesmerized that blonde Belgian into hitting a lot better."

"Do you find her attractive?" Helene said.

"I go for the lanky brunette types," Murdock said. "My idea of a perfect woman is a writer with one hot book who's working on the second book and has your legs."

"You're a devil, Murdock."

"Wonder where Sir Theo gets his tennis shorts."

"They are well-cut, aren't they?"

"Tell you one thing about your British gentleman—he dresses to the left."

"What do you mean, dresses to the left?"

"He's like a courtier with a codpiece. Check it out."

"A codpiece? Don't tell me you're jealous."

Down on Court One, the blonde was giving Theo a big hug. She hung on for a while. Clinging, but also wiggling. And just before she let him go, she brushed his crotch with her butt.

A VOICE FROM BEHIND them, "There you are, and this must be your Mister Murdock!"

The voice belonged to Drusilla Dorn, a woman in her late forties, tall and commanding, with a mane of rich red hair. Helene introduced them. Drusilla squeezed Helene's arm and said, "I want to know the story—where you met, the color of the sky at that moment, the mad twittering of birds, the subtle rustle of autumn leaves. I am such a romantic. Helene has been waiting for you, sir, turning down all sorts of eligible males, one who even had some money, but now that you're here she can get back to work on that project, hmmm? Oh, and we need to get you some proper tennis clothes."

"Let's hit a few first," Murdock said.

"Where's Theo? Oh, there, with his little warriors. He's so busy hosting these tournaments. Shall we?"

THEY MOVED OFF THE bleachers toward the court, where Ulster was chatting with a cluster of teens, three boys and two girls. The boys were well built, some weight work there. The girls were both pretty. As a group, the teens looked like an advertisement for the good life of wealth and privilege.

Helene nudged Murdock. "I saw that pretty one earlier, when we went after your Jeep—she was nailing the bulls-eye with bow and arrows."

"That's Tammy Wellborn," Drusilla said. "Our local archery goddess. People are counting on her to bring home Olympic Gold."

"Is there an archery school here?" Murdock said.

"Very informal," Drusilla said. "But there is a first-rate coach, if you're interested."

WHEN THE TEENS WALKED off, they did not slouch, they did not look bored with the world. They looked coordinated, like they had a common goal, a purpose that held them together. Helene was ahead, shaking hands with Theo Ulster. When the handshake was over, Theo took Helene by the shoulders, murmured something in French, and gave her a two-cheek kiss. When Drusilla introduced Murdock, she called Theo by his rank, Captain.

Up close, Murdock saw that Theo Ulster had warrior eyes. Sharp, perceptive, taking in information. This was a guy who knew how to wait. He was Murdock's height, but leaner, a true Desert Rat with the deep suntan and those solid British knees made prominent by the cut of the shorts. The white shorts were made of a stretchy fabric—enhancing the codpiece effect.

Ulster's handshake was all man. Solid, strong, just enough pressure. He smiled when Murdock said: "Good job on that forehand." Their opening conversation was almost buddy-buddy, like two old soldiers meeting in a distant land after a long period of separation.

"You look like Special Forces, old chap. Am I right?"

"For a while," Murdock said. "And I bet you were a Royal Marine."

"Almost. I had more than a decade serving in her Majesty's SAS."

"What's that?" Helene said. "Sounds like a Scandinavian airline."

"Special Air Services," Drusilla said. "You should see Theo in his dress uniform. Maybe you could wear that tonight, Theo—it drives the ladies gaga."

"Let's have a hit, shall we—get Mister Murdock warmed up. Do you have a first name, or is it just Murdock?"

"That's it," Murdock said. "Just plain Murdock."

THEY WARMED UP AND Murdock felt rusty. His feet had forgotten the moves. He was slow getting to the ball, late on his shots. Theo and Drusilla took the first set, six games to love. In the last game, Murdock felt his timing coming back. On the first game of the second set, with Helene serving, Murdock faked to his right, leaving his alley open. Smiling like a steely-eyed warrior, Theo drove a forehand at the hole, straight toward the alley, but then Murdock hustled back in time to knife a volley that hit Drusilla on the thigh.

She screamed, "You hit me!"

Murdock said he was sorry. Helene gave him a happy smile that told him she was not sorry. Helene had a great twist serve that kicked up to the enemy backhands, a hard shot to control, and Murdock's fakes threw Theo and Drusilla off their game. Helene said, "We're a team, we're a twosome, I love it."

The score was six games all and the teams were 4-4 in the tie-break when Theo's assistant, a blond security guy wearing a Racquet Club vest, called Theo to the telephone. Drusilla was ready to quit. "I'm one-hundred and ten percent sweaty, darlings—and Theo needs to stop anyway, he's the chef for this evening. A lot of people are curious about you, Mr. Murdock. Some of them are coming to dinner."

"White tie and tails?" Murdock said.

"I do love a man with a sense of humor—shall we say sevenish?"

II

Murdock

THEY CAME INTO THE member's bar and a woman in slacks grabbed Helene's hand. Her name was Marina Ramsay, her accent had a Spanish lilt, and she led them to a double-table of Dallas Rich, people who were dying to meet Murdock. He shook hands with the Latimers, the Goldens, the Jansens, and the Grahams. The men looked powerful. The women looked cared for. Helene was chatting with the blonde from Little Galilee, Elise Something, the mother of the archery girl. A big round-faced man handed Murdock a business card. Gerald A. Ramsay, CEO of Ramsbanc. Headquarters in Dallas. Murdock had seen him before.

"Heard good things about you," Ramsay said. "Maybe we could talk sometime."

"Talk about what?" Murdock said.

"Is Murdock for hire?"

"Depends on the job."

"Sleuthing," Ramsay said. "That's your thing, right?"

"Thanks for the card," Murdock said.

HELENE WAS SIGNING COPIES of her book, so Murdock

grabbed a tiny table in a dark corner. He ordered two draft beers and surveyed the crowd. The Dallas people controlled the center of the room. Against the south wall, serious looking people pecked away at laptops—writers here for the weekend conference. By the north wall, there was a cluster of young female tennis players, late teens and early twenties, tanned, smiling and giggling, enjoying their butterfly youth on the circuit. A table overlooking the tennis courts had a sign that said, "Theo's Table, Reserved."

Helene sat down beside him. "Book marketing," she said. "It never ends."

"The Ramsay guy gave me his card," Murdock said. "I feel like a baseball player about to be sold."

"I met most of them at Angel's Nest," Helene said.

"That's where I saw Ramsay," Murdock said. "Through the binocs. He was sporting a shoulder rig, playing Wyatt Earp."

"Drusilla knows the Ramsays," Helene said. "When she's in Dallas, she gets invited to their parties."

"So how do they mesh with Ulster the tennis pro?"

"What are you driving at, Mister Detective?"

"How many times have you been up there—to Angel's Nest?"

"Once. Theo kept inviting me, so I went with Drusilla. The food was to die for—all those exotic meats and sauces. I remember talking to Elise Wellborn—I had forgotten her last name until today—she's divorced, a single mom trying to raise a teenager. She's lucky, because her daughter has this drive to be a world-class archer."

"Olympic Gold," Murdock said. "How long have Drusilla and Ulster been close?"

"They were chummy when I arrived," Helene said. "Drusilla told me, in confidence, that Theo is really well-endowed. She even used the F-word, big surprise, and she should know—four marriages, four divorces—Drusilla likes her sex."

"How much money has she got?"

"Enough to fund this club. And she owns a lot of real estate."

"Does Ulster always talk like that?"

"Like what?"

"Old chap, old boy, old fellow—like an actor in a movie about the ebbing of empire."

"Women love it," Helene said.

"What about you?"

Helene Steinbeck grinned. Murdock felt her knee under the table. She put her hand on his. The hand was warm; she was warm and smelled earthy. Murdock took a deep breath. The light streamed in from the west. One side of her face glowed, the other side was in deep shadow, like a moment rendered by an artist. When she leaned closer, he felt the steady pulse of her body heat. Her face wore the look from last night, when she had called Murdock to the bed. The waitress swooped over, shattering the moment with menus for dinner. Helene said "No thank you." They finished their drinks. Two female tennis players came in.

"There's Ulster's lesson," Murdock said. "Do you know the other one?"

"Sonja Vasic," Helene said. "She's Serbian, playing well, moving up."

"Reminds me of you," Murdock said. "When you were that age."

"You didn't know me then," Helene said. "And I was never that slender, or that sexy ... but aren't you sweet? We should get going. I need a shower and maybe you can scrub my back. What are you thinking?"

"Thinking about the shower," Murdock said. "Scrubbing your sexy back."

"No," she said. "I know that look. It's pure Murdock P.I. Tell me."

"I was watching Ulster down there with the Belgian—and I flashed on Sophie Orff."

"Why?"

"Blonde hair," Murdock said, "but also the body type. They

were both chubby girls, still carrying some baby fat. They both looked … I'm not sure. Innocent but still sexy? And Theo had on his mask of disdain."

"Wow," Helene said. "Mask of Disdain. With archetypes like that, you could be a writer."

"Maybe it was the sunburned shoulders," Murdock said. "Two chubby girls, twin sunburns. Not sure it goes anywhere."

They passed the tables where the tennis players sat, chatting away in a dozen languages. Helene said, "I see sunburn on a lot of shoulders, Murdock."

"Sometimes even a world-class detective screws up."

The parking building for Apache Junction had four floors. The Jeep was on Four. When they were headed down the ramp, Helene said, "What body-type is your friend, Barbi Bellini?"

"More like the Serbian," Murdock said. "Tall and lean and Italian-dusky, with a Roman nose."

"Let's move it, Murdock. Can't be late for Drusilla's."

12

Murdock

THE MAIN COURSE FOR Drusilla's dinner party was Theo Ulster's chili, but the side dish that got all the attention was Theo's fire-roasted meats—venison, pork, turkey, rabbit—paper thin slices, accompanied by three secret spices, your choice—Hot, Medium, or Mild. As a sign of autumn, there were sweet potatoes and fresh vegetables from the Taos Farmer's Market. A Caesar salad, Taos style, three kinds of lettuce topped off with shreds of Monterey Jack cheese. College kids in aprons kept the wine carafes full.

Murdock sat across the table from Theo Ulster. Drusilla sat between them, the hostess at the head of the table. Miss Marie-Claire Benoit, the chubby-cheeked Belgian tennis star, sat between Theo and Sammy Savage. From the way she shoveled in the food, chewing with joy, you could see the reason for her chubby cheeks. Her blonde hair was almost platinum. She had a deceptive, TV-savvy smile and straight white teeth. You saw the teeth a lot because she was laughing at Theo Ulster's jokes with her mouth wide open.

As Murdock listened to the conversation, he saw Theo Ulster slather butter on a wedge of cornbread and set it on the girl's plate. She nodded, and here came the giggles. The girl was so young. And Theo, the perfect Brit, was so nonchalant.

The Serbian tennis star—Sonja Vasic—was the polar opposite of the chubby Belgian. Sonja was tall, stately, and calm. She was in her early twenties, serious instead of silly, and she kept asking Murdock questions. Was he perhaps a man with Indian blood? Did he know any Indians well? How many guns did he have? Would he please pass the venison?

Sonja sat between Murdock and Helene, who sat next to Sally Jo Catton. Sally Jo had led the Santa Fe forensic techs to the crime scene on Angel Mountain. Murdock wanted to be down at that end of the table, listening to Helene and Sally Jo.

Drusilla said, "Sally Jo? Helene? Yoo-hoo? What are you two talking about down there?"

"The dead girl," Helene said. "The one on Angel Mountain."

"Oh," Drusilla said. "Please do share it with the table."

"Murdock," Helene said, "they didn't find any arrows—"

"Arrows?" Drusilla said. "Do you mean bows and arrows?

"We're still processing," Sally Jo said. "Agent Savage says nothing gets out until we've have those test results back."

"There were no arrows found, Drusilla," Sammy said.

"We saw four arrows," Murdock said. "Three fletched arrows mean a longbow. One bolt means a crossbow. That's some heavy artillery."

Beside Murdock, Sonja said, "Someone is dead? Killed by arrows? Is it your Indians?"

"People, people," Sammy said. "Come on. We got us a great party going here and this meat is first-class—Let's change the subject, *comprende*?"

"What about the dead girl?" Murdock said.

"We found what was left of her," Sally Jo said. "Now we wait for the lab."

"What was left of her?" Murdock said.

Sally Jo looked at Sammy. He was busy eating. There was sweat on his forehead and when he chewed, he looked around the table like a man at his own funeral. "She was all torn up," Sally Jo said. "Terrible tooth marks."

"Are you thinking dogs?" Murdock said.

"Well, Johnny Sanchez thinks so. He's a park ranger."

Sammy said, "Sergeant, all this talk is ruining my dinner."

"What time did you guys make it up there?" Murdock said.

"I checked my watch," Sally Jo said. "Two-thirty-three."

"It was nine-thirty when we got off the mountain," Murdock said. "Forty minutes to Taos, where we reported the crime. That was just after ten. That left a three-hour window."

"Wild dogs?" Drusilla said.

"That's what Johnny said."

"Did anyone mention wolves?" Theo Ulster said. "That seems an obvious choice. Or coyotes?"

"Johnny said dogs."

"I know Johnny," Theo said. He's a competent man, but did he absolutely rule out wolves?"

"Johnny didn't say wolves," Sally Jo said.

Theo kept going. "Not a single trace of the Mexican Gray Wolf?"

"That was the Gila," Sally Jo said. "Down south."

Sammy looked up from his food and stared at Sally Jo. His eyes flashed and his jaws worked. When he swallowed, his Adam's apple seemed to double in size. When he spoke, his voice growled. He looked right at Murdock.

"You sure you didn't get a single photo?"

"Sammy," Murdock said. "Are you telling me I made up some story about bows and arrows?"

"Different days, old buddy. We got oversight. We got budget cuts. We got the Governor's boy perched on our shoulder. I got nothing against Julio Calderon personally, but …"

"Surely there is a photo," Theo said. "Any tourist on any given day—why, the camera is *de rigueur*."

Drusilla clinked her fork against her wine glass. "No one is eating? Is everyone finished? Is it time for dessert? Who would like—"

Theo Ulster, his face flushed, knocked over Drusilla's wine glass.

In slow motion, rich red wine splashed across Drusilla's dinner plate, turning the table cloth purple, splashing onto her filmy green dress. Theo Ulster apologized, dabbed at Drusilla with his napkin. Marie-Claire, after a two-beat pause, returned to her eating.

DRUSILLA CALLED TWO NAMES—GAVIN and Samantha—and the two college kids came running. Gavin had the smooth, shaved head of a Zen priest, his chin tweaked by a goatee. Samantha paraded her art on her body—a twisty tattoo that started at her left shoulder and ate up the white skin of her meaty upper arm. Drusilla gave orders. Samantha said, "Yes, Mrs. Dorn." While they were cleaning up, intruders appeared on the patio. Murdock saw them first. A man and a woman, one purple tux jacket and one party dress, carrying wine glasses and striding in like celebrities on an imaginary red carpet.

Drusilla's dining room had a tile floor and French doors that swung open onto a patio, where a marble fountain gurgled. Murdock recognized the man. He was Willy Mapes, a honcho at the art colony, Mapes had refused help when Murdock had asked about Barbi Bellini. The woman with Mapes was slinky, wearing one of those asymmetrical skirts.

Drusilla called her Anais, like the writer, Anais Nin. As she strode forward, Murdock saw her left leg—slender, white, stylish, no stockings. Her blouse was loose and semi-transparent. Her lipstick was a slash across her mouth. Anais looked bruised by life, but ready for more. And she was being watched by Theo Ulster. With eyes of a sniper, slow deep breathing, finger squeezing the trigger.

The college kids brought chairs. But when Anais tried to sit at Helene's end of the table, Drusilla ordered her to sit beside Murdock. With a sad smile, Anais slid into the chair between Murdock and Drusilla. She smelled exciting—Murdock remembered the Paris *poules*—and she had forgotten her bra. She crossed her legs, a cinematic glimpse of lean thighs. As she angled her narrow face to snatch the candlelight, she murmured her last name, Bertrand. Then, in a low whisper, she said, "A meeting, please, with you and your *femme*. Something I must tell you about—"

Willy Mapes finished off his first Scotch, held up his glass for a refill, and Drusilla told him he was drunk, calling him "Willis." They glared at each other. Mapes told Gavin to make it a double. Gavin looked at Drusilla.

No one was moving, so Murdock said, "Hey, Mapes? Did you locate that paperwork on Barbi Bellini?"

"Dru," Mapes said. "What's he doing here?"

"Answer the question. What paperwork is he talking about?"

Willy Mapes was a tall man who looked good in a tuxedo. He had long artistic fingers and a face that was lean and wolfish. A good front man for an art institute or a scam.

"So, Mr. Murdock? Might I assume that this alleged paperwork has something to do with your mission in Taos?"

"It does," Murdock said. "A buddy of mine has a daughter named Barbi Bellini. She's an artist in your art colony and she's gone missing—no word for two weeks. Her dad asked me to look for her. Mr. Mapes's office can't locate her paperwork."

"Listen, Dru," Mapes said. "Don't pay any attention to this claptrap. This bozo threatened me. I was about to call the police when he—"

Murdock took out his cellphone and held it out to Mapes. "Two of Taos's finest," Murdock said. "Right down the table. Agent Savage and Sergeant Catton. You want me to dial for you?"

Mapes grabbed Theo's water glass and glugged it down. Water dribbled down his chin onto his purple bowtie. He glared at Murdock. Then his eyes slid off Sonja Vasic, lingered on Helene—some kind of furtive lust revealed—flicked past Sally Jo Catton, and landed on Savage.

"Samuel," Mapes said. "I've never presumed on our friendship, but I'm asking you, as a citizen of this city, to—"

Sammy Savage tried to stand up, bracing himself by holding onto the table. He swayed, then he wobbled, then sank to his knees. Squeaking, the Belgian girl stood up and backed away. Murdock was out of his chair, moving to help Sammy. A gurgly sound belched from Sammy's open mouth. With a strangled moan, he puked what smelled like all of his dinner and maybe lunch and breakfast, too—right onto the fashionable pavers of Drusilla Dorn's tasteful dining room.

IN THE JEEP, HEADED back to the Sleep Inn, Helene said, "You think your friend Sammy ate too much?"

"Too much and too fast," Murdock said.

"He was pissed at Sally Jo," Helene said. "About the arrows."

"He's in tight with Theo," Murdock said.

"Why did he call you 'Foxy'?"

"It started in the jungle," Murdock said. "With all those swampy marshes and the Southern boys compared me to Francis Marion, a general in the war against the Brits and—"

"The Francis Marion Hotel," Helene said. "It's in Charleston—named for Francis Marion, the guerilla warfare guy. He was nicknamed the Swamp Fox."

"You know your history, Steinbeck."

"And you do have your Foxy side," Helene said.

"What did you think of Theo's venison?"

"I liked the chili better."

"The guy's a real chef."

"Let's do a probing analysis," Helene said. "You start."

"Analysis of what?" Murdock said.

"Of where we are with our case. Of how it might tie into your hunt for the girl from Seattle. You first."

"Gonna go with objects," Murdock said. "We've got arrows and bows. One arrow in Sophie. We've got one flip flop that suggests a missing twin … We've got her wallet and a New York address that Sammy should check out. We've got all that food, special emphasis on venison and chili."

"Venison," Helene said. "That's not in our case."

"It's an object," Murdock said. "Maybe even a clue, and I'm casting a wide net here."

"You are bad," Helene said, "and it's my turn. We've got a camera wanted by both Theo and Savage. We've got Theo Ulster feeding tidbits to that Belgian girl. We've got Anais Bertrand in a slinky skirt that caught your eye—you think she's wearing panties under there?"

"I could do some research," Murdock said. "Undercover stuff."

"Bad, bad," Helene said.

"We've got Drusilla stirring the pot," Murdock said, "led by the aromas of blood and death. We've got Sergeant Catton fretting about the lack of arrow-evidence at the crime scene. We've got Sammy Savage tossing his cookies."

"I was looking at Marie-Claire eating," Helene said. "And I see what you mean about her resemblance to the dead girl."

"Murdock is vindicated," he said.

"Get me back home," Helene said. "I need a shower to wash off this evening."

"Back-scrubbing time?"

"Depends how Foxy you are, Foxy."

13

Helene

HELENE CHECKED HER FACE in the bathroom mirror. Who looked back? Was it a writer? An ex-Town Marshal? A reluctant huntress? A forty-something female dying for love? A victim being set up by a killer?

As she left the bathroom, Helene worked the zipper, closing her down vest. She was still cold from the Jeep ride from Drusilla's house, through the nippy night, back to the Sleep Inn motel. Under the vest she wore a T-shirt and her soft pink pajama bottoms.

She stood in the doorway looking at Murdock. He was wearing his Army T-shirt, sitting on the bed and working on a laptop. On the bedside table was a mini cassette recorder. She was surprised that a tough gun-guy like Murdock—a throwback to frontier days—would have a laptop and a recorder.

Murdock held out his laptop. It had a soft red cover. On the screen was something that looked official. Governmental, bureaucratic.

"I got something on your guy."

"What guy?"

"Captain Theo Ulster."

"He might be *your* guy," Helene said, "but he's definitely not mine."

The room was warm, but Helene still felt shivery. She sat down at the little motel table because she didn't want to sit on the edge of the bed. At Drusilla's dinner party, Helene had picked up on Sally Jo's vibe—she was nervous about the crime scene. In a three-hour window, someone had taken away the arrows, and something wild had mauled the dead girl. Drusilla was a dear—beyond the money and the queenly gestures, vulnerable as a child—but Anais had entered like a film star, making Helene feel dowdy, and the two tennis players—so pretty, so smooth—had made her feel old.

"How did you get this information?"

"I emailed an old Army buddy," Murdock said. "He works for some black-bag intelligence outfit where he can tap into data bases. You want to hear this?"

"Just as long as he's *your* guy and not mine," Helene said.

"That's a roger," Murdock said. "The captain has a long and maybe distinguished military career. Military school, then the British Army, followed by to the SAS, Special Air Services."

"SAS," Helene said. "He said something about that on the tennis court. Like our Special Forces, right?"

"Right," Murdock said. "I met some SAS guys on a training mission. They were Seal Team quality. Tougher than most Army Rangers, with a high-percentage washout rate. Theo's daddy was a low-level diplomat. The mother was an actress, born in upstate New York. Before she married Mr. Ulster, her name was Doris Ellingham Carrillo. The captain served the Queen in Afghanistan, Malaysia, Peru during the Siege. One of his specialties was sniper. When Theo left the Army, he worked as a tennis pro in Santa Fe—that explains his footwork on the court—and then he got into the art business, imports from

Mexico, which could be how he met Drusilla. He's listed as the manager and head tennis pro of Apache Junction Estates, which includes the Racquet Club."

"At the table tonight, what made you think of dogs?"

"It was Jimmy Little Deer's idea," Murdock said. "He said 'wild dogs' and something clicked. Theo's a Brit and England is the home of the fox hunt, guys in red coats riding after a pack of hounds. I've heard coyotes—they yowl at twilight—but I was up there a couple days before you made your appearance, and I didn't hear a single yowl. I think Theo's wolf idea is a crock—a trained sleuth would call it a red herring—and we can check that notion with the wild life folks. How well do you know Sally Jo?"

"She came to Natalie's workshop," Helene said. "She's working on a memoir. I like her. She bought a copy of my book."

"She's been here awhile," Murdock said. "Maybe she knows some dirt about Captain Theo."

Helene watched him close the laptop. He left it on the table where Helene sat brooding. She wanted him to touch her. She wanted him to go away. She didn't know what she wanted. When she was brooding, she hated herself. She hated her need for him. She had known him for two days and he was a permanent itch under her skin. When he moved, Helene wished she had moved first. She watched him tuck the .45 between two cushions. He stretched out on the couch. His bare feet stuck over the armrest. He put his Boonie hat over his face. His chest rose when he inhaled, and then his breathing steadied. Was he asleep already? Helene envied that. Maybe it was the Army—all that boredom split with sudden moments of kill or be killed. Maybe in the Army you learned to grab sleep when you could.

She felt guilty about hogging the bed. After lying awake, staring at the ceiling, running scratchy films of the past life of Helene Steinbeck, she woke Murdock up. The time was 12:33. He came awake in an action-crouch, gripping the .45 automatic.

"What is it, Steinbeck?"
"Come to bed, Murdock."

14

Helene

HELENE WAS DEEP INTO a nightmare about wild dogs and dead girl tennis players when she smelled coffee. She opened her eyes to see Murdock holding out a steaming motel mug. Her first taste made her smile. He had added milk and sweetener, just the right amount. As she propped herself up, she noticed Murdock was dressed and ready to ride. Outside the window, it was pure dark, not a trace of blue dawn. She asked what was going on.

"The crime scene," he said. He was heading back up there.

"Me, too," she said.

"What about your writers' conference?"

"What's today?" she said.

"Thursday," Murdock said. "Yesterday was Wednesday. Yesterday you nailed Captain Theo in his very British privates—a terrorist act he will not forget."

"I have a workshop tomorrow," she said. "And Blue Pencil on Saturday. What about food? Water? Matches? Camping stuff?"

"Your rucksack's already packed," he said.

TAOS CANYON WAS PITCH-BLACK as they drove

through. They did not park at the Cerdo Falls trail-head. Instead, Murdock found a copse of dead trees and scraggly underbrush. It was off the road, behind an old log cabin that looked unoccupied. They started up as the sky cracked open to reveal a slice of deep blue. Murdock did not walk straight up, but sideways at an angle. When Helene followed, she saw he had found an old game trail. After twenty minutes of slow climbing, they came out of the trees into a clearing. There was more light now and Helene saw the dead tree where the arrow had stuck after missing her heart. Murdock walked past the crime scene without stopping. Helene stopped and felt the fear clutch at her throat.

He was marking a line with a dead tree limb. He handed her a flashlight.

"You remember where the bowmen were?"

"Here," she said. "I remember these flowers. What if whoever got the bowmen out of here—what if they sanitized the area?"

"That's why we're turning over rocks," Murdock said.

"Did you come prepared for crime scene work, Murdock?"

"In San Diego," he said, "my fellow cops called me Q-Tip. Here's two for you. And two plastic baggies. We need evidence, like DNA. Where do you want to start?"

She liked it that he was asking her questions instead of ordering her around. He knew how to do his thing and still make her feel like she counted. Like she was not irrelevant.

The rocks hurt her knees. She crawled along the line marked by Murdock. She had a strong fear of the bowman because he had tried to kill her twice. She shrugged off the cold morning, wishing she could change her sweaty T-shirt. She turned over a hundred rocks, two hundred, feeling herself pulled off the trail.

This is where the bowman fell. This is where he stopped to look around, to see if help was coming. Three hundred and twelve rocks. A flat rock, nothing. A round rock, a dark, crusty substance.

She sniffed it. Did it have a smell? Or did she want it to have a smell? She showed Murdock. He nodded. "Good work," he said. She swabbed little bits while he held the baggie. She dropped the rock into one baggie, along with the Q-Tip. Murdock crawled up the trail, hunting, and found another rock. How many samples did they need?

"I'm hungry," Helene said. "And my knees are sore. And I'm hoping three bags of possible DNA is enough."

"I need a look at Theo's lair," Murdock said.

"How far is it?"

"Over that hill," he said. "Then some trees and a big Ponderosa, then a little nothing hill."

"Can I leave my backpack here and pick it up on the way down?"

"We might not come back this way."

"Oh, great."

THEY LAY SIDE BY side on a flat rock overlooking Angel's Nest. Murdock had the glasses. The rock was cold, and Helene shivered from the chill. The time was after seven and the September sunlight made long thin slanting shadows down below. Angel's Nest looked different from up here. The largest building—a solid-looking log structure—sat alone on the east side, its backside dug into the hill. On the north side were two clay tennis courts, and then a smaller building, and then a heavy grove of aspen trees and then a grassy area. Helene remembered Drusilla had called it Gretna Green, after a tube station in London.

On the edge of the grass, Helene saw a group of connected boxy buildings, an L-shaped formation modeled on the Taos Pueblo, with a touch of the Anasazi cliff dwellings. They had stucco exteriors, with visible roofing timbers, like an old Army fort in a western movie. Because of the ridge, the boxy buildings were in shadow. As Helene watched, lights flickered behind a few windows.

Across the green courtyard and nestled next to the aspens

were two one-story buildings that looked functional. Both had green metal roofs.

From up here, the main road to the Pueblo and the town of Taos was out of sight behind the trees. There was a lot on the east side where Helene estimated thirty vehicles were parked: big SUVs, fancy King Cab pickups, two sports cars that looked out of place, and three Hummers.

"I was down there once," Helene said. "With Drusilla."

"How was it?" Murdock said.

"It was a weekday," Helene said. "Hardly anyone around. Theo showed us a guest bedroom. No bed, just a mat on the floor. A wash basin, pitcher, and towel. The bathrooms are communal. Sort of a summer camp for rich people."

"When was that?"

"June," Helene said. "I had just arrived. I didn't know anyone except Drusilla."

15
Murdock

USING THE GLASSES, MURDOCK did a sniper's recon, sweeping the compound, checking for movement. Smoke rose from chimneys. He spent a couple minutes checking out the big log building—had to be Theo's HQ. It had a wrap-around porch, one wide stairway to the main door, a second stairway farther along, and then a loading ramp leading to wide double doors that looked like metal.

A big man in overalls and a boonie hat moved through the cattle pasture, touching rumps, fondling ears. Like they were his friends.

It was tough to judge size and weight from a mile away through binoculars, but Murdock estimated the man's height at six-five and his weight at around two seventy-five. If the guy was bald, he could have been the driver of the black Mercedes. Swinging the glasses to his left, Murdock saw kids streaming into the courtyard. Not little kids, but teenagers with bows and arrows in quivers. Murdock handed the glasses to Helene.

"Tell me what you see."

She was quiet, intense, no talking as she adjusted the lens. The sun was up, but not warm yet, and the frost from last night was just starting to thaw.

"I see kids," Helene said.

"How many? What can you tell about them?"

"A dozen," she said. "They're all wearing shorts and T-shirts, like some sort of uniform. I see lots of longbows. There's one crossbow. Two crossbows. And I think I recognize Tammy, that pretty girl from Little Galilee. Her mother's Elise, you met her in the bar. They're in a circle, sitting down, holding hands. I bet that grass is wet."

"What about the animals?" Murdock said.

"Cows," Helene said. "Nine, ten, eleven. I know zip about cattle breeds, but they've got reddish brown coats and white faces. There's a big guy in the cow pasture, holding a sat-phone. So working from the cow pasture to that big building, we've got goats, fourteen in that herd, then pigs in a pigpen, and next to the pigs a chicken yard. A door's opening. I see a guy in a white apron. He's yawning, carrying a sack under his arm. He's tossing food and here come the chickens. There's another white apron coming out of that same door. This one is female, youngish, dark hair. She just grabbed a chicken. She's got it on the ground. Stepping on its head and tying its legs."

"How many chickens?" Murdock said.

"A bunch," Helene said. "Ninety or a hundred, easy. She's handing the chicken to the guy; he's got a knife. There's a little metal table with a thick butcher block top—hadn't seen that before. He's whacking off a head. She's bringing another chicken. Back to the cattle. The big guy's got a rope around a cow, looks smaller than the others. He's through the gate that leads to the compound and here come the teens. Okay, I see Tammy again,. She's with a tall kid who seems to be in charge. Got that insufferable jock confidence. We need one of those CIA long-distance voice grabbers."

"That's only in spy-movies," Murdock said. "What's with the captive cow?"

"Going back to the grassy area," Helene said. "The big guy's walking away, not looking back. I could be crazy, but I swear he looks kind of sad. The blonde girl's leading the cow across the grass. Someone's watching from a rooftop. It's a woman, dark hair, shorty bathrobe, barefoot, lots of jewelry, —that's Marina Ramsay. Wanna peek?"

"Back to the cow," Murdock said.

"There are two smaller buildings," Helene said. "And a big black gate, a sign I can't read. They've left the grass for a gravel walkway. Some movement by the gate. Bingo, it's Theo himself, wearing khakis and one of those Aussie hats. Theo's unlocking the gate. Saying something to Tammy. She's standing too close, Murdock, like they're got something going."

"We know he likes blondes," Murdock said.

"She can't be more than fifteen," Helene said. "Okay, I see bows and arrows. The tall jock-kid has his arrow aimed at the cow. Jesus, he shot the cow. You see that? The cow's moving. Now another kid shoots, then two more. That poor cow. Here, take the glasses. I'm gonna puke."

Murdock said nothing. Through the glasses, he saw the cow heading away from the kids with bows and arrows. Beyond the gate was a narrow defile with a thin black track that had to be asphalt. Before the cow went out of sight, Murdock counted seven arrow-hits. "Uh-oh," Helene said. "I think we've been spotted."

Murdock swung the glasses. The Ramsay woman was looking up, scanning the ridge. The sun was higher now, and she was shielding her eyes with one hand. She hurried to the edge of the roof and started down, some kind of outdoor stairway. Murdock shoved the glasses into his rucksack.

"Something happening in the big house," Helene said.

Murdock hauled the glasses out. Saw a man in khaki and three dogs.

"How serious is this?" Helene said.

"Depends on the dogs," Murdock said.

He handed her the glasses.

"I'm no dog expert," she said. "But they look like Dobermans."
"That's serious," Murdock said.

16

Helene

JOGGING HELPED HER SETTLE down. One foot after the other, running easy, paying attention to the body, hearing the slap of her daypack. The straps were too loose. At the big Ponderosa, they stopped. Murdock helped her adjust the straps. She noticed her breathing, too fast, *shit*.

"You okay running with the pack?"

"Yes," she said. "Now I am."

"Okay, here's the rough plan. We'll swing by that copse—it's where I made camp a couple days ago—enough cover to get us close to the lip of that ravine, which will lead us down to the Jeep. While there's tree cover, we'll walk fast. When we come to a bare patch, like that meadow near where we found the girl, we'll double-time. We've got a good head start and those teenage Nesters might not come after us—"

"Or maybe," Helene said, "they've got some adult-hunters who are itching for some sport."

"You have a suspicious mind," Steinbeck. "You're the point man. I'm rearguard."

MURDOCK NODDED AND HELENE broke into an easy

jog. The ground was level, then it slanted upward, still running okay. Since coming to Taos, she'd been running in the early morning, so she wouldn't have to control her food intake. The altitude not only made her thirsty, but also hungry. She loved New Mexican food and she always ate too much, but steady running through the sleepy morning streets had allowed her to eat and lose a couple of pounds. Coming out of the trees, she saw the yellow crime scene ribbons and remembered her first sighting of the dead girl. She passed the yellow ribbons and did not stop to breathe until she reached a stand of aspens. When Murdock joined her, he shrugged out of his backpack. Opened the top, and pulled out the rifle with the little exhaust holes in the barrel.

Then she heard the dogs. They were still a ways off—the sound of their baying dim, but persistent. They were hunting dogs, tracking dogs, and Helene was the prey. She shivered.

"Pull out your shoulder rig," Murdock said. "And check your weapon. Make sure it's ready to fire."

"Could these be the dogs that mauled the dead girl?"

"Good guess," Murdock said. "If they catch up to us, don't shoot unless I tell you to. One shot from that Glock and we'll draw hikers and whoever. If I go down, then you shoot to kill."

"Oh, shit, Murdock."

He patted her on the arm. She wanted a hug, but there wasn't time. What had happened to her bucolic existence in this sleepy town in northern New Mexico? One minute she had been worried about running out of money. She'd gone hiking to figure out her next move. When would she be broke? Where could she go then? She was forty-something, too old to sponge off her folks. And then she'd spotted the dead girl and some creep had fired arrows at her, arrows meant to kill, and she had been saved by—

The shoulder holster made her feel better. If they were cornered, she would go down fighting. Protecting Murdock. The hill fell away and she stumbled onto the game trail they had used earlier. She traversed the steep hillside, threading her way through downed trees and thick underbrush.

HELENE CAME TO A clearing. Murdock caught up with her. She heard something crashing through the bushes and she saw a dog leaping over a dead tree. The dog was a huge Doberman, black, with no tail. He looked like a dog from an old Sherlock Holmes story—*The Hound of the Baskervilles*. He let out a low growl and bared his teeth as he charged. Helene heard the spfft of Murdock's rifle. For a long moment, nothing happened. She thought Murdock might have missed, but then the Doberman's front legs gave way and he sagged down to the carpet of pine needles. Then she heard more crashing of brush mixed with menacing growls. A second dog appeared, this one with short black hair and white markings on his face.

She was reaching for her Glock when Murdock handed her the rifle. She shook her head—she had killed with this Glock—but her hands were on the rifle and she thought, *He's teaching me and I like it.* Then the rifle butt was against her body, where the shoulder meets the arm—that little pocket of stability when you are shaking all over, and the bounding animal is a blur in the hexagon's front sight, bright fear dancing in her brain, and her finger was squeezing the trigger because today it was kill or be killed. She didn't know where to aim—the head, the chest? Then she heard the gun's soft whisper.

The Doberman fell away, disappearing from her sights. She looked up to see it on the ground. Not running, but not dead either. The dog was trying to crawl and Murdock told her to finish it. She shot it at close range. Close enough to see the dog's eye, which looked human. She was feeling sick to her stomach when a third dog raced into the clearing. Another short hair. He froze, let out a squeak, took one look at Helene with the rifle, and made a one-eighty turn.

Murdock did not ask for the rifle back, so she clutched it and felt safer as they double-timed past the deserted cabin, back to the trailhead. The Jeep was still there, concealed from the road by the dry bushes. She felt paralyzed, the waves of shock rolling at her as Murdock cranked the engine. They made their way up the hill, and the twisty road made her queasy. Just past Palo Flechado, the shock began to go away. It was a solid feeling, as if she stood strong again, holding the door open for an unwelcome guest.

"What's going on?" Murdock said.

"The shock," she said. "From killing that dog."

"Not to mention what would have happened if you hadn't," Murdock said.

"You didn't coach me or anything," she said.

"You're a good shooter, Steinbeck. Don't underrate your lawman qualities."

"But what if I had missed?"

"You didn't miss," he said. "You did good. And I need pancakes and eggs."

"Yum," she said.

"The thought of food doesn't make you feel like urping?"

"Is that why you said *food*? You were testing me? Oh, you think you're so clever."

She bopped him on the shoulder, Murdock grinned, and the Jeep swerved. They were down off the pass, moving faster, and Helene exhaled. She wanted to talk about Angel's Nest.

She said, "Angel's Nest is Theo's dream-retreat. His idea of Utopia. He has to know what's going on."

"We'll have a talk with Theo," Murdock said.

"Where?"

"Someplace public, lots of witnesses and bright lights. But not before breakfast."

"When?"

"Maybe he'll make an appearance at your writers' conference. Right now, we have things to do."

"Like what?" Helene said.

"First," he said. "Drop by the station, see if Sammy's got your carry permit. Second, eat breakfast. Third, figure out a way to get a DNA analysis of our rocks. We don't know whose DNA it is."

"One of those two archers."

"And we don't know how old it is."

"DNA is like a hot potato," Murdock said. "You toss it to someone, see what happens."

"You'd already seen those dogs, hadn't you?"

"The day before we met," Murdock said. "That same young dog handler we saw today—they were chasing a small animal. Today they were chasing us." Helene shivered. He gripped her hand. He was grinning at her. She liked him so much. It made her feel empty, like she had a hollow place that needed filling and here he was.

"Four things to do," she said. "I have to pee."

"There's a campground," Murdock said. "I see a cookfire, but not many folks stirring."

"And I see a handy forest facility," Helene said.

BEFORE MURDOCK SET THE brake on the Jeep, Helene was on the ground running toward the row of outhouses. Three days ago, she would have noticed the sunlight, the cool morning air, the smell of breakfast cooking. Today, her only thought was peeing to relieve the bladder pressure built up by fear.

The outhouse stank and the wooden toilet seat was cold on her bottom, but Helene didn't care because she wanted to cry about those kids chasing the frightened cow. Crying, however, was not going to solve this crime. When she finished and got herself back together, she exited the outhouse to see Murdock chatting with a man in a plaid shirt.

They were standing by a cook-fire in front of a battered camper mounted on the back of a tan pickup. Murdock was sipping coffee. She walked over and got introduced. She said yes to coffee. It was hot, bitter, and wonderful. When they left,

Murdock gave the man money.

And Helene knew she was falling in love.

17

Helene

WHEN THEY CAME OUT of the canyon, Helene phoned her dad in Florida. He was happy to hear from her and he was very interested in her case. He said he would help with her DNA sample. He even spoke to Murdock on the phone. They stopped at Jack Rabbit Mailers on the Paseo. Helene did the paperwork, Murdock paid for speedy delivery to Florida. As she addressed the package, she felt cop-like. And she loved having her dad on the case.

Back in her vehicle, Helene said, "That wasn't much of a conversation, Murdock. You and my dad barely talked."

"That was guy-talk, Steinbeck."

"What did you think?"

"I like him," Murdock said.

"All you did was grunt at each other."

"He reminded me of my dad."

"Men," Helene said. "You're all impossible."

AT THE POLICE STATION on Placitas, Sammy Savage, looking green and bilious, ushered them into his office.

Blushing, he apologized for throwing up last night at Drusilla's dinner party.

When the apologies were over, Savage had Helene sign for her carry-permit. Murdock nodded and she set the second plastic baggie on his desk.

"What's this?"

"Evidence," Helene said. "Possible DNA from the crime scene."

"Won't fly," Savage said. "There's no chain of custody, all kinds of contamination."

"You don't want it," Murdock said. "Give it back."

Savage poked at the baggie with a yellow pencil, dislodging a bit of dirt. Sweat popped out on his forehead and his grin looked sick. He cocked an eye at Helene, then swiveled toward Murdock.

"You got this when?"

"This morning."

"You were up there again, screwing up the crime scene?"

"Give it back, Sammy."

"Christ. All right. You were always ... Okay. Leave it with me. No promises. You owe me, both of you, for sticking my neck out."

THEY HAD HUEVOS RANCHEROS and salsa verde at Michael's Kitchen, on Paseo Del Norte, which was close to the Welcome to Taos B&B. Murdock refused Helene's offer to pay. She hated to take his charity, but she had to admit she felt relieved.

Helene was packing a bag—underwear, socks, a couple of shirts—when Benny Kline struggled up the stairs with her bill. Three hundred dollars, hand-written on a yellow half-sheet, numbers that made Helene break out in a cold sweat. Without a word, Murdock took Benny downstairs. As they walked away, Helene heard Murdock ask Benny about computers.

Her cell rang. It was Julio Calderon, asking for five minutes of her time. Helene splashed her face with water and ran a comb through her hair. In the bathroom mirror she did not look desperate. She looked tanned, healthy, maybe even happy. As she came out of the bathroom, she heard footsteps on the stairs.

Julio's suit was beige, giving him a military look. His shoes had a perfect shine. As he shook hands with Helene, a stray lock of hair fell across his forehead.

"I left a couple messages for you," Julio said.

"I need a new battery for my phone," Helene said. "And they are very pricey, like everything in Taos."

"Want me to pick one up in Santa Fe?"

"If it doesn't cost me an arm and a leg, sure."

"We got a nibble on that black Mercedes," Julio said. "It's a lease-deal for a guy in Las Cruces. I've got an *amigo* down there who's checking it out. The search took a while because of the plates."

"Las Cruces is south of here, right?"

"Yes," Julio said. "And close to the border. So, Helene, there's this great place, just outside of town on the Paseo del Pueblo Sur. It's called La Encantada—the enchanted place—and well, I was wondering if you would allow me to take you to dinner tonight?"

"Julio, I can't."

"No?"

"No. I've got Drusilla's writers' conference. I'm a presenter. That means I offer workshops. And I signed a contract saying I would mingle with the writers. I was just about to head over there now."

"The Racquet Club, right?"

"Yes."

"I didn't see your vehicle outside, so I thought maybe I could drive you over and—"

There was a soft knock on the door. Through the screen door Helene saw Murdock. She had not heard his boots on the stairs.

"Come in," she called out. As Murdock entered, Helene felt pressure. Her chat with Julio had turned into a mini-flirtation. Her time with Murdock—refuge, shower, being held, feeling safe, loving it when he shot out that tire—had turned into a knot of complications. When the two men shook hands, they were like lions ready to do bloody combat over a single female. Julio's face registered a mixture of jealousy and confusion.

Murdock smiled, as though glad to see the son of his old Army friend. He said, "Saw your ride out there, Julio. How does she drive?"

"Better than your Jeep, Mateo. Looks better, too. What's with the camo effect?"

"It's a kit," Murdock said. "Retails for eight, but I worked the guy down to four. Works great for hunting because it doesn't spook the game."

"It's early for deer season, *amigo*."

"Helene said you were running the plates on a Mercedes?"

"I was just telling her the facts when you showed up."

Murdock nodded, but said nothing. The silence expanded and Helene felt a pounding in her ears. Julio coughed and adjusted his necktie, which was already perfect. Murdock dug into his pocket and brought out the third plastic baggie. He handed it to Julio

Helene listened while Julio questioned Murdock. What was it? Where did it come from? What about the chain of evidence? A conversation that echoed their talk with Sammy Savage. When Julio started to look peevish, Murdock held out his hand.

"Forget it," Murdock said. "Forget we asked. Forget you heard, and forget the mess someone made of the crime scene, on purpose."

The only sound in the room was three people breathing. Helene looked from Murdock to Julio, then back to Murdock.

Two strong men fighting without hitting, without shooting or stabbing, without drawing blood—competing for top dog. Julio held onto the baggie.

Murdock's hand was still out, the palm turned up, and he looked cool and in control. Julio, on the other hand, was sweating. Instead of handing the baggie back to Murdock, Julio held up one finger and said, "*Un Momento, amigo*." He pulled out his cellphone and walked onto the balcony. Before the screen door slammed behind him, Julio was talking to someone in machine-gun Spanish. Helene poked Murdock with her little finger. He grinned back at her.

"Murdock … what are you up to?"

"Testing the waters."

"Who do you think he's calling?"

"Someone in his vast cop network," Murdock said.

"How can you look like you're having fun at a time like this?"

"Where did he want to take you this time? Dinner and soft candlelight, right?"

"La Encantada," Helene said. "It's supposed to be a very nice place. Every now and then, a girl likes to be taken to a nice place."

Murdock nodded, gave her a big grin, like he could care less who she ate dinner with, or where, and then the screen door banged again and Julio was back inside, looking agitated and miffed. He took a deep breath and told Murdock he knew a way to process the DNA sample. When he swung his attention to Helene, it was a massive movement, as if he were pushing a large round boulder up a hill. His shoulders were tense, and Helene could see the cords standing out in his neck.

Julio shook hands with Murdock. Helene followed him onto the narrow balcony. Julio gripped her hand. His eyes were sad, his face defeated. Shaking his head, he said, "Miss Steinbeck. If a picture of the crime scene happens to turn up—I'm just speculating here—then I got first dibs."

She watched him trot down the stairs.

WHEN SHE CAME BACK inside, Murdock said, "Julio's a good dude."

"I see what you mean, about the hot potato."

"Who was more heat-sensitive—Sammy or Julio?"

"Sammy," she said. "Julio was protecting his job in a big organization."

"You look good, Steinbeck."

Murdock's voice was deeper. He was watching her, waiting for her to make a decision. Helene felt the heat in her belly. She was blushing. Was there a way out of this?

"YOU PAID BENNY, DIDN'T you?"

"I reasoned with Benny."

"You didn't hurt him, did you?"

"Your bill is paid. Okay?"

"Just like that?"

"Yes."

"Why?"

"You're a little short right now."

"So it's a loan?"

"I expect you to come into some money, Steinbeck."

"When?"

"Tomorrow. Or maybe next week, or next year."

"Where is this money coming from?"

"Books, bankers, bearer bonds. You never know about money."

Helene was furious. She wrote out an I.O.U. She asked Murdock how much interest and he said ten percent, and she said ten percent of what and he said you look so good when you get pissed. She was hot. She went into the bathroom, looked at her reflection. Had he really said "next year"?

Her face was flushed, what her mother used to call "high color." There was a thin sheen of sweat on her forehead, right at the hairline. She grinned at herself. The grin turned into a smile. She was still smiling when she exited the bathroom, minus the T-shirt, minus the jogbra, a towel around her waist, sarong-style. She closed the front door and locked it. A sharp click.

"I hate you," she said, and threw herself into Murdock's arms. She could feel his readiness—that made her hotter. She ripped off his clothes. The towel floated to the floor. They made hot sweaty noontime love and Helene got off twice. They agreed that she should move her stuff into Murdock's room and check out of the Welcome to Taos B&B. Murdock's Jeep wouldn't hold all her stuff, so they drove back to the Sleep Inn for Helene's SUV.

18

Murdock

MURDOCK STOOD IN THE shadows watching the door to the Mescalero Meeting Room where Helene Steinbeck was conducting her writing workshop. The conference was in full swing, and the corridor bulged with writers eager for fame and fortune from their immortal words. The sign on the door said:

Starting Your Mystery, with Helene Steinbeck, Author of *Murder on Drake Island*.

Murdock saw Theo Ulster coming, chatting with three teens—two muscular boys and the blonde archer, Tammy Wellborn. They stopped outside the door, leaning toward Theo, listening and nodding, like soldiers on a night recon patrol getting last-minute orders from their C.O. The boys went through the door. Tammy lingered. She stood close to Theo. Her smile was smug, flirty. She was fifteen. Theo was Murdock's age. They weren't touching, but they were connected.

Tammy entered the room. Theo Ulster waited until the door closed behind her. He came down the corridor, passing Murdock, and paused in the doorway to the Vestibule.

Murdock came up behind him.

"Captain Ulster, I presume."

"There you are," Theo said. "What about a drink?"

"Great."

MURDOCK FOLLOWED THEO THROUGH the crowd, writers dancing with tennis players. Two right turns brought them to the member's bar, where Theo stopped to shake hands and chat. Murdock heard him setting a time for a lesson, kept on going to Theo's table, with the reserved sign. Theo had a special captain's chair, arms and a swivel action for easy access. It had the best view of the room. Murdock took Theo's chair. He swiveled to his left, then to his right. He phoned Helene, told her where he was. She told him to watch himself.

Theo was fussy, a guy who liked things in their assigned places. Murdock was trespassing, but with a plan. Theo finished shaking hands, turned, and saw Murdock. His smile got brighter. His body stiffened. He grabbed a passing waitress, said something, and nodded at Murdock. When he arrived at the table, Theo did not sit down.

"I hope you don't mind," Theo said. "I ordered for you."

"Very hospitable, Captain. What am I drinking?"

"The usual. Pink gin and ice."

"Like the Brits in Burma," Murdock said.

"What one fights for, old boy."

The waitress arrived with two pink gins. She looked at Murdock in Theo's chair and grinned. Murdock tasted the pink gin, set the glass down, and asked for a Pacifico. Theo made a face. The waitress walked away. Murdock said, "I think I captured your captain's chair."

"Well, if you insist."

Murdock had made his point. He got up and Theo, his smile pasted on, took possession of the chair. Murdock sat across from Theo, on a barstool with no back. Murdock checked his cellphone. No messages. He set the phone on the table. Theo frowned when the waitress arrived with Murdock's beer. The two men toasted without touching glasses. The Pacifico was ice cold going down.

"SO, OLD BOY," THEO said. "I was chatting with some people and your name came up and I was wondering what your job was in Special Forces."

"Recon," Murdock said. "They sent me to language school. I studied Vietnamese and Mandarin."

"You were there, then? In Viet Nam?"

"We did rescue operations," Murdock said. "Knocked out prison camps and brought back the MIAs."

"Jolly good."

"Where were you?"

"The Hindu Kush," Theo said. "Where it became Pakistan. You never knew where you were shooting from."

"You keep a tally of your kills?"

"Command did that, of course."

"And?"

Theo sipped his drink. His eyes got that faraway look, a soldier recalling old battles, distant wars. He looked past Murdock, scanning the crowd. Like he was scanning a brown valley in the wilds of Afghanistan, checking for targets. His smile was bleak. He hoisted his glass.

"Speaking of shooting," Theo said. "The other day on Flatrock Ridge, you shot twice and got two hits—is that really so?"

"Where did you hear that?" Murdock said.

"From you, old boy. Last evening at Drusilla's table. There was all that frivolous talk about arrows and dogs—and I distinctly remember that you claimed two hits from two shots."

Murdock drank some beer. The glass was half full and the beer had lost that first icy edge. Theo was lying. Was he speaking from experience, because he'd been up there? Or had someone told him?

"You train archers up there, Ulster?"

"Up where?"

"Angel's Roost—you got yourself an archery school?"

"The proper term is Nest," Theo said. "Angel's Nest, and the answer is no. There is no archery school, per se, but there are some talented young people and this year they are fortunate to have a coach. Or rather, one of our young people has her own personal coach, who occasionally points out certain techniques to a select few."

"Those meatheads that shot at Helene—they had training from your coach?"

"Surely you're not implying that I or someone in my retinue would—"

THEO DIDN'T GET TO finish his sentence because a woman appeared at the table. Murdock had seen her before, climbing out of the black Mercedes SUV at Little Galilee—the day of the Jeep retrieval. She had black hair, and her face looked classically Italian, the face of an angel in a painting from the Renaissance. The red blouse was tight, two buttons undone, and the white shorts displayed her tan. She sat beside Murdock, her body heat wafting his way.

"I'm Carla," she said.

Her handshake was strong. Necessary for an archery coach.

Theo said, "Do please join us, *Signorina*."

"Thanks."

Carla waved at the waitress. Ordered a gin and tonic, Beefeaters. She shifted her body, bumped Murdock with her hip. Murdock said, "You're just in time."

"Time for what?"

"The Captain here was just telling me you're Tammy Wellborn's personal trainer and that she's on track to win Olympic Gold."

"The kid's got talent, but she needs to practice more."

"Perhaps if you handled her with more aplomb, Signorina Carlini."

"What does that mean—aplomb?"

"It means cocky," Murdock said.

"More precisely," Theo said, "it means self-assured."

"You want to coach little Miss Perfect, Ted, be my guest."

"Carlini," Murdock said. "That's Italian, right?"

"Straight from Palermo, why?"

"A buddy of mine—his name is Bellini—had his daughter go missing from the Art Colony, and I thought maybe, being Italian—and Taos being a small, cozy, gossipy kind of town— maybe you ran into her, or heard her name. Just asking."

Carla shook her head. Her drink arrived. She clinked her glass to Murdock's. She did not clink with Theo.

"Can't help you," she said. "Wasn't Bellini a sculptor or something?"

"A composer," Murdock said.

"Yeah, Italian history, right?"

Silence bloomed at the captain's table. Carla shifted positions, the red blouse opened, and Murdock saw curves and darkness. She gave him a look and he felt her leg under the table. The touch was meant as a distraction. Was she operating solo? Or was she following orders from Theo Ulster?

"Is this your regular gig?" Murdock said. "Coaching Olympic hopefuls in the heart of the Sangre de Cristos?"

"In real life," she said. "I'm a CPA. I was on the team when I was Tammy's age. Brought back a bronze. Didn't make the team four years later so I went to college and got married. End of story. And what about you, Murdock? Where—"

A voice behind Murdock said, "I smell a party." The voice belonged to Sammy Savage, who stood there swaying, holding a champagne bottle in one hand, and two flimsy long-stemmed glasses in the other. His face was red, and his eyes were college boy stupid. He looked like a CIA guy in an action movie— sandals, tan trousers, a short-sleeve shirt left untucked. Sammy jerked his head at the waitress and asked for a chair. She borrowed a chair, held it for him while he sat.

Theo said, "You're drunk, old boy."

"You always talk like that, Ulster?"

"Like what, old boy?"

"Like a fairy from a British boy's school? 'Old boy, old chap, old cock.' Don't answer that. Just kidding. What's Detective Super Sleuth doing here? Cop stuff, I bet."

"You're a cop?" Carla said.

"Army CID," Murdock said. "My C.O. thought I had a nose for homicide."

"A cop in the Army," Carla said.

"That's where I met Sammy. Back then, he had a nose for clandestine intrigue," Murdock said. "Right, Sammy?"

"This fucking champagne is warm," Sammy said. "And going flat."

"Speaking of intrigue," Murdock said. "Are you the spy who leaked the information to Ulster about what happened on Flatrock Ridge?"

"Leak? Information? What is this shit?"

"Tuesday morning," Murdock said. "When Helene and I reported the Sophie Orff murder. You sat behind your desk, asking for photos. We reported the dead girl, the time, the place. We reported the two guys who shot arrows at Helene Steinbeck. I told you that I got off two rounds. We didn't tell anyone else. How soon after we left your office did you leak that information?"

"So now you're accusing me of … what? Jesus, Murdock."

Murdock stood up. He looked down at Sammy Savage. War did weird things to people. He saw a man, once a competent CIA agent, now getting sucked down the tubes. Sammy's face had lost its color. He looked sickly. A wedge of hair slanted across his sweaty forehead. As he raised the champagne glass, Sammy's hand trembled.

"One last time, Sammy. Two shots fired, no mention of any hits. When did you tell Ulster?"

Murdock leaned over, his mouth close to Sammy's ear.

Sammy reeked of booze and sweat and decay. Theo sat there, looking pissed off, holding it in. Carla's knuckles were white from gripping her drink. The silence at the captain's table spread to other tables, where heads turned and eyes swiveled. Sammy's hand reached below the table. It came up holding a Diamondback automatic, six in the magazine, thin, smallish, a good size for an ankle-carry.

Theo said, "Are you mad? Put that away."

Sammy shook his head. His grin was crazed, the last man on the last beach-head, staring into Hell.

Murdock's cellphone buzzed. He checked the window. Helene Steinbeck, texting him. Three letters on the screen. HLP. Help with no E. Murdock said, "Saved by the bell, Sammy."

Murdock left the table. He felt eyes on his back.

* * *

THEO, AWASH IN RAGE, told Savage to put the weapon away. The man was insane. Mad people had to be dealt with.

With Savage back under control, Theo pulled Carla Carlini away from the table. In a tight voice, he asked for her report on the contact in Pueblo. She said a number, 25K. The figure was outrageous, but Theo ordered her to set the plan in motion. He wanted Murdock terminated. She asked again about the 25K. Theo said, "All right, all right, just do it!" He waited while Carla made the call. She spoke, listened, spoke again, and pressed the End button. "Twelve-five by noon tomorrow," she said. "Another twelve-five when it's done." Theo nodded.

Why must everything always be about money?

19

Helene

HELENE'S WRITING WORKSHOP WAS called "Starting Your Mystery." She was using writing prompts borrowed from Natalie Goldberg and a kitchen timer borrowed from Drusilla Dorn. There were forty people in the room, forty potential book buyers. Scanning the group, Helene saw notebooks and pencils and cellphones and a couple of laptops.

Drusilla Dorn sat in the front row with a coterie of her society friends. Behind Drusilla to the left were senior citizens—white hair, blue hair, bald heads—poised and smiling. Helene was nervous talking to groups. The workshop was her way of working through that problem. She was explaining the writing rules—keep the hand moving, don't cross out, go with the heat—when a eight teenagers entered.

Helene recognized Tammy, the archer-girl, and two others from this morning, shooting arrows at that cow. The tall boy's name tag said "Tommy." When the kids smiled, they showed the perfect white teeth that went along with education, good genes, and first-class dental care. As they unpacked their rucksacks, Helene saw a copy of her book and felt better. The tall boy, Tommy, apologized for being late. Helene nodded, and felt her throat contract in fear.

She checked her pink index card. "Intro," it said. Followed by deep breathing, followed by the Warm Up writing prompt—*I remember*. Reading in twos, followed by reading to the room.

Deep breathing was Natalie Goldberg's way of settling the restless writerly body. Close your eyes, take a deep breath, let it out. Feel the air entering and leaving your body. But tonight, when Helene closed her eyes, she sensed danger. Six minutes into the workshop and she was in the grip of panic. She heard her voice, it sounded sepulchral, coming from a long way off: *Let yourself drop down, and let all the air out, and rest at the bottom of the breath.*

When the deep breathing took her down, Helene always felt ideas rushing in, images to jumpstart her writing, but in her first Taos workshop, all she felt was out of breath. She was trapped in a transparent cubicle and the oxygen had run out.

She brought them up too fast. Felt dizzy as she coughed out the first prompt—"I remember," in five minutes—and wrote fast, feeling the words pull her in, closer to the page. This was her life, writing in a notebook, taking deep breaths, watching the words flow from her pen onto the empty white page of her notebook. When the timer sounded she looked up, dazed from her own work. She stood with her back to the wall, her head down, listening as the writers read in twos. This was her world now.

The first to read was a senior citizen. He recited his topic in a droning voice: "I remember what I had for breakfast this morning, green eggs, fat bacon, and the toast was burnt." The second senior read, more droning. The tempo changed when Tammy read her piece: "I remember wanting to kill my best friend," and the room gasped.

Tammy's cheeks glowed when she read. She had a clean prose style, no flourishes. Tammy's best friend, the one she wrote about, the one she wanted to kill, was named Maury Johnson. In her piece, Tammy called him MJ, using his initials.

Those initials, MJ, rolled through Helene like jagged teeth. She felt trapped. A boy read next. His name was Maxwell and he remembered wanting to kill his dad for fucking around. The dad's middle name was Jansen, and he was called MJ—short for Maxwell Jansen—by his wife and close friends. Hearing the boy read, Helene felt better about the workshop. These kids could write.

Helene's cellphone rang. It was Murdock, heading off for a beer with Theo Ulster. "Watch yourself," she said, and turned back to the writers with the next prompt: "I want to write a story about," in seven minutes. This time Helene remembered to set the timer.

In her battered notebook, Helene wrote a story about a young woman in the mountains of New Mexico. The young woman was running, trying to escape capture. She was running from dogs and a gang of hunters with bows and arrows. Helene was not Helene, she was the dead girl, writing from the point of view of dead Sophie Orff. The arrow landed in her back. The timer buzzed. Seven minutes had flown by. Like any beginner, Helene was amazed at what she had written.

The senior citizens loosened up. Their voices were strong with the belief in their own words. Their topics switched from breakfast and grand children to memories of high school and college, lost love and sweet romance. Listening to the seniors read, Helene felt a weight lifting. The process was working; she would make it through.

Before the teenagers read, they held a whispered group meeting. They chose two designated readers, Megan and Skye. Megan was a vibrant brunette with bedroom eyes and, for her age, a lush curvy body. Skye was scrawny and hard, with a strange light in his eyes.

Megan's voice was soft when she started, "I want to write a story about killing my best friend. Her name was Mary Jo," and drew a gasp from the room. As she got into her reading, her voice grew stronger and more cadenced. She captured the room. When Megan finished, she lifted her head and locked eyeballs with Helene, who nodded back. The girl could read. She had nailed it, so what was going down? Then Helene got it. Megan's friend was Mary Jo, initials MJ. The same initials as Myra Jane, Helene's one-time best friend, who was the central character in *Murder on Drake Island*. As Megan sat down, Helene realized that the initials MJ also matched up with Maury Johnson, Tammy's best friend from the first reading.

Helene felt the edge of fear. Maybe not fear, maybe curiosity. The kids were not in the room by chance. They had been sent by someone with a game plan and the sides were uneven. Eight sassy high school kids against one Helene Steinbeck. She was out-numbered, but why was she worried? Over forty people in the workshop. Plenty of adults. She was safe here.

Skye's reading was a skimpy story about killing his number one rival on the high school soccer team. The killing was preceded by a manhunt, where Skye and his jock-friends chased the victim—identified as Manny Jones the Retard, a fat kid wearing a white polo shirt that glowed in the dark— up a steep hill, sharp rocks underfoot, and then through a wasteland wilderness of trees with witches arms for branches. As Skye finished reading and sat down, Helene looked at her group of teenagers. They had read her book and now they were playing with her. Toying with her, according to some kind of plan. There was an hour left. An hour to kill, or an hour to do her job. An hour before she could escape. Helene changed her workshop strategy—more writing, less reading.

For a solid fifty-five minutes, she had them write using prompts called Firsts and Lasts. "My first day at school," for three minutes. "My last day at school," for four minutes. "At my first birthday party," write for five minutes. No reading, no chance to rattle Helene, just writing, switching back and forth—the beginning, the end, the beginning, and when the timer buzzed, Helene thanked them for coming.

Then the bookstore person brought in books for signing and

a line of buyers formed. The senior citizens came first. They paid with credit cards from co-ops and local banks.

"To my sister in Des Moines."

"To my grandchild in Topeka."

The last senior walked away. Helene texted Murdock. "HLP."

The teenagers clustered around the table. Grinning, smug with their sex appeal, confident in their youth, their collective force. The first teen customer was Tommy—handsome and cocky, flashing a black card from Amex that made the bookseller gawk. Tommy signed the ticket with flair.

When Tommy presented his book for Helene's signature, he said, "What a great workshop, Miss Steinbeck. Oh, yeah, right, make it to my big brother, Gerry Junior—use his initials, 'To G.J., from Helene, with love'—just kidding, but listen, Miss Steinbeck, I really want to be a writer, I mean, it's like a lust, a craving, but my folks say no way to the artist's life, so I was wondering, could we buy you a coke or something, like now? Pick your brain? Get your advice?"

Helene said thank you for the invitation but she was tired and maybe some other time. And the next teenage book buyer said the same thing. A yen for writing, parents doing the old roadblock thing, could we buy you a coke or something, pick your brain, maybe?

It was a rehearsed operation with ritual overtones. Automaton teens, mocking her, setting her up, for what she did not know. Helene said "No thank you." She was tired. She was meeting someone. The invitations did not stop. She signed the last book and looked around for the bookstore person. Gone. She turned to pick up her rucksack. Skye was holding it out of easy reach. She reached for her cellphone. Moving fast, Tommy snatched the phone. His eyes looked nasty. The circle of teenagers tightened around her. Her Glock was back in the motel room. Where was Murdock?

Someone came through the door. Not Murdock. A young man wearing a Levi jacket and a red bandana headband. He held up a copy of her book and she recognized Young Winchester, the gawky Indian boy from yesterday on the mountain.

"Hey, pretty lady. I mean Miss Steinbeck. Got a book here. It's for my Uncle Jimmy. You gotta sign it for me." Young Winchester shouldered past two teenagers standing between him and Helene. The closer he got, the better Helene felt. And just then Tommy looked at Skye—they were the leaders of the pack—and together they stood in Young Winchester's path, blocking his next step, separating him from Helene.

"Not now, Chief," Tommy said.

"Hey, man," Young Winchester said. "It's cool."

"Back to the wigwam, Chief," Skye said.

"Don't fuck with me, man."

"What's up, Chief? You packing a knife in your ponytail?"

Tommy shoved the Indian boy, who danced back a couple of steps, light on his feet. Skye threw a punch. With a fighter's knowing grin, the Indian dodged. Then he hit Skye with Helene's book, knocking him to the floor. Someone came at Helene from the side, her teeth bared for combat—it was Tammy Wellborn and her eyes blazed in anger. Helene shoved her away and then Megan, who was taller, grabbed Helene's arm, sharp fingernails penetrating the sleeve. Then Megan nodded, a signal to Tammy, who pulled Helene's hair. At the same time, Megan's eyes flashed and Helene felt sharp pain as Megan's teeth bit into her wrist.

Angry now, Helene remembered hand-to-hand instruction from her police training. She broke Megan's grip by bending her middle finger. Megan kept fighting—she had to be high on drugs—and Helene bent the finger until it made a little popping sound. A sharp cry from Megan, and then Tammy came at Helene again, her eyes wide, followed by Maxwell, heavyset, with longish blond hair. His breath smelled of pot smoke.

With a sideways kick, Helene swept Tammy's legs out from under her, then grabbed the Maxwell boy in a choke-hold.

Another boy had joined Tommy and Skye. They were beating up Young Winchester. Megan was on the floor, her face white. She was holding her finger and calling Helene names—*fucking bitch, you better not mess with us*—and then Murdock arrived, looking like a beach-bum in shorts and sandals, shirt untucked. When Helene released her choke-hold, Maxwell stumbled to a corner, coughing, both hands holding his throat. His face was red. Helene's hands were shaking.

In seconds, handsome Tommy was on the floor with a bloody nose and Skye was in the corner with a white face and pale yellow puke on his shirt. Tommy shook his head like a punch-drunk prize fighter. Tammy sat next to Tommy and Megan, still with an ashen face from her broken finger, and sent hate vibes at Helene Steinbeck. Sue Ellen and Maxwell cowered in the corner.

Murdock called Apache Junction security. When they arrived—two young men with short hair, pistols, and yellow shooting glasses—Murdock and Helene left, their arms around Young Winchester.

AT THE HOSPITAL, THE orderlies took Young Winchester into an exam room and a cute young doctor asked Helene about her last tetanus shot, then wrote on a clipboard. A nurse cleaned Helene's bite wound and as she taped on an artful bandage, said, "It's superficial, but the human mouth is filthy, so if it heats up or gets red, you motor on back to us, okay?" There was no word on Young Winchester, so Helene and Murdock sat in the ER waiting room. She felt drained by the attack.

When Jimmy Little Deer arrived, Murdock briefed him, then said Helene needed rest. As they walked to Murdock's Jeep, Helene noticed her feet were dragging. The desert night was chilly and she clung to Murdock, pressing herself into him. No question in her mind that she loved this man.

20

Helene

HOME FOR HELENE STEINBECK was Murdock's bed in his motel room at the Sleep Inn. Home was where Murdock was. She was being selfish. Someone was after her. She felt crazy. Home for Helene was making love to Murdock, feeling him close, feeling him inside her, a blind wordless act of coupling where she lost herself in ecstasy, tingling, burning, thrilled by her response to this man, herself so open, so willing to surrender and to conquer, in the same breathless instant, feeling the power in one long upward thrust of her thighs. Would it last?

MURDOCK CAME OUT OF the shower, wearing a towel, ready for action. Helene shook her head, not in the mood, and Murdock nodded okay. *What a nice man*. She patted the bed and looked at him. He slipped into bed, wearing boxer shorts and a clean white T-shirt. He smelled good. Helene was still rattled from the encounter with those kids. She snuggled her shoulder against his.

"What do you think will happen?" she said.

"We could get arrested," Murdock said.

"But they started it!" Helene said. "Young Winchester was terribly hurt. The hospital—"

"We're outnumbered in court. They've got the power."

"They planned this, Murdock. They rehearsed it."

"Yeah," Murdock said. "And where there is planning, there is the fine hand of Captain Theo. He was coaching those kids before they went into your room."

"It was weird," Helene said. "They sat together, they exchanged secret signals, and when they read aloud, they were using stuff from my book."

"Like what?" Murdock said.

"The people they wrote about all had the initials MJ—my killer was named Myra Jane. They read to me, not the room, as if they were letting me know they had my number. They're smart, they've been trained."

"Smarmy little pricks," Murdock said.

"How was your beer with Theo?"

"He knows I shot at those bowmen. I'm betting Sammy is the leak. When I pushed Sammy about it, he hauled out his ankle-gun."

"I don't like Sammy," Helene said.

"Then when Carla Carlini arrived, I brought up Barbi's name and the table got real quiet."

"Who is Carla Carlini?"

"Tammy's archery coach."

"Attractive?"

"Not my type."

"What was she wearing?"

"Shorts and a tight blouse."

"Did she give you a peek at her boobies?"

"Yeah, but just then the phone rang."

Helene swatted Murdock. "You lie," she said.

She went into his arms. "I was really scared, Murdock. Those kids—I was outnumbered—it happened so fast."

AT 5:23 IN FULL pre-dawn dark they went for a run. Murdock ran barefoot. *What was he trying to prove?* Helene tried on his bear-claw toe shoes, but on her feet they felt as weird as they looked. Back at the motel, the message light was blinking on the phone. The caller was Sammy Savage. He wanted a meeting at seven.

The meeting took place in the Taos police station. Helene, Murdock, Jimmy Little Deer and Young Winchester sat across the table from Sammy Savage and an Assistant District Attorney named Rocky Benitez. For the meeting, Savage wore a summer-weight suit. Like his other clothes, the suit looked two sizes too small. Rocky Benitez had on a beige, western-style business suit, a string tie, and cowboy boots.

Lawyer Benitez said, "You've got a good case—kids assaulting a lone adult—but it's nowhere near air-tight. And you're up against some big money. The parents will pay big time to keep their kids out of court, out of the system, and out of the pokey. Your bruises are real, but they got a lawyer who's ready to file assault charges against Miss Steinbeck and Jimmy's nephew."

"There were eight of them," Helene said. "They came after us."

"They're claiming the boy had a knife."

"I didn't see a knife," Helene said.

"Who's the lawyer?" Murdock said.

"Fella name of Crane," Benitez said. "Mordecai Crane from Dallas."

"The man who defended the Evil Twins from River Oaks?" Helene said.

"That's him, all right."

"What are they offering?" Murdock said.

Silence in the room. Then Rocky Benitez spoke. "Forty grand, split down the middle."

"Bullshit," Murdock said.

"Miss Steinbeck here was a peace officer," Benitez said. "She had police training and she left bruises and a broken finger. In a court of law, an attorney would weigh your bruises against their bruises. And the broken finger."

Helene shook her head. She hated not having money, hated people who could buy her and sell her. She found a tissue and blew her nose. Then she looked at Young Winchester. His head was bandaged and there were bruises on his face and his crutches were leaning against the wall.

"I'm so sorry to drag you into this," she said.

"Bunch of effing Anglo white-eyes," he said. "They—"

"Easy, son," the lawyer said. "Remember where you're at."

"Is Crane here in town?" Murdock said.

"In the other room. Want me to fetch him?"

"It's their call," Murdock said. "Miss Steinbeck and Young Winchester."

"First," Helene said, "before we deal with this Mordecai Crane, we need to talk."

Savage and the lawyer left the room. Helene pulled her chair close to Young Winchester. She asked how he felt. The boy shook his head, shrugged, and looked at Jimmy, who said they were broke. The ER bill from last night was five thousand dollars.

"We would love to do battle with these people," Jimmy said, "but this is not the hill to die on. I want my nephew back on his feet."

When Savage and the DA came back, they brought a third man, Mordecai Crane.

Mordecai Crane was a thin man in blue slacks, a white shirt, and a red velvet vest. He had a goatee and his mustache was well-trimmed. His eyes devoured Helene. His handshake was warm and genuine. "I found your book very interesting. A good read," he said. "You're quite a writer."

When Crane shook hands with Murdock, Helene could see them squaring off, Alpha males sizing each other up, prehistoric urges still buried in the DNA. When he shook hands with Jimmy Little Deer and Young Winchester, Mordecai Crane made himself look smaller, no threat intended. *What a clever man.*

Crane sat between Helene and Young Winchester and laid out the offer. Forty thousand dollars, to be divided between them. In return, they would sign a paper that nullified their current complaints against the eight teenagers, and a second paper agreeing not to bring future complaints.

There were four copies. Murdock was the last to finish reading. He looked at Mordecai Crane and grinned. "A hundred and twenty," he said, "even split."

"Are you empowered to negotiate for them?"

"Yes," said Helene.

Young Winchester nodded.

Jimmy Little Deer said, "Go Mateo."

"The kid's hurt bad," Murdock said. "If we display him to a judge and get testimony from a couple of medical experts, your clients might avoid jail-time, but their names will get logged into the system. They'll have a lousy year, missing school, getting booted off the track team. They assaulted a lone female; then they ganged up on a juvenile, three to one."

"Is that it?" Mordecai Crane said.

"Miss Steinbeck was a law officer," Murdock said. "And she maintains connections with the law enforcement community. Her dad's a retired cop. He has lots of buddies who are also retired. They're blue collar guys, working stiffs like me. While your clients are sitting in court—or maybe they get to cool their heels in the local slammer with the drunks and crazies—we'll field an army of experienced investigators, working guys who get off on nailing perps with money. No telling what they'll dig up. Maybe another Enron."

"You're threatening a way of life," Crane said.

"A hundred and twenty thousand," Murdock said.

"Let me make a call. If you will excuse me?"

Cellphone in hand, Mordecai Crane left the room. Helene turned to Murdock. She gave him her frown—it had stopped a lot of guys dead in their tracks—but the frown refused to stay put, and she was soon grinning at him. Outside the window, she could see Mordecai Crane, his back turned to the room. At the table, surrounded by victims, he had looked in control. Outside the room, away from the table, he looked tense.

* * *

MORDECAI CRANE WAS OUTSIDE the building, standing in the morning sun, while he conferred with Gerald Ramsay, father of Tommy and Gerry Junior, and the President and CEO of Ramsay Financial, the parent company of Ramsbanc One, a full-service, customer-friendly walk-in bank spreading from Texas into the Gulf States.

Crane's specialty was criminal defense. In his career he had helped two dozen stone killers dance away from the death penalty (the majority went free, no time served)—and he was urging Gerald Ramsay, who had a personal net worth of four billion dollars, to pay the money or waste time in the local courts.

"Whose fucking side are you on, Mordecai?"

"Gerry," Crane said. "This is a no-brainer. The Steinbeck woman was in law enforcement. She's connected to that community. The Indian kid's got beaucoup medical costs. In this town, he'll gather sympathy. You cut a check, the bank slaps on a three-day hold, we've got the weekend coming up. That gives Theo through Sunday to work something out."

"Sunday with Theo. Always a treat."

"The check, Gerry."

* * *

HELENE WAS TALKING TO Murdock when Mordecai Crane came back into the room. He took back the four copies of the agreement. Using a thick-nibbed fountain pen, he changed the numbers on each copy, then handed them back. On Helene's copy, the forty thousand figure had been scratched out and replaced by one hundred and twenty. The split gave her $60,000. To make money in beautiful Taos, all you had to do was break the finger of a spoiled rich girl and get rescued by a brave Indian boy.

Crane handed over the checks. "The parents have suggested—and I heartily agree—that all aggrieved parties sit down at the same table in a gesture of, how shall I phrase it? A gesture of forgiveness and, well—call it accommodation."

"Forgiveness?" Helene said. "No way."

"A small gesture, Miss Steinbeck."

He looked from Helene to Jimmy and Young Winchester. They nodded okay. Then he looked at Murdock, who stood up and stuck out his hand.

"A pleasure doing business with you, Mr. Crane."

"And you, sir. The associated parties are requested to convene in the Assembly Room at nine. Agent Savage will preside. A solid transaction, I think. You sign your name; they give you money. Until nine, then."

When the door was closing behind Mordecai Crane, Jimmy Little Deer gave Murdock a man-hug. Young Winchester shook hands, but his face was filled with hero-worship. They left Helene alone with Murdock.

"Who do you think the lawyer consulted?"

"Some decision-maker."

"Not Theo?"

"Is your dad in good health?"

"For an old guy," Helene said. "Are you thinking about calling him in?"

"Would that be okay with you?"

"He helped me on my last case."

"Cops know about exerting pressure," Murdock said. "They stand there, not doing anything, just looking like cops, and true perps feel the heat."

"I need coffee," Helene said.

21

Murdock

WHEN THEY ARRIVED AT the Assembly Room, Murdock saw three of the nasty kids from last night—Tammy, looking cute, and the two skinny guys who had hassled Helene—standing apart from a cluster of well-groomed adults. A small-world moment: the parents in the room were the people from Theo's Dallas coterie—Murdock had shaken their hands in the members' bar—where they had sported resort sun-wear. Now clustered together like a flock of geese, they had swapped the sun resort daywear for outdoor wardrobes that turned them into models for a fall fashion catalogue. Wherever these people went, the smell of money clotted the air.

Sammy was late, held up by a phone call, so Sally Jo Catton, wearing her Sergeant's stripes, made the introductions. The names came up: Latimer, Golden, Marshall, DeVane, Stewart, Jansen, Ramsay—he was the fat-faced guy with the wife who looked foreign, the lady who had spotted Murdock and Helene yesterday and whistled for the dogs. Ramsay was also the smug father of smug Tommy Ramsay, leader of the Nasty Teens.

The Assembly Room had a long table and folding chairs.

Sergeant Sally Jo Catton was directing traffic. She motioned Murdock and Helene to her right, next to Young Winchester and Jimmy Little Deer. She sat the kids and their parents on her left, facing Helene and Young Winchester. Sally Jo's expression was stony and her eyes were angry. Savage came in. Under the glare of the fluorescent lights, his hair looked dirty white. A bureaucrat who understood crowd psychology, he remained standing until everyone was seated. After stabbing Murdock with a stare, he shook his head.

The parents kept looking over at Gerry Ramsay—dressed in hiking shorts and a fancy leather vest—as if he was their fearless leader. He was sitting between his wife and the blonde woman from Little Galilee, who was short and pretty, like her daughter Tammy. When Gerry sat down, the woman from Little Galilee left her seat, came around the table, and took a seat next to Murdock.

She nodded at Murdock. Her complexion was flawless, smooth flesh over movie-star cheekbones. The eyes were blue and cold. Her shirt, pale purple, had two buttons undone. She wore a vintage leather vest, right out of a western movie. She was Tammy's mom, but where was Tammy's dad? Fifteen parents, and she was the only single mom.

Reading from his notes, Savage summarized the events of last night, the events that had compelled him to convene this morning meeting. He did not use words like "assault" or even "altercation." In a low voice, he said that Miss Steinbeck claimed that her cellphone had been broken, that she had been grabbed from behind, and that Young Winchester had intervened. The teens claimed that Miss Steinbeck had started the trouble, that Mister Murdock had used unnecessary force and that Young Winchester had brandished a knife. As he read from his notes, Savage's face went from pale to flushed, and Murdock noticed that Tammy's mom was snuffling. Porcelain face, real tears. What an actress. Savage ended with words of communion and accommodation.

With faces that showed nothing—no remorse, no understanding—the nasty kids apologized to Helene and Young Winchester. They gave Murdock dirty looks. Helene and Young Winchester signed the agreement. A notary came in with a stamp to make it official. As the kids started to leave, Sally Jo Overton ordered them to wait. She had something to say.

"This could get me fired," Sally Jo said, "but I object to these *ad hoc* proceedings. You young people broke the law. You deserve to be charged, booked, run through the system. You deserve to be tried in a court of law. You're hiding behind your skin color and your money and your wall of—what's it called?—oh, yeah, your wall of privilege. You're walking out here now thinking you got away with it, but be careful out there, in my town. You go one mile over the speed limit, or get charged with underage drinking, and you will get nailed. And—"

"Sergeant Catton?" Sammy said.

Sally Jo stopped. She shook her head, then slid down into her chair. Sammy motioned for everyone out. "Go on, now. Go on." Sammy left, followed by Jimmy Little Deer and Young Winchester. Sally Jo sat there, shaking her head.

"These lousy kids," Sally Jo said. "They have everything. Don't get me wrong—I'm happy you guys got some blood money. I just think it's not enough. There's no way any of us could hold out in a court battle, but I hate it that they can do that to Young Winchester, or any Indian or Latino—and get away with it. There I go, rambling again. See you kids at the conference."

AT THE BANK, MURDOCK waited while Helene deposited her check. A woman at a desk kept looking at him, so he nodded back. Saw "Teresa Tejana" on her nameplate. She walked over, introduced herself.

"You're that detective, right? Julio's friend from Seattle?"

"That's me, Ms. Tejana."

"Julio's all worked up about that dead girl on Angel Mountain and he said you were in town checking on another girl?"

"Yes," Murdock said. "Her name was Barbara Bellini."

"You have a photo or something?"

Murdock dug out the photo. Teresa Tejana took one look and nodded.

"I think she was in here," she said, "maybe three or four weeks back. I remember approving a good-sized check on a Viking Bank in Seattle. I remember making a phone call. She was very pretty, with a lovely smile. She looked like a girl in love."

"Did she say anything?" Murdock said.

"She said something about the art colony. Said she'd found a teacher who was really helping her art."

"Was the teacher Anais Bertrand?"

"No. I've seen her around. It was a guy with a French name. Fran-something? Francis. Or maybe François."

Helene came up and Murdock made the introductions. Then Teresa produced a copy of Helene's book and asked for her autograph.

THEY HAD BREAKFAST AT the IHOP on the Santa Fe Highway, south of town. Murdock had pancakes, eggs over easy, and sausage. Helene had a ham and spinach omelet. He told her about the new lead, an art teacher named François. Helene wanted to talk about the meeting.

"What did you think?" she said.

"We're not going to jail," Murdock said.

"But it's not over," Helene said. "Did you see those kids as they walked out? They looked so cocky. Tommy and Skye and Tammy and that other girl, Megan."

"Not over," Murdock said. "But we took round one."

"And I feel bad about the trade-off," Helene said. "It's like hush money."

"That DA was right," Murdock said. "No way to finance a

court battle. Did you a get copy of that check?"

Helene dug out her copy. The check in the amount of sixty thousand dollars had been drawn on a Dallas bank on an account called Ramsbanc 200. "Three-day hold," Murdock said. "That means you can't get at the money until Monday."

"Ramsbanc," Helene said. "On Monday I pay you back for the room at the B&B."

Murdock looked down at the bank Xerox. Something tugged at his brain, an insight lurking in the shadows. He'd felt the same tug looking down on Sammy Savage eating brunch, mixing with Theo's people at Angel's Nest. He shook his head and the insight tiptoed away.

"I know that look," Helene said. "I smell a hunch."

"Something connects those people, those parents with the naughty kids. It's something basic, maybe even primeval, maybe ugly. When they look at each other, it's like …"

"Like a secret code," Helene said, "I felt it with the kids in my workshop."

The waitress arrived with the check. Helene reached for it— she was feeling rich right now—but Murdock was too fast.

22

Helene

THE ART COLONY OFFICE was on the ground floor of the Mabel Dodge Luhan House, named for the patroness of the arts. The walls of the entryway were papered with photos of writers and artists. Helene recognized D.H. Lawrence and Willa Cather, early visitors to Taos. There were Ansel Adams photos of the desert landscape. There were Stieglitz photos of Georgia O'Keefe painting, and Dennis Hopper writing his *Easy Rider* film script.

The office door said, "Willy Mapes, MFA, Director." When Murdock knocked, there was no answer. No sound from inside. When Murdock opened the door, Helene saw a desk littered with papers. Art on the wall—not famous artists—lots of classical themes. A nude cupid about to loose an arrow at a chubby-cheeked female in a translucent gown. A naked Diana leading her dogs and carrying a longbow. It was Friday morning of a three-day weekend, and the Mabel Dodge Luhan House hummed with workshops. Helene and Murdock passed a room where people were writing in notebooks. They passed a studio where an art teacher in a paint-spattered smock stalked from easel to easel, looming over her pupils.

They found Anais Bertrand on the second floor. Her back was to the doorway and she was working on a painting of a Paris street scene, women in hats and long skirts, men in top hats and tales. Paris from a hundred years ago. The painting oozed nostalgia and loss.

In the morning light, Anais did not resemble the sexy film-noir femme fatale that Helene remembered from Drusilla's dinner party. Instead of the translucent costume that had kept Murdock mesmerized, Anais wore a shapeless blue smock. Her feet were in clumsy-looking clogs. She turned to see who was disturbing her work. Stared at Helene, then at Murdock.

"*Mon Dieu*," she said. "I pray that you bring the coffee."

"We're looking for Willy Mapes," Murdock said.

"Willy? He is never here. You're here about the Bellini girl, yes?"

"Yes," Murdock said. "And a teacher named François."

"That bad boy," Anais said. "He was my lover—until that one stole him away."

"So, you did know her?" Murdock said.

"Not well."

"Why didn't you say so the other day?"

"I must have this job."

"And now you don't?"

Anais gave them an enigmatic look but did not answer. She left her Paris painting and sauntered to a table cluttered with brushes and paints and one white coffee mug. She picked up the mug and stared into it. She said, "Come with me, children," and led them out of the workroom and down the hall to a makeshift teacher's lounge with a window that looked out to Angel Mountain.

As she entered the room, Helene smelled over-cooked coffee. Across the room, there was a coffee pot on a chrome hotplate. Anais filled her white mug. She told them to help themselves and flopped down on a battered purple sofa. Murdock poured coffee into a green mug, handed it to Helene. She said, "No thank you."

Anais was slouching on the sofa like a petulant teenager. Helene sat next to her. Murdock pulled a chair over, turned it around and straddled it, resting his elbows on its back. He looked like a grizzled cop in the interrogation room of an old black and white film.

"If Willy should come," Anais said, "I was never here. Never speaking with you."

"So François knew Barbara Bellini?" Murdock said.

"Knew her in the biblical sense? Oh, yes. He knew her, he had her, he took her indeed—all those workable English verbs. She was quite pretty, not plump like so many girls these days, but more like an athletic fashion model. One day the girl was here, looking totally fucked, floating through the hallways, a dreamy expression on her face, and the next day she was gone, and so was François. Someone said that François had taken her back east."

"Where back east?" Murdock said.

"New York, I suppose. The fabled Village? An artist's garret in Bohemian Soho?"

"Remember when they left?" Murdock said.

"She was here for a week, perhaps more. She started with me—she had talent—.and then she was with François."

"So why didn't Willy Mapes tell me this the other day?" Murdock said.

"Darling," she said. "You'll have to ask him. Though I might suggest—"

"Suggest what?" Murdock said.

Anais Bertrand shook her head. Her face shut down and her throat worked as she swallowed the coffee. She left the sofa, went to the table, opened drawers and slammed them shut. She asked for cigarettes. Murdock and Helene said they were non-smokers. She left the room, her clogs echoing on the wooden floors. When she came back she had a lighted cigarette between her lips. She exhaled, then she coughed.

"I have the proposition," she said.

"Shoot," Murdock said.

"Like François," she said, "I, too, detest this place. To get back to Paris, I need money. There is a large sum of money in Theo Ulster's safe in Angel's Nest. Theo owes me for a lifetime of servitude and suffering. I have the combination."

"How much money are we talking?" Murdock said.

"Currency," she said. "Dollars, Euros, Pesos, Swiss francs, Escudos, Krugerands from South Africa. Theo keeps gold, collectible coins, a sack full of diamonds in the event the gendarmes come to fetch him. When I do this thing, I require a ride back down. There is a term in American films—I forget—I require a—"

"Wheel man?" Murdock said.

"Exactly," she said. "I require a wheel man."

"What else is in the safe?" Murdock said.

"Documents," she said, "and photos."

"Any photos of Barbi Bellini?"

"If there are," Anais said. "They are yours."

"What did Theo Ulster do to you?" Helene said.

"Ah," Anais said. "You are asking for my life story. That will cost you a lunch."

Helene checked the time. At noon she had a panel with a couple of true crime writers. Anais said she would meet them later at a bar called the Brew Pub, on Quesnel. They left Anais pacing the room, smoking a second cigarette.

IN THE JEEP, HEADING through the hot noonday traffic for Apache Junction and the writers' conference, Murdock said, "Theo has cash—where did he get it?"

"Is that your motive for being her wheel man?"

"I like turning over rocks," Murdock said.

Helene smiled. "You do make it fun."

23

Murdock

THE VESTIBULE WAS THE social heart of the Apache Junction Racquet Club. A grand operatic space with pretensions to greatness. An upscale arena, upper class and very A-List, with curved walls that would look, from a bird's eye view, like an enormous peanut-shaped swimming pool.

The Vestibule had red terrazzo floors, cool to the feet, long, thin, leaded-glass windows, and a domed ceiling with a circular skylight at the top that reminded Murdock of the Pantheon in Rome.

At the big end of the Vestibule, a hundred avid readers stood in two separate lines in front of a rough-hewn antique table rife with Taos history. In one line, doting fans bought books from a local bookseller—a hefty woman in a purple squaw dress, lots of ruffles, lots of turquoise beads—who took payment using a portable card cruncher, making sure of a sale before she passed the book to Helene for signing. In the other line were people who had already bought copies of *Murder on Drake Island*, waiting to get the author's signature.

The signing table sat outside the Lecture Hall, the site of the panel on "Writing and Selling True Crime," where Helene, along with two writers and a literary agent from New York, had taken apart the art of making your true crime book a bestseller by maximizing your online presence. Observing the panel from the back of the room, Murdock had played the vigilant sentinel. Helene had the hot book. She had fielded most of the questions.

Murdock leaned against the wall outside the door to the Lecture Hall, admiring Helene's customer savvy as she signed books. They had been up since 4 a.m. and Helene still had on the sandals, the jeans, and the striped shirt that showed off her brown forearms. Murdock was tired, weary from the meetings and the interview with Anais Bertrand, but Helene still looked fresh and cheery as she asked the same questions of each customer. "Who's the book for, please? Are you a writer? What's your favorite word?" Watching Helene, the warm smile, the eyes that looked thankful for the purchase, the strong brown feet in the sandals, Murdock felt connected to this woman. When she turned around and smiled at him, his heart pounded like a military drum on parade. He had just gotten loose from Hana. How much connection was left?

Because he was bodyguarding, and because of the teen attack last night, Murdock kept studying the layout, what corridors led where, just in case. If you followed the curve of the Vestibule around, you came to the members' bar, with the big windows that overlooked the tennis courts. If you branched off to the left, you hit the security gate that led to the condos and townhouses, where you needed a keycard. If you branched off to the right, you got the parking building.

It was Friday, early afternoon at Apache Junction, and the Vestibule was crowded with writers, tennis players, town house residents, and tourists. Across the room, Murdock saw three teens from last night—Tommy, Skye, and Maxwell—chatting with the chubby Belgian tennis player. She had on a tennis dress that looked bedroomy. Thin pink straps crossed her sunburned shoulders and there was a tennis bag at her feet.

From a distance, her bright red lipstick looked like fresh blood.

The bookseller was packing up boxes, stacking them on her hand-cart, but Helene Steinbeck was still signing books. Twenty people in line. Ten minutes to go, maybe fifteen. Murdock saw Tammy's mother, blonde Elise Wellborn, in a tennis dress, carrying a shoulder bag, wearing a cute little tennis hat, as she stopped to speak to Tommy's little coterie. Elise Wellborn looked expensive. Her legs were tanned and the pricey dress was cut to display curves and cleavage. When she came up to Murdock, she introduced herself with a smile that looked genuine. She reminded him that she was Tammy's mother. Then she said, "I'd like to invite you both—you and Miss Steinbeck—to lunch. The invitation comes from Theo."

"Tell Theo no thanks."

"He won't like that."

"How long have you known Theo Ulster?"

"This is our third year."

"What's he like, down under all the British hokey-pokey?"

"You mean, who is the real Theo? He's a handsome Brit who adores being theatrical. An ex-soldier who still enjoys command. My daughter behaves when he's around—and that's a blessing. Are you meeting Miss Steinbeck? I need her signature on my book."

Murdock saw Helene chatting with Sonja the Serbian. Elise Wellborn reached into her bag and pulled a copy of Helene's book. When Helene arrived, Elise apologized for Tammy's behavior, and presented the book and a fancy gold fountain pen.

"If you could say something nice about Tammy's writing," Elise said, "that would be great."

"Your daughter has talent," Helene said. "She's smart—but that stunt last night? That was way out of line."

"I know. And I apologize. It's those kids she runs with. That peer group thing. I blame it all on Tommy Ramsay."

Helene signed her name and handed the book back. Elise

looked at the book, pursed her lips, and put it away.

"Look," Elise Wellborn said. "We got off on the wrong foot here. I'm hoping we can patch this up."

"Give it time," Helene said.

Standing with Helene, Murdock watched her walk off.

"Great legs on that gal," Helene said. "But you probably didn't notice."

"Your legs fill my brain, Steinbeck."

"Oh, sure, Murdock. Let's go. I'm starving. And we've got a date with Anais."

24

Theo

THEO ULSTER MARCHED TO his table in the members' bar. He set down the racquet bag, eased into his captain's chair, adjusted the reserved sign, and signaled the waitress.

His drink arrived, a lovely pink gin. The first sip and he felt his world returning to normal. Theo saw himself as a sociable fellow, a friendly smiling person who had made a simple offer of luncheon—and had been refused. He blamed Elise Wellborn for not being persuasive. He blamed Murdock for the refusal. For the shock, the social slight, the tiny needle of pain.

HE WAS SITTING AT his table, musing on the way of the world, when Florian Fidel appeared in the doorway. One moment Fidel was not there; the next moment, there he was, smiling and confident. The man was in his early forties, lean, hungry-eyed, trying to hide his little pot belly under a Guayabera shirt. When Fidel sidled past the tennis table— seven WTA lovelies—the chatter went into pause mode as the girls gave him the collective once-over. With his nutmeg skin, Indian cheekbones, the drawstring pants and sandals, the ostentatious Rolex, Fidel had the look, and the confident carriage, of a foreign film star. Theo stood up to shake hands. The Rolex flashed. Fidel set the attaché case on the floor. He scanned the room, pointed with his chin at the tennis table.

"Where is she?"

"She's performing on Court One," Theo said. "Just cast your eyes downward."

Fidel moved to the view window. He leaned close. His voice was snappish. "Which one?"

"The tall Serbian," Theo said.

"They are both tall. They both look Serbian."

"The tall one," Theo said, "with the power forehand—*and* the red headband."

"When can you arrange a liaison?"

The waitress arrived. Theo ordered tequila for Fidel and a refill on the pink gin for himself. After a look of appraisal—women always gave him the once-over—the waitress went away.

Theo knew Florian Fidel from the old days, the days of Cielo Azul Escort Services, dicey days when Theo had to make a choice between drugs and females. He could sell drugs and risk incarceration via the DEA or death by cartel. Or he could sell young women to flesh peddlers like Florian Fidel. The question back then was which business had the most growth potential? That first sale had netted Theo a paltry $1,800. Today, by contrast, a man in Mexico was paying $80,000 for the Serbian. The only problem was that Fidel wanted to sample the merchandise, which required a tactical solution, and Fidel's urges were forever pedestrian, forever boring.

"She's even beautiful when shaking hands," Fidel said. "What a pair of legs on that one. I want those legs squeezing me when I ... When can I have her?"

"Where is my money, old boy?"

"In the case."

The attaché was locked. Theo asked for the key. Fidel tossed the key onto the table. Theo opened the attaché case on his lap.

Ten thousand, twenty, thirty, forty. Only half there.

"The price for the Serbian, old boy, is eighty thousand."

"She is magnificent, Fidel said, "Like a wild gazelle."

"You owe me forty thousand," Theo said.

"First, you get us together. Someplace private, for the screaming. After I'm done, you get your other half."

The drinks came. Florian Fidel did not notice. Theo moved the cash from the attaché case to a paper grocery sack. "She's left the court," Fidel said.

"When they finish down there," Theo said, "they come here to suck up the applause."

Fidel turned away from the window just as Marie-Claire Benoit flounced up, her breasts trembling like lemon Jell-O, her blonde hair trapped in a childish ponytail. She had just been eliminated from the singles and she wanted another lesson before her doubles match. Theo made a date for later.

When she walked away, Fidel said, "If you get me a photo, I could arrange a deal with my client. For that one, he might go fifty thousand."

"Bakul? She's hardly his type."

"He would in turn sell her to a man in Bogota."

"She's not for sale."

"Señor Bakul is not happy."

"Not my problem."

"He is not happy because Bellini's not working out. He wants you to lower the price on the Serbian."

"Not a chance," Theo said.

"Or he will pay the full eighty thousand if you throw in a shipment of prime cuts."

"I checked your man Bakul out," Theo said.

"Checked him out how?"

"I checked him out by dining in two of his restaurants—The Blue Parrot, The Crimson Toucan. They wanted an exorbitant initiation fee They grilled me for half an hour, thinking I was an agent from MI-5, because of my bloody accent. After I was identified they brought the menu. Your Señor Bakul is charging one-fifty a slice—a hundred-fifty U.S., one-twenty in Euros—and *he* wants a discount? Ridiculous."

"Customer service is not ridiculous."

Theo was fuming. He was about to respond when the Serbian girl entered, garnering a round of applause, and sat down at the tennis table. She was blushing. Fidel insisted on meeting her. Now. This moment. No time to waste. When Theo hesitated, Fidel said, "You do know her, right?"

"Come with me, Fidel," Theo said, "let me introduce you."

Leaning over, Fidel snatched up his attaché case. Theo broke out in a sweat. What was this Bellini business? He remembered sending the photos of the Bellini girl to Fidel. Photos taken by Mapes. Undressing, taking a shower, sitting astride the toilet having a piss. He remembered the money-discussion—because Bellini was not famous, not a celebrity, she had brought in a mere $30,000-USD. What was all this talk about customer service—when the real issue was Theo's fee?

Desperation launched Theo out of his chair. Desperation drove him to introduce Fidel to the twittery females who surrounded the Serbian girl. When Fidel took her hand, the Serbian started to smile, then looked at Theo, and the smile went away. Her eyes were flinty, sharp, dangerous. Then she swung her gaze back to Fidel. Looked first at his face, then lowering her eyes, she studied the Guayabera shirt, her eyes moving down, her chin lifting—she did have an excellent bone structure—and then her slow, knowing smile. Her voice was sultry, measured.

"What is it that you wish, señor?"

"Do you speak Spanish, señorita?"

"*Poquito*," she said. "Do you perhaps come to me for the autograph?"

"Yes!" he said. "*Sí, sí*, your autograph. I would love it."

"Give me pen," she said. "Give me paper."

Theo's cellphone vibrated. He left Fidel haggling, sweat on

his face, his loins quivering for the Serbian. The caller was Carla Carlini.

"Where are you?" Theo said.

"The Brew Pub," she said.

"Could you call back?" Theo said. "I'm in the middle of—"

"It's your little Parisienne," Carla said. "Anais Bertrand."

"What about her?"

"She's cooking up something with that detective, Murdock. And his lady."

"What about the team from Pueblo?" Theo said.

"The supplier wants the other half."

"We had a deal. Half before, half after."

"He wants small bills in an hour or it's a non-starter."

"Absolute rot," Theo said.

"They're coming now—his team. They know where you are."

"I can't be seen with them."

"Or," Carla said, "I could be your little messenger girl, meet them on the road."

"I accept," Theo said. "And get back here by party time."

At the doorway to the members' bar, Theo glanced back. The Serbian girl still sat at the tennis table, surrounded by her WTA retinue. Florian Fidel was down on his knees, his eyes level with her navel, his nose inches away from those smooth dark legs. Theo saw teeth flashing, heard tinkly laughter rising from the table. The Serbian girl looked amused, like a queen on a throne eyeing a groveling subject. Holding the grocery sack, Theo turned away.

In his office, above the courts, the fray, the treachery of Anais Bertrand, the encroaching danger of Murdock, the unsettling news about the Bellini girl, Theo transferred $12,500-USD to a plastic baggie.

He took the stairs to the parking garage, where he handed the baggie to Carla Carlini. Watching her drive off, Theo thought about inflation and customer service.

The last hit-squad sent by the man from Boulder had cost

fifteen thousand—for a more complex operation. Since the world's economy was a shambles, the cost of this operation, which was far simpler, should have been less, but these people now demanded twenty-five. Where was the customer service in that?

25

Helene

HELENE AND MURDOCK WERE eating in the Brew Pub when Anais Bertrand entered, her handbag slung over one insouciant shoulder. As she sauntered in, passing through a shaft of light thrown by a solar tube, conversation died and people swiveled around to watch.

Anais Bertrand had changed her costume for the meeting. She no longer wore the shapeless art colony smock. Instead, she was back to her feline, femme-fatale persona in a pale blouse, very tight-fitting, under a calf-skin vest that looked like tanned human skin, and a slit skirt that bared her left thigh. Her shoes were strappy sandals with a kitten heel.

There was no smoking at the Brew Pub, but Anais made a show of placing her cigarettes on the table with her gold lighter perched on top. The clientele at the Brew Pub was local—two Mexican guys in short-sleeve shirts at the bar, a gaggle of ladies from a local business, two blond guys who talked too loud about climbing Wheeler Peak.

Anais took a seat next to Murdock and across the table from Helene. Murdock excused himself and headed for the men's room. Helene reached across and patted Anais on the arm.

Helene said, "Did you meet Theo in Paris?"

Anais looked away from Helene. Her chest rose as she took a deep breath. Her fingers were long, with square-cut fingernails. "We met on the sidewalk outside the Café Flor," Anais said. "I was sketching tourist portraits on demand, selling them for a few francs. Theo was quite dashing in his military uniform, a soldier on leave, and he paid me to sketch his portrait. Then he treated me to quite a good lunch. He had money and I was a starving artist. Before we had sex, he put on these little white latex gloves."

Anais stopped talking when the waiter arrived with her drink, a martini on the rocks with three olives. The waiter was a young Latino with slicked-back hair and a sweet smile. She called him Antonio. They seemed to know each other and when he walked away, Anais said, "We are dating. Where was I?"

"Latex gloves," Helene said.

"Ah, yes, to put the finger inside me—that made him feel powerful—and he was quite huge, I suppose Drusilla told you, but while he did me, he stared at this photograph he carried with him, of a woman in a silver dress, pinned to the wall. It was like having two people in my bed instead of one."

"Who was the woman?" Helene said.

"Her name was Eunice Dare," Anais said. "You can find her on the Internet—some kind of actress. He took her with him to war. He brought her to New Mexico. She's in a silver frame now, on the desk in his office."

"How are they connected?" Helene asked. "Theo and this woman in the photo?"

"I asked who she was," Anais said, "and he told me to shut up. That's when he started bringing his girls to my studio. They were German or Austrian or Swiss. Lots of tits and bright hair, all of them twenty years old or younger. When he arrived with a blonde, I would take my sketchpad to the café—he was still paying my rent, you see—and when I returned, the studio would be empty. The sheets would be stripped from the bed. There would be money for the laundry and any broken cups or glasses. He kept a supply of latex gloves in my armoire."

Helene signaled Murdock. He left the bar and started for the table.

"How did you get to New Mexico?" Helene said.

"I was just about to tell you. Ah, here's our *Monsieur* Murdock. Are you ready for my tale?"

Murdock sat down. No expression on his face as he forked in food from his plate and washed it down with beer.

Anais said, "Theo telephoned. He had a job for me, managing his antique business. When I arrived, I discovered he had another business, Cielo Azul Escort Services, where he sent shop girls on dates with clients. By day, I worked in the shop. By night, I became Theo's Madame. The girls were young and quite silly. They were always leaving, flashing engagement rings, and training replacements took time. I hated the work; there was no time to paint. All that ended when Theo met Drusilla."

Helene said, "How many girls worked for Theo?"

"A dozen, perhaps thirteen, I don't know."

"And that's when you went to work at the art colony?"

"Another stupid job," Anais said. "Teaching art to middle-class females with so little talent. Not your Bellini girl. She had talent. She also had François. Are you thinking that Theo has something to do with Bellini going missing?"

"Yes," Murdock said.

"But why? He adores the blondes and Bellini was tall and dark."

"But you do remember her photo in the safe, right?"

"Oh, yes," Anais said, "but of course."

IN THE JEEP, MURDOCK turned to Helene. "What's your read, Steinbeck?"

"Those rubber gloves are spooky."

"Rubber gloves on a guy who fucks while staring at his mommy who keeps girl-photos in a safe? You think she's making it up?"

"She does need our help."

"And I agreed to be her wheelman. On the off-chance of a photo."

"What about that story—displaced by blondes?"

"Like the Belgian," Murdock said, "and the dead girl."

* * *

GRIPPING THE WHEEL OF her Camaro, Carla Carlini turned into the rest stop. At the far end of the lot, past the tourists walking their dogs, Morris Haxton leaned against the beige van. Haxton, thin enough to qualify as skeletal, wore aviator shades and a black suit with a string necktie. As Carla drove up, she saw Muñoz, a Mexican with tattoos. There was a third guy in the van. She could see movement in the rear window.

She parked and climbed out, knees rubbery. She felt eyes on her as she handed over the shopping bag. Haxton's grin was sly, calculating. He hefted the bag. The passenger door of the van was open. He set the bag on the seat. Gloved hands appeared— the guy in the backseat—and the bag went out of sight. Carla turned to leave, but Haxton took her arm.

He wanted to talk about old times. He told her he had six months to live. She felt nothing. He wanted sex, grant a dying man his last wish. She started back to her car and he grabbed her arm again. He was begging now and she felt sick. The voice from inside the van said, "All here. Let's ride."

Haxton said, "Fuck it," and let her go.

She was still shaking when she pulled off the road in Trinidad at a big Walmart. She vomited before she made it to the bathroom.

26

Murdock

IT WAS EARLY EVENING at the Racquet Club and Drusilla's party throng filled the vestibule with sound—laughing and talking. Mariachi music. Balloons hugging the ceiling. A big sign that welcomed party-goers to the Drusilla Dorn Art and Tennis Festival.

Streamers drifting down. Bare shoulders, beards, earrings flashing as heads bobbed, sideburns. Thin female feet in sandals with heels. Frilly dresses.

Murdock stood with his back against a pillar, checking the crowd.

The writers hung out in a group. They wore glasses. They looked depressed, slugging down drinks and muttering, and then the girls appeared—a cluster of fertile females between the ages of eighteen and twenty-three—sweeping into the room like a flock of pretty birds, bringing color and zest.

The writers mingled. They danced. Drusilla worked the crowd, making introductions, grabbing people, pulling them over to Helene's book table. The writers wore name badges from the conference. The tennis players wore name badges from the tournament. The Dallas People wore name badges edged in gold. Theo Ulster's name badge said Theo. Everyone knew Theo. No need for his last name on a tag.

Murdock caught sight of Tommy Ramsay bunched together with Skye Latimer and the surly kid called Maxwell. They were hustling the Serbian girl—Sonja—and chubby Marie-Claire, who was laughing, showing perfect white teeth. Her shoulders were bare, with a blush of sunburn. Her blonde hair bobbed up and down as Tommy Ramsay whispered in her ear and handed her a goblet. She took a sip, held it up to the light, took another sip, and seemed to grow in stature.

Helene Steinbeck walked up, smiling her published author smile. Murdock took her out on the dance floor. Helene wore a dress borrowed from Drusilla Dorn. It was shimmery turquoise, the color of a mountain lake at twilight, with spaghetti straps across her tanned shoulders, and cut halfway down her back. Her skin was warm under Murdock's hands and her eyes blazed with party fervor. He liked his hands on her body. Liked having her in his arms. What would happen to them after Taos? He wore a shirt from the consignment store, his only pair of clean jeans, and a blue bandana for color.

"What are they feeding her?" Helene said.

"Some kind of elixir," Murdock said.

"Captain Theo's Elixir of Love?"

AND THEN SAMMY SAVAGE appeared, wearing his police dress uniform. After another apology for spoiling Drusilla's party by puking on the floor, Savage whirled Helene away, and Murdock turned to see Elise Wellborn in a party dress that matched her green eyes. Without asking, she came into Murdock's arms. She was a good dancer, she smelled good, her skin hot to the touch, and she kept brushing Murdock's crotch with her thigh.

"How well do you know the Ramsay's?" Murdock said.

"We used to be neighbors in Dallas ... before they moved to a bigger home. Why?"

"Is Tommy an only child?"

"Tommy's the youngest, and his mother's favorite. He's got an older brother named Gerry Junior. In school at OU, politics or something."

"Does Gerry Junior ever come to the mountain?"

"He was just here, a week or so ago. He worships Theo and Tammy says he's gotten better with the bow and arrow thing."

"What's he look like, Gerry Junior?"

"Well," Elise said. "He's a junior-sized version of his dad. Big body, a round face that's already looking fat, and he's still in college."

"You're not a fan?"

"He came onto me, not once, but three times. That's when I kicked his jewels. When you're a Dallas divorcee, Mr. Murdock, you wear a sign that says 'Fair Game.' But enough about me. How long have you and Helene been …"

She didn't get to finish her sentence because Helene came up, trailed by Sammy Savage. His face was sweaty and he stank of stale booze. Helene took Murdock's arm. Elise was holding on, but now she let go. She moved away, put her hand on Sammy's chest, right over the heart, and said, "Dance with me, Sammy."

They watched her move off. Helene nudged Murdock. "What was that all about?"

"She wants my virginity," Murdock said. "In return for giving that up, I got some info about Tommy Ramsay's older brother. His name is Gerry Junior. He was up here, but now he's gone. He loves Captain Theo and he's a bow and arrow guy."

"I want your virginity, too. How will you decide?"

"Decide what?"

"Whom to bequeath it to?"

"How about a tryout in the motel shower?"

"It's worth a try. Take me home."

"And leave all this merriment? Look over there."

Across the room, Carla Carlini, her body encased in a gold sheath-dress, had her arm around Marie-Claire, the chubby

Belgian girl. As Murdock and Helene watched, they saw a transfer going on, like a baton in a relay race, as Carla passed the girl off to Tommy and Skye. With Marie-Claire between them, the boys entered the corridor that led to the condos. Tommy and Skye were in the lead, surly Maxwell bringing up the rear. Theo whispered something to Carla, who strode off after the boys.

27

Murdock

MURDOCK WAS DREAMING WHEN the phone rang. A clanging alarm bell from a long way off.

A skinny guy in a loin cloth and turban swinging a fat club against a golden medallion suspended in dark space.

In the dream, Murdock was back in the jungle being chased by army ants led by a mustachioed British dude with a bullhorn calling commands like "Bite his ass! Eat him up! Thigh meat is best!"

He woke up to darkness and voices—and realized that Helene was talking on the phone with her dad. She had her phone on speaker. "Murdock," she said. "It's my dad. Can you take notes?"

He rolled out of bed, fumbled around for his ballpoint and battered old notebook, tools from his PI days. Murdock's handwriting was unreadable. Yawning, he printed out the info in block letters.

The DNA sample sent to her dad belonged to Gerald Ramsay Junior. Dallas address. No record of treatment for a gunshot in any Dallas area hospital. Age: 21. Profession: Student at OU—the University of Oklahoma at Norman, majoring in

International Relations. Parents: Gerald and Marina Ramsay.

Gerry Junior had two citations for driving under the influence. Underage, without a license, not even a learner's permit. A side note: the Dallas police had not been cooperative.

"Anything else?" Helene said.

"Tell your detective hello and good-hunting."

"Okay. I will. Great info, Dad. Thanks." Helene hung up. "Did you get that?"

"What time is it?" Murdock said.

"Two-thirty a.m.," Helene said.

"I meant Florida. What time is it there?"

"Two hours later. Why?"

"Is your dad an insomniac, or what?"

"Tell me you wrote down, what I said—or I'll have to call him back."

"I got it," Murdock said. "Ramsay, Gerald Junior, the brother of Tommy Ramsay, who is Tammy's boyfriend. The same Tommy Ramsay who threatened you and beat up on Young Winchester. I'm going back to sleep."

"Tommy and Tammy," Helene said. "Add Theo and you've got a TV show of people with T-names. You can't sleep now. We need to talk."

"Talk about what?"

"About what to do with this information."

"The world's asleep, Steinbeck. Let's hit it tomorrow."

"We could tell Sammy," she said. "We could tell Julio. What do you think?"

"I think I need more sleep."

Murdock climbed back into bed. Her intensity came at him in waves, buzzing his brain. He could feel her body heat. When Helene Steinbeck got hold of an idea, she pumped out heat like a wall furnace on high. He did some deep breathing, felt himself sliding to the edge, almost there, almost to the land of sleep, and then Helene rolled out of bed and started pacing the floor. Not speaking, not saying a word, but still communicating—

loud and strong. She wanted him up, out of bed, on his feet. She wanted him with her, processing this information.

MURDOCK MADE COFFEE. HELENE drank hers sitting in bed, propped against all the pillows. Murdock sat on the ancient wooden motel chair with his feet on the bed next to hers. She put the sole of her left foot against the sole of his right foot. He could feel the blood pumping through her foot.

"Playing spoons with my footsie?" he said.

"You only think about sex," she said.

"It's not the only thing," Murdock said. "With you half-naked in bed, it's the first thing."

"Let's recreate the crime," she said.

"At three-thirty in the morning?"

"The dead girl was Sophie Orff," Helene said. "New York address. Maybe Soho, maybe the Village. We need to check. Sophie was killed with an arrow shot from a crossbow. A lung shot, which takes training and skill."

"Discovery of the body?" Murdock said.

"In fiction," she said, "it's always an innocent person who finds the corpse—a child or an old lady or a sleepy security guard. But in this crime, it's an ex-cop who shot a photo and a roaming private eye who wounded one or both killers."

"*Alleged* killers," Murdock said. "Maybe they were the clean-up squad."

"Let's bring in the Bellini girl," Helene said.

"She was the PI's motive for being up there," Murdock said.

"Can you describe her? Name?"

"Barbara Bellini. Goes by Barbi."

"Age?"

"She just turned twenty-two in June."

"Profession?"

"Barbi worked as a commercial artist."

"Education?"

"Four year degree in Art History, a year at a commercial art school."

"Height and weight?"

"Barbi was five-eight and maybe weighed one-thirty," Murdock said. "She broke up with her fiancée and got depressed—her dad said she was eating all the time."

"What if Sophie Orff was at the art colony, too?"

"Good idea. We should ask Anais."

"We can assume that Barbi stayed at the art colony," Helene said. "I wonder where Sophie stayed."

"What good would that do?" Murdock said.

"The Victim's Lair scene," Helene said.

Murdock said, "Barbi had that art teacher, François. I wonder who Sophie had to squire her around."

"If they went to New York," Helene said, "my dad has tons of contacts."

"When you call him," Murdock said, "make sure you wake him up. What else does the book say?"

"Make a list of suspects," Helene said. "Who's first on your list?"

"Theo Ulster," Murdock said. "Yours?"

"Willy Mapes," Helene said. "He's so murky-looking."

"What about the lovely Anais?"

"Not the crossbow type," Murdock said. "For her, poison or laying a fancy trap. Who's your second suspect?"

"Your friend Sammy Savage," Helene said. "He's covering something up. Who's your second suspect?"

"One of Theo's underlings," Murdock said. "Remember those guys in the Mercedes?"

"Three men we don't have names for," Helene said, "but the woman had to be Carla Carlini. So, let's summarize. We've got a weapon. A corpse and a crime scene. We don't have a motive. Or an official time of death. The corpse was still warm, so maybe twenty minutes before we got there and—"

"Dogs," Murdock said. "They need to be on the list."

"What category?"

"Crime scene contamination," Murdock said, "by wild animals that cannot be interrogated. How clever is that?"

Headlights sliced through the room. The motel blinds were closed, forcing the brightness through the slit between the blinds and the window frame. Before Murdock could say, "Hit the floor," Helene had rolled off the bed. Murdock crawled to the bed, grabbed the .45 under his pillow.

A ratchety rat-tat sound tore through the room and bullets blew out the front window. Their room was on the second floor. The bullets chopped into the ceiling and dust from wounded sheetrock drifted down. Murdock crawled to the window, waited for a break in the gunfire. Glass shards under his butt. A sharp sticking pain in his right foot as he swiveled around, turning too fast, took a chance, and looked out the window.

Down in the parking lot, he saw the big rear door closing on a battered van. A van that was turning too fast, the driver gunning the engine, the nose of the vehicle ramming into the bottom of the motel staircase, a grinding sound as concrete met sheet metal. The headlight winked out.

Murdock stood up. He needed the rifle, but it was locked in the Jeep.

He laid the hex sights of the .45 on the right front window—just a sliver of a target—and squeezed off three rounds. The window blew inward. The van kept turning, coughing smoke from the spinning tires.

Helene had her Glock out. She went through the door first, wearing panties and a T-shirt.

They ran along the second floor landing.

The van backed up, peeling away a chunk of concrete staircase, dust flying, concrete falling onto the tarmac. The light from the motel was pale yellow and weak—not good shooting light—but Helene opened up from the landing. She was in position, Murdock coming up behind her. He grinned. This woman liked to shoot. And she was pissed.

A tire exploded. As the van reached the street, chunks of rubber peeled away, chewed up by the wheel rim. The slide on Helene's weapon was open, empty magazine.

"Sirens," Murdock said.

"You're trailing blood," Helene said.

KNEELING, SHE PLUCKED THE glass shard from his foot. He heard sirens. He saw headlights, coming fast along the main road. The van was running on three tires and a wheel rim that screeched. As it angled across the asphalt parking lot, it lurched from side to side. The van was almost back on the road to Santa Fe when the first cruiser appeared, red and blue roof lights rotating, markings of the Taos police. The van, swerving to avoid the cruiser, turned too fast to the left and came back onto the parking lot, where it slammed nose-first into the plate glass of the hardware store. The cruiser nosed forward. Gunfire from the van blew out the windshield. Doors opened and two cops scurried around to the back of the cruiser.

Two more cruisers arrived, two black-and-whites from the state police. A riot van parked next to the state police. Uniformed officers huddled for a pow-wow. An officer pointed to the Sleep Inn, where guests in pajamas and robes had gathered beside Murdock and Helene. An officer with silver hair waved a bullhorn. Then he pointed the bullhorn at the van and ordered the people inside to surrender. A moment of quiet and then gunfire erupted from the van. The cops opened up—a miniature war on the road to Santa Fe—and thirty seconds later, when the silver-haired bullhorn man called for a cease-fire, there was silence. Nothing moved; the air was still.

Cops converged on the van. Barking shouts of, "Come out with your hands up" went unanswered. Two more police cars rolled in. Doors opened and cops climbed out. Workers in overalls set up sawhorses for the crime scene tape. Traffic on the highway to Santa Fe got re-routed onto neighboring streets.

Helene said, "Isn't that Julio?"

"Never seen him in uniform," Murdock said.

"How's your wound," Murdock?

BACK IN THE ROOM, Helene checked out Murdock's foot. He took one Arnica pellet, followed by one Hypericum. Helene cleaned off the dirt and dried blood, swabbed it with hydrogen peroxide to kill the bacteria. Then applied antiseptic from his medical kit. Put on a bandage and then an X made with tape. She had the steady hands of a doctor in an emergency room.

They dumped glass from the bed into the trash can. When Julio Calderon arrived, looking wired, Murdock was on the bed with an ice pack on his wound, talking to the night manager of the Sleep Inn about a new room. Helene was on her cellphone to her dad in Florida. She had changed into slacks and a blouse.

"I need coffee," Julio said.

Helene made a pot. While the coffee perked, Julio stared at the floor.

28

Murdock

JULIO CALDERON CHECKED HIS hand-held device.

His silver-gray hair was ruffled. He looked older, no more boyish bounce in his step. The flak jacket hung loose. When Murdock handed him a cup of coffee, he stared at it before setting it down. His thumbs worked the buttons on the hand-held. While Murdock waited, he was aware of the techno-distance separating him from Julio Calderon. They were twelve years apart in chronological age, but a world apart in the new age of information. Julio was the law. He asked the questions.

Q: "What time did the attack start?"

A: "Two-thirty."

Q: "What were you guys doing?"

A: "We were talking about Drusilla's mixer."

Q: "How long did the attack last?"

A: "Maybe thirty seconds."

Q: "When you got outside, what did you see, exactly?"

A: "Saw a beige van. The plates looked out of state."

Q: "You saw the rear of the van?"

A: "Yeah."

Q: "And you fired on the van?"

A: "It was self-defense, officer."

"You don't have to go all prickly on me, Mateo."

Murdock said, "You're coming on like a cop in a sweatbox, Julio. They shot first—with what sounded like some heavy firepower. We returned fire."

"Sorry," Julio said. "I didn't mean to come on so strong. Blame the perps and their heavy firepower."

Julio took a sip of the coffee and inhaled deeply. He had been standing in the center of the room, but now he sat down in the wooden motel chair. Murdock looked at Helene, nodded for her to take over. As she brought Julio up to date, her voice calm, she skirted the teens and the way they treated the Belgian tennis player.

"We were chatting about Drusilla's social skills," Helene said. "How she was so smart bringing a gang of introvert writers into close contact with a gaggle of pretty female tennis players, most of them foreign, all of them exotic—the travel, the beauty of the game, like poetry on the tennis court—and then gunfire blew out our window and Murdock got cut, a piece of glass on his foot."

"So who shot first?" Julio said. "You or Mateo?"

"We shot together," Helene said. "Standing on the balcony. I remember it was cold."

"And you were dressed like that?"

"Things happened so fast," Helene said. "Do you know how many attackers? Or are you allowed to say?"

"There were three perps in the van," Julio said. "One took a round in his shoulder, right up here on top, which could have been one of you guys. Forensics will tell us more. And you guys will have to give up your weapons."

"For how long?" Helene said.

"I'll put a rush on it," Julio said.

"Julio," Helene said, "how did you get here so fast? It was

terrific police work—a roadblock and everything."

"Yeah," Julio said. "Here comes the bad part. On its way here, the van blew through that traffic stop—used to be the old blinking light—the intersection of the Paseo and the ski valley road. Well, the van got stopped by a Taos patrol cruiser. Witnesses heard gunfire, someone called the cops. There was an officer down report, maybe fifteen-twenty minutes before they hit your place."

"Who was the officer?" Helene said.

"Sally Jo Catton," Julio said. "A terrific officer. You might've seen her around. She was an eager-beaver on Taos traffic stops—more tickets per year than any cop in town."

"She's in my writing group," Helene said. "How is she?"

"She sustained a head wound," Julio said. "You know how they are."

"I'm so sorry," Helene said. "That's awful. Where did they take her for treatment?"

"Helicopter to Albuquerque," Julio said.

Helene looked at Murdock and let out a sigh. She pulled the blanket off the bed, shook it, and a tinkle of broken window glass hit the floor. Wrapping it around her shoulders, she sat on the edge of the bed. Her feet were bare. Julio was staring at her legs, not saying a word. As Murdock watched, Julio set the coffee cup on the table and took refuge in his hand-held device. Helene nodded at Murdock—they were playing Julio for information and it was Murdock's turn.

Murdock said, "You got anything on the three perps? Anything on the vehicle?"

"We're running some ID's now," Julio said. "We got a hit on the driver. It's right here on this electronic notebook official issue—man, I miss my little black notebook, always knew where stuff was. Okay, the driver of the van was Leon Trujillo, out of Denver. Nice list of crimes, auto theft, knocking over service stations in the middle of the night. We got nothing yet on his two buddies. One of them had a ballistic vest that looked like military surplus. The plates are out of state, all the way from Wisconsin, and stolen off a Chrysler up in the Milwaukee area. We're running the VIN now. It's an old Chevy, with a bunch of patched-over bullet holes."

"Are your guys questioning the shooters now?" Murdock said.

A weighty silence. Julio stared first at his hand-held, then at the blown out motel window. From his look, Murdock knew the perps were dead. Killed in the barrage launched by Julio's bullhorn command.

"They're gone, Mateo. And don't give me that civilian point of view shit—you know how it goes: 'Officer, did those poor men really have to die?' And how we gotta control police brutality—okay? Well, if you remember, there was this shootout in North Hollywood, like maybe a dozen years back. I was in L.A. doing some training when it went down—seventeen minutes after nine in the morning, lasting forty-five minutes, longest shootout in police history—when these two dudes wearing body armor, armed with automatic weapons and shooting armor-piercing rounds—they hit a bank. When they got outside they found the place buzzing with cops calling out warnings from behind police cars. The dudes said, 'No way,' the shooting started, the cops were majorly outgunned. Eighteen people sustained injuries. Two thousand rounds from the cops, shooting nines and thirty-eights, a shotgun here and there, one perp on foot, one in a vehicle, and because I was there, Mateo, because I remember how it felt, there was no way those crazy hophead *cojudos* in that van last night were gonna pull off something like North Hollywood on Paseo del Sur in Taos, not in my state, not after they'd gunned down an officer, so yeah, I gave the order to shoot. But first I told them to surrender, the whole movie-cop bit. Okay?"

"You really care for her, don't you?" Helene said.

"Care for who?"

"For Sally Jo. She's not just another officer. You know her."

"Some," Julio said. "Yeah, I know her some."

His cellphone rang. The ring tone was a snatch of Mariachi music, a happy party tune. The moment of merriment and celebration sounded out of place in the gloom of Julio's shooting report. He said, "Yeah. *Sí*, I got it, *seguro*, okay?" He hung up. "Okay, please hand over your weapons."

Murdock handed over his .45.

As Helene handed over her Glock, she said, "Without my Glock, I feel naked."

"Didn't I say I'd hurry things up at Forensics?"

With a shake of his head, Julio was out the door, walking along the balcony, his footsteps heavy on the concrete stairs.

Helene said, "Julio gave the order to shoot."

"I was thinking that, too," Murdock said.

"Why did he feel he had to justify his actions? Or was that a smokescreen for taking our guns?"

"We're the loose cannons," Murdock said. "He wants to tie us down, keep us from rolling around, bumping into stuff."

"I really meant that," Helene said. "About feeling naked without my Glock."

"When you said 'naked,' Julio had a coughing fit."

"All you think about is sex, Murdock."

"Your fault, Steinbeck. For looking so toothsome without your—"

She stood up, teeth flashing, and bopped his arm. They moved in sync, like a tag team working from coded signals. Helene hauled out her rucksack, set it on the bed with a thump. Murdock set his rucksack beside hers. The zippers worked in unison. Helene brought out a small pistol, a baby Ruger. Murdock brought out an Airweight 22.

THEY WERE STILL GRINNING at each other when the night manager arrived, all apologies for the mess. He helped them haul their stuff five doors down, to a bigger room—two queen beds, a little kitchenette, two closets instead of one.

"No charge for tonight," the manager said, "and a weekly rate on the rest of your stay." He handed them a small packet. "Here are discount coupons for ten of Taos' best restaurants. Anything you need, *anything*, you call me."

* * *

THEO WAS AWAKE WHEN the phone rang. It was Super-Agent Savage, his voice shaky. Theo had no respect for this fellow. He boasted about his Black Ops experience, but to Theo he was a paper-pushing bureaucrat, lost in the decadence of women, drink, and drugs. Drugs supplied by Theo.

"Samuel?" Theo said. "What?"

"Your fucking house guests," Savage said. "The boys from Boulder—well, they've all bought it."

"How?"

"Murdock and the writer-woman blew out a window and a tire. That slowed your house guests down until that fucker Calderon arrived. He was pissed about his ex-squeeze—Sergeant Catton, who took a bullet in the head—and ordered the guys to open up."

"Where were you?"

"At home, fixing my alibi."

Enraged, Theo hung up. Ten years ago, he would have slammed the phone into its cradle. But with cellphones and wireless phones, you only pressed a button. The old days were better.

29
Helene

THE DELIVERY CAME AT 6:02 in the morning.

Helene was asleep. Woke up with the sound of a car door slamming, then bootsteps on the concrete stairs, then the same bootsteps on the walkway outside their room. New room number 237—five doors down from their old room—which had no window glass now, its ceiling pockmarked by automatic weapons fire.

She said Murdock's name, got no answer.

She reached for her Glock, but felt the Ruger and remembered handing the Glock to Julio. Feeling the morning chill, she grabbed her down vest. She padded to the door, opened it a crack, and saw Murdock talking to a man in a bent sombrero.

The man had a package.

Murdock had a roll of money.

Helene watched the exchange.

Murdock came back to the room with the package. He wore a shirt and jeans and an old pair of moccasins.

"Who was that?"

"Santa Claus," Murdock said.

"From the North Pole?"

"From Bernalillo," Murdock said, "another small town about to be a suburb of Albuquerque."

"Who's your friend?"

"Michael Roto," Murdock said. "We served together in Uncle Sam's army. He's a helluva tracker. He brought something for Jimmy and something for you."

"For me? From Albuquerque?"

"Open it," Steinbeck. "I'll make coffee."

"What are you looking at?"

"Your magnificent ass."

The package was heavy. Not flowers, not candy or jewelry. The paper was pink and thick, the kind old-time butchers used to wrap meat. She uncovered the packages. One long, one short. The big one had Jimmy's name printed in block letters. *J Little Deer*.

"Yours is the short one," Murdock said.

She opened the shorter package to find a Glock nine—identical to hers, but older and gleaming—and mounted with those hexagonal sights. It felt terrific in her hand, comfortable, like an old friend who had gone away and then returned. She wondered how much it had cost.

"You can't," she said.

"I already did," Murdock said.

"I can't afford it," she said. "I can't even afford a room of my own."

"Pay me when you cash our Ramsbanc check," Murdock said. "Right now, I need a bodyguard. And a bodyguard needs a weapon and you keep giving yours up to good-looking cops."

"I thought you were body-guarding me!" she said.

"Not guarding the whole body," Murdock said. "Just those legs. And maybe that fine ass."

"What about this part?" she said. "Worth guarding?

"How does it work?" he said.

"You asking for a test-drive?"

"Can I drive it now and pay later?"

She unzipped his jeans, saw that he was not wearing underwear. She shucked the jeans down. Walked him backwards to the metal chair. Sat him down and then sat on his lap. Teased him until his nostrils flared. She wanted him to say he wanted her. Not just her legs and her ass and her sex, but the whole of her, the sum of body parts, brains, and emotions that was Helene Steinbeck.

"Say you want me."

"I want you."

"Say my name."

"Helene."

"Say you want me and use my name."

"I want you, Helene."

Then she took him inside. It was so easy, so smooth, so right. And, she had to admit, she liked being on top.

THE MORNING FELT CRISP on the drive through the sleepy town. On Saturday mornings, Taos traffic was light.

Helene was feeling great until they came to the blinking light intersection and the crime scene ribbons surrounding the place where the creeps in the van had attacked Sally Jo Catton. Helene phoned Albuquerque. Sally Jo was out of surgery in Recovery.

Murdock turned at the sign for the Pueblo. Adobe houses on both sides of the road. Each house had a vegetable garden. Helene saw rows of corn and fruit trees. At the quarter-mile marker, Murdock made a right turn onto a country road, orange clay and rocks. Two more rights and then up a little hill, past a fence where three horses stared at the Jeep, up to a little adobe house with a blue door.

Jimmy Little Deer came out grinning, slapped palms with Murdock, shook hands with Helene. He asked about last night, gunfight at the Sleep Inn. While he listened to the play-by-play, Jimmy stood silent, shaking his head.

"Who were they?" Jimmy said.

"Three shooters," Helene said. "A beat-up van with Wisconsin plates. Murdock didn't tell you, but he caught a piece of glass in his ankle."

"Makes a fella think about moving out of town," Jimmy said. "I got coffee, how about some doughnuts?"

They said okay to the coffee and Murdock handed over the package. They sat at a wooden table under an arbor where bees buzzed while Jimmy pulled the rifle out of the nest of pink butcher paper. Jimmy smiled. "Hey," he said. "Thanks. I owe you."

The rifle was a De Lisle, a twin to Murdock's. It had the same fat barrel with the little exhaust holes. The same folding stock. The same stubby, businesslike look. And it was equipped with hex sights.

THEY WALKED UP AN arroyo that opened into a small box canyon dotted with cottonwoods, where Jimmy had already set up a line of tin can targets. They took turns shooting the De Lisle. When Helene shot, she felt the ease of holding the gun and was still amazed that it knocked over a can with only a whisper of noise.

Jimmy said, "I gotta pay you for this, man."

"It's a gift," Murdock said, "from Santa and his elves."

"You got me in a hammerlock, man. If you don't take my money, then I'll be bound to deliver help when you get your white Yankee ass caught in a crack. That happens, you give a holler, hear?"

"It's a deal, amigo."

"How's Young Winchester?" Helene said.

"The bruises are already turning yellow," Jimmy said, "and he's swapped the crutches for a cane and a blue boot—the young bucks heal so fast—but there's this little old girl up to the Nest who's got his head whirling."

"What girl?" Helene said.

"Cute little blonde," Jimmy said. "You might've seen her at

that pow-wow with the rich folks. She was sitting right across from you guys, knives in her eyes. A Dallas gal, named Tammy. Her last name is something Anglo and rich. I warned him off, but YW is young and the chick is hot and I'm just his uncle and she must have fluttered them eyelashes, because they made peace yesterday while I wasn't watching and she invited him up to the Nest for Ulster's shindig. You guys going?"

"No," Murdock said.

"Yes, we are," Helene said. "We're driving Drusilla."

"Well," Jimmy said. "If you do get up there, keep your taste buds alert—see if you can taste my beef cattle in Ulster's famous chili."

BEFORE THEY LEFT, JIMMY showed them the patches in his fence—three breaks where the barbed wire had been cut to make a hole and then mended. In the last couple of weeks, he said, he had lost five head of cattle. Not much for a rich gringo, but the loss of five animals cut Jimmy's little herd by thirty percent. He tracked the hoof prints up the Mountain, toward Angel's Nest, where the trail ran out on some rocks.

"They got fancy fences up there," Jimmy said. "With them sensors, like a federal prison."

"You think it's Ulster grabbing your cows?" Murdock said.

"Whoever it is," Jimmy said. "They gotta be picking up cow shit before it hits the ground. I was tracking a lost yearling last week when I come onto the rocks, and right then the signs changed—no more hoof marks, and not a trace of cow flop. Pardon me, ma'am, but that's bread off my table."

"It's okay, Jimmy."

"You think your cows end up on Theo's table?" Murdock asked.

"His herd keeps growing," Jimmy said. "I lose three cows; his herd grows by two, with one left over to feed them Dallas folks."

"Have you told the cops?"

"I told Savage," Jimmy said. "He was an okay dude when he first got the job—there were stories in the paper about his experience in the intelligence community—sounds like a bad joke to me—but the last couple of years, he's been acting weird. He's always half-plastered and when I tell him about a cow gone missing, he blows me off, like a missing cow is too far below his pay grade. He says he'll handle it. Then nothing happens. The only cop showed any interest was Sergeant Catton. I was down there last night, at the blinking light, watching her get hauled away in that ambulance. You guys hear how she's doing?"

MURDOCK TOOK KIT CARSON Road, skirting the town, and drove into Taos Canyon, into a cul-de-sac off the road to Valle Vidal, where Helene practiced shooting the new Glock with the hex sights. Where Murdock kept moving the tin cans farther away, where she kept knocking them over. Where she was elated by her success.

"Why isn't this thing more popular?" she said. "Cops, the military?"

"Cops think it impedes the draw," Murdock said. "The military is scope-happy. They spend millions in product development—field testing, consulting—and when the scope doesn't cut it, they spend more millions, and they wholesale the hardware to brokers, who get rich arming the third world."

"Why did you say no to Theo's party?"

"Being on his turf makes me nervous."

"What about Anais? You said you'd be her man of the wheel, remember?"

"I am interested in Theo's safe. And we could check on Young Winchester."

"That Tammy is a sorceress," Helene said, "and only fifteen."

"You're out of ammo," Murdock said, "and all this talk has made me hungry."

"But we just had coffee and doughnuts at Jimmy's."

"That was a mere snack," Murdock said, "and you've made this into a workday. I need huevos rancheros."

30

Helene

DRUSILLA DORN, RESPLENDENT IN ecru slacks and a purple shirt, sat in the Jeep's passenger seat. "How exciting," she said. "It's like being on safari."

Murdock was driving. Helene sat in back. They were headed up the hill to the annual Theo Ulster Chili Fest at Angel's Nest. They passed the crime scene ribbons at the blinking light, where the shooters had wounded Sally Jo Catton.

"Taos used to be so peaceful," she said. "There were hippies and Indians in the plaza, wearing their blankets, and the occasional animal hit by a vehicle, but it's all changed now. Sally Jo was my dinner guest two nights ago, I hate to think of her in hospital ... and that poor dead girl, turning up like that. How do you feel about it, Mr. Murdock?"

"Sorry?" Murdock said.

"We were wondering where you had gotten to."

"Focused on the road."

"I was wondering what it feels like to kill someone."

"Depends who it is," Murdock said.

"You sound like Theo. He was a sniper, you know. Have you and he bonded yet?"

"Not yet," Murdock said.

"Do you think you might? I'm asking because he's so lonely, and you do have soldiering in common, and men have so much difficulty making friends, and I was curious."

"Guys need a common goal," Murdock said. "Like a sports team trying to score, or a squad executing a mission."

"Perhaps Theo could assist you in your hunt for the Bellini girl?"

"Good idea," Murdock said. "Could you mention it to him?"

"I'd be happy to."

THE PAVEMENT RAN OUT and the ride got bumpy and Murdock slowed down. A sudden breeze blew Drusilla's hat off. It was brand-new, with a chin strap. Helene caught the hat and handed it back.

"Thank you," Drusilla said. "I know I should follow your lead and use that little strap, but it seems so ..."

Helene spoke from the backseat. "What was Theo like when you first met him?"

"Handsome," Drusilla said. "He was the pro at the Triangle Racquet Club in Santa Fe. He was on the court in his tennis whites, tall and lean and tanned, and I remember thinking—now there's a man I could wear high heels with. Two of my husbands were short and fat. So Theo certainly gained points in that department."

"So you chose him?"

"Females are happier if we can choose, and I have this little secret measuring scale of 'Goods' that I try to follow. First, good genes."

"Genes means he was tall," Helene said, "good-looking, witty."

"Excellent. Second is good behavior."

"He was polite," Murdock said. "He opened doors, he paid attention."

"He wore a suit on our first date," Drusilla said. "The third scale is good resources."

"Money," Helene said.

"And there, poor Theo fell short. But with a man, two out of three is usually all a girl gets."

THERE WAS TRAFFIC UP ahead, a line of vehicles winding toward Angel's Nest. The sun was behind them now, off to the left, an orange wafer sliding toward the horizon, ending another gorgeous autumn day. Helene could feel that Drusilla wanted to talk about Theo.

"Of course," Drusilla said. "I had already heard the gossip about Theo being very well-equipped. Ladies of the club spoke of him as a catch, telling fish tales—was it this long? No, it was this long. Women can be so silly. But I was rebounding from my last divorce and Theo courted me with energy. He had a little side business in South American artifacts. He wanted out of that, so I found him a position in Taos."

"Why did he want out of the artifacts business?"

"Who can say?" Drusilla said. "I think he wearied catering to those salesmen from Mexico. They were short, they wore suits, they pestered Theo to get them dates with his little shop girls. He was much happier in Taos, especially when he started construction up here."

"So Angel's Nest was his idea?"

"Theo's dream," she said. "But I had title to the land. It came to me as part of the settlement for my second divorce."

"I thought Angel's Nest was Indian Land," Murdock said.

"It was, but my second husband won a bit of acreage in a card game. And I was thinking about selling it back when Theo saw his dream come true."

"How many divorces have you had?" Murdock said.

"Four husbands, four divorces."

"And is Theo on deck for number five?"

"Oh," she said. "I shudder to think, as Grandma used to say.

Theo is fun. But he does have a roving eye. Look at the way that pretty Belgian girl simpers when he's around. I admit he is a marvelous host, a world-class cook, those meats, those sauces, so very French, and until another tall man comes along, well…"

THE ROAD TURNED RIGHT, a long curve, and the going was bumpier now. Helene knew Murdock had more questions. She caught his eye in the rearview mirror and nodded.

"How well do you know the Ramsays?" Murdock said.

"Purely social," Drusilla said. "They've been to my house. They reciprocate when I'm in Dallas."

"What do you think of their boys?"

"That Tommy Ramsay is a rascal. He pulls pranks, he's terribly oversexed. For that one, I see a dark future. The older boy, Gerry Junior—everyone calls him G.J.—has a bright future in government. Or so the gossip goes. He speaks Spanish. His mother was some sort of Latina beauty queen."

"Has G.J. been around this summer?"

"I saw him only briefly."

"Do you remember when?"

"A week, two weeks? Is there something I should know?"

"Gerry Ramsay mentioned a job."

"Really? What sort of job?"

"Yet to be determined," Murdock said.

"Would you like me to put in a good word?"

"That would be great," Murdock said.

Helene said, "So who owns the land now?"

"Why, I do. Or I guess it's really the Drusilla Dorn Trust. It's managed by a little man in Houston. He knew my daddy. He doesn't like Gerry Ramsay. He won't tell me why. I get quarterly reports."

"So you leased it to Theo?"

"Actually, the lease is held by a consortium."

"A group of investors?" Helene said.

"Yes. Several individuals have banded together. People who

enjoy this area. A lot of them have cabins in Little Galilee, which is a Dallas stronghold. Also people from Los Angeles and Miami."

"So you get income from the consortium?"

"That money pays for scholarships," Drusilla said. "It funds the writers conference and the tennis tournament that brings in all these beautiful young women. It's paying your way, dear, so that I have the pleasure of your company. Oh, here we are at last. The sun is barely down and it's practically winter."

THE ROAD LEVELED OFF. There were shallow parking lots carved out of the mountain. Murdock turned on his left blinker, but then a teenager in an orange vest handed him a piece of cardboard that said Parking Lot A.

"I phoned ahead," Drusilla said. "I told Theo I wasn't walking a half mile on these treacherous rocks."

They kept moving. Helene saw a gate with a sign that said Quarry Way. Through the gate was an asphalt track wide enough for a golf cart. Helene asked about it.

"Quarry Way started as a mining venture," Drusilla said. "Then it became a ski run, but Theo wants something for snowboards and those awful ATVs. The A-lot is just there, and here's Corporal Simpson to guide us."

Simpson had a British accent, a short haircut, and strange blue eyes. Helene recognized him as the dog-handler the day she had killed those dogs. In his military khakis, he seemed innocent as a boy scout. He directed the Jeep to a parking slot beside a big Mercedes SUV.

Helene remembered a similar vehicle from Wednesday morning, in Little Galilee, when they had gone to fetch Murdock's Jeep. Helene also remembered a damaged grill. The grill on this Mercedes looked okay, but seeing the big machine up close still made Helene shiver. She looked at Murdock, then lifted her chin and glanced at the Mercedes. When Murdock nodded, she knew they were both thinking the same thing—

Could this be the Mercedes that had spooked Helene on the Paseo? Was this the same Mercedes that Murdock had disabled by shooting out a tire?

SIMPSON HELPED DRUSILLA OUT of the Jeep. She mentioned the cold again while she extracted a down vest from her shoulder bag. Murdock was doing his soldier-thing, asking Simpson where he had served. Simpson mentioned someplace in Central Asia, but then he said that his uncle had served with Captain Ulster.

In the Gate House. Simpson hung the Jeep keys on a keyboard painted white. "It's the custom," he said, "in the event some cars need re-parking."

As they walked with Simpson toward the Media Shack, Helene heard applause. "It's the archery competition," Simpson said. "There's this young girl at the Nest who keeps winning all sorts of tournaments. Perhaps you've heard of her? Tammy Wellborn, only fifteen. The Captain's grooming her for Olympic Gold."

31
Murdock

THERE WERE THREE LINES for ID photos at the Media Shack. One for UTES—young people up to 22. One for Yuppies—parents of the UTES. And one line labeled OLDIES AND WEAKINGS—a phrase Captain Theo had discovered on a T-shirt in China. The T-shirt, explained Corporal Simpson—with homage in his eyes—had faded away, but the words had survived and usually occasioned an interesting anecdote about the Captain's past as a soldier for the Queen. Drusilla Dorn darted away, carrying Simpson's black sat-phone.

Murdock pulled Helene into the line for Oldies. The name-taker was a teenage girl with upper-class teeth and a name-tag that said "Sue Ellen." Murdock remembered her from Helene's workshop, sitting on the floor, looking scared. With a steady hand, she printed their names on little cards. Helene gave the girl a compliment on her penmanship. Sue Ellen blushed as she apologized for the other night in Helene's workshop. "We were out of line," she said, "and I'm really sorry. Tommy Ramsay has a lot of wild ideas."

Murdock and Helene were third in line, behind an old man with glasses wearing a straw boater and two society women with blue hair in tight helmet hairdos. The UTES line was the longest. Murdock saw Marie-Claire chatting with two boys from Friday night's assault on Helene. Marie-Claire's friend, the tall Serbian girl, waited in the Yuppie line, a red rucksack slung over her shoulder.

The girls waved. Marie-Claire turned back to the boys, but the Serbian girl gave Murdock a shy smile. Still on her sat-phone, Drusilla was complaining about the security stuff. Murdock heard the words "racial profiling" and "sexual discrimination."

"What beautiful girls," Helene said.

"Theo works fast," Murdock said. "Meets them on Wednesday, lassoes them into his party on Saturday."

"Theo's not that good-looking," Helene said. "How does he do it?"

Drusilla came back, waving her name badge. Her face was flushed, her eyes bright from verbal combat. She handed the sat-phone to Simpson. "Would you believe they had my badge with my name on it locked in a drawer? What a farce. What absolute rot. Who else could wear my badge? And what's going on with Theodore? I'm going to find him."

When Murdock and Helene were tagged and photographed, they exited the Media Shack with Sonja Vasic. Helene asked about the red rucksack. "Pajamas and toothpaste," Sonja said. "My roommate, Marie-Claire, insists on staying the night."

"Are you perhaps sleeping here also?" Sonja said.

"We're leaving early," Helene said. "What are the rooms like?"

"Number Two-Oh-Three, at the Anasazi Cliff House, is quite primitive," she said.

Marie-Claire came up, wobbling on her high heels and looking squeezed by her tight-fitting party dress. Her shoulders, creased by the spaghetti straps, still looked sunburned. She shook hands—"Hello, how are you?"—and then swept Sonja away, "to meet some people," she said. The people were Gerald and Marina Ramsay, from Dallas. Three groups away,

Murdock saw Willy Mapes, surrounded by a knot of Goth girls—harbingers of Halloween.

TWO HUNDRED PEOPLE SWARMED the grassy area called Gretna Green. The rich people sipped cocktails from fluted glasses. The mountain people guzzled beer from mugs that looked as if they had come straight from Munich. At the edge of the crowd, Willy Mapes was chatting away with a clutch of girls—not tanned tennis players with smooth biceps, but arty girls wearing ultra-Goth black. One girl had a purple streak through her hair. Another wore performer face-paint. The right side of her face was bone-white, the left side was a gleaming black, with a reversed red C-curve. The tip of the C-curve touched her blood-red lips.

"If you can separate Willy from his vampire babes," Murdock said, "I can ask him again about Barbi Bellini."

Murdock stood in the shadow of the Maintenance Shack, watching Helene Steinbeck swing into action. She shot a smile at Willy Mapes. Smiling back, Willy introduced his retinue. During the introductions, Helene grabbed Willy's hand and whispered into his ear. Willy nodded, said something to the girls, and left the circle. Helene threaded her arm into his as she guided him toward the Maintenance Shack. Willy was laughing. He was looking at Helene. She was holding his attention, keeping his eyes away from Murdock.

"That's so crazy," Willy said. "Where's that awful Murdock?"

"We broke up," Helene said.

"Well," Willy said. "That was very smart of you because—"

Murdock grabbed Willy's jacket and jerked him under the shadows made by the overhang. Hauled him around the building to the rear. From here, Murdock could see gleaming grills and expensive headlights from the pricey vehicles in Parking Lot A. The Jeep was out of sight, lost in a forest of high-dollar chrome and curved Plexiglas.

Willy kept struggling. Murdock popped a fist into his solar

plexus. Willy made a sound like *woof*, sagged against the wall, clutched his chest as he fought for air. Murdock shoved the photo under Willy's nose. It showed Barbi Bellini, tall, graceful, wearing shorts and a tank top, striding into the front door at the art colony.

Willy nodded. He was wheezing as he spoke. "Bellini was here; I recognize her now. I heard she was shacking up with that fucker, Francois—that boy was equipped like a swordsman— chicks flopped down and begged for it. One day she was here, the next day she was gone. No forwarding address. No request for a refund. Okay?"

"When did you notice, Willy?"

"A week ago. No. Ten days or a maybe couple weeks. You're hurting me. When Theo hears about this—"

Murdock gave Willy a shove, then jerked his head, the signal to scoot. Helene came up as Willy scooted away, coughing and wheezing. And checking his wristwatch.

"Willy's got a date," Helene said, "and I'm ready to head back down the mountain."

"We just got here," Murdock said.

"We need to tell Drusilla," Helene said, "make sure she has a ride."

"We need to find Anais Bertrand," Murdock said.

"As I remember," Helene said. "Anais was thinking of not coming tonight."

"She needs money," Murdock said.

"She makes me nervous."

"She's survived Theo this far," Murdock said.

THEY WERE STILL ANALYZING when Corporal Simpson arrived, a fake smile on his face. "There you are," Simpson said. "The Captain would very much like to see you for a moment, in his office. It's in the Smokehouse, just up the hill. Let's walk, shall we, and please allow me to indicate points of interest along the way. You are here, at the Maintenance Shack. It's where we repair the vehicles—quite a number of tires getting torn up by this rocky terrain. To your left across the Green we have the Lodges—your Pueblo Hogans, your Zuni Wickiups, and your Anasazi Cliff House—accommodations for two dozen families on the ground floor, a dozen up top. The grassy area in front of the lodges where the guests are gathered is called Gretna Green, not named after the London tube stop, but rather a favorite city of the Captain's. Just there, the little lorries are being unloaded. Chairs and banquet tables, for after the game."

"What game?" Murdock said.

"It's called Indian Shoot, Mr. Murdock, and it's become quite a favorite of the crowd. Now then, checking my watch, it's time for your visit to the Captain. Please follow me, single file."

They followed the corporal along a gravel path that wound through a copse of aspen trees, their yellow leaves fluttery-fragile in the late afternoon breeze, up a slight hill, away from the lodges and the wide expanse of Gretna Green. They came out of the trees, animals grazing to their left, a dozen head of cattle, two dozen goats—more animals than Murdock had seen from Flatrock Ridge. They passed a building that said "Spa." Then two clay tennis courts. The Smokehouse came into view through the trees. The path turned to asphalt, leading them to a set of stairs made of railroad ties. The Smokehouse was a sturdy-looking log structure with a steel roof. Murdock recognized the building as another landmark he had seen from the ridge on Wednesday morning. As they climbed the stairs, Murdock smelled meat cooking, pungent and sweetish. Roasted meat. Beef or goat? Deer or wild turkey?

Simpson led the way up the stairs onto the veranda. The door was heavy timbers, and not locked. Going through, they passed double doors leading to a meeting room, outfitted with tables and metal fold-up chairs that would seat maybe a hundred guests. At the front of the room was a giant TV screen. Simpson led them past the meeting room, around the corner. Two doors here, one closed, one open. At the end of the hallway was a sign that said "Theo's Kitchen."

A voice called out, "Is that you, Simpson?" and then Captain Theo himself was standing in the open doorway, smiling and nodding like an English country squire, holding out his arms to receive welcome guests. He wore a khaki officer's uniform, a pistol in a Sam Browne belt, his chest crowded with service ribbons.

When Simpson shook Murdock's hand, the gesture was terse and dismissive, as if Murdock did not exist. Done with Murdock, Theo gripped Helene's right hand in both of his, smiling like a schoolboy, locked into his country squire role— Foxes and Hounds, old chap—and drew her into his office.

The office door was steel, sturdy and thick, with no window onto the hallway. As Murdock passed through the door, he noticed the decoration—an old bas-relief engraving of a soldier, maybe a Roman Centurion, wearing a plumed helmet with an exaggerated ear protector to shield the side of the neck. Centurions, the world's first mercenary soldiers.

Theo's desk was two metal floor cabinets bolted together to form an L-shape, with one edge pushed tight against the wall. The cabinets were equipped with metal casters, for easy moving. No papers on the desk, no pencils in a pencil holder, no paper clips, no open ledgers, no laptop or box of Kleenex— only a single photo in a silver frame, turned to the wall, its subject hidden from the visitor's view.

Mounted on the wall above the desk was a locked metal cabinet. To the right of the cabinet was a full size relief map that named the mountains surrounding Angel's Nest. Taos Mountain, Wheeler Peak, Angel Mountain. There was a window in the outside wall. The sun was lower now, the shadows gathering. On the wall next to the window Murdock saw black and white photos of men in uniform, cradling weapons. The men looked young and thin, starved by war.

Under the map was Theo's floor safe, big and clumsy-looking, with a black stove-polish exterior, and a little frame that looked like embroidery rope. On the door was a colored engraving of a naked woman curled around a lily in a glass flute. The dial was brassy. The thick door of the safe was ajar, but not enough for Murdock to see inside.

Standing before the map, Theo was using a swagger stick to point out landmarks to Helene. He looked like a relic from an old war movie. "Here *we* are," he said, "that little circle of green. This, of course, is Pueblo Road, our main link to the outside world. If you turn left here, at Quarry Way, and climb a bit, you'll intersect the overland trail that leads around Blue Lake and winds up at Little Galilee—and this bleak escarpment to the east is Flatrock Ridge. Can you show me, Helene, where you encountered that poor unfortunate girl? We could really use a photo. I can't believe you were up there without your camera."

Helene shook her head. No camera. Theo swung around. His eyes gleamed. "I say, Murdock, where was your corpse, exactly?"

Murdock held out his hand and Theo gave up the swagger stick. Murdock laid the tip on the map. "The corpse was here. The archers were up here, on higher ground."

"So you fired at them uphill?"

"Yes."

"And where had you just come from?"

"Downhill," Murdock said.

He handed the swagger stick back to Theo. Theo's eyes blazed, he shook his head. He was not in the office. He was off somewhere else—a battlefield, a parade ground—and then, like an eye-blink, he was back in the room.

As a soldier, Murdock knew where Theo was coming from—he had felt the same telltale trembling, the same alienation from civilian life, the powerful tug of the soldier's way—but something always brought him back and then Theo was present again. He set the swagger stick on the desk and took Helene's arm. Let me show you my kitchen."

Corporal Simpson held the door, and the smell of cooking meat flooded Murdock's senses. Pungent smoke, super-tangy spices, a strange sweetish quality to the smell. As Murdock went out, he checked out the photo on Theo's desk.

Encased in the silver frame was a woman, beautiful, in a silver gown, looking straight into the camera. The gown bared her shoulders, showed the tops of her breasts, and outlined her hip and left thigh. She was sitting on a chair draped in velvet. The photo was in black and white, but the velvet was dark, maybe purple-colored. The throne-like divan gave the woman a regal appearance—and Murdock had the impression that she was posing for a role, a stage play or a film. There was handwriting in the bottom right hand corner. Murdock bent down. It was an inscription. "With Love," it said, "from Eunice Dare."

Corporal Simpson was waiting, standing at attention. Murdock pointed to a closed door.

"What's in there?"

"Captain's closet, sir. Shall we?"

The kitchen was L-shaped, with ovens built into the wall, half a dozen restaurant-sized cooktops, and butcher block cutting tables. One oven door showed a faint light. When Murdock looked in, he saw a chunk of meat rotating on a spit. It was light meat, not dark, and had a pale tan color, suggesting that it had not been cooking for long. At the butcher block tables, four chefs in toque hats—two men and two women— were slicing thin cuts of sandwich meat from haunches that had been roasted to a gleaming bronzy-brown. The meat looked like what Drusilla had served at her dinner party. The last two ovens in the chain were dark inside. One of them was padlocked. A little hand-written note said, "Out of Order."

Smiling like a born restaurateur, Theo fixed a plate for Helene—slices of meat, sauces, a celery stick to clear the palate. There were three heat-levels for the sauces: Mild, Medium, and Hot. Theo named six kinds of meat—pork, chicken, turkey, antelope, goat, and venison. "The sauces are needed," he said, "because white meat tends to dry out."

Helene took a bite and smiled. She took another bite with a different sauce and asked for water. "That's hot!" she said.

Corporal Simpson was chatting with a female chef, her apron stained with meat juice. The female chef left Corporal Simpson and came over. Her face was college-girl young. Her name badge said "Chef Diana." She took Murdock's plate, arranged three meats in a triangle, and dabbed on the three sauces. Murdock took bites. He liked the green sauce best. The meat was not chicken or pork. The slices came from a haunch that looked processed, like the smoked turkey Murdock bought at Costco in Seattle.

"What's with the sauces?" Murdock said.

"Some kind of secret code," Diana said. "You're that detective guy, aren't you? The one who found the dead girl?"

"Yes," Murdock said. "Did you know her?"

"The Captain's a real party animal," she said. "The girls are my age or younger. He mingles them with his groupies. You hear stories."

"What kind of stories?"

"Strip-poker," she said. "Clouds of doobie-smoke."

"You one of his groupies?""

"No way," she said. "I'm staff, and not a jock. Those kids are the chosen."

Chef Diana went back to work. Across the room, Helene was sampling the meats. Murdock moved from table to table, dipping his meat slices into little pots of sauce. He stopped at a cooktop where a guy in a white apron was doing a taste-test on a big iron pot with a spicy smell. The guy said he was doing the final taste of Captain Theo's Chili—the heart and soul of the Chili Fest—before sending it on to Gretna Green. Murdock took a taste. Spicy and not bad.

"Does Theo do his own sauces?"

"Not sure about that," the guy said.

The guy turned away. Murdock went around the corner of the L, where he saw a set of double doors—"Storage, Authorized Personnel Only." The doors were white metal—they reminded him of hospital movies, where sweaty orderlies piloted a life-and-death gurney through bat-wing swinging doors as they rushed to the emergency room.

As Murdock tasted the next sauce—he preferred the green sauce on the pork—the double doors burst open and a short guy in a toque hat came through in a rush, pushing a metal cart. Before the doors swung closed, Murdock caught a glimpse of boxes on shelves, a shiny conveyor belt leading to a door that said "Waste Room." Before the door closed, Murdock saw construction in progress—a steel frame for a box, a pile of bricks, a steel door equipped with a round window, a portable cement mixer. In the far corner was a smaller box that had to be an incinerator. Theo Ulster torched his own garbage.

The short guy stopped his metal cart and stood in front of Murdock.

"Back away, friend. This is staff only, off-limits to the public."

Murdock said nothing. The doors closed. The cart was empty except for a butcher knife with a curved blade. Murdock stood there, holding onto his plate. The short guy looked like a street punk who had survived the gang wars and was now employed by the Sicilian Mafia. His name tag said "Marius—Iron Chef," and he was steamed up about something. Behind him, Murdock heard Simpson call, "I say, Mister Murdock, there you are."

When Simpson appeared, Iron Chef Marius shrugged and backed away. The threat was over, but not finished. To be continued. With a glare at Murdock, and another glare at Simpson, Marius rolled his metal cart away.

"Hey Simpson," Murdock said.

"Yes?" Simpson said.

"What's cooking with the ugly Iron Chef?"

"Always on edge, sir. All these meals, all this pressure, each time the Captain adds another kind of meat."

Before they left the kitchen, Theo called the chefs over for an upbeat message. Theo laid on a last rah-rah compliment. Then he said, "We must be going," and nodded at Corporal Simpson, who led Murdock and Helene down a hallway, past more ovens, passing the storage room, toward a door with a sign that said, "Loading."

Simpson opened the door that led to a loading dock. Theo gave Helene a kiss on the cheek, gave Murdock's hand another dismissive shake, and was saying goodbye when his sat-phone beeped. He apologized for the interruption, and said, "Ta-Ta for now." He was on the sat-phone as he climbed the ramp back to the Smokehouse. He climbed fast, legs young and springy, with no effort, no gulping for breath at the top. Captain Theo kept himself in shape.

32

Murdock

ON THE WALK BACK to Gretna Green, with the crowd noise rumbling, Helene Steinbeck told Murdock she was really ready to leave the party, head back to town, have a hamburger, not Theo Ulster's beef or veal or goat, rent a movie, spend some quality time. Murdock said okay. They were hunting for Drusilla Dorn—they needed to make sure she had a ride back down—when a woman from Helene's writing group asked about Sally Jo Catton, "Is she doing okay?" Then the woman said, "There are people who want you to sign books." Already leading Helene away, she added, "Only take a minute, hon."

Murdock got a Modelo Especial at the drink table. He stood near the entrance to the Anasazi Cliff House with his back to the wall, observing Theo's guests. The city people were drinking out of real wine-glasses. The mountain people were drinking out of real beer steins. Lots of dishes to wash and the constant danger of broken glass. Murdock saw Marie-Claire, the chubby Belgian, holding hands with Tommy Ramsay and feeding herself a chunk of meat. Her bare, round shoulders gleamed. Her mouth glittered with laughter. Standing there on

Theo's grass, Marie-Claire was surrounded by nasty rich kids from Dallas—the same kids who had rousted Helene at the writing workshop.

Murdock turned away from the party as Sonja the Serbian girl came up. She was hugging herself as if chilled.

"That man, that Mister Mapes. Do you know him?"

"What's up, Miss Vasic?"

"He follows me," she said. "He says things. How beautiful I am. He invites me to a big fiesta in Mexico. Just across the border, he says, and offers me five thousand dollars to play an exhibition in Mexico, in a private club. So I find Marie-Claire because I wish to leave this place and she is angry with me. 'What is wrong with you?' she cries."

"You're worried about your friend," Murdock said.

"She is too much at parties," Sonja said. "And the drinking is killing her chance at serious tennis. In every city on the tour—Paris, Gstaad, even here in Taos—Marie-Claire finds so many boys to be among. She has this photo from the beach at Tenerife, many copies. She is wearing the bikini, but the bottoms only, with her back to the camera, looking over her shoulder. She has a wonderful smile, so warm, and it beckons the boys. All summer, the photos," Sonja said. "All summer, the boys."

"And, oh..."

She stopped talking and Murdock looked up. Helene Steinbeck had finished signing books, and was now walking through the crowd with Drusilla Dorn, shaking hands, stopping to say hello, moving on toward Murdock and the girl. Murdock watched her. A woman who knew how to handle herself.

The girl from Serbia walked off, straight back, long legs, wearing her Taos trophy, a new cowboy hat. She stopped to shake hands, first with Helene Steinbeck, second with Drusilla. Looking thoughtful, Helene Steinbeck joined Murdock. Drusilla chatted with Sonja.

"Twenty-seven books," Helene said. "Signed and sold. I get ten percent of each one and the damned check won't arrive until next March, and I don't know where I'll be and—"

"How about Seattle in March?" Murdock said.

"Whoa," she said. "Did you just invite me to see your humble man-cave?"

"Can you cook? Murdock said.

"Steinbeck's secret casserole," she said.

HELENE GAVE MURDOCK A squeeze. She pulled him closer, and then she settled her hip against his. He could hear her breathing. Could feel the pulse of her blood from her hands holding on. He had come to Taos feeling empty. With Helene Steinbeck, he felt full. Her breath was warm on his cheek.

Drusilla came up, smiling sadly, then turned to watch the Serbian girl, who was walking fast, her arms folded, her ponytail swinging. The tennis players greeted the girl as she joined them. Giggles rose from the group.

Drusilla was telling them about her conversation with the Ramsays—Gerald and Marina, who had a business proposition that needed discussing—when a big bell started clanging, followed by a Theo's voice on a bullhorn, announcing the start-time for the game. Murdock could see people climbing onto bleachers—cowboy boots, loud colors, lots of beer. On the rooftops of the stucco lodges, the city-people sat in chaise-longues, drinking champagne cocktails.

"Can you catch a ride back?" Helene said. "Murdock and I are—"

"You can't leave," Drusilla said. "The fun is just getting underway."

"I'm beat," Helene said. "Okay?"

"Ah, the course of true love," Drusilla said. "Not to worry. Oh, there are the Ramsays again. Wait right here."

MURDOCK STOOD WITH HELENE, watching Drusilla

grab Gerald Ramsay by the arm. Marina took Helene aside. She wanted to chat about a book she had in mind, and Drusilla rushed off to say hello to someone. Murdock was alone with Gerald.

"What's up with you and Willy Mapes?" Gerald said.

"He's got something I need."

"Mind telling me what?"

"Information on a missing girl."

"And her name was something Italian, right?"

"Bellini," Murdock said.

"Willy is so small time. Did you get what you needed?"

"You know something, Mr. Ramsay?"

"Call me Gerry. And the answer is no—I don't know anything. Sorry about that. But I'd like to talk with you about a real job."

"A real job doing what?"

"Doing what you do best," Gerald said. "Sleuthing. Checking people out, digging up the dirt. I could offer a starting salary at two-fifty per annum. Benefits package. Interested?"

"You have two boys, right?"

"Tommy and Gerry Junior," he said. "Something you need to share?"

"Tommy got in my way the other night. I thought it might run in the genes."

"We settled all that, didn't we? At the meeting hosted by Sammy Savage?"

"What about Gerry Junior," Murdock said. "Is he here tonight?"

"He's taken himself off to school," Gerald said. "Tell you what, when you're done here, when your current case is solved, when you finish up with this *cherche la femme* thing, or whatever, give me a buzz. I've written my private number on the card. That's twenty-four/seven—day or night, you buzz me. We'll 'set up a meeting, work out a deal."

"Sounds terrific," Murdock said.

The two men shook hands. Gerald's grip pulsed with confidence and leadership. As he did the strength test again, Murdock squeezed back, thinking, if he broke Gerald's hand now, if he put this rich arrogant prick on his knees on the wet grass, he could disable an enemy combatant—a wrist twist packed with torque, holding on until he felt Gerald's hand losing strength.

Murdock let go.

Gerald's grin glowed with the power of money.

He wanted to own Murdock.

33

Helene

THE BLEACHERS WERE FULL, so Helene and Murdock grabbed some folding chairs and sat on a hummock with a good view of Gretna Green.

The adobe buildings were laid out in a U-shape and stacked together like boxes added onto boxes. The buildings were two stories—two boxes tall—and Helene spotted the Ramsays, sitting in chairs on the roof of the Zuni building. They were chatting with Elise Wellborn, Drusilla, and the stunning archery coach—Carla Carlini.

"Like spectators at the Roman arena," Helene said.

"Have you seen Anais?" Murdock said.

"Not since we arrived," Helene said. "Are you thinking what I think you're thinking?"

Murdock gave Helene a soft shoulder bump. She answered with a smile. Then she turned to examine the compound. Theo Ulster's Gretna Green, with its skin of freshly mowed grass, resembled a well-kept polo field. As she watched, two dozen teenage kids trotted onto the grass carrying rubber hammers and little metal stakes. As the teenagers drove stakes, Helene watched three circles forming. The outer circle was white, the middle circle was red, the tiny inner circle was black.

"Oh," Helene said. "There's Anais. She's waving."

"And looking furtive."

"Are we going to help her?"

"Let her take the lead," Murdock said.

"Maybe she's waiting for the game to start."

"She's a smart lady," Murdock said, "knows a diversion when she sees one."

THERE WAS A RAISED platform at the far end of the compound, close to the Media Shack. On top of the platform was a little roofed structure, like a guardhouse in a prison movie, and Theo Ulster was on top with a bullhorn.

Theo spoke into the bullhorn, "As you can see, the two outer circles—one red, one white—give shape to a track for keeping our runner on course. The black circle in the center is a cage to contain the eager archers.

Marie-Claire Benoit was ready to run. She had replaced the pink party dress with shorts and a tight top. She joined Theo, who was down off the platform at the edge of the white circle. She did a couple of leg stretches, then shook out her shoulders to get loose, like a swimmer preparing for a race. She left Theo to stand with the other runners.

Helene was watching the runners line up when Anais Bertrand appeared, wearing dark slacks and sensible shoes and a man's shirt under a dark blue sweater. Her eyes were nervous, her face tight with apprehension.

"Theo is here," she said, "surrounded by his admirers. Now is the perfect time for the little floor safe. Are you still my wheelman?"

Helene looked at Murdock. He nodded okay.

"Do you want help with the safe?" he said.

"If there is a photo of your Bellini friend, I shall bring it."

Helene watched as Anais faded into the shadows, then entered the Aspen Grove. She gripped Murdock's arm. He patted her hand.

34

Marie-Claire

MARIE-CLAIRE BENOIT WAS DOWN on the grass, down on one knee, waiting for the gun. The grass was cool and soft, easy to run barefoot. The ring on her finger caught the light. She thought of Tommy, his strong body pressed against hers, his tongue in her ear, the whisper of marriage, sweet chills up her spine. She saw him in the crowd, standing between his parents. Tommy gave her the Texas thumbs-up. How could she be so lucky?

Marie-Claire, the girl from Belgium, felt totally at home in the mountains of New Mexico. What a surprise! She was eighteen, her tennis life was sinking, anyone could track her fall on the WTA computer, but here on the soft grass she had a new beginning, tonight, running this race called Indian Shoot, running to honor the memory of the noble people of these sacred mountains.

Down on her knees, feeling relaxed, Marie-Claire checked out the track, an oval created by stringing white wires through white stakes driven deep. She checked out the competition— five girls from the WTA tour, six boys from the writers' conference—and knew she could beat them. She checked out the four archers inside a small circle in the center of the track. She knew two of them—a boy named Skye, Tommy's friend, and the pretty blonde girl named Tammy. To win, you had to run three laps and cross the finish-line without being shot.

A voice came over the loud-speaker as Theo Ulster, the Head Pro, gave instructions. "Runners, ready to run? Archers, ready to shoot? Remember that the arrow tips are only rubber suction cups. If you get hit, clear the track. Ready? One-two-three, Go!" The starter pistol made a little pop and Marie-Claire was up and running, remembering her school days as a sprinter, moving ahead of the pack, in full stride, taking the lead. Her speed drew the first arrows. She dodged two, then dropped back, letting the arrows fall on the pack. Her legs felt strong, her heart was buoyed by the boy, the ring, the marriage promise, love at first sight. She was in the Zone, running for her life.

Two laps completed and only one competitor left as Marie-Claire stumbled, faking a fall, hearing the writer slow as he came up behind her. His name was Whitworth. He was thin, with a scraggly beard, and he wrote poetry. Out of the corner of her eye, Marie-Claire saw arrows arcing down. One came from Tammy's bow, one from Skye Latimer. When Whitworth was close, Marie-Claire rolled to the side. One arrow fell to the grass. The other one hit Whitworth.

She did not wait to watch him fall. Did not pay attention to his yelp. "Hey, bitch! I tried to help you!" She ran because this was her chance. This was her night, her time. She dodged two more arrows and made the finish line, where Sonja was there with a hug, where Theo was there with the prize, $500 in dollars. Easy money, but nothing compared to the wealth of Tommy's parents. And they were being so nice to her.

Like now, as Tommy's mother grabbed Marie-Claire in a hug. "Honey," she said. "You were magnificent. How about a shower and a cool drink?"

"Where is Tommy, Mrs. Ramsay?"

"He'll be right along. But right now you must meet the girls—and please call me Marina. Mrs. Ramsay is my mother-in-law."

MARINA, SUCH A PRETTY name for a mother. She found Marie-Claire a robe. They walked away from Gretna Green toward a building called the Spa. The night was chilly and Marie-Claire was sweaty and she was looking forward to a shower. The Spa building had stairs and beside the stairs a metal ramp. Inside the Spa Marie-Claire saw signs above doors. One sign said, "Men." One said, "Pool." Marina took her through the door that said "Women." The room was lovely— smooth white tile and soft wooden walls. She saw lavatories, toilet stalls, bidets, a shower room, massage tables with wheels, robes on wall hooks, and a sign that said "Sauna."

IN THE SAUNA, SHE met two other women, Lilith and Eve. Marie-Claire accepted a drink. It tasted good and she needed to hydrate. When the glass was empty someone handed her another. How relaxed she felt with these women. They were rich, they were twenty years older and still beautiful, they moved like sleek cats. They possessed the secret of staying young. Three more women came in. Celia. Madolyn. And Elise, the mother of Tammy.

They wanted to know about Marie-Claire. What was life like on the tennis circuit? How many of the tennis players were gay?

"When did you start playing tennis, hon?"

"I was nine," she said. "I ran on the track team. A tennis coach put me onto a tennis court, for a try-out, he said. I ran down every ball."

"When did you turn pro?"

"I was fifteen. I had my first manager. Her name was Mrs. Delacroix. She cheated me, so I found a new manager. His name was Yuri. I love this drink. What is it?"

"It's iced tea and something to smooth it out. Was Yuri handsome?"

"He was rough with me. He had big feet and very large— hands."

The women laughed. They asked about her other coaches. After Yuri, there was Alex. After Alex, there was Tomaso.

"What happened with Tomaso?"

"I fired him when I caught him fucking a skinny bitch from Belarus."

The women applauded. They cried, "Attagirl!" They asked about penises. Was Yuri bigger than Alex? Was Alex bigger than Tomaso? They asked if Marie-Claire had seen Theo's penis. It was quite tremendous, they said.

"How do you know?" Marie-Claire said.

They laughed again and Marie-Claire laughed with them.

The woman called Madolyn said, "Honey, the first time with Theo, that bastard split me wide open and never smiled once. I was sore for a week. What a memory!"

The women sat close together on the bench, their thighs warm against hers. Someone rubbed her back. That felt good. Someone rubbed her calves. That felt better. The drink was gone and a another drink appeared, like magic. How many drinks was that? Her head felt light and the room was spinning. The women talked about cars. Which was better—the Mercedes or the Lexus? They talked about men in bed—two of them were fucking the same tennis pro, back in Dallas. She felt a hand between her legs. She felt lips licking her breasts. She felt loved.

35
Murdock

THE RACE WAS OVER. A few big-bellied eaters were going back for seconds. Other guests had left the tables and were walking toward the parking area. There was no sign of Marie-Claire.

Across the compound and just up the hill, Murdock saw his old jungle buddy, Sammy Savage, towering over a circle of short guys who looked prosperous and well-groomed. Two of the guys were bald, three had pricey haircuts. Sammy wore a cowboy suit—boots and a Stetson, pearl-snap buttons on his western shirt, a leather vest with fringe. The Stetson was pushed back on his forehead. His face was sweaty. "I see Tammy," Helene said. "She's making friends with Sonya Vasic."

To kill time while they waited for Anais, they strolled over to Theo's portable bar. Helene spoke to some people, signed another book. Looking past Helene, Murdock saw Willy Mapes walking with a guy in a fancy Guayabera shirt. With his Aztec cheekbones and full head of pretty black hair, he could have been Julio Calderon's younger brother—Latino, maybe South American. At the main entrance of the Anasazi Cliff House, Mapes pushed through the door. Señor Pretty Hair followed.

Murdock checked his watch. Nine minutes since they had seen Anais Bertrand. Two minutes for her to get through the Aspen Grove to the Smokehouse. That would leave her seven minutes with Theo's floor safe. How much time did she need? Anais had refused their help. Helene nudged Murdock toward the Cliff House.

"Willy Mapes and his pal," Helene said.

"Sonja and Tammy," Murdock said.

"Three against one," Helene said.

"Let's check it out."

THEY STAYED IN THE shadows, Helene ahead, Murdock scouting the rear. The big front door was heavy, with black wrought-iron hardware. A tiny squeak as Helene pushed it open. There was no office, no soft drink machine, no movement in the downstairs corridor. Except for the adobe walls, the inside of the Anasazi Cliff House looked like any old motel. A sign on a door said: "Meditation Room. No shoes permitted." Sounds came from the second floor, voices, feet scuffling, something hitting the floor. Helene led the way up. Murdock admired her hustle. No hesitation, no sign of doubt.

At the top of the stairs, Helene stopped to pull her baby Ruger from the ankle holster. Murdock checked the load of his Airweight. Wished he was holding the .45. Hoped he would not have to shoot. Anasazi 203 was around the corner from the stairwell. The door was locked. From behind the door came grunts, a stifled scream, then more scuffling sounds. Helene tried the door. It was locked. She stepped back.

Murdock had never liked kicking down doors. It was movie-cop stuff and the doors in real-life had not been rigged by Hollywood film-technicians to blow open with one fake Karate kick. He aimed the Airweight at the latch, held his hand to shield his eyes, and pulled the trigger. Wood splinters nicked the back of his hand. The sound of the Airweight echoed loud in the corridor. One easy kick from Helene and the door swung open.

SONJA THE SERBIAN LAY half on the bed, half off. Her slacks had been pulled down around her thighs. Her panties were torn. Señor Pretty Hair was holding her shoulders, pushing her backwards. Her new western shirt lay crumpled on the floor. The brassiere straps were off her shoulders. Tammy Wellborn was behind Sonja, tugging on a bungee cord around Sonja's throat.

Willy Mapes, eyes wide, was back-pedaling away from the bed. Helene Steinbeck quick-stepped to Willy, drove her fist into his throat. He went down.

Murdock clipped Señor Pretty Hair with the Airweight. Not hard, just enough to get him off Sonja. Tammy Wellborn screamed, a warrior's cry. and leaped at Murdock. He felt the scratch of her claws. Tammy's eyes were crazy; she was one stoned girl.

Helene grabbed Tammy's hair, jerking her sideways, then slamming her against the wall. As she went down, Tammy screamed curses. "Fuck! You cunt! You're fucking dead, both of you—"

Helene helped Sonja to her feet. Helped her shrug into the blouse. The girl was shivering and her chest was heaving. Then she looked around, saw Willy Mapes on the floor holding his throat. Her eyes lit up. She charged. Willy rolled away from her. Moving fast, her feet doing the little dance steps from tennis, Sonja lined up, as if Willy was a soccer ball on a flat green field. Then she kicked his nuts. Willy groaned, wrapped his arms around his legs.

Señor Pretty Hair shot a death look at Murdock. He said, "You are dead meat, *pendejo*."

Using the bungee cords, Murdock lashed Pretty Hair and Mapes together, facing each other, close enough for a kiss. Murdock motioned for Helene to leave the room. She went out, her arm around Sonja. Using his knife, Murdock cut strips from a towel. He used the strips to lash Tammy to the bed. Before he left the room, Murdock grabbed a wallet from Fidel's drawstring britches.

SONJA STUMBLED ON THE stairs. Helene caught her, steadied her, then helped her through the thick wooden doorway, into the night. Murdock was impressed with Helene's quick strength. Outside the Cliff House, the night air felt cooler. They kept out of sight behind the bleachers. Fifty feet away, seated at tables on Gretna Green, Theo's guests sat at tables, scarfing down the food. Murdock heard the clink of flatware on crockery. He heard voices.

"Hey, down there. Pass the meat."

"This platter's empty."

"I think maybe Captain Theo wants us out of here."

With Helene and Sonja leading, they skirted behind the Pueblo Hogans to the Aspen Grove, where they found Anais Bertrand waiting. She was grinning as she held up the Trader Joe's bag. "I was moderately successful inside Theo's safe," she said. "Not rich, but enough. And tomorrow I say goodbye to Taos. Ah, this pretty tennis girl. What have they done to you?"

Anais gave Sonja a quick hug. She whispered to her in French. Murdock detected sounds of sympathy and understanding. As they moved through the trees, he kept expecting the alarm to sound. Where was Theo?

36
Marie-Claire

MARIE-CLAIRE DID NOT REMEMBER leaving the sauna room, but she saw the ceiling moving and knew she was rolling along; she heard the wheels. She was on her back covered with robes. The wheels rolled on wood, then fallen leaves. The moon came out from behind a cloud. She was outside. She heard cars starting, voices from far away. The bed she lay on tilted up, three women pushing. They wore robes. They wore masks. It was All Hallow's Eve and she was ten years old.

The moon went away and she was in a room that smelled of dead meat and ashes. She felt herself being lifted and set down again and there was someone in a white robe staring down at her and she knew those eyes because they belonged to Theo Ulster and he was wearing the same white latex gloves.

37

Murdock

MURDOCK AND HIS CREW arrived at Parking Lot A. The Jeep still sat between the Mercedes and the Cadillac Escalade with the gold grille and gold handles. Even in the dark, Murdock saw that the Jeep was tilted to the left. Kneeling down, he used his pencil flash. Two tires had been butchered to the bone. A big jagged slash in the left rear, a cleaner slash in the left front.

Helene remembered seeing keys on a keyboard inside. They trotted to the Gate House. The door was locked. It was a flimsy door—it collapsed with one good kick.

As Murdock entered, a red light started blinking. *On-off. On-off*. He listened for an alarm. Heard nothing. Just the red light blinking like an evil eye, filling the little shack with light from Hell. More than a dozen sets of car keys hung from little hooks on a piece of plywood painted white. Above each set of keys was a little metal plate that held a name and a license plate. Murdock saw Ramsay, Maxwell, Steck, Latimer. Helene grabbed the keys on the left. He grabbed the keys on the right. The key to the Jeep was gone.

She said, "Let's take the Mercedes."

Back in Lot A, they pressed remotes, working in tandem, Helene popping a lock, then Murdock. Beeps in the night as car doors unlocked. The Mercedes beeped on the eleventh try—a sedate, refined sound. Helene loaded Anais and Sonja in the back. She tossed the remote to Murdock. Told him she was too nervous to drive. She sat in the passenger seat, holding the remotes in her lap.

As he eased out of Parking Lot A, Murdock saw a flashlight beam in his rearview mirror. He was pissed about his tires.

"How many remotes?" Murdock said.

"Nineteen," Helene said. "Are you thinking what I'm thinking?"

Murdock grinned. Helene rolled down her window. As the vehicle went downhill, she tossed keys and fancy remotes into the night. Anais spoke from the backseat.

"I am wondering about this Mercedes," Anais said. "In this I could ride to the airport in a grand style."

"We can drive you," Helene said.

"Oh," Anais said. "You are too kind. I accept."

Helene went through the wallet. "The man with the pretty hair," she said, "is Florian Alejandro Fidel. He's an officer in the Colombian National Police. I see credit cards and cash and a hotel key card. Why don't you take the cash?"

"A policeman, did you say?"

"Yes."

"Thank you again for the help."

"What's up with Marie-Claire?"

"All summer she is often away at night," Sonja said. "In the morning, she always returns. I will see her tomorrow. At this moment I am very tired."

38

Theo

THEY ENTERED WEARING ROBES, masks, and white latex gloves.

Men in white. Women in black. Two women rolled the service cart, a metal table with wheels.

The Lookalike lay on the metal table. Her eyes were heavy-lidded, drowsy. The drugs were working. Two parts Ketamine. One part Cantharis. Theo stood on the dais, looking down.

There was no talking. Silence kept them focused. Silence ripped them from their bloody everyday worlds—banks, betrayals, boredom—and welded them together in a sacred space where the only act was a ritual older than civilization.

The slaying of a virgin.

Five of the men were veterans. There was only one neophyte. All six females were veterans. Theo knew who they were, not from the faces—they wore masks—but from the way they moved, the confidence born of practice, the feet beneath the robe, the shuttered looks of trepidation.

They kept coming back because they were made free by Theo's ritual, the delicate dance of death. The precise steps, the anonymity, the unity of purpose, the release, knowing that you had triumphed, because you were alive looking down at death.

If they did speak, the walls would explode with accents—Texas, Georgia, Florida.

The Lookalike whispered something. Theo leaned down. Her lips whispered a few words. "Where is Tommy?"

The men lined up according to height. The tallest man came first. His name was Latimer, a Dallas banker. The shortest man—Gold, from Miami—took the sixth position. Women spread the legs of the Lookalike. Sexual sound-effects were forbidden. No grunting, no foul language, only silence. One by one the men took their turns, except for number three, Ramsay, who lost his erection. Theo smiled at this failure to perform. Another demerit for the overweight banker from Dallas.

The women lined up according to height. The shortest woman in front, the tallest in the sixth position. Each woman held a knife. Blades glinted in the light. Theo knew them by their knives. He trembled with each wound. He was the knife. He was the sharp penetrating blade.

The Lookalike shivered, then was quiet. The eyes stared at the ceiling. The men exited the room, followed by the women. Theo removed his robe. He checked his wristwatch for the butcher, late again, and then he heard footsteps from behind, turned to see Frieda Holst in her school uniform, plaid skirt and white middy-blouse, holding out her knickers, the same contorted smile, the same bloody trick and Theo backing off, get away from me, slamming into the metal cart, and fell to one knee, fresh bright blood on his trousers.

The door opened and the butcher entered, wearing a white jacket dotted with old bloodstains. Blood never washed out. Theo gave instructions. The butcher looked bored. He wanted payment now. This was his last job. He was leaving the mountain. Theo owed him back wages. No matter who it was, they always wanted money.

CARRYING THE ROBE, THEO left the butcher in the Waste Room and walked through the kitchen, along the corridor to his office. He unlocked the door, entered. His head whirled and he grabbed the wall for support and remembered he was here for money.

Going to his knees before the safe, Theo smelled the scent of the intruder. Someone had been in the office. Someone unauthorized had twirled the dial on the safe. With the door open, Theo sensed disarray. He kept his cash in three steel boxes. Dollars, Euros, Swiss francs. There was money missing from each box. Perhaps there was just enough money left to placate the greedy butcher.

As Theo replaced the steel box, he saw that a photo folder had been moved. He flipped it open. A dozen photos gone, a dozen Mummy lookalikes. Dark girls who shared one observable attribute with Mummy. A curve of calf, a coil of hair, a look in the eye, a way of walking. The Bellini photo was gone. He ran through a short list of suspects, people who knew the combination, and stopped when he came to Anais Bertrand. Who hadn't heard how much she hated Taos? Who hadn't heard her whine about getting back to Paris, City of Light?

BACK IN THE WASTE Room, Theo handed the money to the butcher.

"That's not even half what you owe me."

"The rest is down the hill, old boy."

"Fuck that old boy shit. Where's my money?"

"Finish up here, I'll take you down."

"You're a sick fuck, Ulster. Mess with me, I'll chop your dick."

"Have your cellphone on. We'll fetch your money."

"What time?"

"On my count, old boy."

THEO LEFT THE WASTE Room, walked through the kitchen

and along the corridor. Safe inside his office, Theo tossed the robe into the closet. He checked the bed. It was ready for action. He changed his trousers and put on a fresh shirt. He stared into the mirror above his wash basin.

His eyes looked harried, a weary rabbit chased by hounds.

There was more work to do.

He sat at his desk, pencil in hand. Time for a list, get things organized. First, there was that bit of business down the hill, ending the connection with that troublesome French whore. In every culture, there had to be penalties for stealing. Then there was tomorrow and the Quarry Hunt, a fitting climax to a bad week. Then there was Frieda Holst, still hovering, still not exorcised—and then there was the Bellini photograph, where had that got to?—but his head ached and he was having trouble organizing his thoughts on paper and there was someone outside knocking on the bloody door.

He flung it open to find Elise Wellborn, shivering in a sweater. Her eyes were puffy. Her nose was red, her face twisted and ugly. Theo hated female emotion. Father had warned him about that when Mummy went away. A woman, Father told him, should exhibit only serenity.

"What?"

"What have you done with my daughter?"

"Go away," Theo said.

"She's with Willy Mapes, isn't she?"

"Tammy can take care of herself."

"I'm taking her off this mountain. You can't stop me."

"Get control of yourself. I'll make some calls."

HE WATCHED ELISE ENTER the office. Watched her tug at the closet door.

"She's not in there."

"Open it. Let me see."

Theo unlocked the closet door. Elise took a quick look

inside. She shrugged, walked across the room, and poured herself a drink.

Theo phoned Sergeant Bolitar on his sat-phone. No answer. He phoned Corporal Simpson. No answer. When he phoned Willy Mapes, he got a buzzing sound. The phone was working but not receiving. That was bad news. Theo strapped on his revolver, a Webley-Vickers service weapon. He told Elise Wellborn to stay in the office. "Finish your drink. Do not move. I'll go fetch your daughter." But as he left the office, he heard footsteps, and there she was, Excitable Elise, her face fraught with female ferocity.

39
Helene

IT WAS SLOW GOING down the mountain in the dark. Murdock was driving too fast, the big Mercedes rocking and bumping, but Helene kept her eyes away from the speedometer. She wanted off the mountain. As the road leveled out and they approached the blinking light intersection, Helene saw the headlights of a traffic jam.

Murdock slowed down, kept the Mercedes close behind a pickup. The traffic jam was caused by a three-car collision at the blinking light. Saturday night in Taos, an autumn chill settling over the valley. Helene shivered, hugged herself to keep warm.

The line of cars moved forward. A police officer in a night-glow traffic vest waved the Mercedes on into town. When they passed Helene's old B&B, she saw a light in the window of her old room. Her room before Murdock. So much had happened since then.

THE TRIP THROUGH TAOS took forty-five minutes. In the art colony parking lot, surrounded by beat-up vans and old VW bugs, Anais Bertrand hugged Helene first, then Murdock, then Sonja. They tried to persuade Anais to stay the night at their motel. Murdock even offered to pay for the room. But Anais, with a secret smile, told them she had to pack. "I have a rendezvous," she said, "one last, memorable love-tryst before I kiss dusty Taos goodbye." As she walked toward the Annex, Anais waved. See you tomorrow. Her figure in the headlights was slight, ethereal, barely there.

On the way to the Racquet Club, they tried the same arguments on Sonja—she must stay close to them at the Sleep Inn—but she was worried about her friend. Better, if Sonja was there at the Racquet Club, when Marie-Claire came back from the mountain. They walked her to her door, where she hugged them both.

IN THEIR ROOM AT the Sleep Inn, Helene gave Murdock the first shower. She was yawning as she emptied the wallet belonging to Florian Fidel. A Police ID card, credit cards, the key card to hotel in Angel Fire. The wallet leather was thin, allowing half a dozen small pockets. Helene emptied the pockets, found two photos. One family photo showed Fidel, two children, and a woman with big hair. The other showed a pretty girl sitting with an arty-looking man. They were holding hands and looking into each other's eyes.

When Murdock came out of the shower, Helene showed him the photo. He nodded. "That's Barbi, all right. Looks like she's sitting in the Brew Pub."

"How tall was Barbi?" Helene said.

"Five-eight," Murdock said. "Maybe five-nine. Dark hair, long legs."

"Okay," Helene said. "So Florian Fidel, a Colombian cop who carries a photo of Barbi, also goes after Sonja. He gets help from Willy Mapes and Tammy Wellborn. How long has Barbi been missing?"

"Three weeks," Murdock said.

"Did Florian Fidel look like a serial killer to you?"

"He looked like a pimp," Murdock said.

"How about a white slaver?"

"Yeah," Murdock said. "Keep going."

"So what if friendly Fidel sold Barbi to some rich guy?" Helene said. "What if the rich guy wants another one, a tall girl like Barbi? What if Fidel gets his girls from Theo? The whole idea makes my skin crawl."

"Mine, too," Murdock said, "but the old crawling skin reflex won't get the cops a search warrant."

"I'm wired," Helene said, "but you're exhausted. 'You lie down and close your eyes. I'll keep talking."

Murdock climbed into bed. Helene rubbed his back, felt the scars, thought about old wounds. Murdock's breathing slowed. He could sleep anywhere. Helene was wide awake. She made a mind-map—words inside circles, lines connecting the circles, Theo's tentacles, dark girls like Sonja, blonde girls like Marie-Claire, money, white slavery, a bank of ovens, hunks of meat turning on electric spits, money, motive, revenge, vengeance, something buried in the past, back to Theo, that photo on his desk, Theo and the woman in the photo, what was her name?—Helene was close to an insight. She could tell because her fingertips tingled. The insight was so—she felt it slipping away.

She stared at her mind-map. A jumble of words, chaotic, frenzied. She felt cold. She turned off the light and snuggled close to Murdock. He was so solid. And he had great body heat.

40
Theo

ELISE WELLBORN DOGGED HIM through the Aspen Grove and across the dewy grass of Gretna Green, through the front door of the Anasazi Cliff House and up the stairs to the door of Room 213. She stood rigid, tears on her cheeks, while Theo brought out his ring of keys. She told him to hurry as he tried each key, one at a time. One fine day, Theo thought, he would get the locks retro-fitted, so that a single master key would suffice. A Universal Key, he thought, to unlock every door in the world, and that made him smile. And then he thought of the cost, and that wiped the smile away.

He opened the door to Room 213 and saw three of his people, trussed like turkeys, their mouths gagged. The nearest one was Willy Mapes, hog-tied with bungee cords, his pants down around his knees. Next to Mapes on the floor was Florian Fidel, the intrepid flesh peddler. Tammy Wellborn was tied to the bed with strips of cloth. Her eyes were closed, her chest rising and falling.

Elise Wellborn rushed to the bed. Tammy opened her eyes. What a good little soldier. Theo liked that she'd been sleeping.

If you're captured and held prisoner, why not catch yourself a kip?

"Mom?" Tammy said. "Theo? What?"

Using his knife, Theo sawed at the cloth strips. He was angry when he saw the strips had been cut from hotel towels. As he freed Tammy, he asked, "What happened, soldier?"

Before Tammy could reply, Elise Wellborn started dragging her toward the door. Tammy said something and Elise let go. Tammy reported to Theo. It was an ambush. Murdock and Helene, with guns. When Elise grabbed her again, Tammy slapped Elise. "You don't know anything, Mom."

"I know I want you out of here—right this minute."

"I'm okay, but you're acting really weird."

"If I leave here without you, I'm coming back with Sammy Savage."

THEO SMILED. HE HAD to admit that Elise Wellborn did look insane. Her eyes moved from her daughter to Theo, and then back to her daughter. She pulled out her cellphone. There was no service. She started crying. She held out her arms to Tammy, but Tammy backed away. Elise exited the room. Theo heard her feet on the stairs.

"She's not kidding—about calling Sammy."

"Ours not to reason why," Theo said.

He had to wait for her response. She was young and spoiled and beautiful—but what incredible warrior material. Was she up to the test? Or was this the end for Warrior Wellborn?

Then she said, "Ours but to do or die."

"Help me free these fools," Theo said. "Then we'll carry out our mission."

THEO LED THE LOSERS down the stairs. The air was rampant with loose talk. Mapes demanded money for the Willy Mapes Travel Fund. Fidel wanted to rape Helene and use a bullwhip on Murdock. Theo was not listening. Two grown men had aborted their mission, endangering the welfare of a fifteen year old girl. Mapes was a loser because of weakness, no moral fiber. Fidel was a loser because of his licentious libido. The girl, a born warrior with no confirmed kill, was Theo's hope for the future.

Theo led them across the grass, through the Aspen Grove, up the stairs to the HQ. He parked Tammy and Fidel in his office. He took Mapes through the kitchen to the Waste Room, with its conveyor belt and an ancient incinerator that cried out to be replaced.

"What are we doing here?"

"Getting your money—for the aforementioned Willy Mapes Travel Fund. Remember?"

"It's creepy in here."

"Don't play the innocent fool. You know what goes on."

"Look, Ulster. Just give me the money and I am outta here."

"Your money's over there, in a tin box, behind that stack of bricks."

Mapes was halfway to the bricks when Theo shot him. The hit was perfect, right behind the ear. He dragged the body to the wall next to the incinerator. It would be better when the new fire-box was up and running. When Theo checked Mapes's pockets, the fake Rolex caught the light. Theo left the Rolex, but took the key-ring—it held the keys to the art colony.

On the way back to his office, Theo phoned Savage, who answered with a sleepy voice. Told him about Elise Wellborn.

"Look serious," Theo said. "Take down her report. Explain that you will require a small army to invade Angel's Nest. Armies take time."

"You woke me up for this?"

"Just do as I say, old chap."

"I need a cash infusion … old chap."

"Tomorrow evening," Theo said. "We'll settle up."

Theo yawned. Even he needed a bit of sleep. Tomorrow was Sunday. It promised to be a very big day on Angel Mountain. That thought made him smile.

41
Theo

ABSOLUTION.

That's what Theo wanted from women. Absolution was what he needed, what he asked for, but not in words so much as in gesture and body language. If only the right woman could read his little book of needs. Mummy could read him. So could Helene Steinbeck. But as he pulled into the art colony lot, Theo Ulster could remember not a whiff of absolution from Anais Bertrand. He parked the Subaru beside her blue VW bug.

Anais Bertrand was a whore passing herself off as a painter. A whore in Paris, a whore in New Mexico. Early morning sunlight filtered through the trees. Theo heard the rumble of a motorcycle. The butcher arrived on his Harley, looking very archetypal in leather vest, pants, and visored helmet. He climbed off the bike with his hand held out, the palm turned up.

"Money, money, money," he said.

"Inside," Theo said.

"That's where the French pussy lives, right?"

"How very astute," Theo said.

"How the fuck did she get money?"

"She broke into my floor safe," Theo said.

"Fuck me," the butcher said.

"Let me get the door, old boy."

THEO WALKED ALONE THROUGH the trees to Studio B. The door was locked. He opened it with a key from Mapes's ring. The narrow corridor was airless.

His feet made little thumping noises on the cheap carpet.

He saw a kitchen, a pile of dirty dishes.

He saw a dining room turned into an artist's studio. Easels, canvases, twisted paint tubes.

Her art was horrid, the work of a degenerate.

He came to a bedroom.

Anais stepped out, holding a table lamp like a club, her idea of a weapon. Her hair was disheveled. The nightgown went down to her knees. Her bare feet were bony.

"You bastard," she said

"I heard you were ill," Theo said.

A noise from the hallway and Anais's eyes showed alarm.

"Who's with you?"

"I heard you were leaving," Theo said. "A triumphal return to the City of Light."

Anais swung the table lamp. Theo dodged and the lamp shattered when it hit the door frame. Theo slapped her wrist, knocking her head sideways, then shoved her backwards into the bedroom, where she sprawled across her messy bed. The nightgown bared her legs.

He heard footsteps, turned to see the butcher behind him. The man stank of sweat, cigarettes, and gasoline fumes. He grinned when he saw Anais.

"Now that," he said. "Is one serious piece of ass."

Theo stepped aside and the butcher invaded the room. Anais shrank back, her arms across her breasts. Theo stood in the doorway watching the butcher unleash his belt. The leather trousers had buttons. The man took his time unbuttoning. He advanced on the bed, took hold of her ankles, and wedged himself between her legs. He looked back over his shoulder at Theo.

"Ulster, you sick fuck. Get out."

Theo exited the bedroom.

In the hallway, he pulled on latex gloves. He checked the hypodermic. He walked to the kitchen, where he found a proper knife. He tucked the knife into his belt and walked back down the hallway to the bedroom.

He heard grunts from the butcher and curses in French from Anais.

Theo re-entered the bedroom. The butcher was buried deep between her legs. The leather pants were down around the man's knees. Anais was squeaking. Theo drove the needle into the butcher's shoulder and he collapsed.

"Get him off me!" she said.

"What have you done with my money?"

"What money?"

"The money from my safe. Dollars, Euros, Krugerrands. Where is it?"

"You owe me," she said.

"Owe you for what?"

"For stealing my life."

"You're a whore. You're insane. You never had a life."

"I got old, Theo. You couldn't stand that, could you, so now ..."

She shook her head. The tears filled her eyes, ran down her cheeks. He pressed thumbs against her throat. In a harsh whisper, she told him the money was in a flour jar in the kitchen. She always lied. He did not believe her. He grabbed her hair, tilted her head back, pulled the knife from his belt, and slit her throat. Blood ran onto the sheets. Holding the knife by the blade, Theo dipped the handle in the blood. Still holding the blade, he closed the butcher's fingers around the handle. For the fingerprints.

The money from his safe was not in the flour jar. Not in the sugar jar. It was in her tiny pantry in a box that said, Virgin Chocolate. Theo did not count the money. He took it and walked outside. The sun was higher now. He heard Sunday morning traffic rising up from the Paseo del Norte. His stomach growled. He was hungry. He had a busy day ahead, he would need his wits about him. He should head back to the HQ.

THEO MADE TWO PHONE calls. The first call was to Savage, who sounded grumpy, his voice slurred by sleep. Theo asked about Elise Wellborn. Savage said that she was in lockup, just for the night.

"What happened, old boy?"

"She was raving," Savage said. "And sounding bonkers. A lot of shit about her daughter being kidnapped. You know anything about that?"

"They had one of those spats," Theo said. "A mother-daughter thing. When will you release her?"

"Maybe noon."

"Three o'clock would be better for my timetable."

"It will cost you, big-time".

"Of course," Theo said.

His second call was to Carla Carlini, who was in her car on the way to fetch the Serbian girl. Theo instructed Carlini to leave a message for Murdock at the Sleep Inn desk. "Use your best French accent," Theo said. "Tell Murdock that Anais is ready to go."

"Go where?"

"To the airport," he said. "After you leave the message, fetch the Serbian."

"Hey. That's not in the plan."

"As you Yanks say, we are now executing Plan B."

42

Murdock

THE MAN STOOD OUTSIDE in the motel parking lot, casting a thick shadow, looming large in the morning sun. He towered over Murdock's Jeep.

Murdock was on the walkway outside his motel room. He could hear Helene Steinbeck rustling around behind him. The man looked up at Murdock and flashed a grin as he held up a key. He was here to swap cars—the Jeep for the Mercedes. Murdock went inside the room for the keys. Helene studied the man through the window, then tucked her new Glock into a Walmart shopping bag.

"That's the same man we saw at Little Galilee," Helene said. "When you shot out that tire. Now he's making you pay with your precious Jeep. What's next?"

"He wants his Mercedes back."

They went down the stairs together. The sun was warm, but Murdock felt cold. His Jeep had two new tires. As they approached the large man, he sent them an executioner's grin, like your head was on the block and his big hand was poised to release the guillotine. It was a victory grin—it spoke of power, force, cunning, and triumph well-deserved. The large man offered his hand and introduced himself as Sergeant Bolitar, first name Derek, an old comrade of Captain Theo Ulster. He spoke with a Cockney accent.

"We were almost introduced last evening," he said, "but as I was on duty, there would have been small chance to swap stories of soldiering and such."

Sergeant Bolitar stood six feet three inches. His head was shaved and tanned. His eyes were hidden behind Desert Rat dark glasses. He wore British Army shorts with a sharp crease, brown knee-socks that girded his massive calves. He wore a Sam Browne belt with a revolver butt protruding from the holster. Another Webley-Vickers service revolver, twin to Theo's. Murdock estimated the man's weight at 250 pounds, maybe 260. From a distance, he looked fat. Up close, Murdock could see a monster built of steel and beefy gristle. Murdock stood six-feet and weighed 200 pounds, but he was no match for Sergeant Derek Bolitar.

"My Captain sends his regards," the man said. "He regrets mightily the damage done to your conveyance, and he takes full responsibility for any hurt that comes to his guests at his functions."

"Thanks for the tires," Murdock said.

"The Mercedes—ain't she a beaut'—if you might relinquish the keys, sir?"

"Where did you get the key to start the Jeep?"

"Had an uncle who taught me a bit of locksmithing." "The Sergeant held out a single key. New brass sparkled. Murdock handed over the remote for the Mercedes. The Sergeant, speaking with pride, said the Mercedes was his own private vehicle, registered in his name, and his first civilian vehicle after driving in military lorries for most of his adult life. He was smiling as he talked, like a new father describing his newborn baby. Murdock could feel the tension, because four days ago, inside the happy Christian community of Little

Galilee, Murdock had blown out the left front tire, dumping the front end of the Sergeant's Mercedes off the road into a Ponderosa. So the subtext here was the Sergeant's pain, which would generate payback. There was no mention of body work in the Sergeant's loving car-speech, but the grill looked new, and Helene had already mentioned the over-buffed front fender.

"She's wearing California plates," Murdock said. "That where you're from?"

"From Liverpool, sir. A lifetime ago, if I may say so. And yourself?"

"Seattle," Murdock said.

"Before I depart," the Sergeant said, "Captain Ulster instructed me to invite you—and the lady here—to a spot of luncheon at his HQ. That would be thirteen hundred hours, sir. He has some people he wants you to meet, and there's a bit of business he didn't get to mention last evening, during the festivities Something about a missing girl?"

"Sorry," Murdock said. "Miss Steinbeck and I already have plans."

"Yes, sir," the sergeant said. He disappeared behind the dark glass of the Mercedes. It started with a whisper. Murdock stood with Helene in the parking lot, watching the big rig merge with traffic on the Santa Fe Highway, heading north into downtown Taos.

"WAS HE FOR REAL?" Helene said. "Spot o' luncheon?"

"There were non-coms who talked like that," Murdock said. "My dad would bring them to dinner. Tough old birds, happy to have a home-cooked meal and a polite manner that was over the top."

"It feels weird," Helene said. "Like boys playing soldier. I got the same weirdo vibe from Corporal Simpson. But with the sergeant, just now, I had a feeling he wanted to be friends."

"We need to check on Anais," Murdock said.

"And Sonja," Helene said. "Maybe she's heard from Marie-Claire."

Murdock was packing a rucksack when the motel phone rang. Murdock answered.

The phone call was from the motel desk. A woman had left a message: she was ready to go. Her name, the desk clerk said, was Anna-something.

43
Helene

HELENE, CLAD IN CLEAN jeans and a pretty yellow blouse, led the way to the Jeep. She was tired of boots and thick sweaty socks. So today she wore Indian moccasins with no sox. It would be good to escape Taos for a couple of hours. The Ruger was in her shoulder bag. Sitting in the Jeep, she had a sudden urge to show Murdock how she would look in a skirt and blouse, bare legs, pumps, a medium heel. She touched Murdock on the leg. He put his hand over hers, kept it there until the next gear shift.

The Sunday traffic was building on the Paseo, so Murdock took the Raton shortcut to the mouth of Taos Canyon, slid through the traffic circles, hung a sharp left on Cruz Alta Road, and raced through the back streets, which looked sleepy on this Sunday morning holiday. He zoomed northwest on Kit Carson Road and turned right at the sign for the Mabel Dodge Huhan House.

There were four vehicles in the art colony parking lot. A rusty pickup. A rusty VW bus with a sign in the rearview mirror that said, "Busted in California." A blue VW beetle with a suitcase in the backseat. And a shiny Harley motorcycle. She saw the

Annex roof through the screen of cottonwood trees. Then the upper part of the huge front window. Of the two doors to the building, the big one was locked. The other had a sign, "Studios A and B."

Helene opened the little door and heard movement. She pulled out her Ruger. A door closed, and then footsteps, coming fast. The man came around the corner. Helene recognized him from Theo's kitchen, one of the chefs. He was dark, stocky, medium height, with a big hooked nose and a scraggy beard. There was blood on his vest, on his arms. His eyes gave her a flat, dead look. A knife flashed in his hand. A kitchen knife with a thin curved blade. She gripped the Ruger with both hands. The man stood there. "Drop the knife," she said.

Behind her, Murdock said, "Don't shoot him, Helene."

"Why not?"

"Julio," Murdock said. "He'll take our guns."

One minute the man with the knife was standing still, lit by a slashing beam of sunlight through a solar tube. The next minute he was charging Helene, the knife flashing. He growled as he made a swipe at her. She hit him with her shoulder bag. He slammed against the wall, then sagged to the floor.

"I didn't do it," he said.

"Where is Anais," Helene said.

"I didn't fucking do it," he said again.

LEAVING MURDOCK TO SECURE the suspect, Helene walked up the corridor. She saw a kitchen, a living room with easels. Anais was in the bedroom. She lay on the bed, her bare legs twisted under her. There was blood on her tank top, blood on the sheets. Her hair was splayed out as if blown by the wind, frozen in a photograph. Her face was turned away from Helene. Above the little table, a window was open. The window had no screen.

Helene's stomach contracted. She tasted bile in her throat. She took a deep breath. Blood had its own coppery smell. She heard Murdock come up behind her.

"It's Anais," she said.

"Christ," Murdock said.

"What did you do with the perp?"

"Towel strips, like last night. I think his name is Marius."

"Did he confess yet?"

"He keeps muttering Ulster's name."

"Who do we call first?"

"I'll call Sammy. It's his turf. You call Julio."

Walking back down the corridor, Helene felt stiff and clunky, like a robot on auto-pilot. When she made it to the door, she burst through, away from death, away from evil, into the bright morning sunshine. Her lungs sucked in air.

MURDOCK STEPPED ASIDE, CELLPHONE in hand. Helene sat on the adobe wall outside the Annex. Half sun, half shade. She phoned Julio Calderon. He answered after two rings. He asked what was wrong. He moaned when she told him about Anais. Julio was in Ranchos de Taos, south of town. "Fifteen minutes," he said. Helene hung up.

The morning sun was hotter now. By noon, the temperature would reach the mid-eighties. When Murdock came back from the Jeep, they sat in the shade of the Annex, putting together what they had so far.

"What did he say about Theo?"

"Nothing specific," Murdock said. "He just keeps saying his name."

"He sounds like he's on something," Helene said.

"Let's show Fidel's wallet to Julio."

"Why?"

"It's the only real evidence we've got—those photos of Barbi Bellini."

"How long do you think Anais has been waiting to get into that safe?"

"Years," Murdock said.

"Waiting for a wheelman," Helene said.

SAMMY SAVAGE ARRIVED WITH a crime scene tech in blue coveralls. Sammy looked nervous, puffy eyes, his face redder than usual. He was almost wheezing as he sent the tech inside. He looked at Helene, then at Murdock.

"Did you people contaminate my crime scene?"

"We know the drill, Sammy."

"What the fuck were you doing here, anyway? And How come you find all these goddamn corpses? I'm going to check inside. Do not fucking move."

Sammy charged into the building. Helene looked at Murdock and used her finger to make the loco sign. Minutes later, when Sammy exited the building, his face was chalky white. He stopped at the support post and stared down at the perp.

"You're Mario, right? From up the hill?"

"Fuck you."

"You ruined my Sunday!" Sammy yelled, and then he started kicking Marius. Murdock walked over, put a hand on Sammy's arm.

Marius said, "This is Ulster's party. You get me on the stand and the shit's gonna—"

Sammy knocked Marius sideways. Blood oozed from his ear. Sammy stood over Marius. His face was bright red and wet with sweat.

JULIO CALDERON APPEARED. HE wore a long-sleeved fisherman's shirt, lots of pockets, and hiking shorts. Before heading inside, Julio shook hands. His handshake was strong, like a man at a funeral holding onto life while remembering death. Julio was carrying a briefcase. He pulled on latex gloves. Marius said Theo's name again. As Julio started for the building, the crime scene tech appeared. They talked for a while. When he came back out, Julio took his time pulling off the latex gloves. He asked the questions. Helene gave the answers.

Q: You two found the body?

A: Yes.

Q: What time?

A: A little after nine.

Q: Why were you here?

A: Anais called us. We were taking her to the airport.

Q: Where was she headed?

A: Paris.

Q: So you got here and met up with this—what's his name?

A: Marius. He had a knife. There was blood on his shirt and jacket. He attacked. We subdued him. We found Anais.

Q: Did you guys touch anything in there?

A: We cut up some towels.

Q: Did you remove anything from the crime scene?

A: Just the towels.

Q: Did either of you discharge a firearm?

A: No.

Q: Okay. You did good work nailing this creep.

Julio opened his briefcase. He brought out Murdock's .45 and Helene's old Glock. Murdock tucked the .45 into his belt. When Helene slipped her Glock into her shoulder bag, she felt the slick leather of Florian Fidel's wallet. She caught Murdock's eye. He nodded. Helene handed the wallet to Julio.

"What's this?"

"There's a photo inside," Helene said. "Along with some fancy plastic and some very official-looking identity papers. The photo is that girl from Seattle, the one Murdock's looking for."

Julio opened the wallet. He was checking the contents.

Muttering to himself. *Colombia? Policia Nacional?* He showed the photo to Murdock. "This the girl you came looking for? Bellini, right?"

"Right. Her first name is Barbi. She's been missing for three weeks."

"What's she got to do with a captain in the Colombian National Police?"

"We don't know."

"What are you doing with his wallet?"

"We found it on the floor of a guest suite at Angel's Nest."

"You're starting to piss me off, Mateo. You, too, Helene."

Julio wanted the story, so they filled him in. The Serbian girl had asked Helene and Murdock to keep an eye on her friend, Marie-Claire, who was drinking too much. They were getting ready to leave the party when they saw the Serbian being led away by Tammy Wellborn. They followed the Serbian into the Anasazi Cliff House, where they heard screams and sounds of scuffling. The sounds led them to an upstairs guest room, where they found Florian Fidel, along with Willy Mapes, holding the Serbian girl down. Her clothes had been torn and she asked for help. There was a scuffle. There was no phone in the room and cellphones didn't work up there. On the way to the Jeep, they encountered Anais Bertrand, who hitched a ride back down the mountain.

"What's the Serb's name again?" Julio said.

"Sonja Vasic."

"I suppose she's tall, dark, and beautiful?"

"Yes."

"How old is she?"

"Early twenties."

"And how old is your girl from Seattle? Barbi?"

"Also in her early twenties."

"I need to talk to Miss Vasic," Julio said. "She's at the Racquet Club, right?"

"Yes."

"Okay," Julio said. "I gotta finish up here. Huddle with Savage, get our jurisdictions sorted out. After that, I gotta make some phone calls—my boss will be pissed, and that Theo Ulster dude is connected to half the politicos in Santa Fe. As for you two, I want you along when I interview Miss Vasic. And after the interview, we'll take a ride up to Angel's Nest. Okay?"

"Bring reinforcements," Murdock said. "Show of force."

"Got a little manpower problem today," Julio said. "There's a drug bust in Rio Rancho. There's a twenty-car collision at the cloverleaf—a semi's blocking three lanes—and a bunch of computer geeks from back east are yelping about the threat to national security if they miss their flights. Now get lost, okay?"

44

Helene

THEY WALKED TO THE Jeep without talking. The sun was warm; the light filtered by the trees. Helene held onto Murdock's hand. She felt as if she was being observed, watched from a distance. Like the trees had eyes. Or perhaps Theo had the trees bugged, little microphones shaped like native insects, hugging the trunk of that next tree, with a WiFi connection to a listening post at the heart of Angel's Nest. Helene shivered. She agreed with Drusilla. Taos was better without the violence.

They were back in the Jeep when Helene's cellphone rang. It was her dad, Frank Steinbeck, calling from New York City. Helene put him on the speaker. The Paseo was noisy with growing Sunday morning traffic, and Helene needed to take notes, so Murdock pulled the Jeep onto Siler, drove past Smith's Food Center on the right, and parked under a giant cottonwood. Her dad came through loud and clear, his deep voice familiar, his humor balanced.

He started with Sophie Orff, the dead girl on Angel Mountain. Sophie's address checked out—a cramped studio apartment in Soho. Sophie's roommate, a girl named Tessa, had emails from Sophie. She'd been working as a barista when she met this guy, love at first sight, and was looking forward to meeting the parents.

"Did the guy have a name?" Helene said.

"Not that Tessa knew."

"So because her friend was in love," Helene said, "Tessa thought Sophie was okay."

"I traced Eunice Dare," Frank said. "Two actor's' workshops led me to a home for old actors in New Jersey. Eunice died last year, survived by two lovely ladies named Florence and Georgia. They said that Eunice had not seen her son for a long time—his name's Theo, right?"

"Yes," Helene said.

Frank Steinbeck said, "When Eunice talked about her son, she referred to him as 'Poor Teddy.' She left home because her husband was a wife-beater. It broke her heart to leave the boy behind. When she talked about him, she always cried, and while she was crying, Eunice would talk about 'girl-troubles,' how poor Teddy would never understand women, how he got hurt by some girl—Eunice always referred to her as 'that blonde doxie.' "

"We're hoping the girl had a name," Helene said.

"When I asked about a name, the ladies shook their heads. The only thing they knew was that Eunice left home about the same time her boy was having his girl-trouble. I asked about photos. They had the same photo you sent me—Eunice draped in silk, looking sexy. When I finished, they begged me to stay for dinner. It's no fun getting old."

"Thanks, Dad."

"One last thing before I hang up. I've got a plane out of JFK this afternoon. The Albuquerque ETA is five-fifteen. I've rented a car and I'm driving up. Where do I find you in Taos?"

Helene said, "We're staying at the Sleep Inn—it's on the Paseo, the main road from Santa Fe—and we're coordinating with a local cop, Julio Calderon. Here's his number."

She recited Julio's number from memory. She nodded to

Murdock. He said goodbye to her dad and welcomed him to New Mexico. Helene hung up feeling the buzz of insight. Mommy called him Teddy.

The motel looked Sunday afternoon sleepy. They were on the stairs, headed for their room, when Murdock's cellphone rang. The caller was Jimmy Little Deer. Murdock stayed on the balcony. Helene entered the room, thinking about the phone call from her dad, Theo all alone, Theo with girl-trouble. Was that enough to make him crazy? When Murdock came in, his face was serious.

"Young Winchester's gone AWOL," Murdock said. "Jimmy wanted to know if we had seen him up there. I told him about the archery competition, the kiss from Tammy Wellborn. Young Winchester checked in last night, around eleven. He'd been invited to spend the night. The kid was due back this morning. Since he hasn't showed, Jimmy's going up there for some recon. His Indian buds are at a conference in Colorado. He needs back-up. He called us."

"He wants me for back-up?"

"He wants you and your new Glock with the hex-sites," Murdock said.

"I need to change."

"I need to call Julio."

IN THE BATHROOM, HELENE dressed in long pants and a clean sports-bra and the long-sleeved khaki shirt from the consignment store. She took extra care with her socks, snugging them tight, no creases, to lessen the chance of blisters.

Standing in front of the motel mirror, Helene tied a bandana around her neck, tried on the Tilley sunhat. She felt shaky as she packed her stuff—water, ammo, crackers, protein bars. She was stowing her new Glock, enjoying the feel, when Murdock finished his phone call.

"So you're trusting him now?"

"We got our guns back," Murdock said. "And he's steadier than Sammy."

AS THEY WERE LEAVING the Sleep Inn, Helene phoned the desk at the Racquet Club. Miss Vasic had gone off with Carla Carlini. There was no sign of the roommate, the clerk said, that rude Belgian girl. Helene thanked the desk clerk.

"What's up?" Murdock said.

"Sonja went off with Carla Carlini."

"Any sign of Marie-Claire?"

"No," Helene said. "So why would Sonja go back to Angel's Nest?"

"Maybe Carla told her Marie-Claire wanted her."

"Wouldn't she be afraid of Florian Fidel?"

Murdock said, "What if Theo wants us back up there?"

"And," Helene said, "What if he's using Sonja as bait?"

"He's after you for bruising his balls," Murdock said.

"He's after you for killing his dogs."

"What if I told him you shot two dogs and I only shot one?" Murdock said. "Then we could be buddies again, me and Theo."

"It would make Drusilla happy. She hoped you two would bond."

"Yeah. We could be chums."

45

Murdock

THEY ENTERED TAOS CANYON, Murdock feeling the tentacles of Theo Ulster reaching out, grabbing up innocent people, squeezing them, dragging them to the maw of the octopus. Murdock was driving over the speed limit, the Jeep leaning on the sharp corners. The time was close to noon and the Sunday traffic was building. On a sharp curve, a big pickup pulling an oversize camping trailer forced Murdock over to the shoulder. The Jeep's right wheels churned up orange shoulder dust, and the Jeep cleared the back of the trailer by four inches. Helene looked over, her mouth in a tight line. She was nervous, too. Helene hauled out her Glock, racked it open, then closed it.

"You okay?" she said.

"No," he said. "I'm jumpy. You?"

"You think I'm wrong about Theo wanting us back up there?"

"Nope. He wants some payback."

"You think we can get up there without being detected?"

"If we came in from the south," Murdock said, "we might fool him."

"He's got to be stopped," Helene said.

THE ROAD TO THE Cerdo Falls Trailhead looked deserted. At every turn, Murdock expected an ambush. Instead of parking in the trailhead lot, he turned right, going past the abandoned cabin then pushing up the little ravine where Helene had shot the dogs. When the terrain got too steep and the wheels started to spin, Murdock wedged the Jeep between two pine trees. He nodded at Helene and climbed out. In the shade of the trees, Murdock could feel the autumn chill. They shrugged into their rucksacks. Helene checked the Glock again. Murdock decided to leave the De Lisle carbine behind.

The climb to the crime scene took twelve minutes. The yellow ribbons were gone. No sign of Sophie Orff remained. Murdock looked at Helene. They skirted the crime scene, heading for Flatrock Ridge. Before they probed for an entry point, Murdock wanted a look at Theo's compound. The pine needles were thick underfoot, and the aspen trees gleamed bright with their temporary yellow. They passed a copse of Aspen and pine. Helene said, "That's where you camped, right? The day you ran into me?"

"That's the place," Murdock said. "Good trail-craft, Steinbeck."

"That's where we first heard Theo's dogs."

THEY LAY, SIDE-BY-SIDE, ON the edge of Flatrock Ridge, trading the binoculars back and forth. Helene reported that the weekend people were toting luggage to the big vehicles, that cars were leaving Parking Lot A and smoke was rising from the smokehouse. She handed the glasses back to Murdock.

Down on Gretna Green, Murdock saw Tammy Wellborn—he recognized the gleam in her blonde hair—pounding stakes into the grass. Across from Tammy, he saw Skye and Maxwell and Tommy Ramsay stringing wire. Off to the left, Murdock saw Corporal Simpson wheeling Theo's generator onto the green. Simpson went to his knees to make some adjustments to the front wheels. When his adjustments were done,

Simpson connected wires to the generator. Murdock wasn't close enough to see colors, but he knew that one wire was red, the other white. In a repeat of last night, the wires formed a narrow, oval-shaped corridor. A track for a runner. Across the green, Tammy Wellborn had finished making her little corral of black stakes and was stringing the last of the black wire. Murdock passed the glasses to Helene.

"It's that same nasty game," she said.

"Indian shoot," Murdock said.

"No runner yet," Helene said.

"Even without the binoculars, I saw Theo Ulster arriving," Murdock said. "He wore his battle fatigues and an Aussie bush hat with the left brim tucked up. Theo was pushing someone along, someone with a crutch."

"It's Young Winchester," Helene said. "He's got one crutch and no shirt and there's a blue boot on his hurt foot. Theo's got his swagger stick again. Ouch, he just swatted the boy's legs. Jesus, Murdock, Young Winchester's wearing an Indian breechcloth."

Murdock saw two people coming from the Anasazi Cliff House. A female who looked naked and a male in khaki, wearing a red cap.

"There's Sonja," Helene said. "She's wearing panties and shoes. Her wrists seem to be bound together. The guy in khaki looks like Florian Fidel. He's slapping her around like a slave."

"We'd better get down there," Murdock said.

THERE WERE TWO ENTRANCES to Theo's compound at Angel's Nest. The east entrance was Pueblo Road, the public entry corridor that came up from the Taos valley through the Pueblo. The north entrance connected with the overland trail from Little Galilee, where Murdock had come in last week, hunting for traces of Barbi Bellini. But there was no well-defined trail coming from the southeast, a steep uphill climb from the Cerdo Falls Trailhead. They climbed down off Flatrock

Ridge. Murdock knew where they were—he had scouted this approach last week, the day before he'd met Helene—and when Murdock found the dim track of the game trail, he thought, *Too easy*, but he kept going because of Young Winchester and the Serbian girl. A ten-minute uphill climb got them within echo-distance of the compound. They could hear the distant chug of Theo's generator.

As they closed in on the compound, the chugging sound of the generator was punctuated by shouts of "Olé!"

Murdock moved easily through the trees, watching the ground, a modified sniper-walk, planting each foot, scanning for bandits. Helene was off to his right. He hunkered down when he saw an adobe roofline, looked over at Helene. She nodded. The building was the Anasazi Cliff House, where Tammy Wellborn had taken Sonja Vasic last night. He heard another "Olé!" The crowd sounded small, a dozen voices. The generator kept chugging.

Murdock saw movement to his left, then a flash of color. A girl appeared. She was unarmed. Murdock recognized Sue Ellen, the sweet-looking helper from the Maintenance Shack. The same girl who had apologized to Helene, who had blamed Tommy Wellborn for instigating the workshop assault. Sue Ellen looked frightened. Helene put her finger to her lips, the signal for silence, and then Murdock saw movement to his right. Tammy Wellborn appeared.

Tammy wore a camouflage shirt—green, brown, black—and a matching cap. Her yellow hair was pulled back into a tight warrior-bun. On her right hand, Tammy wore a three-fingered archery shooting glove. The string of her bow was armed in a full pull-back position. The arrow was set to fly. It had a gleaming tip, metal or maybe glass. Murdock got it now. Sue Ellen in her bright red blouse was the staked goat, sent in to grab their attention. Tammy was the deadly warrior. Her eyes had that same crazy kill-lust from last night. Slitted eyes and a curled lip turned her pretty face ugly.

The generator sound died. There were no more shouts of "Olé!" coming from Gretna Green, part of Theo's ruse. The girls stood there, not speaking, and Murdock admired Theo Ulster's tactics, using them as his point men, knowing that Murdock and Helene would hesitate before gunning down two teenage girls. Tammy was holding on Murdock, but if her shoulders started to swing, she would loose the arrow at Helene.

Murdock was still holding the Airweight. He said, "Here you go, Tammy," and lobbed the weapon at her. If she didn't move, didn't step aside, the Airweight would bounce off her ear. Murdock saw bright alarm replace the kill-lust. But Tammy was quick. She had good footwork. She danced aside, dodging the oncoming Airweight, and aimed the bright arrow-tip at Murdock. He knew it was coming. He turned his side to Tammy, giving her a narrower target. Saw confusion in her eyes. Murdock was already moving when the arrow sliced into his rucksack, inches away from his heart.

Tammy said, "Fuck you!" and hauled another arrow out of her quiver.

Murdock heard Theo Ulster's voice calling, "Warrior Wellborn, stand down!"

Theo was good. One minute he was not there. The next minute, there he was, grinning, looking very soldier-like in his battle dress. Theo was holding the Webley-Vickers. His Sam Browne belt showed a high polish. His hat was indeed an Aussie bush hat with the left brim bent upwards, for the rakish look. In a low voice, Theo spoke to Tammy. She glared at him then loosened the bow string. The only sign of nerves was the rapid rise and fall of her chest. How could so much meanness be packed into such a little girl?

The bushes rustled and Corporal Simpson appeared, his face marked by commando face paint. Carla Carlini, the archery coach, came up on Theo's right. Skye Latimer and Megan of the broken wrist came up behind Helene. Theo ordered Carla to secure the prisoners. She did the job with green plastic zip ties.

In his best uppity British colonial manner, Theo made a brief speech. "So, you clever hiker-infiltrators. Welcome. So pleased you could accept my invitation to luncheon on the veranda, a bit late, as you discern by the position of the sun at high noon, and unfortunately luncheon is no longer being served, but on the fortunate side, you are just in time for the afternoon's manhunt. Now, if you would please accompany me to the gates, we can get started. The hunting party has assembled, and some of them have real lives and real schedules. So we mustn't dawdle, must we now?"

When they reached the compound, Murdock did a quick recon. The stakes were still strung with wire. The generator had gone silent. The bleachers were empty of spectators. Young Winchester lay on the grass. He wore no shirt, no shoes, and no shorts—only an Indian breech-cloth that barely covered his crotch. And his right foot—the same foot that had been injured the night he came to Helene's rescue—was encased in a calf-length blue boot. Lying in the grass was a metal crutch.

The Serbian girl crouched beside Young Winchester, looking winded and pale. She was naked from the waist up. She caught Murdock's eye and shook her head. There was no sign of Florian Fidel.

"Corporal Simpson," Theo said.

"Yes, sir?"

"Secure the bait, Corporal. Irons in the waste room, and then get to your post."

"Sir!"

Simpson hauled Young Winchester to his feet. Handed him the crutch. Simpson pulled Sonja Vasic up. She looked down at the grass. Simpson looped a leash around her throat, gave her a shove toward the Aspen Grove. She started walking. "Captives," Theo said, "follow me."

MURDOCK SAW WHAT THEO was doing. It was psychological warfare, getting into the enemy's head. They were trapped in Theo's world. They were no longer citizens, no longer people. They were captives. Theo made the rules. Theo defined your place in his world.

Calling out, "One-Two, One-Two, step smartly now, there you are, together now!" Theo marched them past the maintenance shack and the Gate house, through the parking areas to the big iron gates Murdock remembered from yesterday. Attached to the left gate was a metal sign mounted on a pole that said, "Quarry Way." Another word from the arsenal of psychological warfare, another sign of Theo's power. Beyond the gates, Murdock saw an asphalt track leading up the hill. After the first thirty yards, the track narrowed, with just room enough for a small vehicle—an ATV or a golf-cart. There was a curve, and the track went out of sight. Beside the iron gates was a lean-to. Under the lean-to were people sitting in canvas camp chairs. They were sipping drinks and chatting away. Murdock knew them all from last night—the Ramsays, Gerald and Marina, Florian Fidel. And sitting next to Marina was a guy with his arm in a sling. Had to be Gerry Junior, the shooter on the mountain from last week, the guy who had taken one of Murdock's .45 rounds. Gerry Junior shot Murdock a nasty look. Gerald and Marina Ramsay were chatting with Florian Fidel, who wore dark glasses, a black baseball cap, and a safari outfit just like Gerald's. Fidel and Gerald were equipped with fancy, high-polish shoulder rigs, expensive and macho. Marina carried her weapon in a holster with a quick-release belt-clip. Marina whispered something to Gerry Junior, her mouth tight, brow creased with worry. As Tommy Ramsay came up with three leashed dogs, Murdock did a quick count. If you added Tammy Wellborn, Tommy Ramsay, and Corporal Simpson, the hunting party numbered seven. Add Theo and you had eight.

FLORIAN FIDEL STOPPED TALKING and turned toward Murdock. His expression changed from sociable to hostile.

At a fast trot, with a jungle growl, Fidel headed straight for Murdock. Using his parade-ground voice, Theo shouted at Florian to halt.

"At ease!" Theo cried. "He's not yours just yet!"

Fidel kept coming, moving fast for a city guy. He clawed at his shoulder rig, came up with the pistol, nine mil, Sig Sauer. His toe hit a rock. He stumbled, got his legs under him, and kept coming. Fidel was moving too quickly for a good shot— unless he'd been trained to run and shoot and hit the target. That was something you could sense about an opponent's training, but Murdock had observed Fidel's moves last night. The guy was mean and he was strong—but then he stumbled and Murdock felt better.

Murdock waited until the last second, seeing the wild attack strategy forming in Fidel's eyes, the pistol raised, the dull chrome pistol catching the light, giving Murdock a split second to act. His wrists were held by the zips. He stepped close, got inside Fidel's circle of supposed safety, snapping his wrists up, catching Fidel's exposed elbow. Fidel grunted. Elbow hits could send electricity zinging through the arm, shoulder, neck.

The fingers loosed the Sig. It hit the ground with a thump. Fidel, really pissed now, ran at Murdock, the head-butt technique. Murdock turned sideways, sending Fidel into the dirt. As Fidel went down, Murdock saw a purple bruise blooming on the left cheek, near the ear. A bruise from last night's scuffle.

Theo grabbed Fidel's safari jacket, hauled him to his feet, and gave him a shake, like a schoolmaster would deliver to a naughty boy.

"Old fellow," Theo said. "Do be patient! Remember that the death-blow must be savored, tasted, as it were. Your opportunity will come."

"Fuck you, *pendejo*," Fidel said.

"Quarry," Theo said. "On the ground with you. It's shoes and socks removal time."

USING A LITTLE SHARP-NOSED wire cutter, Carla Carlini snapped off the zip ties. Murdock and Helene sat in the dirt to unlace their boots. Another way of cutting you down, reducing your size, taking away weapons, identity-words, protective footgear. This was a manhunt and they were the quarry. Because they were quarry, they had to run barefoot. They sat there waiting. Carlini took their boots, their socks, their sunhats. Theo handed over two bandanas and two pairs of flimsy green flip flops.

Theo's introduction to the manhunt was formal, very British, very old-world imperial. The key word was "quarry." The introduction was delivered with a mocking tone that made it sound like a walk in the park, like a run for your life. The introduction roused Murdock's hate-meter. For Theo Ulster, Murdock's hate was twelve on a scale of ten. Murdock was sweating from fear. He was sweating from the sun. He was worried about Helene's feet. Barefoot on those rocks. How long could she last?

Theo's voice sliced the air. "Quarry," he said, "will be granted a twenty-minute start before the hunters are let loose. Quarry will attempt to avoid capture until sundown. Upon capture, quarry will face sentencing and punishment. Surrender is possible, but frowned upon—who amongst us wishes to lose face? If quarry manages to evade capture until sundown, then a celebration will be in order. The last celebration was two years ago. That particular quarry evaded capture with a mad leap from the jagged lip of Flatrock Ridge."

With a smug smile, Theo handed Murdock a survival tool. A rusty Swiss Army knife. The knife blade was dull and the pointed tip had been sawed off. The corkscrew was broken, no chance of sneaky quarry stabbing a hunter. The little scissors were rusted shut. Theo gave Helene a snaky smile. "Ready, my dear?"

"Why are you hurting me?"

Theo Ulster stared at Helene. He stepped closer, gripped her arm, looked into her eyes. As Murdock watched, Helene's face changed, going from hard to soft, from bleak fright to a pleading slack-mouthed expression edged with abject surrender.

Theo was still gripping Helene's arm. He said something, then gave her a little shake. Smiling like an Aztec demigod, Theo said, "Don't worry, my dear. You're much too old to eat."

46

Helene

THE COURSE OF THEO Ulster's merciless manhunt was an uphill trail marked by little metal plaques mounted on steel posts driven into the ground. The asphalt topping was warm and rough. When the asphalt ran out, the trail turned rock-hard, with sudden pockets of loose shale and pine needles, where the footing felt tricky, and where Helene tripped and fell, skinning her bad knee. The flip flops would not stay on. Her feet burned. Only minutes into the hunt and she was holding Murdock back. Another hundred steps, and the pain would be too much to bear. She hadn't told Murdock, but Helene had a plan. A way into Theo, a way out of this mess.

Murdock gave her the knife. Using the knife, Helene cut strips from Murdock's left shirt sleeve and used the strips to lash the flip flops tight to her feet. The terrain was tough; the lashings would not last. Helene felt panic. She willed herself to be calm. She thought about her dad. Would he get here in time? Would she be alive to greet him?

She helped Murdock build a landslide. Two large round rocks, teetering, held in place by small flat rocks used as wedges. Atop the rocks, two dead trees with thorny branches, limbs from bushes, broken off by Murdock.

Murdock was sweating, grunting, giving everything to the work of building the landslide. She could not see his eyes behind the dark glasses. His arms were getting red. Theo Ulster had taken their hats. "Get some sun," he had said. "You both look pale as ghosts, ashen is the death-shade, you know. Any questions? Too bad. The Q and A period is over. Ready, set, go. You have a thirty minute head start. Let's make that twenty-one minutes. How about fifteen? Quarter of an hour for two woodsy honeymooners. Off with you now."

UP THE SLOPE FROM Murdock's landslide prep was a huge yellow boulder. Helene cleared a track downhill, from the big boulder to the pile of rocks and trees. Murdock used the knife and a sharp rock to dig a trough on the downhill slope, digging under the lower side of the yellow rock. The knife blade broke. Murdock cursed. The yellow boulder was their starter, the ignition for the landslide. They had to free the boulder from the mountain, send it downhill to the hunters. "First strike," Murdock said. "First blood to us. Confusion for the enemy. Loss of confidence."

Murdock thought like a soldier. Helene's thoughts flitted from the corpse on Angel Mountain to the body of Anais Bertrand to the hopeless track she was scratching in the dirt. If she did not survive this day, she would cherish her time with Murdock through all eternity. Even under the stress of Theo's game, Helene and Murdock worked together. They came to the same conclusions at the same time. No explanation needed. They divided the chores, no bickering about his and hers.

She studied Murdock's yellow boulder—it looked huge, inert, impossible to move, even with the dead tree as a lever. Murdock was checking her channel. Sounds floated up from the trail down below. Voices, the barking of dogs. Helene remembered shooting that dog the day she had found the blood on the rock. Remembered the comforting feel of the De

Lisle Carbine. If she had the little rifle now, it would even the odds.

Helene looked out from behind the escarpment. They had chosen this spot for the landslide because the trail made a sharp turn and they could work out of Theo's line of vision. Looking out, Helene saw Theo in his floppy sniper hat. Tammy Wellborn now wore a dark baseball cap. Tommy and his brother Gerry Junior, the only man with a sling, were bare-headed. In the hot sunlight, they looked like typical golden boys.

"How you doing?" Murdock said.

"Scared," Helene said, "and my feet are on fire."

"Sorry about your feet," Murdock said.

"I love you," Helene said.

"And I love you," Murdock said.

"What are we doing here?" Helene said. "Why aren't we—"

"This will slow them down," Murdock said. "Slowing down will piss Theo off. If we're lucky, the rocks will break his leg."

"How far to the Jeep?" Helene said.

"Couple miles," Murdock said. "If we take the shortcut."

"Two miles on this ground," Helene said. "My feet will be down to the bone."

"I'll carry you," Murdock said.

"If I surrender," Helene said, "then—"

"Then he'll kill you. And rape you. And—"

"I can handle Theo," she said.

"He's crazy," Murdock said. "He won't let you talk. Won't listen."

"Quarry that surrender has until sundown," she said.

"He's lied about everything else," Murdock said.

THE VOICES WERE CLOSER now. The dogs were louder and more strident. Baying, barking, a picture of sharp teeth stabbing Helene's brain. Helene watched from behind a rock. The heat beat down on her head. She remembered Theo's grin when he confiscated their sunhats.

When the hunters were closer—it looked to Helene like thirty or forty yards away—Murdock wedged the dead tree under the backside of the big yellow boulder. The veins stood out in his neck. His face reddened with the effort. At his nod, Helene added her weight. The dead tree made a groaning sound, but the rock did not budge. Murdock told her to keep pushing down. He scurried around to the downhill side, pulled at the dirt with his hands. Then he rejoined Helene, put his back to the rock, braced his bare feet against the slope, grunted, cursed, panted.

The voices were so close; the dogs sang a song of triumph. Winners and losers. Hunters and quarry. She heard a shout from down below, and then Murdock let out a roar and the dead tree broke under Helene's weight. The big yellow rock moved forward, one inch, two inches, its rumpled front side finding Helene's track. She was proud of that, watching the rock gain momentum as it traveled downhill. It slammed into the pile of landslide stuff, a big grunt when it made contact.

A munching sound, like huge jaws biting bone. A rumble of rock on rock. A shout from down below.

A girl's bright scream

Shaking and feeling grim, Helene squeezed Murdock's hand as they looked down from behind the escarpment. The ravine below was filled with dust. The dead trees flopped like broken windmills. Shouts, a dog yelping, a cloud of dust. A voice calling for help.

Murdock said, "Let's go." He grabbed his flip flops and led her up the trail. She hadn't gone twenty steps before the burning started. The pain sang through her brain like a burning coal. Frantic, Helene looked around for a place to hide, gather her courage, and surrender. She wanted something off the trail, something that would draw the hunters away from Murdock. He knew where he was going. She knew what she had to do. Their first his-and-hers argument.

47
Theo

U P UNTIL THE MOMENT of Murdock's pernicious landslide, Theo Ulster was having a better than average day. The sun was warm, a perfect Indian summer Sunday in the glorious Sangre de Cristo Mountains. He was on the hunt for a real adversary, not some frightened Frieda lookalike with milk-white thighs. The walk-in freezer at the Smokehouse was stocked with meat for winter. The trail vehicles—golf cart four-wheelers—had narrowed the quarry's fifteen minute lead to eight minutes. If Theo's planning was on target, the woman would fail before she had reached Mile Two. The man, Murderous Murdock, would either surrender with her or make supper for the dogs.

THEY HAD RIDDEN UP in the golf carts to the end of the asphalt. After parking the vehicles in formation, they had formed themselves into a happy, well-focused group marching up the defile. Theo had assigned Tammy Wellborn to be the Warrior on the Point. Tammy was so eager for her first kill, and Theo needed to debrief Gerry Junior about the healing progress of Howard Whitbread, his downed comrade from the initiation, still in hospital suffering from Murdock's lucky shot on Flatrock Ridge.

Theo saw that Tommy Ramsay had joined Tammy on the point. Gerald and Fidel were having a discussion about exchange rates and the safest banks offshore. Marina was handling the dog named Mark Anthony. Corporal Simpson had control of the other dogs, Cassio and Brutus. When the debriefing was over, Theo ordered Simpson to release one dog. Simpson chose Cassio. Things can happen so fast. The dog, unleashed, caught the scent and bounded up the trail.

Then came the landslide.

ROCKS BIG AND SMALL, dead trees, a blinding swirl of dry New Mexico dust, the whole messy mass propelled by a giant yellow boulder that slammed down the ravine with a deadly intent that seemed personal. The dead trees rotated like insane windmills, and their dry branches turned into staves that sank their sharp barbs into the leg of Tommy Ramsay. The boy screamed and went down. Tammy Wellborn, quick as a water-nymph, danced aside and took shelter in an alcove.

Theo watched her from down below. The intuitive female, with her fluid intuitive grace. Supple at fifteen. Luscious. Marina Ramsay loosed her dog. Theo did not see it happen, but seconds before the landslide, he heard Cassio's trademark yelp as the dog charged past Theo and up the trail. Cassio had a superior nose for quarry. The poor beast ran headlong into the landslide, turning as he heard the rocks coming down. Before the dust had cleared, Cassio was dead, a lifeless lump of bone and fur, killed in Murdock's landslide. Brutus was hurt, and Tommy Ramsay's leg had been twisted, the foot turned at an odd angle. Marina was in shock. There was no sign of her dog, Marc Anthony. Gerald kept muttering, "What the Fuck, What the Fuck." Of his five civilian hunters, only Tammy kept her head. The girl's eyes were slitted as she scanned the mountain.

Theo, furious at being ambushed, snapped orders as the dust

settled. He sent Marina back to HQ with Tommy. He was her son, after all. He gathered the remaining hunters—Tammy, Gerald, Gerry Junior, Fidel, faithful Simpson—and delivered a pointed lecture before starting up the hill. "No shooting until the order is given," Theo said. Tammy nodded, but Gerald and Fidel, in defiance of the command, racked shells into their respective weapons.

As they climbed, Theo felt a pain stab his left knee. He looked down to see blood and dirt on his trousers. He did not remember taking a hit. As the leader, he could not stop the column to examine the wound.

* * *

HOT SUN. DRY AIR. Thirsty. Panting. On the edge. No time left.

Murdock felt sick to his stomach. He hugged Helene, felt her heart beating against his chest. He did not like the look in her eyes. Halfway between doom and sacrifice.

He helped her climb up to some rocks that gave shade. She stumbled on the way up. "Shit," she said. "Shit, that hurts."

Helene's frantic pain sang through Murdock as he helped her ease down between two big gray rocks. There was dirt crusted in the blood from her feet. In a weak voice, she ordered him to go. "Hurry," she said, "before they see you leaving."

"Bash Theo in the throat," Murdock said. "While he's choking, take out his eyes."

"I can handle Theo," she said again. "Now split."

* * *

THEO AND HIS HUNTERS came to the landslide site—a twist in the trail where Murdock and the woman had fashioned their little trap. Theo could see the clever channel used to guide the big yellow rock into the ramshackle pile of stones and dead trees. The hunting party filed past with no comment. A quarter mile up the trail and Theo saw the trees that marked Mile

Two. Sergeant Bolitar was up there, off the trail in a concealed location.

Theo pressed the button on his sat-phone—cellphones had no service in his domain—and gave orders to Sergeant Bolitar. Theo wanted both quarry alive. The man and the woman. Use only necessary force.

Bolitar said, "Yes, sir, Captain, sir." But when Bolitar growled, Theo knew. Murdock had wrecked the big Mercedes and Bolitar wanted revenge.

A hundred meters past the landslide site and Theo saw the woman. She was off the main trail and up the hill. She had followed a dim game trail that led to a pile of jagged red rock. Theo saw her little blue blouse. Theo put his finger to his lips, —no talking—and led his party up to the woman.

SHE LAY IN THE fetal position on her right side. When he drew closer, Theo saw that her feet were raw and bleeding. Good planning on his part. The flip flops lay in the dirt, along with some strips of khaki fabric, the same color as Murdock's shirt.

Theo prodded the woman with his boot. She did not open her eyes.

"Helene," he said. "Where is Murdock?"

"Fuck you," she said.

He gave her left foot a nudge with his boot. She groaned, pulled the foot back. He repeated his question. She said, "Fuck you" again. Theo grinned. A woman of spirit, half-dead, bloody and beaten, and still trying to sound defiant with the F-Word.

Gerald Ramsay sidled up next to Theo. In the wild, Gerald always forgot his place. Always pushing Theo, manipulating, throwing his banker's weight around. The man had a bloated ego, an exaggerated sense of his own importance. Theo steeled himself. The barter was about to begin.

"Nice ass," Gerald said. "For a lady writer."

"She's my prisoner, old boy."

"A hundred grand off your debt," Gerald said. "Right off the top, Captain, for ten minutes with the—what do we call her?—with the Female Quarry."

"I told you," Theo said. "She's mine. I go first. You come after me."

"Two hundred grand," Gerald said, "and I'll shave the interest on your whole loan from seven to six."

Theo poked Gerald's chest. He took off his dark glasses. The sun slammed into his eyes. Theo's one weakness in the desert was being born with blue eyes. For that weakness, he blamed his mummy. To shield his eyes from the sun, Theo put his face close to Gerald's.

"In your air-conditioned boardroom," Theo said. "At the head of your polished table, surrounded by your minions in their business suits and soft chairs, you are king. In my world, however, I am king. I give the orders, you follow them. If you play nice, you may have second helpings."

Theo watched Gerald's eyes. The fellow was high on meth or PCP—like so many civilians, he could not venture into the bush without a crutch, something to boost his courage, some potion to turn a slimy banker into a temporary mountain man in boots that cost fifteen hundred dollars. Gerald's eyes glared back at Theo. When you were on the proper drugs, Theo remembered, you felt invincible. You were Beowulf slaying the dragon. You were bare-chested Conan boffing the Queen of Night. Knowing this, Theo did not give up an inch of ground. In less than a second, he could have the knife out—he wore it on his back, the hilt next to his right ear—and Gerald would be on the ground, gutted like a tusked boar, bleeding out.

A moment of decision, Tammy silent, Gerry Junior sneezing, Florian Fidel looking impatient, and Theo saw the drug-fueled glare fade from Gerald's eyes. Gerald grinned. He looked dazed. He shook his head and backed away, leaving Theo alone with the woman. Theo sank to one knee. He ignored the sudden dart of pain. He had her. Now, how to get her to the HQ?

"Helene," Theo said, "can you walk?"

"Fuck you," the woman said.

48

Murdock

MURDOCK'S FEET WERE BURNING, but they were tough enough to last another hour. As he left Helene, he could smell trouble up the trail called Quarry Way. He could smell an ambush laid by Theo. An ambush with burly Sergeant Bolitar in charge.

The main trail—the one marked by little metal plaques that winked in the sun—led up the hill to a line of trees on the lip of the next ridge. The trail snaked up to vanish between a pair of matching rocks, boulders the size of railroad cars. The ambush would be there, just as the quarry topped the hill and started to feel better. Boom, you're dead.

A HALF MILE FROM the top of the ridge, there was a sign on a metal pole that said "To Little Galilee." Murdock turned right, off the main trail, and crouched down behind a rock outcropping, expecting to hear the crack of a rifle. Nothing. Scanning to his right, he saw the dim traces of a game trail that meandered toward the crime scene. His khaki shirt was the same color as the rocks. He knew they were watching for him. Maybe they already had him in the crosshairs. He crawled along the game trail until it was safe to run bent over. His back hurt. His feet burned. He remembered moving bent over in combat. It seemed easy back then. Not so easy now, and the odds were worse, the stakes higher. When he was out of the line of sight from the opening, Murdock shifted into a soldier's trot, following the gentle zigzag of the game trail. Animals were smarter than people. Animals took it easy, turning, twisting, keeping the slope to a minimum. Humans liked going straight for the goal. If the shortest distance from A and B was straight up, then humans went straight up.

Murdock checked the sun. Three-fifteen, maybe three-thirty. He had no wristwatch. Theo had confiscated that along with their sunhats. He figured twenty minutes to get on top, another ten minutes to the crime scene, five minutes to the campsite, maybe three minutes to the Jeep for the De Lisle. He was feeling his feet now, jabbing pains with each step. There were camp moccasins at his old campsite, buried with clothes and food and ammo. If the backpack was still there, he had a chance. The campsite had trees and underbrush. Easier to defend from there.

The game trail led him onto a bare expanse of mountain, where he would be exposed before he made it up top. He was too beat to run, so he shuffled along, heading for the trees. The first shot whanged the trail, kicking up dust to his right.

Murdock kept moving. If he had to die, he would go out in motion.

He changed speed. Slow to fast. Since they were shooting off to his left, there was no percentage in running zigzag. The second shot slapped a rock just behind him as he made the trees. The bullets stopped. He was breathing hard and his feet burned. He still had the flip flops around his neck. No time to stop and strap them on.

HE WAS FIFTY YARDS from the crime scene—it was closer than his campsite—when he heard the dogs. He estimated tree cover for a quarter mile. Trees would not slow dogs down—Murdock needed a weapon. He had the little knife with the pointless blade. Not good for stabbing. But he remembered that morning at the crime scene, he and Helene on their knees hunting for blood. He remembered unearthing several wedge-shaped rocks sticking up from the hard ground. Remembered thinking they were giant arrowheads from an earlier age. If he could grab one of those rocks, it would be heavy enough, and maybe sharp enough. If he could lift it. If the dog got close enough. If he could slug the dog before he felt the teeth. Too many ifs could drive you crazy. If you were quarry.

As he crested the rise, Murdock saw the place where they had found the dead girl, the dead tree that had caught an arrow. Still no explanation for her death, why she was killed. *Have to beat the info out of G.J.* As he trotted ahead, Murdock ran a mind-movie of their return to the crime scene, early morning, on his knees searching for DNA. In his mind-movie, he saw Helene on her knees, turning over rocks. The image of Helene brought back the worry. He had to stay sharp. He saw the tip of a rock. The dogs were closer. Dogs were faster than hunters. Theo had three dogs with his little group of hunters. How many dogs for Sergeant Bolitar? Murdock heard one dog voice—a big sound, maybe the alpha male—and two yelpers chiming in. Three dogs was two too many. Too many to kill with a rock. If he even found it. If he could keep moving.

49
Theo

USING HIS HAND AXE, Theo felled five trees. Runty little things, two inches in diameter. He used straps from his rucksack to fashion an Indian travois. Two main poles strapped together in an elongated X, with the bottom legs twice as long as the top. They strapped the woman across a platform of smaller trees. She kept her eyes closed. Theo used Gerry Senior and Simpson as pack horses. They pulled the travois down the hill. Theo and Florian Fidel walked close behind, helped lift the travois over the larger rocks. When they reached the parking area for the golf cart four-wheelers, the woman sounded delirious. They loaded her into Theo's golf cart. He handed over a sat-phone, told them to rendezvous with Sergeant Bolitar.

"Bring Murdock to me," Theo said. "Alive."

They trudged off. Gerry Ramsay walking with Fidel. Corporal Simpson walking with Tammy and G.J., who was courting Tammy like a fool, not knowing that she was eager for her first kill.

Theo started the golf cart. With the little engine purring, he left Helene sitting while he opened a medical bag and pulled out a hypodermic. He fitted the hypo with a needle, filled the tube with a solution from a rubber-topped vial. He came up on Helene's left side, smiled at her, and started down. The hypodermic was in his left pocket.

"You're a real bastard, Theo."

"And you, my dear, look good enough to eat."

50
Murdock

SCREENED BY A RIDGE of ragged rocks, Murdock watched the dog break from the woods. A Doberman, maybe sixty pounds, running easy. Murdock heard the dog's voice, saw the teeth. And found the rock. It jutted up from the ground, waiting to be wrestled by a crazy man. That man was Murdock. He pulled the wedge-shaped rock from the earth. Ten pounds, maybe twelve. Too heavy to throw. The dog was fifty steps away. Happy in the hunt, what he was bred to do, hunt down the quarry, use those teeth. Kill.

Murdock saw the dog in slow-motion. Launched in flight, paws forward, claws out, bright teeth bared. A low growl in his throat.

Murdock held the rock low, near his knees. When the dog closed in, Murdock swung the rock, arcing upward, catching the dog under the chin. Used momentum and all his savvy, fighting gravity, remembered to follow through, hearing the crunch of rock on jawbone. With a whimper, the dog collapsed. Murdock slugged him on the ear. Saw blood in the fur. The dog whined. Shook its head. Did not get up.

Murdock ran for the campsite. A hundred yards or so

exposed, then into the trees, Aspen and pine. As he crashed through the brush, he could hear the baying of Dog Number Two. Still no shouts from the hunters. Dog Number Two was sixty steps away and closing when Murdock came to his campsite. The strength was leaving him. His legs weighed a thousand pounds. Once inside the trees, he did a quick check. No footprints, no sign of visitors. The campfire was still marked by a ring of blackened stones. The brush pile where he had buried his gear looked untouched. He checked the sun through the trees—close to four o'clock, and sunset came fast in these mountains. At sunset, Theo would kill Helene.

Murdock tore at the brush pile. Dug down, reaching for the camp shovel. Felt the blade, hauled the shovel out of the dirt and locked the blade in place just as Dog Number Two blew through the tree cover and launched his killer-leap at Murdock. In one jerky motion that should have been smooth, Murdock rammed the shovel upward, aiming for the throat. Murdock was late, the dog's teeth too close, and the blade connected with the dog's belly. He let out a woof and collapsed. Murdock hit him twice with the shovel. Goddamn Theo Ulster for keeping these great-looking dogs.

Feeling the adrenaline from the two kills, Murdock tore through the trees to the Jeep. His hands were shaking as he unlocked the compartment and extracted the De Lisle. Grabbed an ammo belt. Fought the pain in his feet as he started uphill toward the campsite. He had camped there for two nights. Back then the only problem was tracking Barbi Bellini. Since then, things had changed. He had met Helene and fallen in love, and now Theo had Helene and Murdock had to use rocks to fight for her life.

Carrying the De Lisle carbine, Murdock stumbled up the hill. He needed an observation point with cover. He passed the campsite, got to his knees, and crawled until he saw the meadow. No sign of the hunters, but the afternoon was still and he could hear voices. His feet were hurting. Across the open field, he saw movement as Dog Number Three broke from the trees. Not running, this old dog, but trotting along, sniffing the air, tracking the quarry. Murdock hunkered down behind a fallen tree that had turned into a nurse log and was now sprouting branches.

Dog Number Three was big, the perfect alpha male. Big and handsome, wise with his years. Maybe he would back off. Murdock watched him, cautious, sniffing the body of Dog Number Two. The old dog made what could have been a sound of sympathy, then sniffed his way up the hill toward the campsite, zigzagging, nose to the ground, stopping at the brush pile that covered Murdock's buried backpack. When the big head turned toward Murdock, his eyes were sad, as if he regretted what he was about to do. Murdock could feel him thinking, analyzing the situation with his dog brain. Putting the evidence together. The smells, the blood, his dog-buddy down, the enemy close.

Murdock shot the dog when he lifted his head again, nose to the sky, preparing for a baying alert that would bring the hunters. Murdock squeezed the trigger, and the De Lisle made its little whispery sound. Gray gases puffed out from the little holes. The dog stood there for a long moment, looking like nothing had happened, then sank down, butt first. Then onto its belly, then rolled onto its side. Murdock had shot the dog to even the odds. He didn't like shooting this one. The dog was old. Murdock was old. They could have been buddies. The dog looked at Murdock. Still hanging on.

Working fast, Murdock went back to the buried gear. He wanted socks. He wanted boots. He smelled dirt and pine needles and a cold night on the way. He was frustrated at having to move this fast when all he wanted was to lie down and rest. His fingers touched canvas. He dug some more. The backpack emerged. He hauled it out, popped the buckles that held the straps. Extra ammo clip on top. The socks were under the ammo. They were stiff from two days of foot sweat.

Murdock didn't care. He needed boots. He settled for the camp moccasins. They were his; they fit his feet. He remembered Helene's feet, raw and bloody. He heard Bolitar's voice floating through the trees, urging his troops to use caution.

"All right now, lads. Keep up the pace, shall we? Our quarry is close at hand. You doing all right, Miss Wellborn?"

The hunters were in the open, fanned out across the meadow. Murdock was in the trees. This was the time to take action. Two dogs dead in the landside. Two dead and one wounded on the ridge. How many hunters?

51

Murdock

MURDOCK WAS TOO OLD to duck-walk—it killed his knees—so he scurried from tree to tree, away from the campsite, toward the hunters. He was still deep in tree cover when he saw Corporal Simpson in his mountain camos, armed with an automatic rifle. Even in battle dress, Simpson looked like the eternal youngster. Pink-cheeked and innocent, standing on the hummock for a better view. The afternoon sun turned him into a silhouette. As Murdock watched, Simpson twirled his hand in the air and two more hunters came into view. One was Gerry Ramsay Senior, the other was G.J., the eldest son, identified by the bright blue sling for his arm. Simpson, Gerry, G.J.—three hunters, no sign of Sergeant Bolitar, who had to be in command. No sign of Tammy or Florian Fidel.

Murdock waited. He needed them clumped together. He was thirsty. He had left the water back at his campsite. His feet still burned, but the camp moccasins would get him to Helene. Where had Theo taken her? How long had he had her? How long until sundown? Thinking about Helene with Theo gave Murdock the shakes. He saw movement, hunters joining Corporal Simpson. Murdock recognized Bolitar from the size and his laugh. Bolitar wore khaki shorts and a bush shirt. He was walking with Florian Fidel.

Lying prone behind the trees, Murdock saw Tammy Wellborn, walking fast, still in her baseball cap. Her entrance brought the hunter headcount to six. The five men turned to watch her, five men silhouetted by the late afternoon sun, perfect targets. Sergeant Bolitar unslung his rifle and unfolded a map. Went to his knees and spread the map on the ground. As the breeze shifted, Murdock caught snatches of conversation. Words floated by.

"Our quarry was last sighted—"

"Should be hearing the dogs—"

"Deserves a good beating with—"

"See this here—it's where we're at so—"

LOCKING THE HEX SIGHT on Bolitar, Murdock targeted the right shoulder. If the Sergeant was right-handed, he would lose his shooting arm. Murdock was following the unwritten sniper rule: if there are troops, take out the leader, no more tactics, no more tongue of fire. Murdock had killed four dogs—three today, one last week. He had wounded G.J. and his pal, the other bowman. But as of this moment, Murdock had not killed a single person in New Mexico. Of the six hunters, Bolitar had to be the best shot. Take him out now, as he got to his feet.

Murdock squeezed the trigger. The De Lisle whispered. A hundred yards away, caught in slanting autumn sunlight, Sergeant Bolitar turned, stared in Murdock's direction, reached for his pistol—he wore a Sam Browne belt, he reached with his right hand—and then sank to his knees again. At the same time, Gerry Ramsay Senior sat down, hard, clawing at his butt, and the other hunters—four remained—hit the dirt and lay flat.

Before the return gunfire slashed the underbrush, Murdock was moving again. Away from his shooting spot, deeper into the trees. He kept low. Automatic fire chewed trunks, whined off rocks. Branches dropped down, pine needles flew up, hung in the air. Gerry Ramsay keeled over, going from a sitting position to prone. What had happened? Murdock had fired one round into Bolitar. He had not shot Gerry Senior. Had the fat banker shot himself in the foot? Or was Jimmy Little Deer trying to even the odds?

Murdock heard Tammy's voice, "I see him! I see him!"

The girl was up now, nocking an arrow, running right at Murdock. She had good eyes, this little girl, or maybe a good nose for the kill. When Tammy was thirty yards away, she stopped. Hauled back on the bowstring, and loosed an arrow. It sang in the air. Murdock shifted, scooting back, keeping low. The arrow landed where he had just been. Uncanny. He didn't want to shoot her. She was pretty and petite, with a long life in front of her. She loosed the second arrow. It hit the tree he was standing behind. Murdock was in shock. Immobilized by a teenage female. He was too old for this shit.

Tammy was yelling again, "Come on, you guys! Come on!"

52

Murdock

SIMPSON WAS ON HIS feet, moving toward Tammy. Before he had gone three steps, Simpson dropped, hit the ground, and grabbed his leg. Now Murdock knew for sure. The second shooter was Jimmy Little Deer. Murdock remembered Jimmy's phone call. Young Winchester was AWOL. Jimmy wanted help finding him. Their rendezvous time had been one o'clock. The time now was after four. Another arrow from Tammy Wellborn slashed through the trees and stabbed the dirt an inch from Murdock's moccasin. As he looked up, Tammy was fitting another arrow. And she was a dozen steps closer.

Murdock stared at her and she stared back. Her eyes were crazy. Her face looked cruel. The torturer's apprentice. The smile spoke of invincibility—being a girl made her safe. Tammy could shoot at Murdock, but he would not shoot back. Theo had trained Tammy to kill with a bow and arrow. Tammy Wellborn stood between Murdock and Helene.

Before Tammy loosed her next arrow, Murdock laid the hex sights on the bow-frame and squeezed the trigger. The bow exploded. Tammy screamed. "I'm hit! I'm hit! You dirty bastard!" She was dancing up and down, holding her right hand between her legs. There was a dark splotch on her hair, near the right ear. The baseball cap was gone, but Tammy Wellborn would live.

Murdock swung the rifle to cover Simpson, who was just young enough to make a dopey attempt to avenge the girl. Simpson lay still, but Florian Fidel was running back down the hill, toward Quarry Road. When the odds were six to one, Fidel was ready to kill Murdock. When the odds shifted, the bastard hit the road.

Sergeant Bolitar, wounded but still in command, called off his troops. Murdock collected the weapons and checked the wounded. Tammy Wellborn had lost a finger and Murdock fashioned a tourniquet. Blood from her right ear was clotting. Gerry Ramsay Senior wheezed, but he still had color in his face. Simpson had a shattered kneecap. G.J. sat in the dirt, crying. When Murdock had the hunters secured and the weapons in a pile, he hollered to Jimmy Little Deer, who came loping in from the north, grinning, carrying his De Lisle at port arms.

"Murdock," the sergeant said. "You've won and we've lost and I'm wanting to be off before the officers of the law arrive. So might I be surrendering with some conditions?"

"What conditions?" Murdock said. "You're shot, you need a doctor, you've got my girl."

"I know the captain. I can get you closer. And with more speed, sir."

"Where's he got her?"

"In his office. He's got a closet with a bed."

"So what do you want out of this deal?"

"First," Bolitar said. "I'll be wanting my share of the treasure in the Captain's floor safe. Second, I want my lovely Mercedes. Third, I want to be on my way before the arrival of the local constabulary. That Savage fellow is no friend of mine."

Murdock said okay. Bolitar talked too much, he was stagey,

like a Sergeant Major in an old movie, but Murdock liked the guy. Almost.

THE HUNTERS' WEAPONS FORMED a little pile. Tammy Wellborn's longbow. G.J.'s Police Special. Corporal Simpson's Beretta in an ankle holster. Gerry Senior's Glock nine. When he disarmed Gerry Senior, Murdock noticed the banker's boots. The brand was Kenetrek, fine leather, high tops to support the ankle, terrain-tough soles, already broken in.

Gerry Senior grunted when Murdock took the boots. Murdock pulled them on. The fit was perfect. What a world— he and this greedy overweight shit-head banker wore the same size boot.

"You cocksucker," Gerry said. "Taking the boots off a wounded man."

"I could fix the wounded man part," Murdock said.

"Oh, yeah?"

"I could turn you from wounded into dead."

"Get the fuck away from me! This is not over yet. I'll have your balls for breakfast."

When he checked Sergeant Bolitar for weapons, Murdock found only the regulation Webley top-break revolver. It was a heavy piece of artillery, a .455 caliber, solid and well-made, viewed in hundreds of British army films. Starting with NATO, the world's armies were armed with automatic nines and the Brits still sported six-shot revolvers.

Murdock was impressed with Bolitar's size and his fitness. The guy was stout and solid, past fifty and hard as a mountain boulder. His fist could down an ox.

Murdock took Jimmy aside for a parlay. Jimmy was a tribal cop. He would call for help and herd the wounded hunters down the hill, leaving Murdock free to go after Helene, Young Winchester, and the Serbian girl.

Murdock and Jimmy shook hands. "Find my boy," Jimmy said.

Murdock and Jimmy helped Bolitar to his feet. As Murdock left with Sergeant Bolitar, he heard Jimmy on his tribal police sat-phone.

Murdock turned to Bolitar. "Sergeant?"

"Sir?"

"Call your boss," Murdock said. "Tell him Murdock is dead."

53

Helene

THEO'S ARM HOVERED AT eye-level.

The hand held a hypodermic. The needle glimmered in the harsh sunlight. Helene's hands were tethered. Her feet screamed with pain. Something stabbed her thigh. When she looked down, she saw the hypo sticking out.

"Bitch," Theo said. "You killed my dogs."

Heat spread from the needle. Ripples of heat, with Helene's thigh at dead center. Pain and heat and then she was floating, late autumn moth. Fog curled in her head like a soft kitty. The road went away, the rock shimmered. The asphalt was a black pool. The golf cart was a Nile barge and she was Cleopatra.

She stared at the man. His face shimmered. The needle glimmered. He was the Needle Man. A hole appeared in the fog. She saw buildings, grass, Aspen trees with soft golden leaves. A ramp, a doorway, a key in a lock. A tilting motion, floating up the ramp, and the fog closed in, an envelope of swirly gray. She was cold. Freezing. Shelves to her left, boxes on the shelves. Letters on the boxes said "Captain Ulster's Prime Cuts."

A voice said, "Bound for Guadalajara."

Her mouth said, "What?"

"Destination Mexico," the voice said.

"You sick bastard."

The fog grabbed her by the throat. She saw a door marked "Waste." The light flickered, turned to shadows. The golf cart kept moving. She saw ovens in a wall, one lonely oven with a padlock she remembered seeing before. A hundred ovens in a wall and only one with a padlock. What did it mean?

Images swam at her. Door, corridor, bulletin board, door. Now she was rolling, trundling along a runway, moth wings beating the air. Her body soared over the fog, Helene aloft. Coming down in a room with a bed and black sheets. Through a doorway she saw a flag furled on a long wooden pole. A desk with a photo. The Needle Man was holding a silver blanket. The silver shimmered like wet glass.

"Sick bastard," she said.

SHE WAS LYING DOWN.

She knew she was lying down because the object above her was a light hanging from the ceiling. Ceiling was up. Her body was cold. Her arm reached for the shirt—to pull it tighter. There was no shirt.

Hands touched her body. Her belly felt the hands. Her breasts felt the hands. She had four hands. Two belonged to the Needle Man.

He grinned at her like the man in the moon. He was wearing a white robe that looked Japanese. Her brain registered a kimono. Her ears heard a snapping sound—Needle Man putting on latex gloves. She recalled hearing about white latex gloves from a French woman with a slit for a mouth. Her brain reached for the name of the French woman. The name dripped wet with fog.

A sensation of something entering her way down there through the wet.

Not pain, not heat, but something invasive.

"Feel that?"

"What was in that hypo, you sick bastard?"

"Ketamine for lovers," he said. "And a dash of Cantharis. Here, sit up. Your quim is frozen. Put this on."

She could not sit up. She could only float.

She was a fog-shrouded moth flapping her wet moth wings, attacking the light that hung from the ceiling. Her skin felt silky. Through the fog, she saw that the silky silver blanket was a dress. She remembered the dress on a woman looking at her from a photograph that perched on the edge of the desk.

"I saw her," Helene said.

"Who did you see?"

"The woman in the dress."

"Where did you see her?"

"I'm not telling any sick bastard."

"See this?"

Her eyes peered through watery fog. Her lungs stopped breathing.

"See this?"

She saw a needle. It caught the light from the hot lamp that hung from the ceiling. The lamp attacked by a wet moth flying. The needle was close to her eye. The eye felt danger.

"Do you see this, bitch?"

"What is it?"

"Mummy's hat pin," he said. "It complements Mummy's silver dress."

"I saw her," Helene said.

"Who did you see?"

"I saw Mummy. She wore the dress."

"Remember Marie-Claire?" he said. "She was one of them. One of those busty blowsy buxom blonde Harpy tarts. Did you know that she was chosen?"

"Chosen for what?"

"Not just chosen," he said. "A better word would be 'selected.' The Harpy Tart was selected for our amusement. She was selected to satisfy an old debt."

Helene's eyes followed the hat pin. Her skin felt it traveling down. Shoulder, breast, belly. Pausing at the navel.

"Feel that?"

"I feel nothing."

Her brain could tell that her mouth was lying. The hat pin left her navel and scraped its way to her thigh. His hand moved, a pressing-down motion, and her thigh felt the hat pin. On the end of the hat pin was a little purple knob that caught the light from the ceiling lamp where the wet moth lay dead from burning.

A ringing noise ripped through the ears, stabbing her brain.

"Turn it off."

"Be quiet, bitch."

The ringing noise came from a Sat-Phone.

Her brain knew that word.

The Needle Man answered. "Ulster," he said. "Yes, Sergeant. Quite. Is there Intel? You did? I say. Excellent work, Sergeant. So let's transport the corpus to the HQ. Make sure you knock. And Sergeant, your prowess will not go unrecompensed."

Helene's ears heard again the snapping of latex. Not white gloves this time, but instead a slick white condom.

The Needle Man sat on the edge of the bed. The Kimono was loose and he was fiddling with his manhood. He was huge. He gave her the shakes. Her lungs sucked at the air. They felt no air, only more fog. Her nose smelled the Needle Man.

Smelled his anger, his contempt, his power over her.

He turned to her. He was holding onto himself. Rubbing and squeezing. He looked down. "There you are, old boy. Just in time, because Mummy's back, and we've got some raffish boffing to do." He raised his head and smiled until his eyes were narrow slits. Helene's legs tried to close, but he forced her knees apart. He knee-walked closer. She tried to escape by flapping her wings. Wet wings, dead. He got between her legs. Pushed himself forward.

"Feel that?" he said.

"I feel nothing."

"That phone call," he said. "It was my Sergeant, reporting. *Votre ami est mort.* Your companion is dead. They're transporting the corpse for your pleasure."

54
Murdock

THE GOLF CART BOUNCED downhill at top speed. There was a tightness in Murdock's chest, his mind on Helene. A dip in the asphalt threw the golf cart sideways, slamming into the rock wall on Bolitar's side. The big man made a face. He was sweating, breathing hard. His hands were secured with straps. As they went past the iron gates, Bolitar started talking, the words spilling out like a penitent at confession.

"I knowed I was done for," Bolitar said, "when you shot out my front tire, and sent my lovely black Benz beauty to the body shop. I seen you up there, above me shooting down. You could have killed the lot of us. You didn't. No one had heard the report of a rifle, but it was a real reach, you and that De Lisle carbine. That's a British weapon, you know. I seen one when I was a lad—my uncle Declan brought it back from North Africa."

The blood splotch on Sergeant Bolitar's right sleeve stretched from his shoulder to his elbow. His right hand was stuck into his tunic, a Napoleon pose. His voice was calm and edged with respect. The road smoothed out when they passed the Gate House.

"There's three things about you and me, sir. Three things that let me know you was not the Captain's average sort of enemy. First was that tire shot. Second was the way you nicked my black beauty, the night of the party it was."

"And the third thing?" Murdock said.

"It was the way you shot that little girl," Bolitar said. "Myself, I would have shot to kill. She's a warrior and a nasty bitch. She's made her choice, and killing her would be the soldier's way. But you merely disarmed her, and foolish it was to spare the girl and put your mission at risk. You took a finger instead of a life. She's a crazy one, a true kinswoman of Captain Ulster, taken from her mum and trained by him, and—"

"Where's the Indian kid?" Murdock said. "The Serbian girl?"

"In the Smokehouse," Bolitar said. "They're together, you see, in the storage room. I wonder. If I rescued her, and made her grateful-like, and then asked for her hand—but it's too late for that. Too late for …"

Engine whining like a meat-grinder, the golf cart rolled past the Media Shack into Theo's compound. The light in the west was pale orange now with a layer of bluish-purple clouds. No sign of the nasty parents or their nasty teen offspring. The golf cart wheezed up the gravel path. Murdock's hands were sweating. Fifty yards to Helene.

"Where are the keys?" Murdock said.

"In my right hand pocket, sir. Loose me from these bonds; I'll lead you to him."

Murdock stared at Bolitar, reading his big soldier's face.

"You want your lady, sir. I want what's due me, after all these years. The captain's not the same man I served with out there—why he even started bragging how he could tell one of them girls from the other by the taste, wearing a blindfold. I ain't no deserter, but being on the wounded list gives me a soldier's excuse. The clock's ticking, sir, and I'm your man."

Holding the De Lisle steady on Bolitar, Murdock unbuckled the canvas straps. Bolitar grunted as he climbed out of the golf cart. A lesser soldier with the same nasty arm wound would

have fainted. Not Bolitar. Murdock kept the De Lisle on Bolitar
as he lumbered up the steps to the veranda.

Murdock fished the keys out of Bolitar's pocket. He smelled
sweat and blood, the soldier's legacy. Standing this close,
Murdock expected a fast move from Bolitar. Once a soldier,
always a soldier. Nothing happened, no elbow to the head,
no knee to the balls. The key worked, the door opened, and
Bolitar led the way into the Smokehouse.

55
Theo

THEO PUSHED FORWARD, DRIVING into the female. She moaned, the trap door opened and he fell through. He landed on the bed in the master bedroom, next to blonde Frieda, who was boffing Theo's Papa.

"You're not Mummy."

"Get undressed," Frieda said. "You're next."

There were two beds in the master bedroom, side by side. Mummy lay on the other bed, her legs closed. Theo vaulted across. Nothing could stop him.

"I'll send for you," Mummy said.

"Where are you going?"

"America," she said. "I promise to send for you."

"Why are you leaving me?"

"It's your father," Mummy said. "He's fucking that girl of yours. What's her name again?"

"Her name is Frieda."

"Get off me," Mummy said. "I have to dress."

HIS BRAIN FLICKERED. HIS memory sent him spinning, and he saw himself reaching for Frieda Holst, naked except for her plaid schoolgirl skirt. He felt the pain of her fingernails clawing his face. He watched her mouth open, pink lips, teeth, heard her scream for help, and then the bedroom door opened and the muscular housemaid pulled him off the bed. He fell onto the floor and Frieda rushed out, that white skin, those chubby thighs, a cruel smile on her lips. On her way through the doorway, Frieda passed Papa coming in, brandishing the cane from Hong Kong. Followed by the Monsignor in his purple church robes.

Theo dodged the cane and knocked the Monsignor down. He stood at the window watching Mummy enter the taxi while the driver held the door.

Mummy climbed inside and the skirt climbed up her leg. She was wearing the stockings with the red shoes that Papa hated, and the leg inside the stockings was so beautiful it took Theo's breath away. He stood at the window, frozen, watching the taxi turn the corner. The red lights winked at Theo and his heart exploded. *I promise to send for you.*

"WHY DIDN'T YOU SEND for me, Mummy?"

"I did send for you. And here you are. And here is a photograph to remember me by."

"Who signed this? Who is Eunice Dare?"

"Eunice Dare is my stage name, dear. Every actress has one."

"Why do females always lie?"

"It's not a lie, dear. It's a stage name. For the theater. Tell me you're happy to see me."

"What is this place?"

"This is America, dear. This is New Jersey. This is my home now. You look so handsome. Where have you been?"

"Fighting for the Queen," he said.

"Get off me, she said."

56
Helene

THE NEEDLE MAN WAS inside her.

She didn't see him get inside. He kept calling her Mummy.

There was wetness on her face. She opened her eyes. The eyes saw a face with a silly mustache. A drop of drool on his lips. His eyes were lit up, bright with conquest.

"Mummy," he said. "So happy you came back to me. I have longed for this day, this moment."

"I saw Eunice."

"There you go again, seeing things."

"I saw her in the Actor's Retirement Home in Englewood, New Jersey," Helene said. "She was waiting for you to visit and she looked just like the lady in the photograph."

His eyes slid to the left. They locked on the Eunice Dare photograph. "You left me here with Papa," he said. "He stole my girlfriend. He locked me in the cellar and boffed the girl in your bloody bedroom. When you left, Mummy dear, you promised you would send for me."

"I did send for you," Helene said. "And here you are."

"You lying bitch."

"Get off me," she said.

He started doing push-ups. Hands pushing her shoulders, grunting. Now she felt him ramming her. The fog was lifting. Her body rose up. The fog was thinner, the bright light hurting her eyes. She sagged down again, like a water-logged moth.

"Feel that?" he said.

"I feel nothing."

A KNOCKING ON THE metal door.

A hard steel door, she remembered, a door painted green. The Needle Man stopped doing push-ups. He turned his head. "Sergeant Bolitar?" he said. "One moment, if you please."

But the voice on the other side of the green door was not the burly brogue of Sergeant Bolitar. It was a nervous voice on the edge of hysteria, high-pitched, with a Spanish accent. "Teodoro Ulster," it said. "Open the fucking door! I want my money."

"Fidel," the Needle Man said. "He's deserted the hunting party."

"Teodoro?" Helene said. "Is that your real name?"

"Shut up."

He slapped her. He backed away. She felt him exit her body down there. Leaving her feeling invaded. He did not remove the condom. He used the belt to secure the kimono. He marched across the room.

Helene watched him from her place on the black sheets. Both palms were sweaty. Both wrists were bloody. Her nose smelled the blood. Her wrists felt the pain. She craned her neck, eyes straining, looking up past her forehead, seeing her wrists tethered to the bed frame. The tether looked looser on her right wrist. Fresh blood was slick like oil.

Teodoro Ulster stood in front of the steel door, watched by the eyes of the Centurion, a copper medallion nailed to the door. The revolver was a vintage Webley-Vickers. It looked out of date, a weapon from another time. Helene knew her guns.

Her dad was an ex-cop.

She contracted her right hand, making it small.

The Needle Man fired through the wall beside the door. He aimed low, knee-level. From behind the door, Florian Fidel screamed. Bullets tore through the wall. Glass from the shelf rained down on Helene's head. She closed her eyes. Sharp shards stunned her face. Her right hand came free.

"Teodoro Ulster, you *cojudo cabron*! Why do you shoot me?"

Teodoro kept firing. The explosions were measured and steady. Helene's brain counted the shots. Two, three, four, five. Helene's right wrist came free. There was no more gunfire, no more broken glass, but the Needle Man was back, the kimono shimmering.

"You do so resemble Mummy," he said. "I saw the resemblance, and here is your chance to—"

"Teodoro," she said. "I have to pee."

"Filthy, foul-mouthed bitch!"

He slammed the revolver on the desk. The kimono opened as he climbed onto the bed. He forced her legs apart, eyes narrowed, focused on his re-entry.

Helene punched his throat. She aimed for the Adam's apple. A straight punch, uncoiling from her shoulder.

She heard a crunch.

He grabbed his throat and fell off the bed. A good solid thump when he hit the floor.

Her right hand freed her left hand. She rolled off the bed. Her feet touched the floor and her knees went away. She hauled herself up by grabbing the bed.

The British Flag leaned against the wall. The flag was rolled up. It was heavy, awkward and Helene was weak, her muscles turned to water, the drug still boiling in her veins.

She swung the flagpole. It caught him on the ear.

He went down.

The revolver made a clunk when it hit the floor. Her left thigh burned. She looked down, saw the purple tip of Mummy's hat pin. The Needle Man was crawling away. She jabbed him with the flagpole. He grabbed the revolver. How many shots left? She stared into the muzzle. Her arms were so tired. She had strength for one last thrust. The flagpole rammed his pistol hand. The explosion was loud in her ears. He kept pulling the trigger, but nothing happened. He dropped the pistol and crawled toward the wall where his saber was hanging.

Helene fell, pinning him with her weight. He tried to speak and a gurgle came out. Pulling the hat pin from her thigh, she poked his face, going for the eye. He turned his head and she rammed the pin into his cheek. There was a knocking at the metal door.

She heard a voice calling her name. "Helene!" it said. "We're coming! Stand clear of the door."

GUNFIRE FROM THE CORRIDOR. Voices of men. Murdock was dead. Killed by the Needle Man's men. More pounding on the door. She didn't care. She pulled the hatpin out of his cheek. He was not the Needle Man. Not even Teodoro. He was Captain Theo Ulster, SAS. He killed girls for sport, for entertainment, for revenge, for meat.

She stabbed down. The hatpin drove into his eye. His face turned red.

His frantic knees hammered her lower back.

She heard the door open. A voice that sounded like Murdock, who was dead.

He was kneeling beside her. "Helene, are you okay?"

She had both hands on the hatpin, pushing, hurting, hating, seething—

Killing Theo Ulster.

57
Helene

HELENE WAS DRESSED. HER teeth chattered, and her muscles kept writhing into spasms. She was hugging herself for warmth.

The khaki hiking pants were too short, too big in the ass. The man's blue shirt was covered by a turquoise cardigan. The cardigan was covered by a down vest that had belonged to some dead girl. She wore clean white socks and a pair of Indian moccasins—white leather, garish red stitching, one size too big. Her feet burned. It was full dark outside. There was no use hunting for her boots. Goddamn Theo Ulster.

He lay on the floor in a pool of dried blood.

The hat pin was buried in his eye. Six inches long, a hat pin for the history books.

Had it really belonged to Theo's mummy?

MURDOCK WAS GOING THROUGH Theo's desk drawers. When he finished with a drawer, he wiped off his fingerprints. As Helene watched, he dropped a small red stick into his pocket. Helene sat in the straight chair, trying not to shiver. The little stick had a name. What was it? Her brain slipped away. She knew you plugged the little sticks into computers. Ports? Something flashy, but what?

Maybe her head was still floating on Ketamine. Maybe she should do research on Ketamine. Since she felt tired, maybe she should lie down, but the only place to lie down was the terrible bed with the bloody black sheets. If she lay down on the bed, the memory would suck her backwards in time. Sergeant Bolitar sat on the floor, dumping papers from the safe, making little whimpering noises. Why wasn't he dead? Why wasn't he cuffed?

Helene heard footsteps. She turned to see Murdock holding the De Lisle, covering the door where Sonja Vasic stood, wearing a man's safari jacket. Her legs were bare and splotched with blood. Her face looked swollen, her lips bruised, her eyes haunted. She was holding a pair of fireplace tongs. She leaned against the doorjamb. Her eyes went from Theo on the floor to Bolitar at the safe. Then to Helene, then to Murdock, then back to Helene.

Helene stood up. She felt shaky. It hurt to get out of the chair. Sonja gave her a hug. Helene felt friendship and understanding. "I was afraid you were dead," Sonja said.

"Are you okay?"

"You are needed. Come with me. Please?"

HELENE AND MURDOCK WALKED with Sonja, down the hallway, following the blood trail, toward Theo's kitchen. The door was unlocked. No need for a key. She led the way past the wall of ovens. Looking to her left, Helene saw the oven with the padlock.

They passed through the storage room, where the shelves held little boxes labeled "Captain Ulster's Prime Cuts." The storage room was freezing and Helene shivered. Sonja led them through a door marked "Waste." Not so cold in here.

YOUNG WINCHESTER SAT ON the floor, one leg bent at

a painful angle. He was holding a pistol in his hand. He said, "Hey, white people," and then started crying. Sonja knelt down, put her arms around him. One foot wore a sock. The other was still wearing the blue support boot. Young Winchester had on khaki safari trousers and a fancy hunting shirt, pale yellow, with lots of zippers and flap pockets. Helene had last seen that yellow shirt on Florian Fidel.

Fidel himself was naked. Strapped down to a metal table that was connected to one end of a silvery conveyor belt. In the corner of the room, Helene saw a black-iron frame shaped like a rectangle—seven feet long, three feet wide, and raised three feet off the floor, the same height as the conveyor belt. Next to the iron rectangle was a large pile of bricks, sacks of cement, sacks of sand. Beyond the sacks was an electric cement mixer, silent for now, its mouth gaping open. Helene's brain was slow on the analysis. Cement and a boxy frame and thick glass in a fire door and dead girls.

She looked at Murdock. "My God. He's building another incinerator," she said.

Auschwitz at Angel's Nest. Murdock squatted down beside Young Winchester. The pistol was on the floor between the boy's legs. Murdock did not touch the gun. They talked in low tones. Sonja stood up, walked over to Helene. Helene's legs were shaking, forcing her to brace herself on the metal table where Fidel lay, naked and shivering. His right knee was bruised. There was a knot on his head. A shiny metal chest strap held him down.

Fidel's left eye opened. "Fucking *putas*," he said.

Sonja Vasic stood on the other side of the table. Her eyes were cold as she poked Fidel's swollen knee with the fireplace tongs, bringing a gargled scream. Murdock came up beside Helene.

Sonja dropped the tongs, and they hit the floor with a clunk. "You're a Colombian cop, right?"

"Fuck your mother," Fidel said.

"You buy girls from Theo and sell them to your buddies south of the border."

"Fuck your mother, *pendejo*."

"You sold a girl named Barbi Bellini," Murdock said. "Who was the buyer?"

Fidel spouted a stream of Spanish. Murdock ran his fingers up Fidel's throat, stopping above the Adam's apple. Murdock pressed down and Fidel stopped saying "Fuck You" and started coughing. Murdock let up and Fidel stopped coughing.

Murdock said, "This bone in your throat, the bone I'm pushing on right now, is called the hyoid. The hyoid bone connects to the larynx. If the hyoid bone gets pushed a little more, you won't be able to breathe. If you can't breathe, you'll die. Nobody in this room gives a shit about that. Where's Barbi Bellini?"

"Fucking *cabron*," Fidel said.

"I'm gonna count to three," Murdock said. "Give you some time to think about my question. Ready, set, go."

The move was fast. Before he uttered the word "set," Murdock's thumb pressed down on the hyoid and Fidel's good eye bugged out, tears gushing. He could not cough, but he managed a nod. Murdock let up on the pressure. He leaned down, his ear next to Fidel's mouth. It took awhile before the man could talk. Then Helene heard him whispering. Murdock straightened up. He reached under the table, did something that loosened the metal band around Fidel's chest. Fidel nodded.

"Barbi's in Guadalajara," Murdock said. "She's being held by the same guy who's buying all that meat we saw in Theo's ovens. His name is Eduardo Bakul."

"So she's still alive?"

"According to my buddy Fidel."

"He could be lying," Helene said.

"He said that city to me," Sonja said. "Guadalajara. He said we would fly there and I would very much enjoy the soft life."

"Thanks for not killing him," Murdock said.

"You think he's got his own plane?" Helene said.

SERGEANT BOLITAR APPEARED IN the doorway. His eyes lingered on Sonja then shifted to Murdock and Helene. "What is it, Sergeant?"

"The captain's money, sir. It just ain't there."

"Where's that key ring?" Helene said.

Murdock handed her Theo's key ring. She led the way out of the Waste room, into Theo's kitchen. It was a creepy universe of cutting tables and sharp knives, a closet for chef's uniforms, and a long row of ovens built into the wall.

HELENE WALKED ALONG THE wall of ovens to the back of the room, to the oven with the padlock. She found a light switch. The padlock was black, the hasp stainless steel. She tried two keys from the key ring. The second key worked. She freed the lock from the hasp, tried to open the door. Her strength was not there. She asked Murdock to help. He had been standing back, watching her solve this problem of Theo's money. She did not know how she knew. Perhaps it was because she knew Theo. She could sense his isolation, feel his depression. Had she known about Theo that first day, when they shook hands on the tennis court? Had she seen the craziness in his eyes? Had she been overly impressed by his British accent? By his graceful moves on the tennis court? As she shook Theo's hand, was he already confusing her with his mummy?

Helene shivered. Theo was dead. She was alive. Murdock had the oven door open. Inside, Helene saw three cash boxes. Each box had a label stuck on the lid. One box said "Euros." One box had a dollar sign. The third said "Other." The boxes were locked. She handed the key ring to Sergeant Bolitar. Before he opened the boxes, the big man clasped his hands together, as if he was praying, and lifted his eyes to the ceiling. Helene looked closer. In this light, for the first time, Helene saw the blood stain on the Sergeant's jacket. The stain was two feet long and a foot wide. It darkened the right side of the jacket.

"Would you like me to open the boxes?"

"Please, ma'am. If you would."

Each box was filled with cash. Bolitar chose the box labeled "Other." It contained Swiss francs and British pounds and a roll of gold coins that Bolitar identified as "them French roosters, ma'am." He handed the box of dollars to Helene. He handed the box of Euros to Sonja Vasic. She blushed when she accepted the box. They were talking in French. She seemed to be thanking him. Now the Sergeant was blushing and smiling. Reaching out, Sonja touched the wounded arm.

"Enough talk," Murdock said. "It's time for the hospital. We need two conveyances, one for Young Winchester, one for Fidel. There's a golf cart in the office."

"Some of those meat tables have wheels," Helene said.

Murdock grinned. He saw the irony.

SONJA WENT WITH HELENE to the kitchen to fetch a table with wheels. On the way, she told Helene about the fury of Fidel's rape, and how gentle Sergeant Bolitar had been when he locked Sonja and Young Winchester in the Waste room. "That big man," she said. "He did not hurt me. He seemed to care for me."

They found the table with wheels. They rolled it back to the Waste room, where Young Winchester sat in Theo's golf cart. They were loading Florian Fidel onto the table when Helene heard voices. Footsteps coming from Theo's kitchen. Then a voice called out, "Mateo? Don't shoot, bro."

Jimmy Little Deer came through the door. Behind him were two Indians, both armed, both from the Tribal Police.

"Mateo," Jimmy said. "You look like shit, bro."

Then Jimmy was standing at the golf cart, gripping Young Winchester by the shoulders, talking in Pueblo, or whatever language they spoke. Nodding and grinning, Jimmy shook hands with Murdock. They beamed at each other, old comrades celebrating another victory. Jimmy pumped Helene's hand. Jimmy's eyes lit up in appreciation when he shook hands with Sonja. The eyes narrowed when he nodded at Sergeant Bolitar.

Murdock asked about Theo's hunters. Jimmy said they were under guard, watched over by guys from the Tribal Police. Julio Calderon was on the way up and Jimmy, who hated paperwork, would be happy to give Julio credit for the bust. As Jimmy talked, two Indians entered. Jimmy introduced them, Tribal Police. They wheeled Florian Fidel out. Jimmy sat in the golf cart with Young Winchester. Helene hugged herself. She was shaking again.

When they passed Theo's office, Helene looked in, just to make sure that Theo was still dead. Seeing him, she took a deep breath. Murdock was holding her arm. She patted his hand.

"What was that little stick you took from Theo's desk?"

"Evidence," Murdock said.

"A memory stick, right?"

"Also called a flash drive," Murdock said.

"Flash drive or memory stick," Helene said, "if we take it, then we break the chain of evidence—and it becomes—the damn words are slippery, they keep sliding away. Got it—the word is *inadmissible*."

"If we leave it behind, Sammy will make it disappear."

"Maybe Julio will get here first."

"Sammy's in bed with Theo," Murdock said. "With Theo dead, he'll do whatever he can to cover his ass. The flash drive goes with us."

"I am so tired," Helene said.

OUTSIDE THE SMOKEHOUSE, HELENE saw three pickups and a four-wheeler with big mountain tires. Jimmy Little Deer introduced three more Tribal Policemen. In the lead pickup, Helene saw the blonde hair of Tammy Wellborn. Beside Tammy was Corporal Simpson.

Murdock and Helene led the way to the parking lot. Sonja

and Bolitar followed—she was driving the other golf cart.

"Is that man courting her?" Helene said.

"He said he was going to propose," Murdock said.

"The sergeant gave her a knife," Helene said. "She gave it to Young Winchester. That's how they got loose."

"Looks like she's remembering okay," Murdock said.

THEY WERE IN BOLITAR'S big Mercedes, heading out of the parking lot, when Helene saw headlights coming up the road from the Pueblo. The lead vehicle was an unmarked Crown Vic cruiser. The ranking cop in the cruiser was Julio Calderon, who brandished an arrest warrant for Gerald Ramsay, Jr., based on DNA evidence and Helene's photo of the dead girl at the crime scene. Julio looked at Helene, asked if she was okay.

"Theo raped me," Helene said.

"Jesus Christ," Julio said. "Where is he?"

"Dead," Helene said.

"You hurt?"

"Cuts and bruises," Helene said. "And I'm freezing to death and you're holding my door open."

Wearing his cop's stone face—no expression, don't give anything away—Julio closed Helene's door. Then he climbed into the backseat with Sonja and Bolitar. He asked questions—"How you doing? How bad are you hurt?"—then listened to their answers before climbing out. Julio stood there in the headlight glare, his fists clenching, his chest heaving.

Julio's voice was terse. "Mateo," he said, "get these people to the hospital. I'll phone ahead, let them know you're coming. I'm glad you guys are okay. From this moment on, consider yourselves sequestered. Do not talk to anyone about what went down up here. Do not say one word at the hospital. Not one word to Savage or the press or any state people from Santa Fe. Understood, Mateo?"

"Where is Savage?" Murdock said.

"Down the hill," Julio said, "doing traffic control."

Julio stepped away from the vehicle. Murdock went into gear and they started down the hill, toward Taos. In the backseat, Sonja and Bolitar were murmuring in French.

Past the Pueblo, Helene saw red and blue roof lights—the Taos cops setting up a roadblock at the blinking light intersection. A cop named Jimenez waved them to a stop. Sammy Savage emerged from a dark SUV, stumbled toward them, and motioned for Murdock to lower the car window. Light from his flashlight forced Murdock to turn away. The light played across Helene, then powered into the backseat.

"Foxy! Where the fuck you think you're going?"

"The hospital. Orders from Captain Calderon."

"This is my town. I give the orders."

"Miss Steinbeck's wounded, Sammy. She's bleeding—probably got a concussion. She needs a doctor."

"He's already up there, isn't he? That fucking Calderon is up there, taking over, marking his territory like a dog pissing on rocks?" Then he said, "What about my buddy Ulster? Been trying to raise him on the sat-phone. What does he say about this invasion?"

"Better check with Captain Calderon," Murdock said.

Behind the bluster, Sammy Savage was shrinking. He kept trying to loom large, but then he would recede, like a man walking backwards out of dimming light into deep shadow. He whispered something to Officer Jimenez, who waved his hand at Murdock. The signal to drive on through. The last thing Helene heard was Savage on his sat-phone, yelling about closing the crime scene.

58
Murdock

THE TAOS HOSPITAL WAS one roundabout exit off Highway 585—Paseo del Canon East, before it enters Taos Canyon. When they arrived, Murdock saw the ER team waiting outside. There were gurneys for Helene, the Serbian girl, Young Winchester, and Sergeant Bolitar. The doctor in charge of the triage was a handsome, strong-featured Latina woman named Cisneros. She knew Young Winchester, she had seen the Serbian girl on TV, and she had bought a copy of Helene's book. The doctor's eyes glittered with speculation when she saw Sergeant Bolitar.

Murdock sat in the ER with Helene, staying by her side—worried, hating that bastard Theo, grateful that they had come through—until Helene's doctor ran him off. A nurse gave Murdock pills and an injection that dulled the pain. He lay on a narrow white table while they cleaned up his cuts, took pictures of his battered feet. They sewed up his butt where Tammy Wellborn's glass-tipped arrow had hit.

One nurse asked a question, "You been wearing those weird barefoot shoes or what? They got these little finger-gloves for the toes, huh?"

When they left him alone, Murdock dozed. He woke up from a dream—back in the jungle, his feet being eaten by giant army ants—and his mouth tasted like camel piss. On a shelf in the bathroom, he found a cheap blue toothbrush and a mini-tube of toothpaste. He brushed and still felt unclean. Theo's dirt was getting to Murdock.

He found Helene in a third-floor room with two beds. Helene, speaking in a voice loopy with pain-killers, told him about the costumes, wearing the silver dress, the slaps, the latex gloves, the hatpin, the Q and A session where she had played the role of Theo's mummy, her feeling of triumph when he had lost his erection, her drug-laced fear that Murdock was dead. Her voice was shaking.

"In my mind," Helene said, "I kept seeing you lying on a rock filled with a hundred arrows. You were trapped inside a cage of yellow crime-scene ribbons. That's why I fought to get loose. If you were dead, I had nothing to lose. Theo was a dragon. I had to kill him. One more thing."

"What?"

"When Julio comes, let me answer the questions."

"You feel up to that?" Murdock said.

"Just don't ride to the rescue, okay?"

"I hear a plan being set up," Murdock said.

"I'm gonna make him a deal," Helene said. "One that leaves us out of the great media onrush."

Watching Helene, hearing her voice, being with her, Murdock was amazed. This woman had been battered, bruised, abused, raped, wounded, driven close to death—and yet she was ready to take on the head cop and his questions. She was thinking ahead. She needed to nail things down with Julio before the news hit the media.

"You're a wonder," Murdock said.

"Drusilla called," Helene said. "She knows about my feet needing rest, no tripping around town, so she invited us to stay at her house. She was in Albuquerque, at some Sunday event.

She saw something about Angel's Nest on TV. She said that she dumped Theo the night of the party, because he had ignored her and paid too much attention to Marie-Claire. Can you get me some coffee?"

Murdock went to find coffee. When he came back to the room, he found Julio Calderon sitting in a chair, looking weary, shoulders rounded and gray hair mussed. Julio kept yawning as he worked the buttons on his electronic gizmo. Julio asked if Murdock was okay. Murdock nodded, took the other chair, and waited. Silence is strange stuff. If there's no sound, your ears strain to hear something. Murdock heard himself breathing. He heard Julio's thumbs jabbing tiny keys. He heard Helene's heart beating. He looked over and saw that she was already watching him, her face a mask. Murdock had fallen in love with a woman of mystery. Julio started with motive, standard cop stuff.

"So," he said. "One more time. What were you guys doing up there? At Angel's Nest? What was the plan?"

Before Helene could answer, her dad came into the room. Frank Steinbeck had Helene's nose, her generous mouth, the same wide-set eyes. He greeted Julio like they were old friends. He shook hands with Murdock, but did not make small talk.

"Dad," Helene said, "could you and Murdock leave me alone with Julio?"

"You sure about that?"

"Julio's not only a top cop," Helene said, "he's also a gentleman."

LEAVING THE ROOM, MURDOCK led Frank Steinbeck to the visitor's lounge. The guy at the coffee kiosk was happy to make two Americanos. Murdock paid, left a good tip. They sat side-by-side. Frank Steinbeck wore a sharp wool suit, a blue shirt, a red necktie. His hair was thick and going from gray to white.

He took a sip of coffee. Questions on the way, a father

looking out for his daughter. "How you doing?"

"Better now," Murdock said.

"Are your feet chopped up like my daughter's?"

"Yes," Murdock said, "but I lasted longer up there because I've been running barefoot."

"How long did she make it on that trail?"

"Half an hour. Things were moving fast by then."

"Whose idea was it to split up?"

"Her idea," Murdock said. "She said she could handle Theo. My job was rescuing her. Before I could do that—rescue her—I had to cut Theo's troops down to size."

"You're sure he's dead? You saw it with your own eyes?"

"When I came through the door," Murdock said, "she was sticking a hatpin into his eye socket. That's six inches of steel aimed at the brain. He used his last ten seconds to gloat. Then he was gone."

"What's going to happen next?"

"She'll make a deal with Julio."

"He came onto her, didn't he?"

"Julio takes a run at anything female," Murdock said. "But your daughter told him to go away. He's behaved ever since."

"She speaks highly of you."

"She's a wonder, Mr. Steinbeck."

"Call me Frank, okay?"

"Yes, sir, Frank."

"Do you love her?"

"Yes, I do."

"You guys thinking marriage?"

"I am," Murdock said. "Not sure about her."

"Helene's tried marriage twice. Did she tell you?"

"She mentioned it," Murdock said. "No details."

"Helene takes after her mother," Frank Steinbeck said. "She was a no-nonsense woman. She passed that trait along."

"You're a lucky man."

"Ready to get back? Maybe we can eavesdrop on the interrogation."

MURDOCK HAD KNOWN A few men like Frank Steinbeck. Some in the Army, some when he was a cop. They were tough men, resilient, smart, honest. Guys who would cover your back. As they approached Helene's room, Julio Calderon was making his exit. He stopped to shake hands. His smile qualified as rueful, like he'd been out-maneuvered.

"I don't want her in court," Julio said. "That Ulster *cabron* is dead, no way we can prosecute him, so we're going after the live ones, starting with that college kid, Gerry Ramsay Junior, because Murdock and your daughter gathered DNA at the crime scene. Did you have a hand in that, Mr. Steinbeck?"

"Will I have to testify?"

"No, sir," Julio said. "It stops with me."

"I played a small part," Frank Steinbeck said.

"But the D.A. might need you, on that Sophie Orff info."

"I feel like a cop again."

Julio shook hands with them. He told them something they already knew—Helene Steinbeck was one hell of a woman. They watched Julio walk away. When they came into the room, Helene was staring at nothing. She brightened when she saw them.

"Did my dad ask about your intentions?" she said to Murdock.

"He did," Murdock said. "What did you work out with Julio?"

"I hit the high spots on my time with Theo," Helene said. "Julio turned off his little machine; he did not take notes. If there's any other way to get the cannibal story out, Julio won't force me to testify. But—"

"But what?"

Helene said, "Agent Savage closed Angel's Nest—no one gets in there unless cleared through him. Julio told us Savage was acting crazy. The guy gave Julio a court order stating that nothing from the crime scene could be removed. So all that stuff in the Smokehouse—the ovens, the storage boxes, Theo's closet—is' out of play. Did I just say that? I sound like someone else. I am so tired."

"Murdock's the angle guy," Frank Steinbeck said. "I bet he's already on it."

"Private eyes never sleep," Murdock said.

Murdock kissed Helene's forehead. He shook her dad's hand and then left them alone, Frank Steinbeck sitting on the edge of her bed. They were murmuring.

Murdock walked the halls, checking on Sonja and Young Winchester, who were both sleeping. When he asked about Sergeant Bolitar, the nurse said he had left.

"I wheeled him out to that big Mercedes," the nurse said. Her eyes brightened at the memory, and Murdock wondered what had attracted her more—the big man himself or his impressive ride. Both, he guessed.

59
Murdock

THE HOSPITAL BED WAS hard and Murdock was stiff. His feet hurt. He wanted to tuck Helene into the Jeep and hightail it out of town. He wanted to escape what he knew was coming when the media got a whiff of what had gone down on Angel Mountain—cannibalism, Theo's manhunts, white slavery, fat cats driving gas-hog cars, reporters in your face, cameras and microphones—enough to keep the CNN screens full for two weeks.

Before first light, Murdock was up hunting coffee. He bribed the cooks for three cups and a ceramic pot. Rode the elevator to Three, where he found Frank Steinbeck guarding Helene's door.

"How are you doing?" Frank said.

"Stiff and sore," Murdock said. "How did Helene sleep?"

"Couple of nightmares. Called out for you a few times. You got plans for today?"

"If you'll stay on the door," Murdock said, "I thought I'd run over to Angel Fire, check on an airplane used by our buddy Florian Fidel."

"He's the white slaver guy who grabbed your friend's daughter, right?"

"Fidel was flown in here—he needs a plane to transport Theo's prime cuts—so there's gotta be a pilot. I want to get to him before he hears the morning news."

"You better hustle," Frank said.

"How are you doing?"

Frank Steinbeck held up his cellphone. He grinned at Murdock and his eyes crinkled at the edges. "I called a couple buddies for backup. Retired cops like me. We'll rotate the door-guard duty, keep the media circus at bay."

"I remember," Murdock said, "when a cop had a couple days before getting ground into hamburger by pundits and talk show hosts."

"Good times," Frank said. "Thanks for the coffee. I'll tell her you were here."

MURDOCK FOUND THE PILOT of Fidel's Lear Jet sipping his early morning wake-up coffee at the Angel Fire Ski Lodge. The pilot's name was Eddie Flack. He was a couple years younger than Murdock, curly red hair, a small pot belly, an uneasy grin. Eddie was a guy who'd been around, who knew how to handle himself.

In the corridor, Eddie swung on Murdock and wound up on his ass, his nose dripping blood. Murdock fastened Eddie's wrists with a green zip tie, then used the key card taken from Fidel's wallet. In a fancy briefcase, Murdock found girl-photos and cash. One of the photos showed Sonja Vasic looking good in her tennis togs. On Fidel's laptop, Murdock found a string of messages in Spanish, from someone who signed his name BKL. Murdock brought out the photo of Barbi Bellini. Eddie Flack nodded. He had seen Barbi Bellini in Guadalajara, at the home of Señor Eduardo Bakul. Before leaving Fidel's room, Murdock grabbed some underwear—Fidel wore Calvin Klein bikinis, skimpy and tight to display the crown jewels—and two pairs of socks.

BACK IN TAOS, MURDOCK got a lecture on proper police procedure when he turned Eddie and the briefcase over to Julio Calderon.

"Goddamnit, Mateo," Julio said. "I can't use tainted evidence in court."

"I don't want Eddie," Murdock said. "I want Barbi Bellini. And this guy Bakul has her."

"She could be dead."

"Yeah," Murdock said. "And she could be alive."

"How you gonna get her back?"

"We'll buy her back," Murdock said. "Maybe throw in the airplane and pilot to sweeten the deal."

"What do I get—my ass in a sling?"

"Your picture in the paper," Murdock said, "handing the Bellini girl over to her grateful dad. I can see the headlines now—'Gubernatorial Candidate Calderon Rescues Missing Maiden from White Slavers.' "

"Speaking of headlines, we got the media calling already."

"Let's grab Rocky and talk to Florian Fidel," Murdock said.

"Why should you be there?"

"Fidel's my buddy," Murdock said. "We have an understanding. I want him to talk to this guy who's got Barbi."

"What have you got cooking, Mateo?"

"A present for Fidel."

FLORIAN FIDEL, WEARING AN orange jailbird jumpsuit, sat across the table from Julio Calderon, representing the State Police, and Rocky Benitez, the prosecutor. Fidel's hair was a tangle—it needed a wash and a set. His face had worry lines and his eyes were red around the edges, as if he'd been crying. He complained of cold feet and begged them to get him some socks. Fidel's lawyer, a thin man from Denver, sat on Fidel's right. His name was Rebus Hodge and he wore a western cut suit with a string tie and a silky shirt with pearl-snap buttons.

Murdock sat at the end of the table, on Fidel's left, his chair tilted back, arms crossed. The plastic bag with the socks and underwear was on the floor beside his chair. The lawyers sparred first. Rebus Hodge wanted the white slavery charge to go away. Since his client had been wounded and then held against his will, he was bringing suit against Murdock, Helene, Sonja, and Young Winchester. Watching the lawyers fart around, Murdock felt the clock ticking. Murdock believed in truth and justice. He also believed in revenge, an eye for an eye. He'd paid his dues by testifying in more than a hundred trials—and seen guilty defendants walk. Murdock caught Julio's eye and nodded.

Julio cleared his throat and said, "Guys."

The lawyers stopped in mid-sentence, and Julio said, "Extradition."

"What?"

"Mexico wants him back," Julio said. "After Mexico, then Colombia. They need U.S. dollars down there to finance the fight against the drug lords. Señor Fidel is soft. A Bogota jail will turn him into mincemeat."

Rebus Hodge turned to Fidel, whose face was pale green. His eyes watered. When he shook his fists at Murdock, the manacles clicked together.

Rebus Hodge wanted to be alone with his client. He asked for the room and Julio shook his head. Rebus took his client into the corner. Gripped his arm and slammed him with some tough-talking words. Florian Fidel was having trouble breathing, but he nodded okay and they came back to the table. The deal they wanted was no extradition in exchange for a reduced sentence if Fidel pleaded guilty to attempted kidnapping.

Fidel agreed, but his teeth were chattering now, and he kept reaching down, an awkward motion because of the manacles, to warm his cold feet. Murdock brought out the plastic sack and emptied it onto the table. Fidel made a grab for the socks, but Murdock snatched them away.

"One more thing," Murdock said.

The lawyers started in again. Julio frowned at Murdock. Fidel nudged his lawyer. "Amigo," he said. "What does this cocksucker want?"

Murdock wanted two things. First, he wanted Fidel to testify against Theo Ulster. To explain how Theo led the manhunt for Murdock and Helene Steinbeck. And be sure to mention that it started out with eight armed hunters against two barefoot quarry. Second, he wanted a telephone introduction to the man who was holding Barbi Bellini.

"Do those two things for me," Murdock said, "and you get the socks."

FOR THE DEPOSITION, THEY called in a court recorder. Murdock waited a half hour while Florian Fidel answered questions about his business dealings with Theo Ulster, buying girls, selling them in Mexico and South America. Fidel did not see himself as a white slaver—the girls he transported were always well-treated. Then he answered a second set of questions about Theo's manhunt. The hunters he remembered were the blonde girl—he called her *La Rubia*—the fat man, Gerry Something, and the young soldier, Corporal Simpson. Theo Ulster, of course, and yes, perhaps he was crazy. He remembered two young men and a woman, the wife of the fat man. She was from Brazil, Fidel said, and very beautiful. Seven hunters plus Fidel made eight armed hunters.

THE PHONE CALL TO Señor Bakul, the big man in Guadalajara, was conducted in Spanish first, then English. They used Julio's Smart Phone, on the speaker. Fidel talked to two men and a woman before he got to Bakul. One man growled, the other chirped. The woman spoke with a low-level control. After a moment of waiting, Bakul came on. He did not address Fidel. Instead, he asked to speak to Murdock.

Bakul's English was excellent, his voice sounded educated. He explained that the *Americana*—he meant Barbi Bellini— was unhappy, as was Bakul. For a price, he would let her go. They tossed numbers around and came up with forty thousand. They set Saturday as the day for the transfer. They would fly down and be guided to the home of Bakul. There was no mention of the pilot, the plane, or the thigh-meat of dead girls. As he listened to Bakul talk—his calm, educated voice—Murdock felt like he was in a movie, black and white, a ghost moving across a surreal landscape toward a castle that shimmered in the fog. He was curious about this guy Bakul.

"Bring a woman," Bakul said. "*La Americana* hates all men, including her father."

There was a soft, muffled click and Bakul's voice went away. Murdock had to phone Charley Bellini for the money. He shook hands with Julio and Rocky, then headed for the door.

Fidel said, "Where are my fucking socks?"

Murdock was at the door. He reached into the plastic sack. Grinning, he tossed the socks to Fidel, one pair at a time, spinning in the air. Fidel scooted his chair around so he could pull on the socks. Murdock still held the bikini underwear, an apt symbol for a white slaver who wore sexy clothes and sampled the merchandise. One more contemptuous toss, and the undies hit Fidel's cheek and fell to the table.

"Cocksucker," Fidel said. "*Pendejo, pelon!*"

60

Murdock

EARLY SATURDAY MORNING, WITH court in recess for the weekend, Murdock and Helene and Julio Calderon sat in Fidel's Lear Jet while Eddie Flack left the Angel Fire airfield and headed south across the border. In his backpack, Murdock carried forty thousand dollars in cash, from Charley Bellini in Seattle.

At the Guadalajara airport, they followed a DEA guy to a black Suburban. The vehicle had leather seats, tinted windows, and a ceiling mount gun rack that held three Ak-47s and two Uzis. Under his blousy Guayabera shirt, the DEA guy packed a Sig Sauer in a belt holster. Two SUVs with blacked-out windows trailed the Suburban through the streets to the home of Eduardo Bakul. Five minutes and a body-scan to get through the front gate. They checked the rucksack that held the money.

AT BAKUL'S MASSIVE FRONT door—it was decorated with Baroque filigree, leafy vines of pale metal—the guards handed them over to a forty-something woman in a business suit. "I'm Mrs. Lund," she said. "I'm Eduardo's sister. Please follow me."

Mrs. Lund had smooth skin, dark hair that she wore in a bun, and a confident walk. She left them in a library, where they found three walls of books and a picture window overlooking the peanut-shaped pool. It was decorated with four girls—two in bikinis, one buck-naked, and one who looked pregnant. The girls were tall and twenty-something, like Barbi Bellini. They moved like athletes.

"Good genes," Helene said.

"We got a pattern here," Murdock said.

"Yeah," Helene said. "Eugenics by Bakul."

Mrs. Lund came back with Señor Bakul. Murdock had expected a short guy with a fat neck and greasy chops, a guy who had bad teeth and farted a lot. But Bakul was the picture of suave. Tall and lean, with blond hair and blue eyes. He shook hands and invited them to sit. He sent Eddie Flack, who seemed right at home, out with Mrs. Lund. Bakul did not leer at Helene. He asked about their trip. Would they like coffee? Water? Alcohol?

Murdock got coffee. Helene got hot tea. Julio Calderon got a Coke. Bakul took Murdock aside.

"You came for the Bellini?" he said.

"Yes."

"And you have the money?"

"In the rucksack."

"Is it all there? The whole forty thousand?"

"Would you like to count it?"

"Do you vouchsafe its contents?"

"We counted it three times."

"Is the news from the states accurate? The man Ulster is dead?"

"Yes, sir."

"And the inventory?"

"The cops have it."

"What sort of man is your client, señor? The father of Bellini?"

"Charley Bellini is a self-made man. His folks were immigrants. He's got a construction company. He wants his daughter back."

"May I say something?"

"Shoot," Murdock said.

"When Bellini arrived, I was shocked to learn that she was already with child. My purpose in life does not include rearing the offspring of another male. Her health began to deteriorate and I became concerned. I am therefore satisfied with our transaction—all's well that ends well, as they say, and if there was more time, I would request a longer chat with you—but there is an anxious father waiting, so perhaps another time."

Bakul turned away from Murdock and said something in Spanish. Murdock caught one word, "*Bruja*." Murdock heard female voices and the click of heels on stone. Then Mrs. Lund came in with Barbi Bellini. She wore a loose yellow blouse that did not conceal her pregnancy. Her lips were too red, her eyes too dark. She shuffled along like she was hurting. She kept her eyes down as she approached Bakul. Her smile was forced. Her hands were shaking. She had not seen Murdock yet.

Bakul said, "The money, señor."

Murdock handed over the rucksack. Bakul passed it to Mrs. Lund, who passed it to a twenty-something guy in a suit. Bakul's face was bleak stone. He spoke to Barbi in Spanish. It sounded like a lesson from Spanish 101.

"How are you?"

"I am fine. And how are you?"

"I am fine. Thank you. What is your name?"

"My name is *La Americana*. I am called *La Bruja*."

"Do you recognize this *hombre*? This man who has come for you?"

Barbi raised her head. Her eyes swept the room. She saw Murdock, then looked at Helene. Then she looked back at Murdock.

"Uncle Matt? What are you—"

Bakul took Barbi's arm. She did not resist. He handed her off to Murdock. Murdock remembered hugs from the past, but there were no hugs today. Barbi was keeping her distance. She was still inside the house of Bakul. In her mind, she still belonged to him.

Helene said, "Hello, Barbi. I'm Helene."

The two women hugged. Murdock watched them walk out. He had unfinished business with Bakul. He didn't know what kind of business. The guy didn't say much. He let things speak for him. Things like the house, the gate, the metal detector, the goons with guns, the immaculate Mrs. Lund, the heifers hanging out at the pool.

Bakul spoke, "You and I, señor. We did not make the world."

"That's for sure."

"You were smart to bring the woman."

"Just following orders, señor."

"My airplane is at your disposal. And sometime I would like to get your perspective on the Ulster business and also Señor Florian Fidel. This is not the time. Mrs. Lund will accompany you to the airport. She will give you a card for her email. A pleasure, señor."

They shook hands, Murdock and Bakul. Bakul and Julio exchanged a few words in very fast Spanish. Mrs. Lund appeared. Bakul exited, talking on his cellphone. Mrs. Lund rode with them to the airport. The Lear Jet had a new pilot at the controls.

Before she left, Mrs. Lund handed over a business card with an email address. "My brother wishes to stay in contact," she said. "He finds you both very interesting."

ON THE FLIGHT BACK, Murdock and Julio had the front seats. Helene sat in the back with Barbi. When they landed, Barbi's dad, Charley Bellini, was waiting with an ambulance. At the hospital, Charley asked Murdock about the trip.

"He let her go," Murdock said. "Savor that. She's in shock.

She needs time and soft hands."

"Why didn't you kill that cocksucker?"

"It wasn't a movie, Charley. They had the guns."

"If I ever see him, I'll kill him."

"Go to Barbi. Tell her you love her. Give her time."

61

Helene

THE METAL DETECTOR WAS broken, so Helene and Murdock got patted down at the courthouse entrance by two cops. A line of hopefuls curled away from the door, past the TV vans.

It was opening day of The People v. Gerald Ramsay Junior, the charge was homicide, and the Taos County courtroom was packed—spectators drawn by the rumors of cannibal activity on Angel Mountain. The trial had pulled the media spotlight away from Theo's accomplices—the sleek women, the powerful men, and hangers-on like Corporal Simpson. He was in jail, in a cell next to that of Florian Fidel, waiting to be extradited back to England on an assault charge.

Helene sat beside Murdock, behind the railing and behind the prosecutor's table, where Rocky Benitez took notes on a yellow pad. To her right, at the defense table, Helene could see Gerry Junior, aka G.J., in a jacket and tie. G.J.'s arm was in a sling, underlining the damage from Murdock's .45 slug, and he had walked in on crutches—part of Crane's strategy to twist the truth, casting G.J. as the victim shot by Murdock instead of the stone-hearted killer of Sophie Orff.

Because Helene had found the body, she testified first. And Crane, with his little death-smile, shredded her testimony. Using her photos from the scene—the corpse, Gerry Junior reeling from Murdock's gunshot—Crane made Murdock look like the perpetrator, the man who should be on trial.

"This is your photo of Mr. Ramsay," Crane said. "Please describe what you see."

"He was just about to shoot an arrow when—"

"Just describe what you see. No conjecture please."

"He's bending over."

"And can you tell the court why?"

"He'd just been shot, but …"

Crane grinned, stepped away from the witness stand. Helene felt awful. Crane's voice echoed through the courtroom. "May it please the court, the reason for his bending over—so aptly put by the witness—was that he had been shot by Miss Steinbeck's companion, Mr. Murdock. The forensic evidence on this shooting has already been entered and tagged. No further questions."

Sally Jo, a police sergeant and an expert climber, was the next witness for the prosecution. She had led the forensic team to the crime scene. In his cross-examination, Mordecai Crane kept asking Sally Jo to speak up. Her voice stayed soft, her answers sounded tentative. In a cryptic tone, Crane summed up Sally Jo's testimony. "So in summary, Sergeant, your team was tardy arriving at the scene, where you found a mutilated body, no alleged arrows, no murder weapon, and questionable DNA?"

"That's not what I said."

"Did your team find even a single alleged arrowhead?"

"No, but—"

"No further questions, your Honor."

Crane floated to his table and sat down. He was in control and loving it. The Judge asked Rocky Benitez if he wanted to cross-examine. Sally Jo sat there waiting. Her face was deathly pale. She was not up to more questions. As Rocky stood up to answer, there was a commotion at the door.

Helene Steinbeck recognized the voice of Sammy Savage.

"Hey, Murdock," she said, "it's your old jungle pal."

"Out from under his rock," Murdock said.

They turned around. Sammy was already inside, flanked by the two cops, Ruiz and Jimenez. Ruiz was a new hire, young, good-looking, and over-serious. Jimenez was older, heavier, a cop who used his badge as an excuse to bully people. They were going through the motions of a pat-down and Sammy was grumbling about it. For his courtroom visit, Sammy appeared in a jacket and tie.

The Judge rapped her gavel. Her name was Esmerelda Quisneros. She was mid-fifties, a local girl from Questa, just up the road from Taos, with a rags-to-riches story—working her way through school, cutting a path for women in judgeships across the greater southwest, awards, scholarships, connections—that gave her icon status in the media. They called her Judge Q—Quisneros from Questa—and her first order of the day had been to ban any use of the word "cannibalism." It was an inflammatory term, she said, and therefore misleading. This was a murder trial, not a three-ring circus.

"Agent Savage?" she said.

"Yes, your Honor?"

"What is the purpose of interrupting these proceedings?"

"New evidence has surfaced, your Honor."

"New evidence pertaining to the case before us?"

"Permission to approach the bench?" Sammy said.

The Judge said very well. She asked the two attorneys to approach the bench. Mordecai Crane had lost his smarmy smile. He got up and looked back at the doorway, where the cops were poking Sammy's chest, checking for weapons. Nothing inside the jacket, but when Ruiz reached down to do the ankle check, Sammy shoved him away. Ruiz called after him. Sammy kept walking. He half-turned, gave Ruiz the thumbs up and lumbered toward the front of the room.

"Did you see that?" Helene said.

"Didn't perform the old ankle check," Murdock said.

"Sammy looks deranged," Helene said, "maybe even suicidal."

"Maybe now's our chance."

Murdock reached into his jacket pocket and brought out the red memory stick from Theo Ulster's desk in the office at Angel's Nest. He held the stick in his palm, grinned at Helene.

"No way," Helene said.

"What I need from you, Steinbeck, is a tiny distraction."

"Who am I distracting?"

"Eyes of the crowd," Murdock said. "Where's the nearest gun?"

Helene looked to her right, where Farley Doran, blonde and muscular, leaned against the wall, his weight-room arms folded across his chest. Doran was thirty-something, new on the force—he'd transferred in from Albuquerque—and getting a lot of appraising looks from women. Farley grinned at Helene. His message was sexual.

"Farley Doran," she said, "against the wall. Packing a Glock."

"He digs you, Steinbeck."

"So?"

"Gotta admire a man with classy taste."

Sammy Savage gave Murdock the thumbs-up as he passed. He had on aviator shades, so Helene could not see his eyes, but the skin on his face was stretched way too tight, and the smile looked forced. He was wobbling as he walked, a little unsteady, maybe from drugs or booze or both. Sammy stumbled, made a face, caught himself on a chair, went down to one knee, and time froze.

MURDOCK SAID, "ANKLE-GUN!" AND started for Sammy.

Helene went the other way, toward Farley Doran, who wasn't watching Sammy because now he was making flirty eyes at a pretty girl in the fourth row. Helene got right in Farley's face.

"Savage has a gun!" she said.

Farley said, "No chance, baby." Then his eyes got big and he said, "Fuck it. Get outta my way." He shoved Helene aside, took a step forward, rested his hand on the butt of his weapon and called out. "Agent Savage, you stay right there. Let me see your hands. In the air, sir! Right fucking now or—"

And Sammy, holding the ankle gun, shot Farley Doran.

The movement was jerky, the gun-arm wavering. Sammy did not wait to see Farley fall, but instead turned on Mordecai Crane, who had joined the Judge, using the bench as cover. Sammy's voice was gravelly. "Crane, you slimy cocksucker, where's my hundred grand?"

Sammy fired again, shot number two, the explosion booming. Women screamed. Men bellowed. Mordecai Crane sagged down behind the Judge's bench. Sally Jo Catton slipped out of the witness chair.

Rocky Benitez threw something at Sammy. Sammy dodged, grinned, fired again, shot number three. Sammy's big hands made the gun seem toy-like. Rocky was behind the Judge's bench.

Next to Helene, Farley Doran slid down the wall. His weapon, a Glock Nine, was in his holster, strapped down. He was right-handed and he fell on his right side, burying the gun under two hundred and thirty pounds of weight-room beef. Helene, sweating now, tried to roll him over.

The door cops were blocked by spectators trying to get out. Sammy fired again, shot number four. Ruiz grabbed his shoulder. "Jesus, he shot me!"

Helene saw Murdock tackling Sammy. The gun went off again, shot number five, breaking a window, and glass shards fell. She could not see Murdock—he was lost in the crowd.

SPECTATORS CHARGING THE DOOR jostled Helene. She grabbed a man's sleeve. Asked for help moving Farley. The man was middle-aged, with a mustache and anxious eyes.

He grunted as he rolled Farley over. "Big beefy cop," he said. Helene unsnapped the safety strap, the Glock came free. The weapon felt good in her hands. She stood up, back to the wall. A woman holding a child blocked Helene's shot. Murdock was on the floor.

But Sammy was on his feet again, swaying back and forth, aiming at Murdock, his voice low, burning with anger. "Goddamn you, Foxy. Why didn't you back off? Why did you come to me with that fucking corpse? Was that fucker Ulster paying you, too?"

The Judge flew out from behind the bench. Her hair was tousled, her face angry, her robes flying as she charged Sammy Savage, waving her gavel. Sammy didn't shoot her; he just knocked her sideways with one swing of his arm. She crashed into a row of chairs. Murdock stood up, not straight, but hunkered over. His ear was bloody. He held out his hand to Sammy. "Give it up, man." The little gun pointed right at Murdock. Helene remembered five shots. The gun was an automatic, at least six in the magazine.

Helene did not say Freeze.

She did not give Sammy a warning.

Murdock was between Helene and Sammy.

HELENE HELD THE GLOCK with both hands—the approved FBI shooting stance, arms aligned with shoulders to form the isosceles triangle for stability. She had learned to shoot from her dad, the NYPD cop, who taught her about guns while her mother said "Tsk, tsk," because shooting was for men, not women. Murdock was still in the way.

"Murdock!" she cried. "Get out of the—"

And then Sally Jo Catton rose up, an avenging angel gripping her hospital cane with two frail hands. Sally Jo swung at Sammy. The cane missed his head, but clipped his shoulder. Sammy turned on Sally Jo, aimed the pistol. "You skinny-assed bitch! You were always sneaking—"

It was the moment for Helene's shot. She looked along the barrel, lining up the front blade in the little V, wishing that the borrowed weapon was equipped with Hex Sites—so much quicker—telling herself to get out of the way, let the trigger finger do the work.

The Glock kicked in her hands. Across the room, Sammy Savage torqued to his left. Helene had aimed for the chest, the body shot, hoping he was not wearing kevlar, but the shot had hit the left shoulder. She shot again, cooler now, more deliberate. Sammy went down. Murdock gave Helene a look. It felt like admiration, that little grin of his.

MURDOCK WAS ON HIS knees, leaning over Sammy. The Judge was hurt, calling for help. Helene saw Murdock slide the red memory stick into Sammy's chest pocket. Sally Jo was on her knees, blocking the Judge's view of Murdock and Sammy. Rocky Benitez was behind the Judge's bench, holding onto Mordecai Crane. There was no sign of G.J. or his crutches. Sally Jo was whispering, the Judge was nodding.

"Get the medics," Rocky said. "Crane took a hit."

"Where's your defendant?" Helene said.

"Looks like he split," Rocky said. "Can you guys get him back?"

Sally Jo was on her feet now, talking on her cellphone, calling for help. A sheriff's deputy came through the door, followed by an EMT person in a blue uniform, carrying a medical kit—white, with a red cross. Helene squatted down beside Murdock. Sammy's ankle-gun was a Diamondback nine, thin, no-nonsense, deadly.

"Nice tackle, big boy."

"Nice shooting, Steinbeck."

"I was counting the shots," she said. "The gun had six in the magazine, one in the chamber. He fired five. That meant there were two left."

Murdock squeezed her hand. Someone tapped her shoulder

and she looked up to see Sally Jo, who said, "Help me find Ramsay."

Murdock said, "Go. Make big speed."

HELENE AND SALLY JO found Gerry Ramsay Junior in the parking lot with his parents, standing next to the Hummer with Texas plates. Marina Ramsay's face had no color. She looked shattered. Gerry Ramsay Senior had lost his banker's bluster. No one said anything. They marched Gerry Junior and his crutches back inside, handed him over to the sheriff's deputy. They stood with Rocky Benitez, watching the Judge being wheeled out on a gurney, talking to Sally Jo. Two men in blue coveralls starting lining up the chairs. A woman in blue came in pushing a mop bucket on wheels.

"THE JUDGE WANTS A meeting," Rocky said. "You three guys, Mordecai Crane, and yours truly. As soon as she gets settled at the hospital. Maybe this afternoon, maybe this evening. She told me to tell you."

"What's up?" Murdock said.

"Something about new evidence," Rocky said. "But I tell you what—the ass she saves first will be her own."

62

Helene

THEY MET WITH CHARLEY Bellini in the Anaconda Bar at the El Monte Lodge on Kit Carson Road. The Lodge had a pricey feel, luxurious, the best that money could buy. The chairs were welcoming. From here Helene watched the snake sculpture coiled along the ceiling. A waiter in a white coat brought coffee and Danish. Charley Bellini was dressed in business casual—khakis and a sweater, loafers with no sox—and his smile was filled with thanks.

Helene liked his handshake, solid, no hidden messages. She didn't like the reason she was here—to tell Charley what she knew about Barbi's stay with Eduardo Bakul—but she understood. This was woman's work. Barbi had talked to Helene on the plane from Guadalajara.

"She won't tell me anything," Charley said. "She's my kid, but I ask her something and she turns away. My wife's got two sick kids at home. And she's taking care of her own mother, so she can't get down here. The docs say Barbi might get discharged next week, no specific day. Thanks for coming."

"You sure you want to hear this?"

"I gotta know," Charley said.

Helene sighed. "Okay. Well, they grabbed your daughter at the art colony. The director let them into her room. He worked for Theo Ulster, who worked for Florian Fidel—he's the man in jail—who worked for this man Bakul. They flew her to Guadalajara. She was drugged on the flight. When the drugs wore off, she met Bakul's children—three pretty little girls, like a welcoming committee. They spoke English, Italian, German, and some Russian. The oldest girl told Barbi she wanted to be a mathematician.

"It was a household of women. There were two Brits and two Russians. The Brits were swimmers. One of the Russians was a tennis player on the way up, the other was a standby for the Soviet Olympic team. All the harem girls were Barbi's height or taller. They had lovely skin, Barbi said, and thick healthy hair. Both Brits were pregnant—they got treated very well. A special diet, dinner with Bakul, where he inquired about their families and bloodlines. Barbi was the newest addition to the harem."

"Jesus," Charley said. "Listening to you, I got to thinking—Barbi's five-eight. She swam in high school, went to college on a tennis scholarship. What's going down with this guy?"

Helene said, "Your daughter told me that sex with Bakul was regular and uneventful. He never hurt her. He didn't try to frighten her. He was calm, she said, and businesslike. He seemed to be more interested in one of the Russian girls. She laughed at his jokes. And she was eager to learn Spanish. Everything changed when Barbi started throwing up. Bakul brought in a doctor. The pregnancy test showed positive, and Barbi's household status took a dive. Bakul had three girls; he wanted a boy-child, but he refused to spend his resources on another man's offspring. When she lost status, Barbi got depressed. She was certain he would kill her. She moped around, tried to study Spanish. She was hungry all the time, a mother-to-be eating for two, and throwing up. Her only friend was Mrs. Lund, Bakul's sister, who managed the girls. One day, out of the blue, Mrs. Lund told Barbi to dress for a trip. Barbi threw up, big time. She knew she was dead. She told me when she saw Murdock in the library, she thought she had died and was looking at an angel."

"That bastard," Charley said. "If I ever see him, I'll cut off his nuts."

"You've got your girl back," Helene said, laying a hand on his shoulder. "She needs you. She needs love and one hundred and ten percent of your deepest fatherly understanding."

Charley hauled out his big checkbook. He wrote out two checks, both in the amount of $25,000. One check was for Murdock, one for Helene.

THEY RETURNED TO DRUSILLA'S, where Helene found an email message from Sonja Vasic. She was back home in Monte Carlo, applying to universities for graduate work. Berkeley, Stanford, and the University of Washington. Helene told Murdock. He was lying on the bed with his eyes closed and a blanket over his feet.

"Anthropology, right?"

"She's switched to medicine," Helene said.

"Smart girl."

"Yes," Helene said. "And very beautiful."

Murdock opened his eyes and looked at Helene.

"Steinbeck," he said. "Come over here. Let's take a nap."

I love it when you call me Steinbeck."

63

Helene

IT WAS EARLY EVENING when they drove back to the hospital, where they huddled with the Judge in a staff conference room. White walls, a long table, a plastic water pitcher, plastic glasses, and a medium-size computer monitor connected to a laptop. Helene sat between Sally Jo and Murdock, who sat next to Rocky Benitez, who sat across from Mordecai Crane, who had a bandage on his head to verify his wound from the wood splinter ripped from the Judge's bench by Savage's bullet.

The Judge sat at the head of the table in a wheelchair, dressed in a hospital robe. She looked pale; maybe it was the shock from her wound.

The Judge said, "Sergeant Catton claims to have new evidence. Let's see it."

Sally Jo Catton passed her the flash drive. It was red, the grainy exterior that would not hold a fingerprint, with a little chrome tongue that plugged into a USB port.

The Judge held it up like a trophy. A look of suspicion flickered in her eyes. She spoke to Sally Jo. "And this came from?"

"From Agent Savage, your honor."

"From his person?"

"From his pocket."

"When did it surface?"

"At the courthouse, after the shooting, when we had time to check him out."

"So it's been entered as evidence? And tagged?"

"Yes, your honor."

"Just speculating here, Sergeant … Why do you suppose Agent Savage neglected to enter this thing into evidence some time ago?"

"I don't know, your honor."

"Have you seen it?"

"I saw enough to know it has a bearing on this case."

The Judge paused, as if weighing her future, as if standing at a crossroads trying to decide which road to take. Then she shrugged, the first shrug Helene remembered from her, and handed the flash drive back to Sally Jo, who plugged it into the laptop.

The screen flickered. The slide show started.

The first still photo showed an outdoor scene—Angel Mountain in the morning, a field of rocks and flowers about to become a crime scene.

Helene took a deep breath.

She had seen these photos before, she knew the sequence, but they still made her feel creepy. Creepy and helpless and afraid.

Then she saw herself from that terrible Tuesday morning. Walking with her camera, shooting photos of fall flowers. She wore shorts—the weather was still warm enough back then—and a long sleeve shirt with the sleeves rolled, and her Tilley sunhat. Sitting there in the Judge's chambers, holding her breath, seeing herself from a distance, captured by Theo Ulster's secret camera, Helene watched the whole sequence. She saw Gerry Junior loose his arrow. She watched as Murdock made his tackle. Remembered her disbelief as she fell onto the corpse. Remembered her shock when she realized that Gerry Junior's hunting pal was aiming an arrow at her. Felt the flood of relief when Murdock fired two shots—short puffs of smoke from his .45—and both hunters went down.

Helene did not like watching herself come close to getting killed.

In the photos on the screen she looked slow, indecisive, robotic. Helene the automaton. Murdock, on the other hand, looked like an action hero. Quick, no wasted motion. She couldn't see him talking to her but she remembered his calm voice. "Roll sideways. Plug your ears. Check the corpse."

Beside Helene, Sally Jo was breathing hard.

Down at the end of the line of folding chairs, Mordecai Crane was fidgeting. For the first time, Crane's face showed signs of stress. If these photos made it into court, his clever defense—pinning the blame on Murdock—was toast.

The arrow shooting sequence stopped.

The setting shifted from the crime scene to Angel's Nest—tables and chairs and diners on the grass of Gretna Green. Morning light, the camera shooting guests seated at a long table, drinking coffee, slapping jam on toast, chewing. The crime scene photos had been shot with a zoom lens. The breakfast table photos, on the other hand, were shot in close-up, showing the faces of people Helene knew. She recognized the Ramsays—Gerald and Marina—the Latimers, the Golds. The camera caught Sammy Savage in conversation with Carla Carlini. Next to Carla was Elise Wellborn, chatting away with Mordecai Crane. The diners looked up as Chef Marius arrived with meat slices on a silver platter. Silent applause from the table. Tanned hands raised champagne flutes, toasting the meat. Helene's stomach felt crampy, twisted into knots.

Marius handed the platter to a blonde girl. Helene recognized Tammy Wellborn.

Tammy wore short shorts and a skintight leather vest. One

photo showed her bare legs. Another showed her face, bare of lipstick, smart-alecky, sexy. Not the face of a fifteen year old girl. Another showed Mordecai Crane with his hand on Tammy's bottom.

The Judge pushed a button on her laptop. The image of Tammy and Mordecai left the screen.

The Judge looked at Helene. Then at Sally Jo. Then at Murdock, then Rocky Benitez. When she got to Mordecai Crane, the Judge's eyes turned dark. She swung her gaze back to Murdock. "Mr. Murdock?"

"Yes, ma'am."

"It seems you have been falsely accused."

"Yes, ma'am."

"Are you aware of any duplicates of this flash drive that might be floating around? That might find their way onto the Internet? What's that thing called, where they show clips?"

"Would that be YouTube, your Honor?"

"I know people in California," the Judge said. "People who know of your exploits—they say you are very clever. They say you teeter on the edge between law and lawlessness. That you flirt with good and evil. That it is good to have you as a friend, that it is dangerous to have you as an enemy."

"What people, your Honor?"

"Never you mind. I have my sources. Be aware, Mr. Murdock, that we are a lot alike, you and I. Like you, I can be a good friend. I can also be a dangerous enemy. And let me say that if there are other copies, and if one of them found its way onto that YouTube, I would hold you personally responsible. I would incarcerate you while investigators tear your life apart. In other words, you would not be my friend."

"I understand, your Honor."

"Some advice for you," the Judge said. "Do not darken my door again. Help your clients, but help them elsewhere, out of my jurisdiction. Are we clear?"

"Thank you, ma'am."

"Everyone out," she said. "I need a word with Mr. Crane. Don't leave the building. Just give us a moment here."

She waved them out with a shooing motion. Rocky Benitez started to object. The Judge cut him off. There was hardness in her face. Stone face, steel eyes, rigid jaw. Showing no mercy.

THE FOUR OF THEM—HELENE, Murdock, Rocky, and Sally Jo—huddled together outside in the corridor while the Judge conferred with Mordecai Crane. Helene sat on a bench next to Sally Jo, taking the weight off her feet. Rocky kept looking at his watch, shaking his head, pacing the floor like a matador waiting for the bull. Murdock sat on the floor, his eyes closed.

"She knows," Rocky said.

"She's guessing," Helene said.

"My ass is toast," Rocky said. "Burnt toast, crumbling into ashes. How can you just sit there, Mateo?"

Murdock stood up, motioned for them to gather. He spoke in a low whisper. Helene had to lean forward to hear. "Let's talk about what the judge wants."

"A seat on the Supreme Court."

"What do you want?"

"I want a murder conviction," Rocky said. "I also want Theo and his little circle."

"Think back," Murdock said. "When did the Judge stop the slide show?"

"When she saw Crane's hand on that little girl's butt."

"Good," Murdock said. "What if the Judge knew what was going on at Angel's Nest? We know Sammy was covering for Theo. He invaded the Judge's courtroom asking for money. What if the Judge—along with Sammy—was part of Theo's cover-up operation? What if she's in there crafting a deal that will make her look good in the media?"

"And what if," Helene said, "she knows there's a duplicate flash drive?"

"Yeah," Sally Jo said. "That's why she came down on Murdock."

"You people are dreamers," Rocky said. "Judge Q is gonna mince me like an onion, fry me up, and have me for breakfast. With my luck, I'll wind up down south, right on the border, dodging cartel bullets and spending my days processing illegals. I gotta pee."

Shoulders rounded, Rocky headed for the Men's Room. Sally Jo gave Helene a bleak smile. She whispered that she wanted to apply for the Chief's job, but had heard they were bringing in a man with more experience, from Arizona. Helene touched Sally Jo's shoulder. Then she gave her a hug.

THE JUDGE'S DOOR OPENED and Mordecai Crane came out. His face was gray, the color of ashes. Before the door closed, Helene got a glimpse of the Judge. She was watching the monitor.

"Where's Benitez?" Crane said.

"Rocky went to the head," Murdock said. "You want to sit down, counselor? You don't look so good."

"You must feel pretty good about yourself, Murdock."

Murdock said nothing. Down the hall, Helene saw Rocky Benitez approaching. Crane went to meet him and the two lawyers got into it. Helene knew what they were talking about—the case, the future, jail time—but she was dying to hear the exact words. She looked at Murdock. His eyes were closed again, his face had a Zen calmness. How did he do that?

When the lawyers finished, they shook hands. Helene never understood that. Two enemies, both schooled in the law. They fought, they tore at each other, then they shook hands. Crane walked away, his cellphone to his ear. Rocky came over to report.

"We got us a deal," he said.

"What kind of deal?" Helene said.

"The fucker gave me Theo Ulster," Rocky said. "We'll do it

in court, using the Ramsay kid. The Judge wants to make it public."

"What about the Ramsay kid?" Helene said.

"Plea-bargain," Rocky said. "A minimum security facility— fresh air, Wi-Fi, his own espresso machine, babes in bikini bottoms. What is the world coming to?"

"So your job is safe?" Helene said.

"And Mateo is off the hook for assault. As deals go with the higher-ups, not bad."

64
Helene

THE METAL DETECTOR WAS working again, but the line to get inside the courtroom still stretched out to the Paseo. As witnesses for the prosecution, Helene and Murdock were given priority for entry. A cop Helene didn't recognize led them to their seats behind the prosecutor's table. They had just settled in when the Judge entered, using a cane instead of a wheelchair, and shadowed by a bodyguard, a tough-looking woman from the state police.

When the Judge was halfway to her bench, the applause started. Spectators stood up, like patrons in a theater. The sound of clapping filled the courtroom.

The Judge blushed. In a stern voice, she admonished the crowd. She reminded them that this was a court of law. A man was on trial for murder and homicide was a serious business.

The spectators grinned at her. The Judge had taken on a crazed killer with only her trusty gavel. She had survived a gunshot wound in the course of her work. Her face had been on TV, and reports of the shooting had filled newspapers. There were rumors that Judge Q would soon replace Judge Judy.

The Judge introduced her bodyguard. Detective Torres wore

a business suit. Her hair was cut short. She carried her weapon on a belt holster under the blue jacket. She was a tall woman, very fit, with high cheekbones and an icy smile.

The Judge reminded the spectators where they were in the progress of the trial. The prosecution had presented its case against Gerry Ramsay Junior. Today was the start of the case for the defense, and, she reminded the court, Mr. Ramsay and the prosecutor had agreed on a plea-bargain in return for his testimony.

The Judge made a little speech. "It is not only the mandate of this court to affix sentences that fit the crime; it is also the mandate to uncover foul and evil acts, to make them visible and real in the public eye. We also have an obligation to you, the citizens of the state of New Mexico, to keep you informed. Mr. Crane, the defendant may take the stand."

The Defendant, Gerry Junior, aka G.J., was still on crutches. The arm-sling was gone, and with it the reminder that his arm-wound had come from Murdock's .45 automatic. Gerry Junior was six feet tall, but the crutches made him look shorter.

AS G.J. TOOK THE stand, he still radiated an air of smug superiority. From the news reports, Helene knew that he spoke fluent Spanish—the papers kept bringing in his mother, who had, when she was eighteen, been first runner-up for Miss Universe—and he was studying Chinese with the intent to serve his country in the U.S. Foreign Service. His body language sent the message that this puny trial in a small town in New Mexico was nothing much—just a bunch of misguided and backward country bumpkins harassing a harmless city boy, blocking his path to the international big time.

Mordecai Crane, G.J.'s attorney, was not on crutches, but he still wore the head bandage—to remind the spectators, and the media world, that he, too, was collateral damage from the courtroom invasion of Agent Sammy Savage. Watching Crane move toward his client in the witness box, Helene could see a change. Instead of the blue power-suit, Crane wore a soft-looking sports jacket and baggy corduroy trousers. The necktie was brown. To open the case for the defense, Mordecai Crane asked questions that only required a yes or no answer.

"So, G.J., did you find yourself on Angel Mountain on the morning of September 10th of this year?"

"Yes."

"Were you accompanied by your good friend, Howard Whitbread?"

"Yes."

"Were you up there on Angel Mountain on orders from Captain Theo Ulster?"

"Yes."

"Were you armed with a longbow?"

"Mine is a recurve."

"Were you on Angel Mountain for a specific purpose?"

"Yes."

"Was that specific purpose an action, which, if completed properly, would gain you Warrior status in the company of Theo Ulster?"

"Yes."

That was Crane's last question. Helene thought he looked a little green, a little "liverish," as her mother used to say. Mordecai Crane turned away from his client. The gesture was almost dismissive. A washing of hands. Crane stepped away from his client, leaving him alone in the witness chair and Helene saw sweat on G.J.'s forehead. Crane nodded at Rocky Benitez. "Your witness, counselor."

In contrast to Mordecai Crane's modest courtroom uniform of corduroys and lumpy sports coat, Rocky Benitez had on a new blue power suit, three-piece. A gold watch chain attached to a handsome gold pocket watch dangled from the pocket of the vest. It had belonged to Rocky's great grandfather.

"Mr. Ramsay," Rocky said, "picking up where your attorney left off, because you wanted to be a Warrior and not a Wimp, you therefore hunted down a girl, whom you called a target. You have stipulated that the target was selected by Theo Ulster. My question is—on what basis did Theo Ulster select this particular girl?"

Gerry said, "She fit the profile."

A murmur ran through the courtroom. Spectators shifted in their chairs. Rocky waited for quiet. Then he said, "Mr. Ramsay, would you please describe this Victim Profile?"

Gerry Junior hesitated. He looked past Rocky, fixed his eyes on Mordecai Crane. There was the scraping of a chair being pushed back and then Crane, looking fatigued and leaning on the defense table with one hand, objected to the term, "Victim Profile." It was hearsay, he said. It had not been established yet.

The Judge said, "Sit down, Mr. Crane."

The court recorder repeated the question. Gerry Junior didn't want to answer, so the Judge ordered him to answer or be held in contempt.

G.J.:	Okay. Okay. This is really basic stuff. The target female was a twenty-something. On the plump side of one-fifty, blonde with pale skin. She worked as a barista, lived alone. Took courses at the Art Colony.
Rocky:	Tell us about the art colony.
G.J.:	There was this creepy guy there, Willy Mapes. He fingered the targets.
Rocky:	Willy Mapes? What did he get out of the deal?
G.J.:	He got paid.
Rocky:	Paid by the head? Like buying a cow or a pig?
G.J.:	Exactly.
Rocky:	So to summarize—Willy Mapes selected this girl, sent her on to Theo Ulster, who then sent you hunters after her?
G.J.:	Yes.
Rocky:	How did the target get to the mountain?

G.J.:   I collected this one at a coffee-shop. She turned
            out to be a real party animal, drank too fast, ate
            too much.

Rocky: Did you have sex with her?

G.J.   She wanted it, man. She was like—

Rocky: And after the sex, what happened?

G.J.:   Our orders were to hunt her down.

Rocky: And after you hunted her down?

G.J.:   Our orders were to neutralize the target.

Rocky: By *neutralize*, you mean kill her?

G.J.:   Yes.

Rocky: And by killing this girl, Sophie Orff, you would
            gain Warrior-Status?

G.J.   Yes.

Rocky: Tell us why Warrior-Status was so important,
            Mr. Ramsay.

G.J.:   Warriors got inside. Everyone else was outside
            looking in.

Rocky: Inside what?

G.J.:   Inside the inner circle.

Rocky: And what happened inside the inner circle?

G.J.:   It was so real. No more fakery, no more pretense.
            Inside there, you knew you had arrived. It was
            just like Theo said. To become a Warrior, you
            had to walk through fire. You got inside the
            circle and the person on both sides of you was
            a Warrior, and the person next to them, and the
            person across the circle. You'd taken a risk. You
            were up there looking down instead of down
            there looking up. Got it?

Rocky: What was Captain Ulster's role—once you got
            inside?

G.J.:   Theo was the man. He was different from other
            people, other adults, because he'd lived through
            battle. He called it *forged by the fires of war*. If

you were a Warrior, he trusted you. Because he was a Warrior, you trusted him. Everyone on the outside—you couldn't trust them—until they got the discipline and made it to Warrior.

Rocky: So you sat around a campfire?

G.J.: Yeah, right.

Rocky: Then what?

G.J.: Then Theo would tell these stories. How he got his first kill. How he took out enemy snipers from four hundred meters. How he survived in the bush. He told about the time he was wounded and hung there on the edge, knowing he was dead. He told these stories, and you knew who the guy really was. You knew where he was coming from. Theo was a real hero. Not like some big-assed overweight nobody in a suit carrying a briefcase, riding to the office in a limo, getting fat behind a desk. Everyone wants real. Everyone wanted in.

Rocky: So there you were, around the campfire, surrounded by Theo's Warriors. What did you drink? What did you eat?

G.J.: There was this unbelievable meat. The smell really churned your juices. There was the bonfire, the circle of Warriors. You'd be holding hands—the Warrior on your right was ranked above you, the one on your left was below— and Theo would go around the circle, holding the meat on the tip of his K-Bar, and while you were chewing, he would say your name first, then dab your forehead with grease. And then, he would tell you—this is the really real part— he identified who you were eating.

Author's Note

I FIRST CAME TO Taos when I was twelve.

The road through Taos Canyon was gravel and orange caliche. Our family vehicle, a brand-new 1947 Dodge with Fluid Drive, blew a tire on the Palo Flechado Pass above tiny Angel Fire.

My mother hitched a ride. Came back with a handsome guy in a Texaco pickup. He had white teeth and a new tire for the Dodge.

I wanted to get there. Itchy to reach Taos, the plaza, the history, stone-faced Indians, their loins girded in blankets of baby blue. I was itchy for civilization, New Mexico style. I wanted a fountain coke with crushed ice and access to comic books—Plastic Man, Daredevil, Terry and the Pirates, and Steve Canyon. At twelve, I had no idea that comic books would teach me about structure in storytelling: action in boxes, dialogue in a bubble.

Taos has changed since those early days of rough roads and fountain cokes. Today's roads are paved. There is more traffic. People piloting giant SUVs build giant homes with great views.

To write my sixth Murdock mystery, *Murdock Tackles Taos*,

I made a few changes. You can see them as you read. In these pages, you can have a drink at the Member's Bar in Theo Ulster's Racquet Club while you watch world-class female tennis players slam the ball on Court One. Racquet Club guests can park in the shade of the Parking Building.

In these pages, you can drive past the Welcome to Taos Inn, the B&B where Helene Steinbeck sleeps until invaded by nasty teens in cahoots with the killer. You can drive the same main road south—it changes names at the stoplight to Paseo del Sur—past Eske's Brew Pub and the courthouse where Helene shoots Sammy Savage (in self-defense), heading south past the Visitor's Center, and arrive at the Sleep Inn, found only in these pages, where Murdock and Helene survived the attack from the black van.

If you leave town, heading north toward the Blinking Light, where it used to be, you'll pass the *ranchito* of Jimmy Little Deer, then the Taos Pueblo, your vehicle climbing a rocky road to the gate that leads to Angel's Nest, the enclave-kingdom of Theo Ulster, who is backed by the money from those same SUV people, who are paying big bucks for a special experience, sought after by those who have seen everything, sampled every flesh pot, drunk every arcane vision-bringing beverage, smoked every illicit pipe-cigarette-toke-hookah, and tasted every exotic food. After all that, what can one possibly do for a zing?

To reach Angel's Nest in a clandestine way, you park your vehicle at the Cerdo Falls Trailhead—found only in these pages—and you climb through trees to Flatrock Ridge, and from there you belly up to the edge, where you can look down on the roofs of the Theo Ulster's Anasazi Cliff House, ancient adobe buildings turned into motel rooms for chosen guests.

To keep the action moving toward the climax, I built Quarry Way—the nasty uphill road where Theo Ulster conducted his girl-hunts, where he sends Murdock and Helene wearing flimsy flip flops. You know the story. You were there. Your trained detective eye looked down the barrel of Murdock's DeLisle, peered through the Hex sights, focused dead center on evil. You felt the pull of the trigger. You fought off the dogs. You saved the day.

I hope you enjoyed your read.

CAMEL PRESS

Matt Murdock Mysteries from Camel Press

Bloody Murdock (1986)

Murdock for Hire (1987)

Dial "M" for Murdock (1988)

Merry Christmas Murdock (1989)

Murdock Cracks Ice (1992)

Murdock Tackles Taos (2013)

For more information,
please visit www.camelpress.com
murdock.camelpress.com

ROBERT J. RAY is the author of seven previous novels: *Cage of Mirrors, The Heart of the Game, Bloody Murdock, Murdock for Hire, The Hitman Cometh, Dial "M" for Murdock, Merry Christmas, Murdock* and *Murdock Cracks Ice. Murdock Tackles Taos*, issued by Camel Press, is the sixth book in the Matt Murdock mystery series.

Ray is also the author of a popular non-fiction series on writing, "The Weekend Novelist" and he shares writing techniques at bobandjackswritingblog.com.

A native of Texas, Ray holds a PhD from the University of Texas, Austin. Tuesdays and Fridays he writes at Louisa's Bakery and Café in Seattle.

For more information, go to murdock.camelpress.com.

Made in the USA
Charleston, SC
23 August 2014